The Somerby Tree

By David E Merrifield

The Somerby Tree

©David Merrifield 2017

Published by MindsEye,

an imprint of

Catberry Press, Lowestoft

ISBN 9780995478176

A catalogue record of this book is available from the British Library

Acknowledgements

I would like to thank Josh Cooper from East Coast Colleges (Great Yarmouth Campus) for the cover design, and Mat Dale (Art Design and Photography) for his help.

Thanks also to Jo at Catberry Press for her help and support in getting this book to publication.

www.facebook.com/catberrypress

Author's Note

The Somerby Tree is a reworking of a previous novel of mine, The Tree Doctor. It is not fundamentally changed, but has undergone what you could call 'cosmetic surgery' to improve upon the original manuscript.

Contents

INTRODUCTION – About Time

This is a little story all about time. To some, it may appear to be just a simple story but to others, I hope it opens up your minds so that you might question just exactly what you know about the subject. I think it is fair to say that most of us take time for granted. We may think we know time, its little peculiarities, its rules, its definitions. But when we look at it from another angle it could be said that in fact we know very little about time at all.

It is also quite likely that once you have read this book, you will consider the story to be completely impossible or at least highly unlikely. But can you be sure? Really sure? Can you *prove* that it is impossible? Can anyone prove that it is impossible? I doubt it. You see, I am only presenting one view of what I consider to be possible. I might be right, I might be wrong, I'm sure we'll find out eventually. I can't tell you when that might be. One day in the future perhaps, who knows? In time.

The story takes place in the village of Somerby. It is just an ordinary village in England, a rural village with a fairly normal, everyday, growing population. Somerby isn't the real name of the village, but it is based on a real village. When the story begins, the village is going through some changing times. It's a time of modernisation, a time of prosperity, a time of growth. There are two distinctly different types of growth affecting Somerby now. First, there are the families that have been living in the village for many years. You could call them locals and they have ancestors who have lived in or near the village. Whatever you call them, these families are expanding due to normal population growth. It is a general trend found all around the country, which has seen families getting bigger and living longer. This means that families are growing compared to a few decades ago, but alongside this natural expansion, the village is enlarging at a slightly quicker rate because of certain other factors.

One of these reasons is people migrating from the big cities to start new lives in the country. Like the villages of England, the cities have also grown and the trouble with the cities is that they don't have enough room to build homes for all these growing families whereas the rural areas have lots of space.

It could be anywhere in the UK, east, west, north or south, but that doesn't really matter. There is a mass exodus from the concrete jungles that English villages have not seen the like of since the Second World War evacuations. As always, there is some friction between the old established rural families and the newcomers, neither seemingly having any time for each other. That isn't really the case but sometimes it isn't easy communicating with people you don't know. The two types were brought up quite differently but eventually, in time, they will all come together and help each other. Sometimes, of course, this takes a lot longer to achieve than one would hope. Sometimes it is too late to get to know someone properly because of the different ways that people are. In time, we all get to realise what other people are trying to do. Time. That's all it takes. Time.

The Riddell family are just another typical London family. Father, mother, son and daughter. Their roots, for the last couple of generations anyway, have been in London. They are no different to many other families in England, those that live in the cities at least. They are a family who have decided that it is time for them to move away from The Smoke, as they describe it. They are not criminals or confidence tricksters but a lot of people who were brought up in the country seem to think they are. There is a certain distrust of people who move into their little villages from London. A lot of the local people also find it quite hard to be friendly with strangers. It isn't anything personal, it's just the way the locals in Somerby are. They take years to confide in anyone they don't really know, because that's just the way they are. There will always be the odd one who is friendly and happy to talk to anybody, the sort in fact who wants to chat to all newcomers, to find out a bit more about them and what lives they lead. It is a way of educating yourself, asking questions, but then you will always get one who is too friendly.

The Somerby Tree

David Riddell and his family are looking forward to their new life, a new chapter in their book. It's an opportunity to start anew, not that there is any sinister reason why they need to. It is really an exploration, a safari into the realms of what is almost a completely different country. The way that life will change for them is yet to unfold. His parents have no idea what lays in store for them and nor does his sister Louise have any concept of what this move means. When they looked back on it, none of them had much idea of what was about to happen but that's quite natural. They might have had some vague concerns but nothing that they could put their fingers on. How could they? Nobody knows how things are going to turn out. Only time will tell.

And so, we come back to Time. How we talk about it as though we fully understand it. What exactly does the word mean? The dictionary definition is "a non-spatial continuum in which events occur in apparently irreversible succession from the past through the present to the future". This is, in fact, not the only definition, as time means many different things depending on the context. It actually has very diverse meanings. It can mean a split second, and it can mean a thousand years. It can mean now at this moment, or it can mean long before. What a word it is. Very powerful, very strict but it can also be forgiving. I think if we were honest with ourselves, we'd admit that there's a lot about time that we don't know.

It is also incredible how sometimes the decisions we make can change our lives in such a dramatic way. Should I catch the early bus or get the train? It's a decision that we might make every now and then. To choose the early bus, and meet someone special who is also on the bus. To chat to them and fall in love. To get married and have children. The fact that someone is born is down to the fact that you decided to catch that early bus. Does that seem far-fetched? It could be that that special person only caught that bus on that day, so if you had chosen to catch the train you would never have met them.

Let's take this a step further. Say there is a terrorist working in your city who wants to cause a disaster and get some news coverage. They might have already decided to blow up the nine o'clock train. That decision is, of course, out of your hands, as it has been made by someone else. You decide whether to catch the early bus or the train. Now you can see that a very simple decision might make a big difference. You might be saying that you don't make those sorts of decisions, but next time you're on a train look around at some of the other passengers travelling on the train, and ask yourself if they had a choice whether they caught this train.

We haven't even considered other types of

transport. Cars are full of ifs and maybes. Whether to use the car at all. When to use the car. To leave early and travel slowly, or leave late and take a few risks? To take the shorter route or stick to the main roads which should be faster? To turn left, or right? There are numerous decisions that can affect what happens in your life in just one simple journey. That's all it takes. One simple journey.

The Riddells are just like any other family. They make these decisions all the time, usually without much regard for the consequences. Of course, they are unaware of the consequences. You don't know what is going to happen in the future, do you? It's just that sometimes the things we do can have such a lasting effect. You don't always know when you do things just how significant they might be. It's only after a time that you realise what the consequences were. Over time. So, as I have said before, only time will tell.

Chapter 1
A STRANGER

Tuesday 30th August 1994

Sue busied herself in the kitchen making sure that tea would be ready as soon as Michael walked through the front door. She looked out of the kitchen window and took in the lovely summer's evening as she briefly checked the time on the oven.

"What's for tea, Mum?" David asked as he bounced past the kitchen door on his way to the lounge.

"It's one of your favourites, darling. Lasagne."

Sue took the big salad dish from the fridge and added some finishing touches by grating on some Italian cheese. The kitchen clock said 6:10.

"Can you set the table, David? And where's your sister?"

"Louise is in her bedroom."

"Tell her tea will be ready as soon as your father gets home."

"I'm just watching the telly, I'll tell her in a minute." David replied, guessing he'd be told to do it straightaway, but to his astonishment there was no response from his mum who hadn't properly heard.

A couple of minutes later, the sound of Michael's key could be heard unlocking the front door. It was almost like an alarm for both David and Louise to go crazy, as they both made their way towards the front door to watch their father take off his overcoat.

"Hello, Dad," David said, as he gave his Michael a hug. "Now we can have tea."

"Daddy," Louise ran down the stairs, jumped into her father's arms and gave him a big kiss.

"Hello Louise. Hello David. I hope you've been helping your mother."

"I have, but Louise hasn't," David said, glaring at his sister. "Mum said you have to set the table for tea." David barked out the order, but Louise did not respond. "Louise," he repeated, "Mum wants you to get the table ready for tea."

As the family sat around the dining table, the television churned out the latter part of the day's news. All four of them were looking forward to salad and David particularly liked the lasagne that Sue made to go with it.

"Mum, this is fantastic." David spoke with his mouth still half full.

"Of course it is, I made it!" Sue allowed herself a little self-praise.

"What's going on in the world today then?" asked Michael, expecting the family to listen to the news.

"Well, Spurs are playing at Ipswich this evening. They should win that one."

"No, I meant the news, David."

"Oh. Well Klinsmann should score tonight, that's all I know. Can you test me on football, Dad?"

"Not tonight, David, I just want to sit down and relax."

"Oh Dad! Please?" David pleaded. Michael thought

of a couple of questions but he wasn't really in the mood for quizzes. He hoped the kids would settle down soon so he and Sue could relax together for the evening.

"I've got a question for you, David," Sue interrupted.

"Oh, Mum, you're no good at questions," replied David.

"Who won last Wednesday when Everton played Spurs?"

"We did, two-one."

David decided he wouldn't hang around waiting for his mum to think up another stupid question, so went off to his room. Michael and Sue were finally able to relax.

***

Sunday mornings in the Riddell household were busy. David was getting ready to play football, whilst Louise just played. She would probably go off to a friend's house later, while Michael spent most of Sunday mornings working in the garden. Today was no different. The Sunday paper had been delivered and Michael was reading it while David scanned the sports pages.

"Billy Wright has died!" David spoke out loud.

"Oh, has he? That's a shame," Sue replied as she cooked the breakfast. Michael folded the paper up to read what David had seen about Billy Wright.

"Oh yes, it says here he died yesterday. David, do you know who Billy Wright was?"

"Yes, he was the captain of England, wasn't he?"

"He was and what club did he play for?"

David thought briefly.

"Wolves, I think," David replied, adding "definitely, Wolves."

"That's correct, and what team did he manage?"

"Oh, I don't know that. Was it a low league team?"

"No."

"It wasn't a Division One side, was it?"

"Yes, it was," said Michael, chuckling as he replied.

"You're joking with me," said David. He looked at his mum. "Was it Everton?"

"No, it was Arsenal."

"Arsenal!" David replied, astonished. "I never knew that."

He went off upstairs to look up Billy Wright in one of his football books.

Sue looked at the clock. It was nearly nine. She served up fried breakfasts for the three hungry people at the kitchen table.

"Can I have David's egg?" Louise asked. She didn't like fried bread, only ate a little bit of bacon but did like eggs.

"No, darling. If you want another egg you should ask for one." Sue replied. "David, breakfast!" she shouted. There was the sound of movement upstairs.

"So, can I have another egg, please?" Louise asked.

"No. There's enough on that plate for a young girl." David joined the table, hearing the end of the conversation.

"Louise can have my egg if I can have her bacon."
David thought that his sister would most likely go
for that and he wasn't wrong. Sue thought it was
good to get all the family around the table at least
once during a weekend, it didn't happen that often,
she thought to herself.

***

The weekend went very quickly and Monday was
busy. It was the last day of the summer holidays for
both David and Louise. By Tuesday Sue felt that
things were at last getting back to some sort or
normality and she could do many of the things she
loved doing, like baking cakes. The kids both
arrived home from school and Sue was finishing off
a sponge cake that she had been trying make all
day. Sue stirred the mixture, then all of a sudden
realised that there was something missing. She
searched in the cupboard, but there was nothing that
would do.

"David, darling, will you do me a favour?" Sue
called out. David walked halfway downstairs and
leant over the bannisters to reply.

"What is it, Mum?"

"Will you just pop round to the shop and buy me a
big bar of chocolate, please?"

"Can I go in a little while?"

"No. I need it now for the cake I'm baking."

"Can't Louise go?"

"David, I'm asking you."

"But I'm in the middle of my homework. It's just
up to the sweet shop, so surely Louise can go?"

David spoke in his begging voice. "Pleeease, Mum!"

"Where is Louise?"

"I'll go and get her."

David didn't wait, but shot back upstairs to his sister's room. "Louise, Mum wants you."

Sue wasn't totally happy with her son when Louise came down.

"You wanted me, Mum?"

"Yes, darling, will you be a good girl and go and buy me a big bar of Cadbury's chocolate from the sweetshop around the corner?" Sue wiped her hands on a tea-towel as she spoke. "Can you do that for me?"

"Yes, Mum, I can do that." Louise was quite happy to go.

"You should get some change," Sue said, as she handed Louise a fiver.

Louise clutched the five-pound note and made her way out of the front door. The street was fairly quiet although the main road at the end was full of traffic as usual. She passed a number of shops but stopped briefly, noticing a make-up kit in the window of one of them. Within moments she had set off again and made her way into the sweet shop. There was only one other customer in the shop, a man who seemed to be looking around aimlessly, so she decided to take a quick look at the pick'n'mix before asking for the chocolate. She wasn't sure whether she dared buy a few sweets with her mum's money, but before she could decide, the woman behind the counter spoke.

"Can I help you, dear?" It was Mrs Gardiner who owned the sweet shop, a sweet old woman who Louise had met many times before.

"No thanks, I'm all right," Louise replied, still looking at the pick'n'mix sweets.

"Loose!" the other customer exclaimed. "You're Loose! Are you okay?" The man seemed to be talking to Louise but she wasn't sure. He seemed nice enough but she had no idea who he was.

"Sorry, are you talking to me?" asked Louise, needing to confirm if indeed he was. She spoke politely as she had been taught. He didn't reply immediately, he walked towards her as if he might tell her off, but then stopped in his tracks, and put his arms back down by his side.

"Hello, Louise. It's good to see you!"

The man spoke softly, which instantly warmed Louise, but she couldn't exactly place him. He didn't look like one of her teachers, but he knew her name.

"Er...I don't actually know who you are."

Louise swiftly turned around and spoke to Mrs Gardiner. "Can I have a large bar of the Cadbury's Dairy Milk please?" she asked courteously.

Mrs Gardiner grabbed a large bar from the shelf behind her but kept an eye on the man, as she wasn't sure exactly why he was in the shop. She handed the chocolate to Louise, who gave her the note as payment.

"You'll be moving home soon," the stranger said to Louise. She heard him, but it meant nothing to her so she ignored the comment. "To the seaside," the man continued as she took her change from Mrs Gardiner. Louise was worried that she might drop the change so held on to it and started toward the door. The stranger made another comment about something being loose, that she half heard, but Louise was more intent on getting back home so made her way out of the shop and back down the High Street.

Louise skipped back home with the chocolate in one hand and her mum's money in the other, but the make-up in the other shop's window was just too much too ignore. She looked at what was included. She could see a nice bright lipstick, and a compact mirror with some coloured eyeshadows in it, but there were also some other items that she was trying to identify. She thought that she had better not be too long or else her Mum would be annoyed but just at that moment a voice spoke next to her.

"Louise, I just wanted to say hello."

It was the stranger from the sweet shop again. Louise turned to look at him and he touched her arm in a seemingly friendly way. She meant to be polite again and tell the man that she had to get home but her words didn't really come out properly.

"Must get home," were the only words she uttered as she turned and skipped the rest of the way, leaving the strange man observing her. He didn't follow, just watched her as she turned the corner into her own street.

When Louise got home, she thought again about who the strange man might have been. She had run the last hundred yards or so and was quite out of breath as she shut the front door.

"Ah, thank you darling, that will make a lovely cake," said Sue gratefully as she collected the chocolate bar and change. Sue noticed that Louise was out of breath and seemed a bit flustered. "Are you okay, my dear?"

Sue patted Louise on the head and gave her a hug, but Louise started to cry. "What's wrong, my love? Have you fallen?" Sue was confused about what might have occurred. Had something in the shop upset her?

"No, it's okay Mum. I was talking to some nice man, and I know I mustn't talk to strangers."

"Where, my darling, where were you? In the shop?" Sue was immediately concerned about what might have happened. She held Louise even closer.

"No, outside the shop that sells lipsticks and make-up."

"What, Fiona's Boutique, just around the corner?"

"Yes. Oh, well, in fact in the sweet shop as well."

"So, what did he say to you?"

Sue wasn't sure she wanted to hear her daughter's answer but she needed to ask.

"He just said hello, and some weird stuff about

being loose, or he was calling me Loose, I don't know." Louise just gave another sob as she tried to think back on what had just happened. She remembered back to what she had been taught at school about strange men and it worried her, although she had never felt that she was in any danger.

"Did he touch you, Louise?" Sue's voice grew sterner as she asked.

"He touched my arm."

"Did he grab you?" Sue gave Louise another hug.

"I don't know. He was in the sweet shop and then he was outside with me." Louise was getting anxious as she tried to explain to her mother what had taken place. It was hard enough trying to work it out for herself.

"Are you okay?" Sue felt the best thing was to try and treat the incident as if it was all nothing so that Louise might calm down a bit.

"I just want to help you make a cake, Mum." Louise dried her tears and calmed down. Sue thought that keeping her close in the kitchen was the best thing for both of them, but she was angry at the thought that some pervert had made a grab for her daughter.

Sue's thoughts were confused. She wanted to keep her family safe. Well, her children at least. Another part of her was seething, and wanted to get out there and confront this man. She considered leaving David and Louise with a neighbour but then she would have to explain and that was the last thing she wanted to do. She looked at the time and realised that Michael would be home in the next half an hour. 'Blast!!' she thought to herself. She hadn't made a start on tea, and her cake had been stirred to death.

"Louise, darling, I need to make a start on tea as Daddy will be home soon."

"Alright, Mum. I'm bored with baking anyway. I'm going up to my room."

"Okay, but I'm down here if you need me," said Sue, trying to reassure her. Louise went straight back up to her bedroom and read one of her magazines. The next thirty minutes or so went very quickly, and although it might be a bit late, Sue would have tea ready almost as soon as Michael got home.

It was almost as if Sue had talked him up. Michael came through the front door and the kids both ran down to say hello before making their way back to their rooms.

"Dinner will be ready in ten minutes, kids," Sue shouted up the stairs as she greeted Michael. She could see that there was an inner smile in him trying to break through.

"Darling," he said, as he took off his coat, hung it up and got ready to give Sue a kiss. "I have some news for you."

"Ooh, some news," Sue replied, in a coy manner. She gave her husband a big hug. "So what news, exactly?" She didn't want to spoil the mood and was keen to hear what he had to tell her. Michael grabbed her hand, and looked into her eyes.

"I've been offered the chance of a promotion."

"Promotion, that's great." Sue kissed him as a reward. This would mean more money, she thought.

"I've been asked to apply for the post of Customer Services Manager," Michael added.

"That's superb news." Sue tried to keep positive but Michael knew her as well as she knew him, and he sensed she had something to tell him.

"Is there a problem?" Michael was straight to the point. Sue couldn't keep it back and she told him every detail that Louise had told her. Their enjoyment of Michael's promotion seemed to evaporate very quickly.

Sue told Michael not to say anything over tea, but it was obvious that he wasn't happy about things and just wanted to ask his daughter if she was okay. He kept looking at her, but true to his word he didn't say anything out of turn. As soon as tea was over, Louise knew it was time to start getting ready for bed, and David was happy to play in his bedroom, which gave Michael and Sue a few moments to themselves.

"I think I should ring the police."

Michael was fairly sure that this was the right action to take.

"But Louise seems to be okay, and that would only stir everything up again. I think we should just leave it for now." Sue put her point across in a determined voice and Michael listened. Their discussion continued for at least another twenty minutes until Louise shouted down that she was now going to bed. Michael wasn't convinced his wife was right, but he agreed to do nothing for now at least.

***

A couple of days passed and the incident seemed to have almost been forgotten. Michael mentioned it to Sue a couple of times, but Louise never said another word about it, and the Riddells got on with being a normal family again. It was a Wednesday evening and England were playing a football match against the USA. It was on telly and David was keen to watch it, so the whole family sat around, even Louise.

"I'm hoping Teddy Sheringham scores tonight, Dad," David announced.

"I think Terry Venables knows how to motivate him, so there's a good chance." Michael thought England should score a hatful of goals so there was every chance Teddy would score one of them. He knew it would make David happy if he did. Sue was happy to watch the game and Louise just enjoyed being able to sit up late with everyone. She had no real interest in the football, but was pleased to see England win.

***

Thursday was a bit of a wet miserable morning as Michael made his way to work on the tube. He was used to crowded trains and the lack of seats on his journey, but some mornings seemed to go quicker than others. Today was one of those days. He had a lot on his mind. Louise was still a worry, but the promotion was his priority. Michael worked as a bank clerk in the City. He didn't think it was the best job ever but he was good with figures and he picked up all the new rules and regulations a bit quicker than some of his counterparts, which might be why he had been given the chance to go for something higher. He'd been in his present job nearly five years and felt that a change was probably overdue.

He and Sue had been able to give the situation a bit of discussion, and with the way things were they both felt that perhaps the time was just right. The only thing was that he had been told that this would probably mean a move out of London. Again, Michel and Sue had discussed several friends and relatives who had moved out to Chelmsford or Harlow, and who had found things perfectly okay, so neither really considered the promotion as anything they couldn't deal with. Michael wanted to mention the possible promotion to his mum and the rest of the family, so he decided that although there was no match this weekend that they would travel to North London on Saturday.

***

The Riddells settled in at Michael's mum's for the day. They wouldn't stay into the evening, but his Mum wanted them to stay for dinner so that was what they did. Michael managed to tell his Mum about work, but although she said 'yes' and 'no' in the right places, she didn't really take it in. Michael's younger sister Anne took a bit more notice.

"So where will the job be?"

"I don't know yet. All I've been told is that it'll be out of the City, because at least to start with I need to be in a smaller branch, but I understand that I get the position first, then look to see where there's a vacancy."

"So it could be anywhere, then?"

"Yes, I suppose so."

Michael, David and Louise helped carry chairs in from the front room so that there were enough to sit five around the table, but this still meant that two had to sit elsewhere. Twenty minutes later the food was almost ready. Tomato ketchup, brown sauce and salt and vinegar were plonked on the table. There was an old scruffy cloth over the table and a big plate of buttered bread slap bang in the middle. Michael's mum then returned with a collection of knives and forks which were just dumped for anyone to pick out as they wanted. There were a couple of sets of cutlery, some that actually matched, but most of them were a mish mash from the various sets that the house once had. Louise looked long and hard at the cutlery on the table.

"Mum. What's that yellowy stuff on those knives?" she asked, pointing.

"Well, it's supposed to be ivory. I don't think it's the real thing, probably some imitation," Sue answered.

"Ivory. Same as pianos?"

"Yes, darling, same as pianos."

The whole family had tea. It was a minced beef meal with boiled vegetables and gravy. Michael's mum came through with a big saucepan full of mince and dished out a big spoonful on to each plate.

"Grandma?" Louise looked at the meat on her plate.

"Yes, dear, what is it?"

"Is there onion in with the meat?"

"No, I don't think so, dear. The butcher never puts onion in with his mince," she lied, knowing full well she had cut up a small onion to cook with it.

"But I can see some onion in mine." Louise wasn't going to be fobbed off with a simple answer.

"It must have got in there from the vegetables, dear." Grandma continued to serve up the minced meat as she was explaining. As she finished the last one she went back to Louise's plate and took a spoonful of mince away.

"You've taken half of mine away, Grandma!" Louise exclaimed worriedly.

"I thought you wanted me to take the onion away?"

"No, I'll eat it Grandma."

The meat was returned to her plate. Next came the vegetables, potatoes, cauliflower, carrots and turnips. There were more complaints from both David and Louise, mainly about turnips, but in the end they accepted them. Gravy was poured and the dinners were complete. Michael and his dad sat in their armchairs to eat whilst the rest sat round the table.

"So, tell us more about this new flat of yours," Sue asked Anne.

"Hasn't Michael told you anything?" Anne replied, in a cheap dig at her brother.

"Yes, Dad has told us about it." David stood up for his father.

"Well, I have to say it is a very modern flat. Two bedrooms, living room, kitchen and bathroom," Anne started.

"Is it high up in the sky, Auntie Anne?" asked Louise.

"Well, it's on the second floor, but not really that high."

"You've got a lift, I believe?" Sue added.

"Yes, and so far, it's working. A lot of people tell me that it breaks down but I haven't seen it out of order."

"And your neighbours?" Sue asked again.

"Well, that's a bit of a sore point. Most of them are from abroad. Three doors down there's a Romanian, I think he is, and he can speak English," Anne paused and thought about who was listening, "but I don't like to hear the words he knows."

Sue raised her eyebrows in Anne's direction.

"What words does he say, Auntie Anne?" Louise knew that Anne meant swear words, but took advantage to put her in a difficult situation, mainly to see how she got out of it, but quite interested to see if her auntie would in fact repeat the words.

"Words little girls shouldn't hear!" Anne thought that was a pretty good answer while Louise thought it was the answer her mother would give. "To be honest, I quite miss living here, Mum."

"Well you can always come back, you know that," Anne's mum replied in a supportive way. "You know you'd have to be in by eleven o'clock though."

"Of course, Ma. And you know I would always be in by that time."

"Yes, but this time I'd lock your bedroom windows so you couldn't climb in through them."

Anne's mum knew what her kids got up to most of the time.

"I never used to do that, Ma." Anne pleaded her innocence.

"One of you used to."

Hearing his mum's reply, Michael ducked as if to keep his head down. "That Mrs Jackson said she would call the police next time she saw anyone breaking into our house." There were a few giggles round the table. "Nosey cow she is."

"Anyway, although there are some nice neighbours in the flats, most keep themselves to themselves. They are all different races and seem to have their own little groups. I don't know where they all come from. Hardly any of them speak English."

"How do you know?" David asked.

"Well, when I walk past them they are always talking in some foreign language. And as for those bloody Romanians..." Anne rolled her eyes. "There are one or two friendly neighbours, but then I'll get to know more people as time goes on." The dinner continued and then it was time for Michael and the family to make their way home. They had to catch a bus and then a train but it only took about three quarters of an hour.

Chapter 2
IT'S GREAT YARMOUTH

Monday 19th September 1994

A week passed and Michael attended his interview. He was confident in his own abilities, and believed that he had come across well but there was always that nagging doubt in the back of his mind about whether he had said the right things, given the correct answers or the interview panel had liked him. He hoped today he might hear something. As soon as he got to the bank, the manager found him.

"Michael, can I see you in my office please?" The manager shot off up the back stairs, while Michael hung up his coat and tidied himself. He steadied himself and made his way to the manager's office.

Michael didn't find himself in the office that often, and he was always in awe about the size of it. Michael was directed to sit.

"I'll come straight to the point, Michael. I'm not very happy."

"Oh. Sorry sir!" Michael felt a pang of disappointment and it was probably not until that point that he realised just how much he wanted his promotion. His demeanour reflected how he felt inside. His manager held a letter in his hand and looked at Michael.

"Don't be downhearted, man, you got through the interview with distinction!" He laughed as he spoke.

"Oh, right!" Michael sat up straighter. "I thought

you weren't happy with me."

"I said I wasn't happy because I'm going to lose one of my best members of staff. Congratulations, Mr Riddell, you are now a Customer Services Manager."

"Well, thank you." Michael took the offered hand and shook it. "So, what happens now?"

"I have a letter for you here which tells you how well you did." The manager handed him a smart cream envelope. "You need to do some serious thinking now, though."

"Well, I'm going to take the position sir."

"I'm glad to hear it but the places open to you are few, and a couple went last week, so you need to choose today if you can."

"Where is available, then?"

"Nothing in London or Home Counties, I'm afraid. Winchester has a vacancy. It's nice there. Bristol has a vacancy in one of its smaller branches, but I wouldn't recommend that as there is the chance that it may close in a few years. Great Yarmouth, Lincoln, Macclesfield, Stockport and Carlisle are the only others. Ring your wife, see which one you like the sound of best and check out the branch information, but try and let me know as soon as you can, Michael. This is a big step, but it's one you need to take."

As he sat down back in the staffroom Michael felt exhausted. There was so much information to take in and he worried about what Sue would think. He looked at the details of all the different branches, and he decided that Great Yarmouth sounded the best from what was on offer. It was a seaside town which he liked, and the customer base was varied. Michael felt this was the best choice. He rang Sue, told her what was on offer and which one he thought he should choose, and after the initial shock she seemed happy so Great Yarmouth it was.

The next few weeks were frantic and passed very quickly. Michael was pleased to hear that his new branch wanted him as soon as possible and after a bit of negotiation it was agreed that the move would be just after the New Year. Sue was very pleased with this as it helped her to get the children's schools sorted out, but she also talked Michael into another decision.

"I think it's good that you're going to see your new place of work before you move there."

"It was my new manager's idea," said Michael, pleased to see Sue showing interest in his work. "He wants me to go down for a week in late November or early December."

"Yes, that makes sense."

"I'll get a chance to have a look at the place."

"Well, on that point, and as we've picked where we think we want to live, I think over half-term we should take David and Louise to have a look at the place too."

"Err, right." Michael gave her suggestion a bit of thought. "I think that's a great idea."

Sue and Michael were very busy over the next few weeks their bid on a new house had been accepted and a date to move provisionally agreed. Michael and Sue had decided to choose their new house without going to see it in person. It was a bit of a risk but the nightmare of organising viewings and arranging transport was well outweighed by what they had chosen. Sue liked the look of a bungalow in a village called Somerby and this was their final choice.

The weekend at the start of half-term was very much like any other. David was out by ten with some of his mates as Spurs were playing away to Manchester City so he wasn't visiting Tottenham. Louise was upstairs in her bedroom playing games with Jane Barrett, which left Michael and Sue to get on with the everyday chores around the house. Sue hoovered up and down the hallway whilst Michael looked through the pile of paperwork that had accumulated.

At half past four Michael switched on the television to catch up with the latest scores. It didn't look good for Spurs.

"How are Spurs getting on?" Sue knew what Michael was looking for and needed to know for when her son came in. Michael shook his head.

"Not good, but nor are your lot." Michael continued reading another couple of letters while occasionally checking the television. David arrived back home about a quarter to five and made straight for the lounge.

"Oh, hell, Dad!"

"Yes, I know." Sue came into the lounge as Michael gave David the bad news. "Lost, five-two."

"What about the Toffees?" Sue asked.

"They lost one-nil at Palace."

"Not a good day at all."

Sue hoped tea would cheer everyone up.

Sunday morning was also typical. David was up in good time as he was playing football. It was an away match against Melbourne who used to be one of Goodmayes United's closest rivals, but recently Goodmayes had been able to get the better of them.

"What time are you being picked up, David?" Sue shouted up the stairs.

"Half nine. Rob's dad is taking us."

"Okay, have you sorted out your boots and things?"

"Yes, Mum."

"And packed your bag?"

"Yes, Mum," David lied, as he got the last couple of things out of one of his drawers. He checked his bag again and was happy that everything he needed was in it.

Barely ten minutes later the doorbell rang and Rob was there. His dad had the car running so there was no time to waste.

"Bye, Mum, bye, Dad!" shouted David as he slammed the front door, and they were on their way to the football.

"We need another win today," Rob announced as the car approached Valentine's Park.

"We'll win, just you see." David sounded extremely confident and it was a justified feeling. Goodmayes United beat the light blue Melbourne four-nil. Even Andrew Bailey got on the scoresheet, with other goals from Steven Underwood and Alan Storr. It was a convincing win and put them into third place in the league. The whole team was happy and David in particular, after yesterday's results.

Tuesday was soon upon the family. Sue and the kids had done a bit of packing on Monday but they were only going for three nights, so they didn't need much.

"Are we all ready?" Sue talked like a Guide Leader rounding up her pack.

"Yes, Mum," David and Louise answered together.

"Let's get going," Michael added as they left for the station. The journey was a bit complicated, requiring changes on the way, but eventually they were all on the big Inter-City train to Norwich. David found the diesel pulling the train most interesting, while Louise tried out all the different seats, but the journey was a long one taking nearly three hours. Michael was distraught to see how irregular trains were from Norwich to Great Yarmouth, but by four o'clock the family were in The Star Hotel and ready for their evening meal.

***

On Wednesday, Michael and Sue had devised a plan to keep the kids occupied while Michael went to have a look at the Great Yarmouth branch, and Sue visited the Education Office. The day was pleasant, if a bit cold, so for the afternoon they decided to find the famous Great Yarmouth seafront and take a walk along the prom and on the pier. Both David and Louise found it exciting, though a bit windy, and the amusements were full of machines that they both played. The whole day went very well and it wasn't until early evening that they all sat down for their meal. They were all hungry.

"Tomorrow we are going to get a taxi out to Somerby which is where we hope to live when we move," Sue said an excited tone.

"Somerby. That sounds nice," Louise answered.

The family spent the evening sat in the big lounge at the hotel where there was a roaring log fire. It gave off such heat. They sat around chatting about the day when David suddenly remembered.

"Spurs are playing tonight in the Coca-Cola Cup."

"Oh, are Everton also playing?" Sue asked inquisitively.

"Mum, they got knocked out in the first round."

"Oh, did they?" Sue hadn't realised. "So, who are Spurs playing, then?"

"Only Notts County. They're bottom of Division One so it should be a slaughter."

"Let's hope so son, Ossie needs some good results," Michael added. The two of them listened out for the report of the match and couldn't believe what they were hearing.

'*Notts County, three*,' came the first part of the score. Michael looked over at David with some concern. '*Tottenham, nil*,' was the last part.

"Three bloody nil!" David exclaimed.

"Mind your language, David," Sue rebuked him.

"But Mum, Notts County haven't won a game all season. How could we lose to them?"

David listened out for further details and the reporter mentioned that Spurs had a player sent off, but it didn't make the result any easier for David to accept.

Thursday was the Riddell's last full day in Great Yarmouth. Michael had been to see where his new branch was and visited the estate agents while Sue completed all Documentation for the kid's change of schools. Sue was pleased with what they had achieved and the afternoon along the seafront went well as well. All that was left was a visit to the village of Somerby.

Finding a taxi couldn't have been easier as there was a rank right outside of the hotel, so within moments they were on their way.

"Where to, boss?" the taxi driver asked.

"Somerby please," Michael instructed.

"Anywhere in particular?"

"No, just to the village centre please."

The taxi moved off swiftly and after about fifteen minutes they were swinging into the village.

"Wow look at that tree." David called out pointing through the window of the taxi. "I don't think Goodmayes Park has any that big."

"Oh, look, they've got a Chinese takeaway." Sue added, a bit surprised to see one as the taxi swung round and stopped right outside of it. Michael paid the driver after confirming where Hawthorn Drive was.

"There's a coffee bar round the corner. Can we have a coke?" Louise asked.

"Come on then, I could do with a coffee."

Sue walked round to the entrance of a rather large coffee bar. It seemed to be called Doc's and there were plenty of tables.

"David, just sit your sister down at a table. Do you both want cokes?"

"Yes please, Dad."

Very soon Michael and Sue returned to the table with two cokes and two coffees.

"Did you buy any crisps?" David asked. Sue produced a couple of bags.

"Yes, I bought some crisps."

Sue watched as David ate a crisp or two, but he didn't really seem to be enjoying it.

"My stomach doesn't feel right, Mum," David said, the last part with a bit of a cry as he seemed to double over in pain. "My head!"

David held the side of his head and got up on to his

feet.

"What's wrong? Are you going to be sick?" Sue sounded worried.

"I need some air."

David took a few steps away from the table then started to stagger a bit as he looked for the exit. Michael quickly got up to help him and they made their way out of the coffee bar.

"Take a deep breath," Michael instructed. David wasn't sure if he was going to be sick or just die. His stomach churned in a way he'd never experienced before, and despite being very unsteady on his feet he continued to walk away from the coffee bar towards a large oak tree in the middle of a small triangular green. Michael helped him but almost as soon as David reached the tree he began to feel better.

Sue and Louise remained in the coffee bar but Sue kept an eye on what was happening to her son. She saw them make their way towards the tree but then they started to go out of sight. She stood up to see while looking back and smiling at Louise. Back at the tree David was beginning to get back to normal.

"It's weird, Dad. I thought I was going to be sick but now I'm okay."

"You probably need more sleep."

Michael looked over to the coffee shop and tried to beckon Sue out. "Can you stand up?"

"Just about." David wobbled slightly but was regaining his balance. He stroked the tree like it was a dog, and he felt as if it made him feel better. "Can I just stand here by the tree for a few moments?"

"Of course, son. I'll just go and get your mum and Louise." Michael left David next to the tree and went off to discuss things with Sue.

"Is he okay?" Sue was worried.

"Well he seems to have got better almost as quickly as he got ill. Perhaps we should get back to Great Yarmouth and let him get more sleep." Sue agreed. Almost immediately the family returned to the Star Hotel.

***

The trip hadn't been as successful as Sue first hoped with David being ill, but by the time they were travelling home on Friday he seemed to have fully recovered. Sue did wonder if he was in fact putting it on, but she couldn't think why he would have done if he was. By the time Saturday arrived David was fully into football again, ready to go to Edmonton to meet his Uncle John and see the match. Spurs were playing West Ham, so it was a real derby as far as David was concerned.

Uncle John quizzed David on his football knowledge, asking him questions about matches all the way back to the 1960s. He and his brother had been to watch Spurs in the '60s so he had good knowledge of that period. Anything before that, he wouldn't necessarily know. The three of them reached the ground and entered the East Stand. They still referred to it as The Shelf but it was now really just the East Stand. All three of them had a great afternoon, singing, shouting and hurling abuse at the referee. Things went well for Spurs despite David's hero, Teddy Sheringham, being put on the subs bench. Jürgen Klinsmann scored a nice early goal, and although West Ham equalised just before half-time, there never seemed to be any doubt that Spurs would win. They needed to with recent results, and David was sure that Ossie was a happier man after the match. Sheringham scored a goal too, so David was very happy as he prepared to walk back to Edmonton with his family.

After the game, David, John and Michael met up with Robert before making their way back to Grandma's house. As usual, the four of them discussed how the game went and of course wondered how other teams had got on. Michael and John discussed the failings of the current Spurs team in relation to the one they watched as boys, whilst Robert and David talked about how they would both like to play for Spurs one day. Every now and then, John or Michael would throw in a question about football or some other sport to test their respective son's and nephew's knowledge. There were questions on Wimbledon, the Grand National, boxing, and of course several on football. Usually the two boys could get most of the answers. Everton came up in the conversation, and this intrigued David somewhat. His own family had a connection to Everton through his mum, and he knew that although his mum had been forced to support Spurs, she was very loyal to the blues from Merseyside. His grandad on his mum's side had been an Everton fan, David was sure, and it was probably her way of remembering him. His mum didn't speak too much about her younger days and he couldn't remember his grandad too well, but seemed to recall him wearing a blue and white rosette once, though he couldn't recall what the occasion was as it was a few years ago, and time had blurred his memories. Perhaps he would ask his mum. Soon the four of them had made their long trek and were nearly back and were ready to get inside.

As they approached the house, Michael and John found themselves outside the front door of a neighbour's house as it opened and an old woman in a pinafore with a scarf around her head popped out to put some rubbish in her dustbin.

"Hello, Johnnie," the woman called out when she saw them.

"Oh, hello Mrs Wicks. How are you?"

"I'm okay, me duck. Micky is that you?" Mrs Wicks looked hard at Michael as she spoke.

"Yes, hello Mrs Wicks, it's me. Is Alfred better?" asked Michael.

"He's about the same, dearie. Always bloody moaning, you know." Everyone laughed. "I thought your mum said you were moving to the seaside?"

"Wow! That news has got around quick." Michael

was really surprised that his mother had taken in what he'd said and passed it on. "Next weekend we go."

"It'll be nice being near the beach, won't it? Yarmouth you're going to, isn't it?"

"Yes, near there. It'll be cold in the winter but hopefully okay when the sun gets out."

"We all wish you well, Micky."

"Thanks, Mrs Wicks."

Michael and John continued to their mum and dad's house as Mrs Wicks went back in.

November / December 1994

The days went by quickly and November moved into December. Sue sat herself down in the lounge with a hot cup of tea and some biscuits. She tried to remember how things were when they first moved into the house, before they had children. The house was old but they had loved it from the first moment they stepped over the threshold. It was a real family home, full of love and happiness. Full of football Sue thought as she laughed to herself. David had been going on about changing managers recently. Both Spurs and her own team Everton were making changes.

It was a time for change though, and she would make sure that they were ready for it. It would still be hard. She would miss this house.

Chapter 3
TIME FOR GOODBYES

Thursday 5th January 1995
The new year of nineteen ninety-five was welcomed with a lot of partying as usual, and today was the first Thursday of the new year, January 5th, and in less than two weeks the Riddell family will be moving home. January is an unusual time to move, and not when most people would choose, but outside influences held sway. Sue and Michael found things a bit hectic as they both had to keep working right up until the move. Michael was now ready to take up his new post. It brought with it more responsibility, and possibly longer hours, but Michael was quite ready for that.

Michael thought back to the evening when he brought the news of his potential promotion home to his wife and family. Sue knew he was ambitious, and was interested in getting on, but she had always thought that his job would keep the family in London.

Sue never questioned Michael's promotion and was one hundred percent behind him. It wasn't quite the same when the news eventually filtered down to the children. David was the worst. He had a bit of a tantrum about it. Shouting, almost screaming, as if he was being punished. Michael thought back to how shocked he had been at David's response.

After about an hour, Sue had managed to calm him down and he had gone to bed but all night, Michael heard him crying. It was a horrible feeling and one Michael never wanted to have again. He didn't think that David managed even a minute's sleep that night, and in the morning, you could see just how upset he had been.

As Michael went to work that next morning, his excitement about his promotion had completely turned sour. What had he done? It was obvious that he would have to tell his manager that he would for now have to reject the fantastic chance that he had been offered. Michael never quite knew why, but he just couldn't face doing it that day. On the train to work he went over exactly what he would say and how he would try and hope for another promotion nearer to London. The manager was out most of the day, so he had to wait, and there was the twist. Getting home that night, expecting the family to be in absolute turmoil, David had completely changed his mind. It wasn't clear what Sue had said to convince him but he was suddenly all for it. Sue said she hadn't said anything. They had talked a bit but that was it. Michael was certain that Sue was underestimating her part in it.

As for Louise, she was different again. Initially her excitement had waned a little at David's disapproval and enthusiasm for moving seemed to dissipate somewhat. She wasn't against it, just a bit concerned. Despite this, over the past couple of months and the memory of her visit to their new home, she had started to get excited by the idea again. Michael could never quite be sure exactly what everyone thought but eventually they all seemed to look at the bright side of things and they were planning for the move.

The move was a good thing financially, too. Houses were much cheaper in Great Yarmouth, so they would be able to afford a bigger house and have some money left over to spend. Sue was particularly pleased about this as it meant that they could at last afford to have a big family holiday abroad. As soon as they had settled in and made sure that the money wasn't needed for anything else, then she would book a holiday. Summer that year would be the right time for a trip to Florida. David and Louise were not aware of this and Sue wasn't going to tell them, but she was excited at the thought of it. All in all, Sue knew that the move was the right thing to do.

David was also finding it all exiting now. At the offset, he was dead against it. He would be leaving his friends, his school, the place where he grew up and his beloved football team. None of it sounded good to him but after the initial shock, he thought about new opportunities, a seafront, sunshine all day, amusements and the chance that the competition for football team places wouldn't be quite as tough as it was in London.

Louise hadn't been sure either. She thought it would all be quite exciting and leaving her friends wasn't that bad. Being near to the sea seemed to be very much a plus. The beach and the waves were the things she remembered from past family holidays, and to be able to walk to the beach from home sounded almost too good to be true. As plans moved on though, she began to have doubts. Being away from her grandparents was a concern. She would miss their back garden and the shops. Both David and Louise were sad to be leaving their old schools, and when they broke up for Christmas that would be it. They had both been accepted at new schools and Sue had asked if they could have the first week of the new term off to give them a chance to settle in but although Louise was allowed the week off, David was moving at such a crucial time in his GCSEs that it took some convincing, but eventually the authorities saw that due to the only dates that the Riddells could move house, there was no other option and they allowed David a week off.

It wasn't very often that David and Louise found themselves in the same room on their own together but both wanted to watch the television and they were happy to suffer each other for a short time. Diane-Louise Jordan was presenting an article on the differences between town and country living which both David and Louise were interested in. At the end of the article there was a mention of shops, and Louise took a quick look at David to see if he might say something. David saw her looking but was unaware of why.

"What?" David said abruptly.

"I just wondered if you were going to say anything?"

"About what?"

"Shops!"

"Shops!" David replied in a high voice. "Why would I say anything about shops?"

"You haven't been told about the strange man who tried to grab me have you?"

Louise guessed that Mum or Dad would have said something to her brother but evidently not.

"No, what man? He tried to grab you?" David's interest had been kindled. "Tell me, Louise," he insisted.

Louise gave David a brief outline of what had taken place at the sweet shop and on the High Street a few months ago. Now that Louise was more comfortable about the whole incident, she embellished the story to make it sound far more frightening than it really was.

"He talked to me in the sweet shop then followed me outside into the High Street," Louise was in full flow, seeing her brother's interest.

"What did he say?"

"Well, nothing really, just hello, and he kept calling me Loose or Luce or Lucy. Something like that."

"Luce. I like that name." David spoke with a positive voice. "I can see how Louise and Luce could be the same person."

"And not only that, he told me that we'd be moving to the seaside." Louise waited for David's reply to that comment.

"So, he knew we were moving. Is he one of the neighbours?"

"No. What I mean is that Mum and Dad hadn't said anything about the move when he told me."

Louise emphasised that the news of the family's move hadn't been announced when the stranger told her. This part of the whole incident had gone by the wayside with all the fuss of it all. Louise remembered that it wasn't until sometime later that her mum and dad told them that they might be moving. It then dawned on her that she had never actually told her mum and dad about the seaside bit of the conversation. Ah well, she thought, it's too late to tell them now.

"So, was he a bit like a pirate? Big black beard and ugly?" joked David.

"No, he seemed nice, but I'm lucky I ran away when I did because he was one of those men who frighten people. I was frightened." Louise hoped that she had got over her trauma properly.

"Luce," repeated David. "Yes, I like that name. I'll call you Luce, it's a nice name."

Sue had finished work for now, and was busy planning their packing. The removal company had agreed to drop off some chests but Sue had already packed several things into smaller boxes to make life easier. David and Louise were of course off school now and they helped a bit.

"David, have you sorted out what clothes you still need from the drawer in the bed?" Sue shouted.

"Yes, Mum," lied David. To be honest, he had opened the drawer and looked inside but nothing had immediately grabbed his attention so he closed it again.

"So, what have you done with the things you need?"

"There wasn't much."

"But what have you done with it?"

"Oh, I put it in the airing cupboard."

"Whereabouts in the airing cupboard?"

"Can't remember really".

David turned the volume up on the television where he was watching a music channel. Sue knew she wouldn't get any sensible answer out of him, but she had given him the opportunity to remove anything he needed and would remind him of the fact if it transpired in the next two weeks that he wanted to wear something that she had packed. In fact, she could change that to *when* he would want something.

"I'm going to pack everything from that drawer today, you know."

"Yes, that's okay," answered David, not really paying much attention.

"Mum, are you packing the clothes from my drawer?" Louise asked.

"Yes, darling, but I think I know what you will want. Still, you can have a look if you want to." Louise was more interested than David in helping her mum to do the packing. It was pretty exciting. "Mum, what else are we packing away today?" asked Louise showing her eagerness.

"I'm going to try and clear some more things from the dining room today. It's all got to go in that big box over there." Sue pointed to a large cardboard box on the kitchen floor.

"Will everything go in there?"

"We'll see."

"Does the box go in the front room then?"

"Yes darling, with all the other boxes," Sue told her. Louise ran to the front room and looked in. She was surprised to find about half a dozen boxes already taped up and piled together in the front room. There was an old tea chest that was full and had a lid half fastened on the top of it as well as a few other empty chests. David was still watching MTV in his room. It was only his first day off school but he was already bored.

"Mum, is there anything you want me to do?"

"Yes! You can sort out your clothes from the drawer under your bed."

"Is there anything else you want me to do?"

Sue wasn't really surprised at the response but it made her laugh.

"Look, you can go up to the hardware store and get me some string."

"String. We've got loads of string," replied David.

"No we haven't, I need some more, and not that rough sort. I need the nicer white stuff."

Sue looked in her purse for some change that she could give David.

"I'll go, Mum, if you want." Louise volunteered.

"She'll get the wrong type of string."

"No, I won't."

"Will."

The two argued for a few minutes until they got bored. Sue held some change in her hand and wondered which one to send.

"You can both go."

David and Louise didn't often do errands together but for once after they had left the house, they stopped their squabbling and sensibly made their way to the hardware shop. David had been given the money, but Louise was happy with that.

"That's the sweet shop where that bloke spoke to me." Louise pointed across the road.

"What did he say again?"

"Something about 'I shouldn't worry about moving'."

"So he knew you were worried?"

"I didn't know we were moving then." Louise replied.

"And what did he call you again? Luce, wasn't it? Yes, Luce. I actually quite like that name. I'll call you Luce from now on."

"No! My name's Louise. Don't call me anything else." Pleaded Louise, but David had already made up his mind. In the end, she didn't really mind the name either and soon got used to it but only David used it anyway.

Michael was still working. He only had about a week left, but he was determined not to let the move get to him, so he could keep up his good work record right to the end. As he did nearly every day Michael caught the 06:50 train from Goodmayes, and with just a couple of changes on the underground was at work by just after eight o'clock. Trains into London were very frequent during the rush hour so even if Michael was running a little late, missing one didn't mean he was that late into work.

Most of his customers had found out that he was leaving. They had been sent letters telling them the branch would be closing but many had discovered that Michael was one of the first to leave "So, when is your last day, Michael, sir?" asked a customer "Just under a couple of weeks now, Mr Razac." Answered Michael as he took the money bag.

"Jenny tells me that you are to be a boss."

"I wouldn't call it a boss exactly, Mr Razac." Michael laughed a little as he thought about managing a whole bank.

"It is good to be a boss, no?"

"You're a proper boss Mr Razac. In charge of your own company."

"I am not half as clever as you though."

"You earn more money than me."

The Somerby Tree

Michael didn't want to sound materialistic but tried to get his point across.

Michael had thought a little about the type of customer he would encounter at his new branch. Perhaps they would all be farmers? Probably not.

David had spent most of his time looking in the sports shop window at football boots in the sale. He had been offered new boots for Christmas but had opted for computer games instead. He had bought new boots at the start of the season and they were still okay. He only had another couple of games to play so thought he'd wait until he got to his new school before deciding what boots he would need. David played for a Sunday side, and they had a cup game this weekend. It was a crunch match as they were playing a team a place above them in the division. Goodmayes United were currently third in the Barking & Dagenham under-16 First Division. His team were looking forward to the game. It was one of the only things that David was regretting about having to move away.

Michael had talked to him about it and tried to convince him that there were teams in Great Yarmouth who would also want good players. It was like a player in the Premiership having to be transferred. David was happy with this and was determined to go out with a good performance. The sports shop also had a few football kits in the window. Unfortunately, Arsenal and Manchester United seemed to take the prime places in the display but there was a Spurs strip in the window as well. David had been brought up as a Spurs fan by his dad but also persuaded by his uncles and cousins who all lived near White Hart Lane. It was quite exciting when he went to football on a Saturday afternoon. Things had been quite good recently and with a win over Arsenal this week, David was optimistic that the season could bring some more trophies. This Saturday, Spurs were at home to non-league Altrincham. It might be a bit of a banana skin, but he felt confident that they'd win, even if it was just by the odd goal. Pondering this, he made his way home.

"David, is that you?" Sue shouted out as she heard the door opening.
"Yes, I'm back."
"Don't take your coat off, we're going out again."
"What for?" David sounded a bit put out, but he wasn't really.
"I need to go and buy some invitations for the party. I hope you've worked out who you are asking."
"Yes, I've asked them already. Do I really have to send them invitations? It's a bit naff, isn't it?" David knew he would get the micky taken out of him if he was to send out invitations.
"I think you should, David. How else will they know where and when to arrive?"
"I've told them."

"No. You need to send invitations." David shrugged and gave in. He knew he would have to write them, but he wouldn't have to give them out, he thought. Sue had different ideas.

To David's surprise, they turned right at the end of the road and walked up towards the shops past the station.

"Why are we going this way?" David asked.

"There are some invitations I've seen up at Perry's that I think Louise would like for her party so we're going there."

"Oh, and what about my invitations?" David sounded put out again.

"I didn't think you were that bothered about invitations?" Sue gave him a smirk as she put him on the spot.

"Well, no I'm not." David couldn't believe this change of heart from his mum. "Well, there you are then." Sue said in a way that sounded like she had proven a case in a court of law.

"So I don't have to send out invitations, that's great. Thanks Mum." David sounded a bit chirpier.

"No, you've still got to send out some invitations it's just that you shouldn't care where I get them from."

David groaned. Sue and Louise both laughed.

When they got back home, Sue sat the kids down at the dining room table and gave them both a pencil and some paper.

"Right, I need you to write down who you are going to invite to your party." Sue winked at Louise in a knowing way and Louise wrote down her names quite quickly. David had to think a bit before he could complete his list. As he thought he tapped the pencil against his nose. It was a habit he had picked up.

"Don't do that, David." Sue stopped him. "Come on let's sort out your list." It only took ten minutes.

Michael had managed to get away from work a bit earlier today and by 6.30 he was back home. As he unlocked the door, Louise was there to greet him.

"Dad! Hello."

"Hello, dear. Have you had a good day?"

"We did some packing and some shopping, but not much else." Louise gave him a big hug. Sue then appeared at the top of the stairs.

"Hello, darling. I'll be down in a mo."

"Okay. Hello, David, wherever you are." Michael didn't expect to hear from David when he came home from work. David was at that age where he was always too busy doing nothing. There was a groan from upstairs which Michael took as a greeting. Sue came down the stairs and gave him a kiss.

"Everything alright?" she asked.

"Yes. Another day finished."

"I haven't really started the dinner yet."

"That's okay. No doubt you've been busy. There's a lot to be done."

Michael was quite aware that Sue was taking the bulk of the responsibility for the move. He was happy to be able to just carry on going out to work whilst she managed things. He knew that she would consult him on any important issues. It was a very good arrangement as far as he was concerned. "I've told them at work that I'll go out for a drink one night next week. That is still okay with you, isn't it?"

"Yes. Do you know what day yet?"

"No, not really but I would prefer Friday. I know then I don't have to rush to get up the next morning."

"But you promised you would help with David's party on Friday." Sue thought he'd forgotten.

"Yes, I know. I've told them at work that Friday is a non-starter. I'm going to be shattered when I go to bed that night anyway."

"That seems most likely, but don't think you're going to spend all day Saturday in bed." They both laughed.

Friday came and went so quickly that it was almost as if it had not been there at all. Michael and Sue were up reasonably early on Saturday. The whole family was going to Michael's parents in Edmonton again this weekend. Neither David nor Louise had surfaced yet but Sue could hear that Louise had turned her radio on. She was obviously awake, but had decided to lay in a bit. David was likely to be half asleep. He would stay like that all day if she let him. Come to think of it, he was half asleep most days, Sue thought to herself.

"Breakfast will be ready in 10 minutes." Sue shouted up from the bottom of the stairs.

"Okay, Mum." Louise shouted back down.

There was no response from David. Michael was in the back room sorting through some papers. He wanted to take some of the plans and pictures of their new house to show his parents. It was an exciting time for the Riddells and Michael wanted to share it with his whole family. It was likely that his brother John and sister Anne would also there sometime today. They both lived nearby and often called round. Nothing had been agreed but it was likely that John and his son Robert would call round on their way to the ground.

Eventually breakfast was finished and Sue and Michael washed up while David and Louise got ready. David searched for his Spurs scarf which he had put in a drawer in his bedroom, but his mum had been sorting through his things so it wasn't exactly where he thought it was.

"Come on, David, we'll be late for the train," called Michael up the stairs.

"Coming!" David hurried down. The journey was by train and bus with a five-minute walk at the end. The weather wasn't brilliant and it started to drizzle so their walk from the bus stop was quicker than usual. They arrived just after eleven, knocked at the door, and Michael's mum was there to let them in.

"Hello, Lou." Her grandma gave her one of those dry but wet kisses.

"Hello, Grandma," replied Louise, as she wiped saliva from her cheek. David was a bit quicker, managing to give Grandma a hug and make his way down the hall before she kissed him. Both kids went straight in to say hello to Grandad, then David put the television on.

"Hello, Susan. You're looking good." Michael's mum always greeted guests with the same line.

"Thanks, Ma. I'm feeling good too."

"And Michael. You look as ugly as ever!" His mum did have a sense of humour.

"Thanks, Ma. I got all my looks from you."

"If anyone's to blame it's your father. If only I could remember his name." Ma winked at Sue as she replied. "Come on. Let's get you into the warm. I see little David has made himself at home."

"I'm not little, Grandma. I'm fifteen this year." David was annoyed about what she said.

"Aw. Don't they grow up quick these days?" said his Grandma, in her London accent. "Are you going to see Spurs then this afternoon?"

"Yeah, you bet. Cup match today, Grandma."

"Who are they playing?"

"Altrincham," said David with some certainty. Michael came in and sat down on the settee next to him.

"It's 'orrible weather out there for 'em to play in today."

"Yes, Gran, but they won't mind too much," replied David.

"Is John calling in?" Michael asked his mum.

"Yes. Robert is going with his mates apparently, but John's calling in for you two, he said."

"And is Anne due?"

"Well, to be honest, she hasn't been in touch this week, but I left her a message to say you were all coming round and that she was invited for tea. She'll probably call in about five."

Michael's mum left them watching telly and went back to Sue and Louise, who were chatting to Michael's dad.

It was customary for John to test David's football knowledge. Michael would often ask him some questions as a practice, but he didn't know exactly what kind of questions John would have for David.

"Are you ready for some questions, then?" asked Michael.

"Yeah, if you've got some." David knew his dad didn't prepare any questions like Uncle John, he would ask him some off the top of his head.

"Uncle John will probably have the FA Cup as his subject today. Don't you reckon?"

"Yes, I would think so. Ask me some Cup questions, Dad."

"Okay, okay. Who did Spurs play in the third-round last season?"

"Oh, come on, a bit harder than that."

"Well, who was it then?"

"Peterborough," answered David with a confidence that some might describe it as smugness.

"And what was the final result?" Michael thought that this might be a little bit more difficult.

"We won on penalties after two one-all draws." David had no trouble answering that one.

"Easy, eh?"

"I need some a bit harder than that, Dad."

"So, who were the last team to beat Spurs in the FA Cup?"

"Well, seeing as we lost to Ipswich in the next round it must have been them." David answered without even thinking about it. Michael nodded his head in agreement. "We'll be going through Ipswich when we move, won't we?" David was fairly sure, but just wanted some confirmation.

"Not through the centre. The road goes round the outskirts of Ipswich, but we don't actually drive into the place."

"I'm sure the train stopped at Ipswich, we could see the football ground."

"Could we? I don't remember seeing it, David."

"So, I meant, we go past Ipswich on our way to Great Yarmouth."

"Then the answer is yes, we do."

Michael thought about the next question. "When did Spurs last win the FA Cup?" Michael knew David would know this, as they were there at the time.

"They beat Nottingham Forest in 1991."

"Correct, but who did they beat in the semi-finals?"

"Ah..." David had to think at last. "I think we played Leicester City, or was it?" David wasn't convinced.

"No, it wasn't Leicester."

"Don't tell me. Don't give me any clues, Dad, I have to answer them on my own."

"Okay, okay."

"Sorry. I don't really know why I thought Leicester. We beat the scum at Wembley, or at least Gazza did."

"Yes, we beat Arsenal." Michael remembered the game most vividly. It was the fantastic free kick.

"Alright then. Tottenham got to the FA Cup Final in 1987. Who did we beat in the semi-finals that season?"

"That was Leicester City," answered David, immediately.

"Is that your answer?" Michael's tone suggested that David should think again.

"No, of course not. I've got Leicester on the brain. We played a team in yellow." David could picture photographs of the game, but struggled to recall the team. He could say that they weren't a big team. "I remember. Watford," said David though he still wasn't sure.

"And is that your final answer?" Michael toyed with him for a few seconds.

"Yes, it was Watford." David gave his answer.

"Correct." There was a brief silence while David continued to watch the telly. There was a teen programme on interviewing some pop stars. David watched while also answering his dad. Michael meanwhile was thinking hard about his next question.

"The last time Spurs played Altrincham it was in the late '70s. What was the score?"

"Ah, now that's a bit harder." David had to think about this one. "I'm sure we won as I would have known had they beaten us, but I can't remember at the moment." David thought a bit more. "No, I have to say I can't answer that one, although I know we won."

"Well, it went to a replay, and I think finished up 3-0." Michael wasn't certain. "Who were the last team to win the FA Cup two years running?"

"Ah, Dad. You always ask that one. Tottenham of course."

"And when?"

"'81 and '82." David had gone back to his smug tone again.

"Okay, last one for now, how many London clubs won the FA Cup in the '70s?" Michael was finding it hard to think of questions. This was difficult though. Michael had tried to work out the answer and was fairly sure he had it right.

"I don't think Spurs ever won in the '70s. It's the one decade when we didn't win the cup, wasn't it Dad?"

"Yes, unfortunately. Not only that but…" Michael stopped himself, knowing that what he was about to say would give David a clue.

"But what?"

"No, I'm not going to say anything else."

"Right. Well Arsenal won the cup in 1971." David knew that. "That was when they did the double."

"Yes, they did, and had the damn cheek to win at White Hart Lane 1-0 to win the Championship. I'll never forgive them for that. I was going to say that they won the cup in the year when we should have won it."

"Why should we have won it?"

"Because the year ended in a 1." Michael reminded him.

"Oh yeah, of course. I knew that." David thought a bit more. "Spurs won the cup in 1901, 1921 and 1961. We don't normally win in the odd years that end in a 1 though."

"What do you mean, the odd years?" Now Michael was a bit confused.

"Well, the tens, thirties and fifties. Who won the cup in 1911, 1931 and 1951 for instance?"

"Yes, I see what you mean. Perhaps we shouldn't have won it in 1971 then."

David continued with the question in hand. "Chelsea won the cup in 1970 in the first final to go to a replay." David counted on his fingers. "That makes two."

"And what about the other years?"

"72, I can't remember. Wait a minute - that was Arsenal again, wasn't it? They didn't win the cup twice in a row so they must have lost. I think Leeds perhaps. '73 I think was Sunderland and '74 was Liverpool. '75 was the all London final so that makes three. '76 or '77 was Manchester United against Liverpool or was it Everton? No, it wasn't Everton. Mum would have told me. '78 was Ipswich and of course '79 was that Arsenal v Manchester United game they always show on telly." David counted on his fingers again. "I'll say three."

"Yeah, three it is." Michael stood up as if in defeat. "You forgot Southampton in 1976 but I have to say, you know some rubbish, don't you?"

"You know it too."

"Ah, but I'm a bit older. You should be thinking about Maths and Geography."

"Dad, don't be stupid." David shook his head in disbelief.

Before everyone was finished there was a knock at the door as John and Robert arrived. Michael's mum opened the door and there was the normal exchanging of hellos.

"I didn't think you were calling round, Robert," said Michael.

"Just dropping Dad off really. I can't stop, meeting some mates so see you later Uncle Mick." Robert replied as he quickly shot off back towards the main road.

After twenty minutes or so, Michael, John and David had got their coats on and were making their way to White Hart Lane.

The walk down to Spurs took about half an hour, but it was a very easy walk. The drizzle continued to hang around, and everyone seemed to be wrapped up in warm coats. As they walked towards The Angel, there were mainly shoppers about. Mothers and couples, most of them not even aware there was a match on. As they crossed the North Circular, a few more fans became evident. There were still shoppers about, but there was no doubting the fact that there was a football match on. David started to feel a sense of excitement building up in his stomach with the knowledge of tension to come and anticipation of a sense of victory at the end. Football really was a drug. It could make you feel really high one minute, but then in a second you could feel like shit. Only a true supporter would experience both feelings. Even a bad experience one week didn't make any difference, you still wanted to go through it all again next week, always looking for that victory, a feeling of superiority. David couldn't get enough of it.

"Okay then David, let's ask you a few easy questions to get you started," said John.

"Don't make them too easy like Dad does," moaned David moaned as John laughed.

"I'll try not to. In what season did Spurs last play Altrincham?"

"Well that's reasonably easy. It was in 1970 -" David just had to think of the exact year. "- 1979. It was January 1979." David was pretty sure of this, but he thought he would just pretend to struggle with it for effect.

"Yes, correct." John knew David would get that. "What was the competition?"

"Third round of the FA Cup."

"And the outcome?"

"Uncle John! You don't think that Spurs would lose a game like that, do you?"

"Well then, what was the result?"

"Spurs won 3-0. We let them have a replay though." David said this with an air of confidence.

"Ah, but did you know that the original home game was called off because of the weather?"

"Yes, of course I did," lied David.

The game finished 3-0, which was a comfortable win for Spurs, but Altrincham had scored in the second half. The goal was disallowed in the end, but it could have changed things. At that point in the game, Spurs were looking very ordinary, and that goal might have renewed Altrincham's belief in themselves. It wasn't to be, and Spurs scored a third to make the game comfortable. Stuart Nethercott deserved plaudits, as he had not scored many goals before.

At home, they listened intently to the other match reports on the television, waiting with anticipation to see how Enfield got on. The rumours around the crowd on the way out of White Hart Lane suggested that Leicester had won comfortably, but the actual score had not been forthcoming. All of them hoped that Enfield were not embarrassed. They had beaten league opposition in the last round, but Leicester City were a step up. The score came through.

"*Leicester City 2 - Enfield Town 0*," said the sports reporter. All four of them were happy with that. QPR, Chelsea and West Ham all won through to the next round. Everton had also won but Ipswich lost.

"Have you boys washed ready for tea?" shouted Michael's mum.

"Yes," they shouted, even though they hadn't.

"What time did you say Anne was calling round, Ma?" enquired John.

"She said about five. I think she's coming round for tea so she's probably sorting a few things out before she leaves."

"Well, we've got to go really. Our tea'll be ready by now and I can't hang on any longer. Just say hello to her, please." John stood up and put his coat on. He and Robert said their goodbyes and went off home.

"Are we having tea now, Grandma?" Louise asked.

"No, darling. We'll wait for your Auntie Anne. She won't be long now."

Sue came into the lounge to see what David was up to.

"What are you watching?" she asked.

"The cartoons are on, and then it'll be Big Break, Mum," replied David.

"So, was the game okay?"

"We won, Mum, and that's enough." David wasn't really interested in giving his mum a match report.

"You support Everton, don't you? They won today as well."

"I wouldn't say I'm an Everton supporter, darling. I'm a Spurs fan like you." Sue thought this was the answer David wanted to hear.

"No, Mum. I know you like Spurs because Dad and I do, but when you were a girl, who did you support then?"

"When I was young I lived in Runcorn and Grandad was an Everton fan."

"So you supported them as well?" David was curious.

"My dad took me to a few games when I was little. He used to tell me everything about Everton so I suppose I was brought up a fan."

"What games did you go to?" David was interested in specifics.

"I don't really remember," said Sue, trying to think. "I can remember some games, but not many."

"Everton were good in the sixties, though, weren't they?" David knew they had won the cup.

"I do remember going to London on the coach. I must have been about five."

"Do you mean when you moved to London?" David wasn't sure.

"No, darling. Your grandad took me to Wembley when Everton played Sheffield Wednesday."

"You went to see the F.A. cup final?" David was impressed. This was new information. There was he, a regular fan, going to matches most other weekends, and one of his great claims was that he had been to an FA Cup final, and then to find that his mum had been to one as well!

"No. Grandad took us to Wembley, but didn't have any tickets, so we just stayed outside the stadium. To be honest I don't remember much, other than the coach journey and all the people walking along Wembley Way."

David's was disappointed. So, his mum hadn't really been to a cup final. "You haven't been to a cup final, then?"

"Yes, I have. I went with Grandad in 1968," replied Sue with pride.

"Everton lost, didn't they?" David could remember this one.

"Yes, we lost 1-0."

"To West Bromwich Albion. The goal was scored by Jeff Astle, who scored in every round."

David reeled it all off as if he was reading it from a book.

"I don't know who scored. I know Everton lost." Sue told him. "By then I knew what Wembley looked like because England won the World Cup in 1966. That was on the television and Dad made me watch it."

"Did you ever go and see England play?"

"No. I saw most of their games on television, but I wasn't old enough to take it all in, really. You know about the World Cup in 1966, don't you?" She was confident that Michael would have tested David on this subject.

"Yes, I know that England beat West Germany in

the final and who scored. I know we beat Eusebio's team in the semi-finals, that's Portugal of course, and we played against Argentina when that bloke Rattin got sent off. England played Uruguay in the first game of the tournament and it was a boring 0-0. So yes, I know some about the World Cup." David was often asked questions about 1966.

"There were a lot of other things happening in the sixties, you know. Not just football."

"What, you mean The Beatles and mini-skirts and things?" David had often been told how great the sixties were.

"Yes, all that, and other sports. One day we'll sit down and show you some books. It was a period of change, but so were the seventies, I suppose." Sue thought about her own childhood memories, boyfriends and discos. It made her feel good. Just then, the doorbell rang, and someone pushed the door open.

"Hello. Is tea ready?" It was David's Auntie Anne. She poked her head around the door. "Hello, Sue." They hugged.

"Are you okay?" Sue asked.

"Yes, just dandy, thanks," Anne was about to start a full description of her flat when her mum stopped her.

"Hello, Anne. Where have you been, tea's been sat here waiting for you."

"Sorry, Mum. Just bumped into one of my neighbours and we had a little chat, but I'm here now." Anne continued through to where the plates were set out.

Sunday morning was a very important one for David. It was the cup match between Goodmayes United and Morganite Celtic. The two teams were close rivals and would have preferred to have met later on in the competition, but were both looking forward to the game. Kick-off was at 10.30 at Goodmayes Park. It was likely to be a close game, but David was happy to play at home, because in the three matches he had played against Morganite away, they had never won.

Sue made breakfast whilst the family washed and got ready for the game. David checked his gear, and found his favourite football socks, before he was satisfied that his bag was ready.

"Breakfast!" Sue shouted from the kitchen which triggered a stampede downstairs. David was always hungry, but confined his breakfast to just toast and some bacon on match days. Soon the family were ready and David felt a bit nervous. It was a normal reaction and would go as soon as he got to the dressing room. Although it was only a few minutes' walk to the ground, David was pleased to have a lift. He felt more like a professional player when he turned up by car.

By 9.45, players from both teams were arriving at the ground. Morganite were only three or four positions above Goodmayes in the league, but felt this was their year. David stood on the bench in the dressing room and looked out onto the pitch. There were already a few Morganite supporters congregating with their green and white scarves, certain to give vocal backing to their side. Goodmayes meanwhile had several family members spread under the trees on one side of the pitch. If things got exciting there would be some shouting, but usually they remained fairly quiet. The Goodmayes manager gave a last word of support and it was time to take to the pitch.

Morganite dazzled in their pristine kit of green and white hoops, whilst Goodmayes were turned out in red shirts but old dingy white shorts. It was likely to be David's last ever game for them and he wanted to go out with a cracking game. He was keen to rouse the rest of his team to a top performance, but Morganite took a very early initiative and created two chances through their left wing. Both were well wide of the mark but it was obvious that this winger needed attention.

It was in the right back position where Goodmayes had had to make a change, but had to drop their midfield a bit deeper and help defuse the threat. Morganite still used their winger, but if he could get past one man quite easily, there was another just waiting to tackle right behind him and for now the problem was dealt with. It left Goodmayes a bit short in midfield, but David played the centre well, and kept things together. He tackled all over the pitch and appeared full of energy, but Morganite still looked the most likely team to score. Some decent passing created more chances for the Morganite forwards, but Goodmayes' goalkeeper was on top form and equal to anything.

Twenty minutes in and so far, Goodmayes had failed to get a shot on target. The formation they were now playing left the midfield concentrated more on defence than attack, and it was their right sided winger who was being relied upon to create any scoring chances. Keith wasn't having one of his better days and rarely seemed able to get past his marker. The Morganite defence played the ball around with ease and usually found their man in midfield to start another attack but on this occasion the ball was played back to the keeper for him to clear.

As the ball came to him, Goodmayes' centre forward moved in his direction and the keeper took a second touch on the ball to push it a little forward before clearing. The Goodmayes Park pitch had its part to play too. The ball bobbled as the keeper struck it, and it moved only twenty-five yards or so, straight to Steven Hollick, Goodmayes' left forward. He had no other thought than to smash the ball straight back again, and was as surprised as anyone when his shot went right into the top corner. 1-0 to Goodmayes, from the first shot they had. The rest of the half saw Morganite form attack after attack, and Goodmayes found themselves clinging on for half time. Derek Oakman, however, was in brilliant form and made three superb saves to thwart certain goals. The Goodmayes defence tackled and cleared and kept the score at 1 – 0 until the half time whistle went.

As the teams went back into the dressing rooms, Louise asked her dad what he thought.
"A bit lucky to be in front, Dad?"
"Well, I suppose so. Defended well, but Morganite have been the better team. No doubt they'll come out strong again in the second half," Michael told her.
"David's done well." Sue added.
"He's having a good game."

The teams came back out for the second half and straightaway Morganite had a goal scoring chance that Oakman tipped over the bar. It was nearly all Morganite but nothing looked like getting past Oakman. David also stopped many plays with his timely challenges, and words of praise ran around the park. He found himself on the goal line as a corner came across, and he was first to the ball as it reached the goal area. He felt the force of another player also going for the ball, but David was too strong for him and got his head to the cross first. Unfortunately, it was Derek Oakman who was the other player and as the ball dropped to a Morganite forward, Oakman was helpless to prevent them equalising. Oakman blamed David for being in the way, David blamed Oakman for not shouting, and the whole defence started arguing. Captain Phil Hall broke it all up and got the team to concentrate Morganite hit the post, and Oakman made two more great saves, but by now they had stopped trying to get the ball out to their winger as he had been ineffective all game.

Ten minutes to go, and Goodmayes had still only had one shot on goal. It was time for the tide to turn. The ball found its way to Keith Bryant who teased the opposition and for the first time knocked it past his man. As another defender came in to challenge, Keith knocked the ball forward jumped over the tackle that followed. The ball bounced up perfectly as Keith hit in a cross to the far post. Alan Storr rose majestically to meet the ball with his head and the ball looked goal-bound as it beat the keeper completely. Time stood still, but it hit the bar and rebounded. Goalkeeper, defenders and all tried to react but Steven Hollick was first off the mark to volley the ball into the corner. It was 2-1 to Goodmayes, and Morganite were visibly gobsmacked. As Goodmayes celebrated, the confidence left the Morganite players. They had been by far the better team. They probably had ten times the shots as their opponents, yet still found themselves behind. Goodmayes hadn't really created much, but had still scored two goals.

The Somerby Tree

Nothing was going to plan, and they were going out of the cup.

The last ten minutes of the game saw very little creative football and both teams were waiting for the final whistle. The Morganite left winger had hardly touched the ball for the last thirty minutes, and frustrated with his team mates' failure to get the ball to him went looking for it himself. He tackled a Goodmayes man and found the ball at his feet as he started to move in field. Nobody tried to halt his run and he switched his direction goalwards without any trouble. As the first tackle came in the ball just seemed to be stuck to his foot. Another tackle missed and the winger passed him without any trouble. It was all with his left foot, so as David got into a position to try and stop him, he didn't tackle but forced the winger to move the ball on to his right foot. There was nobody to pass the ball to on the right, so the winger kicked towards goal with his right foot. Despite being outside the penalty area the ball swung in and Oakman struggled to get a finger to it. He managed to just push the ball upwards but it wasn't enough and the winger's shot flew into the net. Two all. Morganite players stood in amazement as their player held his arms up in celebration. The whistle went for full time less than a minute later. A draw.

It was a strange feeling for both sides. Morganite had practically accepted that they were beaten, whilst most of the Goodmayes team were thinking about the next round. It was almost in shock that the players shook hands, and began to think about having to battle it out again in a replay.

As the players made their way back towards the changing rooms, an old chap went over to chat to David.

"You had a good game today, son."

David had seen the man a couple of times before, but this was the first time he had spoken.

"Thanks. I didn't manage to stop that bloody goal, though, did I?" David was annoyed that the game hadn't been won today, as he knew it was unlikely he would be available for the replay.

"It was a pretty good goal, and you can't blame yourself." The man touched David on the shoulder. "I've watched you for a couple of weeks now, and I'd like to recommend you to a professional club. Have you ever been for a trial before?"

David wasn't quite sure what to say. He was disappointed with the result, but excited at the approach.

"Er, no, I haven't."

"Well give this card to your dad, and ask him to give me a ring."

The man handed him a small business card which simply said 'Wally St Pier, Football Scout' and a telephone number. David looked at it, and his mind filled with images of him leading a Spurs team out at Wembley.

"Well done, son." Michael broke the dream. "Shame about that goal, but you kept Goodmayes in it." Michael knew that David would be annoyed, and tried to make him feel better. The man turned to Michael.

"Are you the lad's father?"

"Yes."

David handed the card to Michael and left the two of them chatting.

"I've just asked him if he's prepared to have a trial."

"Seriously? Are you connected to a club?"

"Well, I have connections with a few around the area. West Ham is probably the biggest." Wally said the name with pride while Michael nodded in approval.

"We're just about to move out of the area, though."

"That shouldn't matter. How far away are you going?"

"To Great Yarmouth."

"Have you family up there?"

"No." Michael was surprised at the question. "Why do you ask that?"

"Oh, no reason, really. I went for a trial myself at Norwich City in my early days and there was a local lad there who reminds me of your boy. Just thought they might be related."

"No, we haven't got any relations near Norwich."

"Okay. Give me a ring when you can. We'll try and sort a trial out." Wally shook Michael's hand and made his way out of the park.

David went back to the dressing room. The team were all a bit down, whilst the Morganites were high. There was a buzz coming from their dressing room, as though they had won the match. Goodmayes' manager came in and clapped his hands to get the boys' attention.

"Quickly, boys! Just wanted to say that you all battled bloody hard out there today, and deserved to win, but we'll beat them on their ground in the replay just to show them." The team tried to make some positive sounds, but it wasn't easy. David raised a clenched his fist and tried to rally the boys.

"Of course we'll beat them! And they know it." He got a slightly better response.

"As you all know, we might well be without Riddsy for that game," continued the manager. Riddsy was David's nickname, and in fact many didn't know what his first name was. "I would just like to wish him luck where he's going and say that we'll miss him. Thanks for all those crunching tackles you've put in David, and on behalf of the players please accept this little trophy in the hope that you'll never forget Goodmayes United." The manager handed David a small trophy with a footballer on it, as the rest of the team cheered. It seemed to change the mood.

"I just want to see you win the cup this year boys, so do it for me!"

Finally, everyone cheered.

That was only the first goodbye. For the next few days, neighbours stopped on their way past the house to ring the bell and wish the family good luck. The whole road knew what was going on. A few of the neighbours bought Sue a bunch of flowers and a card, reminding her that she was leaving behind a number of friends. Sue was determined not to lose touch.

Friday 13th January1995
Susan knew that Friday was going to be a busy day. Nearly everything was packed up in boxes ready for the removal men, and she had planned for Louise and David to have little farewell parties. Louise's party would start in the afternoon whilst David's was going to be later that evening. With any luck, Michael would be home by then and he would be able to help with the boys while Susan finished with the girls. David's party should be finished by eleven, and she suspected by then they would all be ready for bed. Saturday was set aside for clearing up, and finishing any last-minute packing.

As Saturday morning got going, the Riddell household was enjoying a lie in. It was nearly nine o'clock, and the postman could be heard dropping mail through the door. Michael thought about the next couple of days. The plan was to pack the removal van in the morning, then they would go get their train to Great Yarmouth. They had a family room booked at the big hotel for Sunday night and on Monday morning would pick up the keys. By Monday afternoon, the removal van would be there. Things would probably be all over the place for the first couple of days, but he was sure they would soon be sorted out.

Very soon, Louise was up, and she knocked on their door before entering.

"Alright, darling? Are you okay?" Michael asked as Louise sat down on the bed next to him.

"Yes. A bit tired but okay."

"Did you enjoy your party?"

"Yes. We watched Hugh Grant and I got a book about Princess Diana. I don't think David got anything." Louise wasn't sure whether to be pleased or embarrassed but the former feeling was probably the stronger.

"I need some help with the clearing up today, young lady," said Sue, adding, "Your brother can help too."

"I doubt that," Louise replied. Sue guessed that she was probably right, as David was still asleep. "It feels a bit strange but tomorrow we leave this house forever, don't we?"

"Yes, darling. It's the start of a new page." Michael was a bit concerned that Louise was going to say that she didn't want to go.

"I know. It's exciting. Can't wait, Dad!" Louise gave her father a big hug. "And David has said he can't wait to live near the seaside, with all the amusements and holiday shops."

"Is that so?" Michael pulled a funny face at Sue. "Looks like we're all just waiting for tomorrow to come," said Sue, emphatically.

Chapter 4
THE MOVE

Sunday 15th January 1995
On Sunday, Michael had set the alarm for six. The removal van was expected just after seven. Sue had a suitcase packed with the family's clothes for the next couple of days. By Tuesday they should be in their new house and unpacked. It was just as well that Michael and Sue had got up sharply, as by ten to seven van had arrived.

"Is it Mrs Riddell?" One of the removal men looked at his bit of paper as Sue answered the door.

"Yes, you've got the right house."

"Righty ho, Tom!" The man gave the thumbs up to his colleague, and folded the sheet of paper away in his pocket. Susan let him in. "Have you still got anything left to pack?"

"We have one box in the kitchen to put the kettle and things in after breakfast," Sue told him.

"And is there anything that needs to stay here?" He looked into the lounge and nodded.

"Just one suitcase with our things in. Oh, and we have another box upstairs that I'm putting bedding in, and that needs to go in the van. It should be ready soon." Sue was reasonably well organised. The removal man looked around the house at all the different bits of furniture and measured up one or two things before turning to Michael and Susan. "It should take us about two hours to get this lot packed, so we'll make a start."

It was only just after seven when the first bit of furniture was loaded onto the van. Louise watched for a while. She looked at the furniture and the boxes with her belongings in. David joined her for a short time, but got bored and went back upstairs to see if there was anything he could do. There wasn't. The family had finished their breakfast, washed and dried up, and filled the box in the kitchen with all the last-minute things. Sue finished packing the bed clothes upstairs, and this was the last to be loaded on to the van. Apart from their suitcase, all of the Riddells' belongings had been removed from the house. By nine, the van was being closed and the house was almost completely empty.

"Mr Riddell, we'll be on our way."

"Yes, okay," replied Michael.

"According to my paperwork, we'll be moving you in on Monday afternoon. Is that correct?"

"Yes, we've said about 1 o'clock. Will it be you again?"

"Should be. 'Til Monday then." The removal man touched the tip of his flat cap and got into the lorry. The Riddells' belongings were on their way. Michael went back into the house where the family stood waiting in the hall. Sue had shut the suitcase, and David had carried it downstairs.

"Are we going then, Dad?" Louise asked.

"Let me have just one last look around the place, then we'll get off to the station." Michael had a quick wander around. He almost had tears in his eyes, but he was ready. "Okay, off to Great

Yarmouth!" he announced.

Michael took the case, while the others grabbed their own little bags. David had a rucksack and both Sue and Louise had large handbags. They trekked up the hill to the railway station, and were soon on the platform waiting for the train. It was Sunday, so the trains weren't running frequently. They had about twenty minutes before the next London train was due. There were only a couple of other people on the platform, and the Riddells sat on a bench to wait. Sue kept Louise occupied while Michael tested David on sport, and soon enough they were on their way to Liverpool Street.

After their journey a couple of months ago Michael had found a much better way, or at least quicker way of getting to Norwich. He was happy that the kids had at least been on the same journey before and the planned route was to travel into Liverpool Street to get an Inter-City train to Norwich. Michael had calculated that they would have no problem catching the twelve o'clock train from Liverpool Street and they would be in Norwich by three that afternoon. He wasn't quite sure how good the trains were from Norwich on a Sunday but guessed they would be in Great Yarmouth before six that evening. The journey in to London was no problem and by ten to twelve they were sitting themselves around a table on the Norwich train. Both David and Louise were still excited about the fact that they were travelling on an Inter-City train and this journey was going to be longer than the one they went on in October. They had both seen many of the Inter City trains rushing through Goodmayes station but actually being one of those passengers on a fast train was a thrill and it kept them quiet for a while. Sue knew that once the train got under way both of them would be back to their usual tricks although she was hoping she could keep them interested as far as Romford at least. Perhaps then she would get Michael to buy some food and drink.

"Mum. When is the train going to go?" Louise asked.

"It won't be long now darling!" Sue looked at her watch as she replied.

"Ain't there some bloke got to come round and check our tickets?" David asked.

"I don't think he comes round till the train has started." Michael answered.

"That's a point. Where are the tickets dear?" Sue queried.

"I've got them in my wallet."

Just at that moment there was a whistle blown on the platform outside. After a few seconds, the train slowly started to move.

"Ooh. We're going." Louise said excitedly.

"Of course we are." David replied. He stared out of the window trying to take in as much of the station as he could but within less than a minute the only view was an apparently endless brick wall. The sun outside was blocked and the lights in the carriage were more evident than before.

"I bet you can't name all the stations we go through between here and Goodmayes, Luce." David hoped to put some pressure on his little sister.

"Stratford is the next one."

"Yes and after that?"

"Is it Maryland?"

"Are you saying it is Maryland or not Maryland?" David found some amusement in seeing his sister struggling.

"Yes, darling it is Maryland." Sue answered.

"Oh, Mum. Don't help her." David slumped into his seat a bit more and stared out of the window as the scenery got a bit more interesting.

Fortunately, the kids found many things out of the window to keep them interested and occupied and it was nearly one o'clock before anyone even mentioned food. Michael made a mental list of what everyone wanted and then he and David went to the buffet bar to buy some sandwiches, crisps and drinks but they were surprised to find a queue when they got there.

"I didn't realise there would be as many people on the train as this." Michael said.

"Perhaps it's just that everyone has got hungry at the same time!"

"Yeah could be I suppose. Right let's test you on your FA Cup finals."

"You won't catch me out Dad, you know that."

"We'll see." Michael had a quick think and went straight in with a fairly hard question as far as he was concerned. "So tell me then the name of the goalkeeper who finished up on the losing side in the 1963 Final?"

"Ah!" David was stumped initially but he thought it through. Manchester United won it and they played Leicester City so it must be. David thought out loud. "Gordon Banks," he finally answered with a hint of arrogance.

"Yes well done. Which player became the youngest player to appear in an FA Cup final in 1964?" Michael was thinking hard to try and come up with some reasonably testing questions. David again had to think a bit but he did it to himself this time.

"Howard Kendall for Preston North End," David declared with a smirk as he had found that a bit difficult.

"Again, you're right. Who did he go on to play for?"

"Everton. That was easy."

The queue finally dissipated and Michael got served. The two of them carried various paper carrier bags back to their seats and handed out sandwiches, crisps and both hot and cold drinks. All four tucked into the food as by now they were starting to get hungry again. Sue didn't want any crisps but asked for one of those crumbly type biscuits that she had had before on the train. The two children inspected their sandwiches more like they were laboratory specimens and after the normal comments like 'It's perfectly good food' and 'It won't do you any harm' and 'Just bloody eat it' they ate their food so they could get to their cokes. All four had different sandwiches.

"Hey, this ham and cheese is pretty good," said Michael as he soon started on his second.

"Well of course it's okay. Anglia have won some award for their food." Sue spoke as if she was a spokesperson for the railway company.

"Yes but surely that's their sit-down restaurant meals, not sandwiches."

"No I think they test the buffet food as well." Sue wasn't actually sure but tried to push her point home that the food was okay. The family carried on and seemed to enjoy it.

By a quarter to three the train was arriving at Norwich station. As they got off the train and on to the platform they all sensed the shock of how cold it was. The wind wasn't that strong but it hit them as they stood on the platform waiting to regroup before making their way to the main part of the station. It was one of those winds that you just couldn't seem to get away from but as the family started walking up the platform to the main concourse the wind faded. It was in fact a pretty mild day for January but their arrival in East Anglia was greeted with the harsh reality that they were coming to live on the coast where the weather could be seen at its rawest condition. It wouldn't be the last time that they noticed the wind blew stronger in Norfolk. Sue was quite excited about the journey herself and the family's arrival in Norfolk was a big step. She just wanted to tell Michael that they were doing the right thing.

"Well it says here that the next train to Great Yarmouth doesn't leave till four thirty." Michael was a bit surprised as this meant they would have to wait over an hour and a half.

"There isn't another route that will get us there quicker?" Sue asked.

"No. That seems to be the only way."

"If it hadn't been a Sunday would it have been better?"

"Yes but not much really. We've just got to get used to there not being many trains out here." Michael and Sue gave the news to David and Louise and the four sat down on a bench and tried to prepare themselves for the long wait.

By five o'clock, they had arrived in Great Yarmouth where the weather had taken a slight turn for the worse as it had now started to rain. The Riddell family had taken this journey before of course but this afternoon they seemed to pay a bit more attention of what the scenery had to offer. The sun had more or less set so it was a darkening sky but all four had been looking out of the window on the train to Yarmouth and all had similar thoughts of how bleak it looked with flat fields for miles only interrupted by the occasional broken windmill.

There was also the strange sight of seeing some buildings away in the distance gradually getting more detailed as they got nearer to it. The buildings turned out to be the town of Great Yarmouth. Michael had always intended that they would catch a taxi from the station to their hotel as although the journey wasn't very long the cold evening was becoming more evident to all of them and the trip in a warm car was most appreciated.

The taxi took them to the little by-road at the Town Hall and the front entrance to the hotel where they had stayed previously. The Star Hotel was said to be one of the town's oldest hotels and Michael had been advised by the bank management that it was the best placed hotel for him to stay at which he had found on his previous visits. He liked the hotel so there was no reason to change for this final journey. He booked the family in to the two rooms that were arranged but then also made sure he knew both where and when they were all going to meet.

"Right okay. David and I are in room 217 whilst you girls are in 218."

"Can we walk from one room to the other?" Louise asked.

"No not in between but they are just down a corridor from each other so it won't be that difficult."

"Okay. We're going to have a meal in the hotel tonight aren't we dear?" Sue confirmed.

"Yes. They start serving from six so that'll give us

time to have a wash." The Porter had come and taken the one suitcase they had and led the way to the lift.

"Watch your toes." The Porter said as he slid shut the lift door. He pressed the '2' button and the lift paused before chugging into action and very slowly taking them up to the second floor.

"Shall we meet down in that lounge? I'd like to sit in front of the fire for a while." Sue said.

"Yes okay we'll see you down there about six."

"I'm starving." David added. The family went to their respective rooms and Sue sent Louise to the boy's room with their clothes after she had opened the case. A second trip was required to take along wash-bags but after five or so minutes all of the Riddells were getting ready for dinner.

By six fifteen the Riddells were sat at a table pondering over the menu.

"I want a prawn cocktail starter. Can I have a prawn cocktail starter Mum?" David had heard of prawn cocktail but had never actually ever seen one.

"If you want prawn cocktail then you may have prawn cocktail." Sue replied.

"Any idea what you want Louise?" Michael had given them all a minute to have a look at the menu but guessed that both kids wouldn't really know what to order.

"What's pate?" Louise pronounced it incorrectly.

"It's pronounced pa the." Michael corrected her. "It's basically a meat paste but usually a very strong taste. You might like it."

"And what is whitebait?" Louise asked again.

"Ah. I don't think you'll like that." Michael replied.

"But what is it?"

"They are small thin fish very deeply fried."

"Urgh!" Louise replied.

"Urgh!" David also added. After a few more minutes' consultation, the meals were ordered with a mixture of starters and the usual main courses of mixed grill, steak and fish being ordered. Michael and Sue also ordered some wine which both David and Louise were allowed to have. They were all quite full by the end. David was the only one who considered having a desert but he was talked out of it. Sue and Louise wanted to go back into the old lounge where the open fire was now in full flow but Michael wanted to have a little walk to get to know where he had to go tomorrow and try and get a feel for the town. David borrowed a jumper so he could also go for a walk. They walked out of the hotel and turned right but almost immediately the wind caught them both full on.

"It's always windy here isn't it?" David said.

"Perhaps we'll get used to it after a few weeks."

"Do you know where you're going?"

"Well, the bank is down here somewhere." Michael moved a bit to his left to look further down the quay. "Yes, there it is. I just want to give it a quick look." Michael quickened his pace as he headed towards the bank and David followed, but then there was a sharp stop and Michael turned back to look at another shop. It was an estate agents.

"This is the place where we bought our new house. I mean bungalow." Michael corrected himself just before David was able to. "That's good. This is where I have to pick the keys up in the morning. I haven't got far to go have I?"

"No, not really." David replied out of courtesy.

"Okay, a quick look at the bank and then shall we see what the Market Place looks like."

"Yeah, okay." Michael and David took a gentle walk from the quay to the Market Place via a pedestrianised road called Market Row which had shops on either side of it. Most of them were small old shops and pretty boring but some had interesting things in them.

"Okay, a quick test for you." Michael said as he put his hand under his chin in a thinking pose.

"Who won the World Snooker Final in 1985 in the very last frame?" David looked at his dad with a bit of a frown.

"Am I supposed to know that?"

"Of course you are. You've seen the video a number of times."

"Oh, I know. Didn't realise it was 1985. You mean the bloke with the glasses, Dennis Taylor." David said it with smug confidence.

"Yeah that's right. If you remember rightly they both missed easy pots towards the end." Michael just wanted to make sure that David knew the exact answer. "And who did he beat then?"

"Steve Davis." Michael just acknowledged the

answer with a short nod and got straight on with his next question.

"Name the horse and Jockey that won the 1981 Grand National?"

"Cor that's a bit stiff ain't it?" David immediately assumed he wouldn't know the answer.

"Again no not really. He is pretty famous and once you get the jockey you'll get the horse or I suppose vice versa." David thought for a bit.

"Champion." He answered with a little uncertainty but his Father nodded and he regained his confidence. "Bob Champion and the horse was Alda." David thought hard and sighed as he did so. "Aldaniti."

"Correct." Michael gave him a look of pride. "And name the Frenchmen who won three formula 1 championships in the 80's"

"That would be Nelson Piquet." David was brimming with confidence by now.

"Which British boxer..." Michael fired sports questions at David almost continuously whilst they walked around. David found it entertaining.

The whole family seemed to sleep well and although the rooms at The Star were a bit old fashioned and perhaps a bit small there was no doubt that the beds were very comfortable and warm. Michael and David slept in one room together whilst the girls shared another room. Alarms were set for eight o'clock and by a quarter past nine they were all in the restaurant ordering breakfast.

Monday 16th January 1995

"Now don't forget kids, have a good big breakfast as we may not be able to get much in the way of food tonight." Sue aimed her comments as much at Michael as she did David and Louise.

"Can we have cereal as well as a fried breakfast Mum?" Louise asked.

"Yes of course you can."

"Does that mean I could have kippers if I wanted?" David wasn't going to be left out.

"If you want kippers, you can have kippers." Michael replied knowing David wouldn't touch them. After breakfast was finished Michael left the rest of the family to get the case and bags ready before he walked down to the estate agents to pick up the keys to their new bungalow.

It wasn't long before Michael had returned with the keys and some instructions and he was in the hotel lobby waiting for Sue and Louise to join them. David had waited with a suitcase near to the hotel exit waiting for his Father.

"I was ill last time we went to Somerby wasn't I?"

"Well yes you were son, for a very short while though." Michael tried to remain positive.

"I just remember feeling good around that big tree." David thought about what it looked like. "I hope I see a bit more of the village from now on."

"You should do."

"But yes, the tree made me feel better."

"I don't think it was the tree David." As Michael's words echoed into the morning air Sue and Louise came down the stairs with their bags.

"All present and correct." Sue commented.

Quite soon, the Riddell family were outside the hotel and getting into a taxi again. Michael gave the driver the new address and quite soon they were underway. It was in fact nearly eleven o'clock and David looked up at the clock hovering powerfully over the Town Hall as they departed. The journey seemed to take longer than last time but it only took about fifteen minutes. Louise kept hr eyes open and was the first person to spot the Somerby sign on the road and she shouted it out to the whole car.

"Look we're now coming into Somerby." Louise said.

"Yes, not long now." Michael replied. Michael turned round to talk to Sue. "Did we come in this way when we came last time?"

"I think so." Sue answered.

"I thought you said it was a bungalow?" David said. Michael turned the other way to answer his son as the taxi turned a swift left.

"Wow look at that big tree, Mum." Louise shouted.

"That's my tree, Luce."

"Your tree?"

"Yes, I saw it last time we were here and it was the one that made me feel better," David added. The taxi then turned right. "Hey, look at the flags on the coffee shop." David pointed out of the left of the taxi and Sue turned to look. The taxi came to a stop at a crossroads. Sue turned back and looked at David and then back at the shop.

"Did I read that right David?" Sue asked.

"Read what right?" Michael added wondering what they had seen.

"Well I'm not sure exactly what it said but there was a banner on the coffee shop back there and I'm sure it mentioned our name." Sue was a bit confused.

"It did, Mum. It said Somerby welcomes The Riddells." David confirmed. As the taxi pulled up outside their new home, the family were still talking about the flags and the banners.

"I wonder what all the flags were about?" Michael said to Sue.

"Don't ask me."

"Is there some special occasion today or are there always flags out in this village?" Michael asked the taxi driver.

"Not that I know of. I don't come from the villages so I don't rightly know but thought I would have heard. That place with the banner is a coffee bar. Called Docs." The taxi driver was more interested in collecting his fare. It was the topic of conversation for almost another minute but the Riddells had other things on their minds.

Michael retrieved a set of keys from is jacket pocket and made his way to the front door. The bungalow was quite different to anything that David and

Louise had ever seen before in as much as it had two front doors. One on the front and one on the side. Michael had gone to the front door. He twisted the key and it seemed to turn the lock but the door didn't open. A little push and it gave way.

"Obviously hasn't been opened for a long time." Michael said to Sue.

"Perhaps the Williams used the other door," she replied.

"Is that the name of the people we bought this place from?" David was curious.

"Yes dear. Mr and Mrs Williams." Sue answered. Michael pushed open the front door a bit more but found himself in a small lobby. There wasn't a lot of room and there was another door immediately to his left. He opened this door and it led into a lounge. Sue handed Michael the case and then followed him in closely followed by Louise and then David.

The room seemed quite big but it was empty. There was a brown carpet that was in fairly good condition but generally the whole house seemed very bare and empty. Sue had forgotten the fact that the walls were not wallpapered but just painted.

"Well, here we are kids. Take a look around." Sue wanted them to feel as comfortable as possible and as soon as possible. Louise left the lounge and poked her head into the bathroom.

"It's very small, Mum." Louise wasn't complaining, just commenting.

"It'll be big enough." Sue assured her. David also looked in but said nothing. From the bathroom, a hallway ran off which were the three bedrooms. David and Louise looked in each of them.

"Which one is my bedroom?" David asked.

"Well we're having this first bedroom." Michael replied

"Does that mean I can choose which room I have?" David looked at Louise as he spoke.

"As the eldest we think you should go in to the far room and Louise will sleep in the middle room." Sue wanted to stop any possible arguments before they started. Louise went into her allocated bedroom and gave it the once over. She seemed happy enough with it. David went into his and although it seemed a lot smaller than his old bedroom he was happy enough that it was a bit out of the way.

"Yeah suits me. What do you say Luce?" David asked her as she came in to have a look at her brother's bedroom. She didn't like it as much as hers.

"Your rooms better but I'll take mine." David went into the middle bedroom again. He saw that it was smaller than his.

"I'm the eldest so I take the bigger room." David was happy. Sue was very happy. The four of them entered into the kitchen.

"Wow, it's a big kitchen, Mum." Louise said.

"That's because it is a kitchen diner. We only have the lounge so meals need to be eaten in here." Sue replied. Sue looked around and opened a few of the cupboards. There was a breakfast bar and lots of worktop space. She had remembered being quite impressed with that when she had looked round the place before. It all looked so different now it was empty.

"Right." Michael looked at his watch. "The removal van will be here in about half an hour so we need to sort out where we are going to put everything."

David and Louise were roaming around the place not really doing anything.

"Mum, where's the telephone?" David asked.

"Oh, that's a point. I haven't actually seen one." All three of them walked around the place looking for a telephone but none could be found. "David, get your Father in a minute."

"Dad. Mum wants you." David shouted out the side door. Michael heard and came back in.

"What's wrong?"

"We haven't got a phone." Sue sounded annoyed as she said it.

"Oh, no. I knew I'd forget something." Michael cursed.

"What is it then? Do we need to get a phone fixed in?" Sue was confused as she thought the Williams would have had a phone.

"No, it's not that bad. There should be a cable connection." Michael looked around the kitchen walls. "Yes, there it is." He pointed to the box next to one of the electrical sockets on the wall. "Mr

Williams said that he had tried to get BT to put in a standard telephone for us as he had bought a special phone that he was taking with him. They wouldn't do it. Apparently, we've got to arrange it once we've moved in and had our new number allocated.

At that moment, Louise noticed the removal van driving up the road.

"They're here," she exclaimed. The Riddells all went out together to meet the van. Michael and Sue had listed what was to go in to the garage and what was to come into the house. There were certain things that they thought should come in before others but most things were offloaded in the order that they were on the van. Michael checked his list as things came off the van and directed them either to the garage or inside the house whilst Sue was indoors telling the removal men where she wanted each piece put. David helped in the garage whilst Louise made some tea for everybody. She did make sure that any things going into her bedroom were put where she wanted them to go but apart from that she left things up to her mum to sort out. With a short break for a drink, the unloading took just under a couple of hours so by half past one the removal men were getting ready to leave.

"David, can you just help me lift these boxes?" Michael asked.

"What boxes?"

"I want to move these two from here over to there." Michael indicated which boxes he wanted moving.

"Why are we moving them?"

"Because they are two boxes full of things that I don't think we'll need that soon and reckon they'll stay in the garage for a while."

"Okay." David and Michael lifted the boxes between them and then they went into the bungalow to see how things were getting on in there.

"Sue, where are you?"

"I'm in our bedroom dear." Michael joined her in the bedroom and surveyed the current situation. The bed was where he expected it to be but the dressing table was under the window.

"I thought we were going to have the dressing table against this wall."

"That's where I first put it but it doesn't leave much room to get past the bed so I've moved it over there."

"Oh, all right. But where is the wardrobe going to go when it comes?"

"Yes, you have a point. Have we got the measurements again? I think it might fit in if we put it in the corner against that wall." Sue and Michael measured various walls and corners and finally decided to wait and see when the wardrobe arrived. "Have you left enough room in the garage for the freezer?" Sue was sure he had.

"Yes, and room for them to carry it in. How's the lounge looking?" Michael went into the lounge and was impressed with the way it looked. They hadn't had time to arrange getting a big television so for now Sue had put the small telly in place. "Wow. You've got this room sorted then." Michael said.

"Yes, Dad. I helped Mum do this room." Louise walked in.

"Yes, you did darling, and haven't we worked hard." Sue added.

"Well you've both done well here. The carpet isn't too bad, is it?" Michael said.

"Not the colour I would have chosen but it'll do. Perhaps when we've got sorted we can think about buying a new carpet. What do you think dear?"

"Yeah I don't see why not. I was actually thinking that instead of renting a telly we might look around and see how much it would cost to buy one. We'd probably save money after about a year."

"Ooh, that'll be good." Louise said excitedly.

"Well we will have to see." Sue didn't want Louise to think they were definitely going to buy a new television until they had costed it out. "Are you going to go down to the phone box to sort out BT or do you want me to go?"

"Do you want to go?"

"I wouldn't mind walking down to the Green. I think that was where the phone box was. Is there any reference I need?"

"I'm not quite sure. I have our account number from Goodmayes but we might get a completely different account now we've moved. Take one of the old bills. The number is on there. Once we've got the phone in we can ring the post office about getting our mail rerouted."

"Okay. I won't be that long."

Sue went down to the phone box and with a little bit

of arguing managed to get BT to get an engineer out to them later that afternoon. The appointment wouldn't be until about five thirty or six o'clock but she was happy in the knowledge that at least they would have a phone they could use before the end of the day. Whilst she had gone, Louise continued trying to get her bedroom just how she wanted it whilst Michael asked David some more questions.

"Dad, can you ask me some more questions please. You're good at it." David hoped his dad would help the time pass.

"I suppose so. You are too clever though." Michael thought for a while. "I'll ask you some about the 60's as I know that era better."

"Yeah I know that. I know it pretty well as well you know."

"Okay. First question. Who were the first British football club to win a major European trophy?"

"You don't mean the European Cup, do you?"

"No. A major European trophy."

"In that case it'll be Spurs in 1963 when we won the European Cup Winners Cup." David knew that one.

"Correct but who did we beat and what was the score?"

"Ah I'm not sure about that. It was a big score and I think it was 4-1 but don't know who we played?" David was annoyed his father had asked him a question he didn't know.

"It was 5-1 and Spurs beat Athletico Madrid in Rotterdam. Or was it Amsterdam. Anyway in Holland."

"How was I supposed to know that?" David moaned.

"I can't just ask you questions you know. Anyway you will be able to answer that question next time." Michael kept on the same subject. "Question 2. Who were the first British football club to win the European Cup?"

"Well that's a bit better. Manchester United, beating Benfica at Wembley and the score was 4-1" David sounded quite cocky as he was giving his answer.

"Wrong." Michael was smirking.

"Wrong. Wrong! You're just joking now. It was Manchester United." David got more annoyed.

"No I'm not joking; the answer is wrong."

"Well who was it then?"

"It was Celtic." Michael told him.

"That's not fair. You didn't say we were including Scottish clubs."

"The question asked for the first British club. Scottish clubs are British."

"Anyway, Celtic didn't win the cup before Manchester United, did they?"

"Yes they won it the year before in 1967."

"What the year Spurs won the Cup." David said this proudly

"Yes that's right and what did Manchester United win that year?"

"Did they win anything?" David guessed they probably did but wondered if his father was trying to trick him.

"If you think about it you should know they did."

"Oh of course they must have won the league championship." David felt happy with his answer.

"That's right and how did you know that."

"Because Spurs played them in the Charity Shield match in 1968." David was happier that he had got something correct again. Michael was a bit surprised at his reply.

"Oh yeah. I hadn't thought about that. I thought you would have known because that's how Manchester United played in the European Cup the following season."

"S'pose so."

"The Charity Shield match you're talking about was in 1967 but who won it?"

"What you mean at the start of the 1967/68 season. Yes, okay it was played in 1967, but Dad, nobody won it. The game finished in a 3-3 draw."

"And who scored one of the Spurs goals that day?" Michael knew David would know the answer.

"Pat Jennings scored."

"Correct." Michael paused to try and think of another question. "Alright one last question for now. Who won the League Cup in 1967, what division were they in and what was so special about the game?" Michael felt this might be a bit of a tough one for him and indeed it was. David knew quite a lot about the League Cup but his knowledge of the 60's was a bit vague.

"I know Spurs first won it in 1970 I think."

"1971." Michael corrected him.

"Okay 1971. I know Arsenal lost to Swindon Town

but I can't say I can remember much before that. I know you and Uncle John are always on about them losing to a little club who were in the third division and I've seen some video of the Don Rogers goal. The finals were all two-legged finals in those days weren't they?"

"You're getting warmer." Michael teased a bit.

"Ah right. It was the first final to be played at Wembley." David wasn't sure if this was right or not.

"That's right. And…"

"And probably the winning team again came from the third division."

"Correct. And they were?"

"I don't think I know this one Dad."

"Do you want me to tell you?"

"Please."

"It was QPR." As Michael gave the answer, Sue entered the lounge. They had both been so engrossed with their questions, neither had heard her come in.

"What more questions?" Sue asked.

"Yes, and Dad is making them too hard."

"Alright then, which team won the FA Cup in 1966?" Sue asked. Michael and David both laughed as they knew exactly what the question was going to be.

"Mum, you only ask questions where Everton is the answer." David replied as he was laughing. "Ask me another."

"Okay then. Who won the FA Cup in 1968?" Once

again both Michael and David laughed. "What are you laughing about? The answer isn't Everton." Sue complained.

"No but only because Everton lost. They were beaten by West Bromwich Albion." David answered. Not wanting to be shown up too much, Sue tried to think of another question.

"So, which two Everton players won the World Cup in 1966?"

"Now that's a bit better but it's still about Everton, Mum."

"Well I don't know any other clubs apart from Tottenham I suppose."

"Alan Ball was one and the other must have been one of the full backs. Either George Cohen or Ray Wilson. I don't know which clubs they played for." David thought out loud.

"Yes, it was Ray Wilson." Sue had had enough. "Right no more."

"So, who did George Cohen play for, Dad?"

"Fulham, son. He was a bloody good player as well."

Michael followed Sue back out to the kitchen.

"How did you get on?"

"No problems really. They started off by telling me that we needed to book an engineer which would take about three weeks but with a little bit of arguing I got them to agree to send one out this afternoon."

"This afternoon. You did well there then."

"Thank you but did you expect anything less?"
"Of course not. So when is he coming?"
"They said about five thirty but could be anytime."

As it turned out, the engineer didn't turn up till nearly half past six. Sue was getting a little worried that she would be let down by BT but she wasn't. By seven o'clock, the phone had been installed and the Riddells were getting their new home organised. They were able to sit down and relax at last. There were still no wardrobes of course and hence clothes laying around everywhere but all three bedrooms were able to be slept in so it was just a matter of getting some tea cooked and they were in business.
"We haven't got a lot to choose from folks but I have bought some tinned steak and I can open some vegetables and soup and we can have a hot pot. How does that sound?" Sue asked everyone.
"Sounds alright to me, Mum." David replied.
"That'll be nice." Louise also answered.
"Sounds like hot pot it is. Do you want me to do anything to help?" Michael added.
"No darling. You can set the table a bit later though. Oh and Louise is getting very good at making tea. Now what can we get David to do?"
"Mum, I'm no good at doing anything." David hoped he might get left out.
"I think the washing up for you my son." Sue decided.

As Sue was cooking, there was a knock on the

window. Sue wiped her hands on the nearby tea towel and went to the door. There was a very dark haired woman waiting outside.

"Hello, can I help you?"

"Hello. I'm Mrs Armstrong from next door. We weren't at home when you arrived and I just wanted to greet you." The woman had a gypsyish look about her. Both in her facial features and the clothes she was wearing. Sue was a little wary of her just in case it was a ruse to get in the place but then thought that it wouldn't be good to not invite your neighbour indoors at the first time of meeting.

"Please come in. I'll just call my husband." Sue let the woman in hoping that someone in the family would have heard what was going on and would have come into the kitchen to find out who was at the door. Sue was disappointed to find that nobody had responded. "Michael. Michael just come here a minute please." She turned to Mrs Armstrong and beckoned her to sit down at the table. "I'm sorry, we're just about getting ready to eat."

"Oh, yes. I'm sorry to disturb you and won't stay long."

"Yes dear what is it?" Michael arrived in the kitchen.

"This is Mrs Armstrong."

"You can call me Dawn by the way. I'm from next door. I wasn't quite sure when you were moving in as the Williams moved out middle of last week."

"Oh, I didn't know when they were going." Michael found the situation a bit awkward although he realised in was a nice gesture on behalf of the woman.

"My husband is Nigel. You'll meet him sometime soon I'm sure. If you need anything, please knock on the door. You might not get much help from many of the others but we're usually able to help."

"What do you mean we won't get help from others?" Sue found the statement a bit strange.

"Oh, nothing particularly bad, it's just that most are locals and keep themselves to themselves."

"Oh right. You're not from round here then?" Michael wondered.

"No we're from Yorkshire although my husband is originally from Ireland. We've been here about three years and there are more and more outsiders coming into the village now so there are quite a few people to chat to but most of the locals I don't really know."

"Were the Williams locals?" Michael wasn't sure.

"Yes in a way. They came from Norwich so were Norfolk born but they weren't local to the village. Anyway, I won't stay. Just wanted to say hello and hope you settle in okay." Dawn got up to leave. "And don't forget, if you want anything, just ask."

"Thank you. Bye!" Michael saw her out of the door and then shut it. "Well that was different."

"Yes. Nice of her though."

"Who was that at the door?" David asked.

"Our next-door neighbour. Mrs Armstrong I think she said." Sue answered.

"What did she want then?"

"Just called to say hello really."

"Why did she do that then?"

"Well it's just a way of trying to make us feel welcome." Michael interrupted.

"Oh right." David thought about another question but carried on eating instead.

"So will the other neighbours be calling round?" Louise took up the questioning.

"No I don't think so." Sue answered this time.

"They got the flags out for us, though, didn't they?" David added.

"Yes they did. The village has welcomed us, haven't they?

Chapter 5
SOMERBY

Tuesday 17th January 1995
Tuesday morning saw all of the Riddells sleeping in. Sue was half awake and she had managed to see that it was nearly nine o'clock but as she was certain that all the family were pretty well shattered and apparently still asleep she didn't worry about getting up yet. Michael was laying with his back to her and she touched him gently just to see if he was at all responsive. There was no indication that he was awake so she tickled him a little bit just in a teasing way until he subconsciously moved to avoid the irritation. She smiled and gave him one great big hug and a kiss on his shoulder. She was proud of what they had achieved. This was going to be a new beginning.

It was taking a while but gradually the Riddells were waking up. Louise was the first to wake up and finding her surroundings a bit strange she checked to see if her mum and dad were awake.

"Morning, darling," Sue said as she saw Louise poke her head around the bedroom door.

"Is Daddy awake yet?"

"No, not yet but he soon will be." Sue knew that the talking would wake him up. "Are you going to help me make breakfast?"

"Yes, of course I will. What are we having?"

"To be honest dear, I don't really know. Let's go

and have a look." Sue got out of bed and put on her dressing gown. The house was cold and its newness didn't seem to help the situation much. It was funny, but silly things like having painted walls rather than wallpaper seemed to make the place colder. It was also strange living in a bungalow. Sue followed Louise into the kitchen. "Can you put some water in the kettle and switch it on so we can have some tea please?" Sue pointed in the general direction of the kettle.

"Shall I put some bags in the teapot?"

"Yes please darling." Sue went to the main storage cupboard to look and see exactly what there was to choose from for breakfast.

"Where are the teabags, Mum?"

"Well they should be in the cupboard under the worktop I think." Louise opened the cupboard and found an open box of teabags. David appeared at the kitchen door.

"What's for breakfast?"

"What do you want?" Sue had found some things but not a lot.

"Have we got any eggs?" David said almost immediately.

"Oh, I'm not sure whether we got any. Have a look in the fridge, I mean cupboard." Sue was getting a little bit flustered as she had intended to make this first morning a nice one but of course the house wasn't fully functional yet. The fridge was hopefully arriving later today but for now all the food was in the food cupboard.

"Yes, there are four eggs, Mum. Can I have scrambled egg?" David was starting to get a bit of an appetite and he'd only been up five minutes.

"Well we can have scrambled eggs but I need to see what else we can have with it. We have some bread and tinned tomatoes and there are some sausages we can cook. Will that do?" Sue hoped David would be happy with what she was able to offer.

"Yeah that'll do. I'm going to try and find some clothes to put on."

"Don't empty too many clothes out David as we have a wardrobe coming today."

"Okay, I won't." David answered but didn't really take in his Mum's request.

Michael eventually got out of bed and he too felt how cold it was. He didn't have a dressing gown so he grabbed at his old jumper that was laying across the chair and put that on. He found his way to the kitchen.

"Good Morning all."

"Hello Dad. You're up then." Louise was busy helping with the breakfast as she spoke.

"Mmn. Something smells nice." Michael said.

"You mean me of course." Sue laughed as she replied. "Breakfast will be ready in about ten minutes." Sue and Louise continued with their cooking whilst Michael sat himself at the table. "Do you know what time the deliveries are coming today dear?" Sue asked.

"First one is due about one. I think it is the

wardrobes first then the fridge and freezer will be coming about two."

"Ooh are we getting a freezer?" Louise seemed excited about the thought.

"Yes darling we're getting a chest freezer to go in the garage." Michael replied.

"But shouldn't we be getting a car to go in the garage?"

"Maybe later. Neither of us can drive so it's no good getting a car yet and anyway I'm not sure we'll need one."

"I think you'll find we will." Sue added.

"Breakfast is ready." Sue shouted so that David could hear. Sue and Louise sat down at the table and David was not far behind.

"Great. Scrambled egg, my favourite." David said.

"Everything's your favourite." Louise moaned. David gave his sister a long hard stare and when he had distracted her made a grab with his knife and fork and took some of the scrambled egg off of her plate.

"Mmn! Even more my favourite, Luce's scrambled egg."

"Mum, stop him." Louise complained.

"Mum, stop him." David mimicked his sister's cry for help. Sue hit David's arm quite hard.

"What!" He replied.

"Give Louise some egg back."

"Why should I. It was only a joke." David made no attempt to return any egg.

"Do it!" Sue got angry. David gave Louise some egg back. "And don't do it again." David sulked but carried on eating his breakfast. He pushed his plate away with some sausage and tomato still left on it. "Aren't you eating that?" Sue was a bit concerned.

"To be honest Mum, I don't feel too good this morning. My stomach is a bit weird and I think I've got a headache coming on." David stood up and took a step away from the table.

"Sit back down and wait for the rest of us to finish." Michael ordered. David seemed to have a glared look in his eyes. "Sit down, David." Michael ordered again. David said nothing but just turned his head towards Michael. Michael could see the strange look in his eyes which was a look you think you would see when someone has been stabbed in the back. It was a look of surprise and confusion. David wobbled and then collapsed. He went down with quite a fall and Sue tried to get there to help him but she was too late. He hit his head on the hard kitchen floor and Michael also jumped to try and get round to his son. The whole event only lasted about five seconds but seemed like an eternity. Sue immediately thought back to their visit to the village in October when David felt ill in the coffee bar. It was almost as if he was having some repeat of that illness then but it seemed worse than before.

"David, David." Sue looked for signs that he was still breathing.

"Just roll him on to his side and make sure there's no blood." Michael wasn't trained in first aid but his instincts told him what to do. Sue placed her hand around David's nose and was relieved to find that she could feel his breathing.

"He's breathing." She exclaimed.

"Can you see any blood?" Michael was still worried.

"No, can you?"

"No." As Michael and Sue checked, Louise sat fixed in the chair and started to cry. The tears were small to start with but within a few seconds she had worked up into a bit of a frenzy. Sue stayed with David whilst Michael tried to calm Louise down. He cuddled her as she whimpered away. He tried to comfort her with words like "It's okay darling," and "There's nothing to get upset about," but he knew how silly he sounded as in fact it was a great shock for her. David regained consciousness and saw his Mother looking over him.

"David, can you hear me?" Sue spoke softly.

"Yes I can hear you. Where am I?" David seemed to be speaking quite normally.

"You're in Somerby." Sue told him.

"Yes, I know that, but where exactly. Oh yes, I'm in Rawthorn Drive." Sue looked at Michael who was as surprised as she was with the comment. As she looked back David had closed his eyes again and she was briefly alarmed that David may have lapsed back into his unconsciousness but his eyes opened again. "Mum. My head hurts." David said it in a most soppy voice and it made both Sue and Michael laugh. Even Louise laughed. David sat up and rubbed the front of his head where by now a very big bump was starting to show.

"Can you stand up son?" Michael asked as Sue gave David a bit of support to get him back to his feet. David held on to the table for a short while until he felt capable of supporting himself. "Alright darling?" Michael turned his attentions to Louise who by now had stopped sobbing and gasping and was working to make some sense of all she had seen.

"I think you should go and have a lie down dear." Sue led David back to his bedroom and made sure he laid on the bed. "I'm going to see if we can get a doctor out to see you."

"Yeah, alright, Mum." David felt exhausted and fell asleep quite quickly.

Sue phoned the local surgery and within an hour a doctor was knocking at the door. There was a brief discussion to explain the Riddell's situation about the fact that they currently weren't registered with any doctor in the area and then the doctor went in to see David.

"Wake up David, the doctor is here." Sue said as she shook him gently.

"Err!" David was a bit slow to come round.

"Let's have a look at you son." Doctor Hemmingway said. He felt his pulse and then looked at his eyes. He took out one of those fancy torches that are shaped like pens and shone it in David's eyes, alternating each eye. "Okay David, what day is it today?"

"It's Tuesday."

"And the date is?"

"The seventeenth of January." The doctor seemed happy with David's answers.

"Just open your mouth and say aargh."

"Aargh." As David did as he was told doctor turned to Sue and asked a few more questions.

"You say he went glazed?"

"Well that's what it looked like wasn't it Michael?" Sue replied.

"His eyes were staring and looked as if they were full of tears." Michael tried to explain what he had seen.

"And then he wobbled and fell?" Again Doctor Hemmingway kept feeling David's neck as he continued his interrogation.

"Yes. That explains it." Sue couldn't really add anything else.

"So, David what do you remember?" The doctor stopped inspecting his patient to give him a chance to answer.

"Well, it was a bit strange. I remember having a bit of a headache which just seemed to get worse and then I think I was out in the road, I think, and then in bed but I may have dreamt that last bit. I felt pretty giddy." David seemed to have a bit of trouble explaining his own experiences but tried to report what he could remember as accurately as possible.

"And how's your headache now?"

"Well, it's actually gone now. It only lasted a few

minutes really." Doctor Hemmingway turned to Sue and gave his best prognosis.

"To be honest I'm not quite sure what is wrong with him. He seems okay now and he checks out perfectly alright. Has this ever happened before?" Although the doctor was addressing his mother, David started to reply to the question.

"Well…"

"No, nothing like this has ever happened." Sue interrupted her son to stop him from answering and to give the doctor the reply she wanted to tell him.

"Well, in that case I think he needs to rest a little, but if he feels like getting up, don't stop him. A little air might be good later but wrap up warm of course. Then book an appointment, after you've registered of course, and we'll do some blood tests just in case there are any problems I can't see. Is that okay?" Doctor Hemmingway closed his bag to indicate he was ready to leave. Everyone moved out from David's bedroom and towards the outside door. Michael opened it to let the doctor out.

"I would try and make sure you keep an eye on him for the next couple of days just in case anything like that happens again. I'm sorry I can't be more precise." Doctor Hemmingway shrugged his shoulders.

"Thanks, doctor." Michael shut the door and looked at Sue.

"It's a bloody good job we had that phone installed yesterday," said Sue.

"Yeah. You never know do you." Michael was

worried. "It was a bit like what happened back in October. He hasn't got a temperature at all has he?"

"No Doctor said he was perfectly normal."

"It's just that we have no shops nearby if we need to get anything." Michael thought about all the possible things he could get at a moment's notice back in Goodmayes.

"We'll have to go shopping and get some things." Sue turned to Louise. "Are you going to come out with me to the shop?"

"Yes okay. I'll get my coat." Louise wanted to get some air. She was still upset about the incident and wanted to get out. Sue and Louise walked down to the shop. They had seen it yesterday and wanted to see what they sold. They had been to Tesco's before they arrived yesterday to get some things so hadn't needed to go then. It was an opportunity to meet some of the locals as well Sue thought. When they got there they were a bit shocked as to how small it was. There was a very little fresh food section, a small freezer, basically just one load of shelves with bread and hardly anything at all in the way of medicines. Sue grabbed a basket and put one or two things in it that she could do with but didn't really want and made her way to the counter where a uniformed woman was waiting. She wore a badge indicating that her name was Helen.

"Hello, I can do you here," the woman said. Sue was a bit surprised to find that the woman had a Scottish accent. She was blond but perhaps with a hint of ginger which Sue thought might have suggested her origins.

"Thank you." Sue paused and looked obviously in the direction of the woman's badge. "Helen".

"Oh, yeah. My name's Helen." The woman seemed a bit shocked to be called by her first name but then quickly realised that her badge had given her away.

"Yes hello, I'm Sue and this is my daughter Louise." Louise and Helen nodded at each other. "We've just moved into the village. Yesterday in fact."

"That's nice. Are you from London?"

"Yes, from a place called Goodmayes."

"Oh, I've never heard of it."

"Well it's in Essex really." Sue and Helen chatted whilst the products were being run past a scanner. "Is this the only shop in the village?"

"Well no. There's Coopers round the corner. It's really a newsagent but sells a few other things. We have a butcher and a bakery."

"And a candlestick maker's." Louise just couldn't resist. There was a bit of an embarrassing silence as Helen stopped chatting. Sue wasn't quite sure how the woman would take the comment but Helen laughed and the tension went.

"No deary, we don't have one of those." Helen smiled at Louise and continued. "We have the coffee bar, that's called Doc's, though."

"Ah, is that where we saw the flags yesterday?" Sue knew it was.

"Aye, Doc has just had those flagpoles put up. But he was trying out some lights or something yesterday as well. Did you see them?" Helen had finished adding up the shopping.

"Yes, we did. What were they all about then?"

"I don't think it was anything. Doc was probably getting something ready for spring time. He does a lot of things around the village."

"And there was a banner, I believe." Again Sue knew there was but just wanted someone to confirm what it had said.

"Aye, I didn't see no banner." Helen smiled again at Louise. "By the way we have a Chinese takeaway if you need one and a post office." Helen had almost forgotten what she was telling Sue. "That'll be six pounds forty-seven please."

"Is there a chemist nearby?"

"Ah yes, I nearly forgot. Yes, we have a pharmacy round the corner as well. None of them more than a couple of minutes' walk."

"Thank you."

After shopping they made their way back home. By the time they had returned, the man delivering their fridge and freezer had already arrived and was preparing to start unloading the first of the items. With the fridge arriving, Sue felt that at last the house was getting a bit more ship shape. No sooner had the man finished delivering the freezer that the van delivering the wardrobes turned up. This meant waking David who had slept through the fridge delivery but they left his room till last and woke him gently. He seemed quite refreshed and happy to get up. By the time the delivery had been completed, David was his usual self. He was asking for food and that was always a good sign.

"Do you fancy a little walk around the village?" Michael asked.

"Yes, that would be okay." David was up for that. The four of them walked round by way of the post office, the local pub and then to the collection of shops housing a butcher, bakers, coffee bar, Chinese take-away and hairdressers.

"There isn't a fish and chip shop." Louise complained.

"Perhaps they have a van come round. We'll have to find out." Sue tried to answer.

"There's a fish and chip shop here somewhere. I know because the fridge man said." Michael looked around. "There it is, over there." Michael pointed away in the distance at a small unlit shop which had a picture of a fish on it. It was across another, much bigger piece of green. The four of them continued to make their way to the front of the coffee bar and towards the big Oak tree that stood majestically in the middle of a small triangular green. It was the focal point of the village of Somerby. It must have been there for hundreds of years. There was also a village sign that had a Viking ship on it. There was obviously some connection between the village and old Viking invaders. Sue had purposely come round this way so as to have another look at the banner to see exactly what it said but the banner had gone. The lights had gone too. Only the flags still flew from the top of the building.

"So where was this sign you were talking about?" Michael asked generally.

"It seems to have gone." Sue replied.

"It was up there, Dad, on top of that coffee bar." David looked hard at the building. There was no sign of any such banner or any lights having ever been there. David couldn't quite understand why but there was a nice feeling about the coffee bar. It felt familiar, but obviously he had never seen it before yesterday. Perhaps it was of a similar design to one he had seen on the telly. He wasn't sure.

"I'm sure it mentioned our name. It said Somerby welcomes the Riddells."

"Who would put a sign up saying that?" Michael wasn't convinced he wasn't having his leg pulled.

"Shall we go in the coffee bar and ask them?" Louise enquired.

"Did you see it darling?" Sue replied.

"I saw some writing but didn't look at it properly."

"I don't think we'll go in there today. Perhaps another time." Michael looked inside and saw the place was quite full of kids. He didn't fancy making enquiries at the moment.

"I think we should get going." Sue said. "David, how are you?"

"Okay, I suppose, but can still feel a bit of a headache. It's just come on a bit but I'm okay." David was feeling a bit strange again. He couldn't explain why but it was like there was going to be a thunderstorm soon.

"It is getting a bit cold again so let's get back.

The next morning was hectic. Three people all up at the same time trying to get in the bathroom, get dressed and have breakfast.

Michael and David walked down Rawthorn Drive and after five minutes were walking past the coffee bar known as 'Doc's'. David looked through the window and noticed a few other kids in there who were wearing the same school uniform that he was. There were four distinctly different uniforms by the looks of it and David wondered just how many of them would be getting on his coach.

"There are quite a few in there." Michael nodded towards the coffee bar.

"Yeah, quite a few."

"Do you want to go in?" Michael asked. David glanced at his watch.

"No, not this morning. The coach will be here soon." It was clear that you could see when the coach was arriving from the coffee bar so he assumed that there would be some mass rush when it arrived. David wasn't quite sure what to expect so wanted to be able to move around a bit and make his move as and when he was ready.

"Have you got that letter?" Michael asked.

"What letter?"

"The one that says you can catch the coach I mean."

"Yes, it's in my pocket, Dad. Don't hassle me." David pleaded.

"Yeah, okay. Just making sure you're ready."

"I'm as ready as I'll ever be." David was getting embarrassed about all the questions his father was asking. He was quite pleased to see a coach arriving at the bus stop which he hoped was his. "I think this is the coach now."

"Alright. See you tonight son." Michael knew David wanted to be seen to be on his own and was quite happy to just watch from afar. As the coach pulled up at the bus stop there was a mass of school kids emerging from the coffee bar. There was obviously a fairly respected pecking order of who should get on the coach first. David stood back to see what happened and the elder kids went on first. There were already a number of kids on the coach and again it was obvious that there was some agreed placing from the back of the coach to the front. The last of the queuing kids got on the coach and David was left. He stepped on to the step waiting for the driver to query why he was getting on but to his surprise the man seemed to have no cares whether he got on or not. Not being stopped at all, David made his way to the gangway and looked towards the back for a spare seat. There were a few near to him but most of these would mean sitting next to a much younger kid and he wasn't going to do that. He noticed that there were at least two spare seats close to the back of the coach but there were a couple of lads occupying both spaces and he didn't want to have any aggro on his first day. As he made his way along the gangway, there were a couple of girls about his own age who were sat together that David smiled at. They smiled at him. He had seen one of the girls waiting to get on the coach at Somerby but couldn't be sure if they had both got on there or not. As he looked around again there was another girl sat on her own about two seats back. He looked at her to see if she was normal enough and she seemed okay. He looked again to the back seat and noticed that at least two of the lads sitting on the back seat were watching him. He gave them a nod of acceptance. He was pleased to receive a small nod from one of them in return.

"Do you mind if I sit here?" David asked the girl. She was quite plain faced with pale white skin and longish straight dark brown hair. She turned and looked at him but didn't answer. The coach by now had started to move and David was holding on to the seats with one hand to prevent himself from falling over. That was the last thing he wanted to do on his first day. "Is anyone sitting there?" David asked again.

"No." The girl seemed reluctant to say much more. David took the reply as a go ahead to sit down and he did. As he sat down there was a loud voice heard from behind him.

"We got a new boy." David ignored the remark although he knew quite clearly it was aimed at him. He was quite prepared for a bit of harassment but not knowing quite what form it would take it sent a flutter of butterflies around his stomach. "Oy new boy." A voice from the back seat shouted out again.

David still didn't respond. The girl sitting next to him turned away and looked out of the window. "Oy Carlton boy." The voice called out again. David was now left in no doubt that it was he who was being spoken to as Carlton was the name of the school he was going to. He stayed in his seat but turned to face the back seat. One of the lads on the back seat was half standing or kneeling on the seat and was obviously the one who had shouted. David gave a small nod as if to say he was ready to listen to what he had to say and as he did the coach seemed to go quiet immediately. There were one or two at the front of the coach who must have been completely oblivious to what was going on but generally the whole coach had stopped what they were doing to see what was going to happen next. "What's your name?"

"Dave." There was a pause and David waited to find out what the lad was going to say next. A second seemed to last a minute as the lad thought about a reply but then sat back down. The rest of the kids on the coach sensed that the action was over and got on with their conversations. David wondered if that was all he was going to get from the coach and sat back round. He was happy enough with the attention he had got so far.

"Are you going to Carlton?" David asked the girl next to him.

"No."

"So what school do you go to?"

"Er. St. Nicks." The girl wasn't exactly talkative

and seemed to show an obvious reluctance to join in with any conversation. She certainly wasn't going to ask David any questions. David assumed that this was probably because he was a stranger and thought he ought to ask her name so as to appear friendly.

"What's your name?"

"Mary."

"Mine's David."

"Yes I know." The girl turned to look out of the window again so David gave up. The next part of the coach journey was very much the same. Everyone on the coach was chatting away and just waiting to get to school. The coach turned into some residential area and David guessed they were nearing the school. As another turn was made, he could see ahead that the school was there. There were kids walking along the side of the coach but the uniform didn't seem quite right.

"Is this Carlton Grammar School?" David asked Mary. She didn't reply but shook her head in a negative manner. "Do we all get off here?"

"No." This time Mary actually spoke.

"Are you getting off here?" David thought it was a sensible enough question but Mary just laughed in reply. David couldn't quite make her out. She obviously didn't want to talk to him. That was certain. As the coach stopped, most of the lads from the back seat got up to leave. As they went past David they all gave him a look and as the apparent leader of the back-seat mob went past he stopped and turned.

"Have a good day, Dave." He said it in the most awful imitation of a cockney accent David had ever heard.

"Don't you worry, I will." David replied.

"And bye bye, Mary." The lad said in a manner that sounded quite insincere. David looked at Mary thinking that the two might be boyfriend and girlfriend and in which case he had upset things by sitting next to her but she had cowered away even more into her seat turning her head almost backwards so that nobody could see her. David wasn't quite sure what to make of it. It seemed like the whole of the back seat had vacated the coach and within a few seconds the vehicle was on its way again.

"Does the coach make many more stops?" David asked the girl expecting a one word answer.

"I don't know, sorry." She didn't turn away quite so markedly as before. "The next stop is where I get off and then you stay on for your school." David was taken aback at the length of the reply.

"What school did you say you went to again?"

"St. Nicholas School. It's a Church school." Mary seemed more prepared to chat.

"Where do you live?" David continued.

"Leafby." Mary seemed pleased that David was that interested in her. "I haven't seen you on the coach before."

"No it's my first day."

"Have you changed schools then?"

"Well yes." David thought that was a bit obvious. "I

moved up from London on Sunday."

"London!" Mary gasped.

"You know where London is?"

"Yes but I've never been there. You went to school in London?" Mary seemed impressed.

"Yes in a place called Gidea Park near Romford." David explained thinking that the mention of Romford would make things clearer.

"Oh." Mary replied. It didn't make things clearer. The coach started to slow down again. "This is where I get off." Mary stood as she spoke. David got out of his seat to let her off. As she got out of the seat he just quickly said 'Bye' to her. It seemed like she hadn't heard him or had perhaps ignored him again but then she stopped and turned. "Hope you have a good day, bye." David prepared to sit back down when another voice from the back seat shouted out.

"Oy Dave, you can come and sit on the back seat if you want." David turned to see that there was still one lad sitting on the back seats. He was obviously a Carlton boy.

"Thanks." David went to the back seats and sat in next to the window. "I see you go to Carlton as well," he pointed to the school badge.

"Yas, I'm a Carlton boy. Your first day today?" The lad's accent was very country as far as David was concerned.

"Yeah. Moved up from London on Sunday." As David was replying he sensed that there were two girls also with Carlton uniforms on who had got on the coach at this stop who were making their way towards the back seats. He looked at them and thought they looked alright.

"Hi Phil," the first girl said.

"Hello Jane."

"Phil." The second girl said in way of a hello. "Who's this then?" She wasted no time in trying to find out who the new boy was.

"This is Dave from London." Phil introduced him.

"Ooh London eh." The first girl replied in a sarcastic way.

"Hello." David said. The two girls looked at him and then sat down on the back seat.

"I'm Jane and this is Susan." The four of them chatted all the way to Carlton School and David felt he had made some new friends. As David had not been to a co-ed school previously the whole experience of travelling with girls was new to him. Actually being taught with girls in the same class and seeing girls around the school was even more of an experience but those three friends he made on the bus that day helped a lot.

Louise had a pretty easy day really. Sue had walked with down to the road on which her new school was situated and then she left her to complete the journey on her own. Louise was quite looking forward to meeting some new friends. She had many that she had left behind in Goodmayes but only looked upon them positive side of making new friends here in Somerby. She reported to the office as instructed. Sat at a desk was a stern looking woman.

"Oh you're the new girl, aren't you?" The secretary said.

"Yes, Miss."

"And what is your name?"

"Louise, Miss."

"Louise what?"

"Louise Riddell, Miss." Louise thought she ought to be on her best behaviour on her first day.

"Well, Miss Riddell, I'll take you to see your form teacher now as assembly will be starting in about five minutes." The secretary walked quite quickly down the passage and Louise struggled to keep up.

"Come on, Miss Riddell, we mustn't be slovenly now." The secretary clapped her hands as she paused and waited for Louise to catch up. As she was about three feet away. The secretary set off again, but this time at what seemed like a quicker pace. Louise, still in her coat and carrying a school bag in her hand quickly lost the pace and to make matters worse the school bell rang. This must have indicated that assembly would be starting as children emerged from almost every room and filled the corridor. This made it even harder for Louise to keep the secretary in sight but at last the mass of children who were all walking in the opposite direction finished and the corridor was empty again. The trouble was it was completely empty. Nobody was in front of her. Louise stopped and turned around to see the secretary standing in the doorway of the last classroom. "No wandering off now, Miss Riddell, we don't want to lose you, do we? Well, not on your first day." The secretary stood at the doorway waiting for Louise to enter the classroom, which she duly did. "Mrs Saunders, this is our new girl. Miss Riddell." The secretary looked at Louise. "Say hello to Mrs Saunders."

"Hello, Mrs Saunders." Louise couldn't stand this much longer.

"Thank you, Miss Brown." Mrs Saunders waited for the secretary to make her way down the hall before turning to Louise. "Don't worry about Miss Brown. She's a bit of a fuddy-duddy."

"Oh, right." Louise answered.

"So you're the new girl." Mrs Saunders bent down to talk to Louise. "And you are Miss Riddell."

"Yes, Miss."

"And your first name is?"

"Louise, Miss."

"Well, Louise, you've arrived just as Assembly is about to start so come with me and we'll introduce you to your new class afterwards." Mrs Saunders seemed very nice as she spoke.

Louise was introduced to her class as promised and she made friends straightaway. There was Tina Phillips, Gillian Fortescue, Vanessa Matthews, Melanie Huggins and Olivia Thompson although she was known as Livvy. There was also a boy who made friends with Louise called Peter Masterson but naturally he played with the other boys most of the time. All six were in Louise's class and after school the girls invited Louise to join them at Doc's. They always went there to have a coke or some similar drink, and hang out with some of the boys, and they wanted Louise to join them.

"Come down to Doc's, Louise, after school," Tina asked. She was the first one to make friends with Louise and seemed the nicest of them all.

"I can't, as my mum is meeting me."

"Oh, come on. We don't do anything wild, we just hang out down there. Vanessa has to wait to be picked up so we all go and have a coke," Tina pleaded. The girls were just leaving school and Louise could see her mum waiting for her at the gate.

"I'll go and ask." Louise said.

Sue left Louise at the end of the road and made her way back home. There was still plenty of unpacking to do but first she had to clear up after this morning's activities. There was a bathroom to clear up, bedrooms to tidy and the washing up to sort out but Sue went about her tasks with vigour. The time went very quickly and before Sue realised it was already past three o'clock. She wanted to go and meet Louise today after her first day and knew that she was due out at half past. Sue got ready and made her way to the school. As Louise appeared, Sue gave a little wave but only a little one.

"Mum, do you mind if I go down to the coffee bar?" Louise asked.

"That's okay dear. When?"

"Now."

"Now!" Sue was a bit taken by the bluntness of the request. "But aren't you coming home? I thought you'd want to get changed first." Sue suggested.

"No, Mum. My friends are going to the coffee bar and I want to go with them, please, Mum."

"Okay. What time will you be home?"

"Oh, I don't know. About five."

"Have you got any homework?"

"No," Louise lied.

"Well, your father will be home about six, so I'll be doing tea for then. Make sure you're home in time to get changed and be ready to eat."

"Yes, Mum." Louise ran off before her mum had a chance to change her mind. Sue walked back home, and Louise went to Doc's with the other girls. They giggled and chatted all the way to the coffee bar.

"Have you got any money?" Tina asked Louise.

"I've got some, but not a lot. Why?"

"We have to buy something if we go to Doc's. Don't worry, just stick with us."

Tina and Gillian grabbed some seats at a vacant table and gestured Louise over. The other three girls hung around outside for a few minutes, and joined the others one at a time.

"Are we buying some drinks then?" Louise asked.

"Hold on a minute. If one of the staff looks at us then we go up and buy something," Gillian told her.

"We're all right at the moment," Tina added. Doc's was at its busiest because a lot of kids from school had made their way to the coffee bar, and all the staff were working hard. The younger ones did exactly the same as Louise's friends, and took it in turns to buy things so they could occupy a table for longer. Doc hadn't arrived, but he normally appeared about this time to help out. Either Kathy or Doc would make sure that all the tables were being used.

"Doc isn't here at the moment," Gillian said to Tina.

"No. If he comes out I'll go up," Tina replied. Vanessa was the next one to come in and join the girls at the table.

"Are we ok?" she asked.

"Yes, Ness," said Tina. "Are you being picked up at the usual time?"

"Guess so."

"Have you got far to go?" Louise asked.

"No, not really. I live in Leafby, and my Mum comes to pick me up." Melanie and Livvy were soon also at the table. Kathy looked their way and noticed the six girls. She served the next person in line.

"I'm going to get a coke. Anyone want any food?" Tina asked.

"I'll have a coke as well," replied Louise.

"Don't be silly. We share the drinks," Gillian explained.

The girls spent the next hour chatting about their favourite programmes, boys, music and life in general. After a while some of the older boys from the secondary school came in and the cafe was getting quite full. Louise knew that David's coach would be back any minute and she tried to keep a look out for him. Doc had still not been seen, although the staff were coping quite well so there was no need for him. Nevertheless, it was unusual for him to be absent at this time.

"So, Louise, what do you think of school?" Melanie asked, as the girls passed round a couple of coke bottles.

"It's okay, but I don't like Miss Brown," Louise answered.

"What, the Dragon?" said Melanie, and the other girls laughed.

"She was a bit of a cow when I first arrived," Louise explained.

"Don't worry, you'll get used to her," Vanessa added. "Hey, girls, I've got to go, my mum has just pulled up."

"Alright, Ness. See you tomorrow?" Tina spoke for all the girls. Vanessa left Doc's and the rest of them continued the conversation. From time to time one of the older boys would come over and talk to them. Peter Masterson spoke briefly to Louise. Whilst this was going on, Gillian noticed that Doc had appeared.

"He's looking over at our table," she said.

"But we've already got a couple of cokes," said Tina.

"He is certainly looking at us," Livvy confirmed. "Hey, Louise, that's Doc over there."

Louise looked.

"Oh, him!" Louise replied. "I've seen him before. I didn't know that was Doc."

She continued to look, and she knew there was something about him, but she just couldn't put her finger on what. "He's the bloke who was outside here when we arrived," Louise added.

"No, he wasn't. It's the first time he's been down today," Tina replied. "Well since we've been in, that is."

"No, I mean when we moved in. He was standing outside." Louise tried to correct the misunderstanding.

"Well, he would have been, wouldn't he?" Tina seemed unimpressed.

Louise noticed that more older boys had come in, and she looked out to see if she could spot David. He had already gone past. She thought about running out to get him, but decided to stay where she was. He could come in another day.

By five-thirty, Louise had left the girls and made her way up Rawthorn Drive. She arrived home to find David lying on the floor watching television, and her mum in the kitchen getting tea ready.

"I'll just get changed, Mum, and then I can help you," Louise told her.

"That would be nice, darling. Did you get on all right at school today?"

"Yes. I've made lots of new friends." Louise was really excited, explaining to Sue who each one was.

Sue was pleased that both David and Louise had done reasonably well on their first day at new schools. Twenty minutes later, Michael was also home.

"Hello, darling." Sue stopped what she was doing, wiped her hands and gave him a big hug and a kiss. "So, how's my new Customer Services Manager?" she asked.

Michael told her all about the new job he had taken on. The only downside was that Michael would have to get himself a car and learn how to drive if he was going to do his job properly. The local public transport just wasn't good enough and he couldn't depend on others to drive him around. Sue had to agree. Without a car, they were a bit cut off. Overall, though, she was very happy that all the family had had a good day.

The next day was very similar for all the family. David caught the school coach as usual. He looked around for Mary, but she wasn't where he thought she'd be so he picked an empty seat.

"Hey, Dave, come and sit back here."

It was Phil, standing up this time and inviting him to join the others on the back seat of the coach.

"Yeah, alright," David answered.

"This is Arthur." Phil introduced the lads. "This is Mark, and this is Steve."

"Hi," said David in greeting and all three nodded. He sat down immediately in front of them, but to all intents and purposes, he was part of the back-seat mob.

"You are all from the High School then?" David asked.

"Yus, and you're a Carlton boy?" Arthur seemed to be the main spokesman.

"S'pose so."

"Arthur is the football captain, best player in Yarmouth," Steve said.

"Bloody shut up, you wanker!" Arthur pushed Steve back down on to his seat. "Dave here doesn't want to know that."

"No, I'm interested. A bit," David replied. "Do you play for Yarmouth?"

"No, not exactly. I'm in the youth team." Arthur tried to sound modest but came across pretty arrogant.

"And he's the captain!" Steve added, but then shut up before being told to.

"Well, I'm impressed." David tried to sound impressed. "I'm not even in the school team."

As the coach got to Yarmouth High School the lads from the back seat got off. Arthur gave David a knowing look as he left. It said 'I'm not sure about you'. He stopped halfway down the coach and looked at someone for a moment before continuing off. David dismissed it, but when the coach stopped again in the town he spotted Mary, and it was she who had been spoken to by Arthur. David moved towards the window to try and catch her attention and she saw him as he waved. She looked up briefly and her long hair fell back to reveal a big bruise by her left eye. Almost immediately, she pulled her hair back again to hide it. Mary gave David one more look, before turning and walking the other way.

"Who you waving at?" Phil asked.

"Oh, just some girl." David replied.

"Bloody 'ell, it han't taken you lorrng, has it, boy?" exclaimed Phil in a very Norfolk accent.

"It's the girl I was sat next to yesterday."

"Oh, Mary. You don't want to be waving at her," Phil warned.

"Why not?"

"She's Arthur's girl."

"Arthur's girlfriend? She doesn't act like it."

"Maybe not, but she is. Just be careful."

Phil sounded genuinely concerned.

Thursday was an interesting day for David. They had games in the afternoon. David had already been asked whether he preferred rugby or football, and of course he had chosen the latter. During the lesson, the football coach spotted David's talents. He had shown during the thirty-minute game that he could play football. After a little discussion, David was asked to play in the next school match. On the way home, David planned to talk to Mary, just to see how she was. He took Phil into his confidence. As the coach picked up at the town schools, David looked out for Mary. He waved at her, and she smiled, but she didn't wave back. As she got on, she took a seat towards the front, knowing that David would be at the back but David walked down to sit next to her.

"Hi," said David. Mary turned away from him. "Did Arthur do that?" Again, Mary didn't answer. David guessed that she might be in trouble if Arthur saw her talking to him. "Look," he said, "I'm going to sit back on the back seat before he gets on. I just want to ask if you're his girlfriend." Mary still didn't answer. David left it at that and went back to Phil. "Don't you dare say anything, will you?" David pleaded.

"No, not a word." Phil sounded sincere. By the time David got to Somerby, he was reasonably happy that Arthur would not suspect anything. He said bye to the lads and got off the coach. He daren't look back. Instead he made his way to the coffee shop where Louise had told him to call in.

Michael caught the same bus as the day before. It was on time, so much so that it was pulling away from Somerby just as his watch said eight o'clock. It was going to be another busy day for him today.

Louise's second day was very like the first. She met up with her friends in the playground and spent most of her lessons with them. She was getting on well with Tina Phillips and Gillian Fortescue, both of whom lived in Somerby. They had started to make plans to go into Yarmouth at the weekend, to look around the shops. Louise was very happy to be involved. As usual, after school, they went to Doc's. Louise had arranged that her mum wouldn't come and meet her from school, but she would walk from the coffee bar. Once again, Doc was not working when the girls got there.

"It's not quite so busy today, is it?" Tina said.

"No. I think we might just as well go and get a drink straightaway," said Melanie as they approached the coffee bar.

"I've got enough money to buy a couple of drinks," Louise said.

"You don't need to buy two," Tina told her.

"No, it's okay. I will." Louise left her bag at the table and went to the counter. Brian was serving someone, but Louise was next in line. As she waited, Kathy made her way over to the table.

"Are you girls going to buy anything?" She spoke to them all in general.

"We're waiting for our drinks now, Kathy," Tina replied.

"So, who's buying them, then?" Kathy knew the girls quite well, and was certain that the whole group was sitting around the table.

"Our new friend Louise is buying." Tina pointed to Louise in the queue. Kathy had no response so she gave the table a quick wipe and moved on.

"Ha, that told her!" Gillian said, quietly, so that Kathy wouldn't hear.

Louise was served next, just as Doc appeared. "Two cokes, please." Louise asked. "No, I think I'll have

Pepsi Max instead, please."

"Are both of those cokes for you, then?" Doc asked softly. Louise looked at him as he spoke to her. His voice seemed friendly and warm, although she didn't know why. Louise paused before answering.

"No, they're for my friends as well."

"Have they got you to buy for them?" Doc continued.

"No, I want to buy them." Louise handed the money to Brian as Doc moved back to the doorway. He didn't stay long, but soon retreated to the upstairs office. Louise took the drinks over to her table. Kathy watched, to confirm that they were really drinking, and then went over to Brian.

"Not too busy today?"

"No, not yet. That'll change in a minute, though." Brian replied.

"Do you think that Doc seems a bit subdued at the moment?"

"I think he has things on his mind. Don't know what, though."

Brian's forecast was correct. Within five minutes there were only two tables left unoccupied. Doc came down to help out but as soon as the immediate rush was over he returned upstairs. There were a number of the older kids were in, from the local High School which was situated in the nearby village of Burgh St. Margaret. The school was called Burgh High.

"There's that smelly lad, Gillian." Tina pointed out

a thin boy.

"Oh, no! Hope he's not going to come and sit near us," Melanie replied.

"Who's he then?" Louise asked.

"His name is Tom, or Tommy. I don't think he ever washes though," Tina explained. Without them noticing, one of the High School lads had made his way over to the table.

"Alright, Mel?" he said.

"Yes. Have you got any money you can lend me?" replied Melanie.

"There's fifty you can have." The lad tossed a fifty pence piece her way and sauntered back to his mates.

"Who was that?" asked Louise.

"My brother."

"Oh, he looks quite nice," Louise added.

"Urgh!!" Melanie responded almost immediately.

"Yuk!" Tina and Livvy both added.

"You don't fancy him, do you?" Tina teased Louise a little.

"No, I just said he was nice," replied Louise, blushing. "It's handy to have an older brother who will give you money." Louise tried to deflect the embarrassment a bit.

"Yeah, I suppose so," Melanie agreed.

"You've got a brother, you said?" Tina turned to Louise.

"Yes, where's your brother?" asked Gillian, showing some interest.

"He's not here. He goes to school in Gorleston. I

think he'll pop in on the way home." Louise hoped she was right.

"Will he let you have some money?" Melanie asked.

"Doubt it."

Twenty minutes later, Vanessa got up to leave. "My mum's here."

She searched around for her coat and eventually found it. "See you, girls. You'll have to tell me what Louise's brother is like tomorrow."

"We'll tell you," Livvy shouted.

"He's nothing special, he's just my brother." Louise was getting a bit fed up with all this talk about David. She was beginning to hope he wouldn't arrive, but he did. The school coach pulled up, and off he got. Louise watched him as he made his way towards Doc's and cringed a little as he entered. David spotted Louise at one of the tables and walked over.

"How's it going then, Luce?" David stood at the table.

"Okay." She nodded rather than talked much.

"Do you want a drink at all?" David asked.

"I'll have a Lucozade," Louise replied.

"So will I," Tina added, and Gillian, and Melanie, and Livvy.

"I can't buy you all drinks!" David looked at Louise. He noticed that only two glasses had anything in them. "I'll get you a couple of bottles, and you can share if you want." David duly bought the drinks and handed them to Louise. He had bought himself a coffee and looked around for somewhere else to sit, but there were no free tables. "Shove around a bit and let me sit on the end there." David stuck his coffee cup on the edge of the table, showing his intention to sit there and drink it. Louise pushed the girls round a bit, thinking they might be a little reluctant, but they were already moving the other way so that the space created was next to Gillian and not Louise.

"I suppose you want me to introduce you all?" Louise was feeling a bit jealous but knew David wouldn't be popular that long. "Livvy, Melanie, Tina and Gillian, this is my brother, David."

"Hi, David," the girls said, almost in harmony. As the introductions were being made, one of the Burgh High boys made a comment that the whole table heard.

"Look at him, sitting with all the little girlies!" David turned to see who had made the comment, but there were a bunch of about five local lads and it might have been any one of them. David stared at them as they stared back and sniggered. David had hardly turned back before another comment was heard.

"He's that new London boy." David just ignored the comment. "They're all perverts in London." David again bit his lip. He wanted to react but didn't want to cause a scene with his sister around. He looked around to see if there were any friendly faces about but he was disappointed.

"I think I'll just drink up and go, Luce. Are you going to be all right?" David asked her.

"Yes, I'll be fine. I'll see you at home."

David drank about half of his coffee, and then got up to leave. He said goodbye to the girls but as he made his way towards the door, the group of lads moved to block his path. Not wishing to get into a fight, David carefully stepped between bags to get to the door.

"Oy, London boy, you've just kicked my bag!"

"I didn't mean to, sorry," said David, stepping a bit closer to the door. One of the lads moved towards him, and shoved David quite heavily, while removing one of the bags. David squared up to the lad and one of his friends squared up too.

"Are you going to do anything about it, London boy?" By now the coffee bar was aware of what was going on and Kathy came over from behind the counter.

"What's going on here, then?" she asked, as she saw David and two other boys staring at each other.

"He's come over here and started kicking our bags about, Kathy," one of the lads replied. Kathy wasn't quite sure what had happened.

"Well, they shouldn't be in the way of the door, so move 'em!" she ordered, leaving the lads in no doubt that they should move their bags. David opened the door and went to leave.

"Watch it next time you come in here kicking our bags, London boy." David went home. The Burgh High lads laughed, and moved their bags back.

Kathy told them off for causing an obstruction. It was all over in less than a minute.

When David got home, Sue was in the garage emptying boxes. "Mum, I'm home!" he shouted, but there was no answer. He went to his bedroom and got changed as Sue came back in.

"Hello, darling, good day at school today?" she asked, looking around for David's dirty football kit.

"Not bad, really. They want me to play for the school next week."

"Ah, that's good. When?"

"Next Wednesday. I'll get more details tomorrow." David hadn't had much time to discuss things as he had to get his coach home.

"Where's your kit, dear?"

"I've left it in the kitchen."

"Well, empty it out. I'm not doing it all for you," moaned Sue.

"Yes, Mum!"

"Have you got any homework?"

"Yeah, some French and maths." David opened his school bag to look for his books. "I'll do it now." He laid on the bed and got on with the maths. He hated French, and wasn't going to do much of that if he could get away with it. Maths wasn't too bad, he liked it.

***

Sue was surprised that Friday seemed to come around so quickly. She had started to get some order into the early morning bathroom rush. Michael

would be first up, while she got David awake.
When he had finished, it was Louise's turn. She
didn't have to leave as early. It would take a bit of
getting used to, but Sue thought it would work. She
looked in the fridge, and then in the cupboard.
Tomorrow they would have to go into town and
stock up. Tonight, they could have fish and chips.
Perhaps she would have a quick look around the
village and see if she could buy anything there.

Sue went to the grocers, the butchers and finally to
Coopers, the newsagents, but she didn't get very
much. She was surprised how quiet it was. There
were a few people around, but not many. In
Coopers, she was the only customer which was a bit
awkward since she only really wanted to have a
look, and ended up buying some chocolate she
didn't really want.

When Michael came home he was absolutely
shattered. He was a bit later than usual.
"You're a bit late, problems?" Sue asked.
"No, not really. I wanted to finish a couple of things
so I was ready for Monday."
"What's happening on Monday?"
"I get my first new member of staff, a chap called
John Haylett."
"And what's he like?" Sue tried to appear
interested.
"Seems okay. I've really only spoken to him a
couple of times. Monday I'll get to meet him

properly."

Michael looked around and noticed there was nothing prepared for dinner. "Have I missed dinner, being late?"

"No, I haven't done anything yet luckily. How come you stayed behind so long?"

"Well to be honest, I didn't mean to. I missed my bus by about five minutes and the next one didn't leave for another hour. It's really ridiculous."

"I thought we might have fish and chips, what do you think?" asked Sue.

"Sounds like a good idea. Just let me get changed and I'll go and get some."

"I'll come with you. The kids will be okay on their own. David, we're having fish and chips tonight, what would you like?"

"Plaice, please Mum. Oh, and a sausage," replied David. Louise had heard, and shouted from her bedroom.

"Cod for me, Mum."

"Righty ho!" Sue committed their orders to memory, and with Michael made her way down to the fish and chip shop. They were surprised to find that it wasn't very busy with only two other people waiting for orders.

"Can I help you?" asked the woman serving, as they walked in.

"Yes, please, two cod and chips, one plaice and chips, and what are you going to have, dear?" she asked Michael.

"I fancy a bit of rock to be honest," said Michael.

"Got no call for rock around here," replied the fryer, "only Londoners ask for rock." Sue and Michael didn't know what to say. They looked at each other with raised eyebrows.

"Ah, well, you better make that two plaice, then," Michael smiled at the woman. "You get asked for plaice?" Michael aimed his comment at the man frying, but it was completely ignored.

"Oh, and a sausage please," remembered Sue.

"Battered?" the woman queried.

"Yes, please."

"We're just waiting for chips."

Michael wanted to make another comment about having no call for chips, but he stopped himself. He looked at Sue, who knew exactly what he was thinking.

The weekend meant a bit of a lie in. It had been a busy week, and this was their first chance to do a bit of relaxed looking around.

"We need to go into Yarmouth and do some proper shopping," said Sue over breakfast.

"Where do you want to go?" Michael replied.

"I need to get fresh and frozen, and I need to get some personal things, you know."

Sue had started to write out a list. "Louise, do you need new socks for school?"

"Navy ones, please."

"Okay." Sue added them to her list. "Is there anything you need, David?"

"No." He didn't think about it.

"You two know I want you to come shopping as well," Sue said.

"Do we have to?" moaned David.

"Yes. We need to go round the supermarket and see what everyone wants."

"But you know what we want." David continued to moan. "Can't I stay in and watch the telly?"

"Normally you'd be out at football on a Saturday." Michael interrupted.

"Yes, I know, and it's the football I want to watch." David knew it was a lost cause. Sue had had this argument with Louise the previous day so she wasn't in the mood to give in to David.

"No, we're all going shopping this first time. I don't know what I'll be able to buy yet, so I want you all with me." Sue slapped her hands down on the table to indicate that was an end to the discussion. Half an hour later, all four were on their way down to the bus stop.

As they got nearer to Doc's, Louise spotted Tina and Gillian.

"I'm just going to say hello to my friends," Louise said.

"Okay, but don't be too long, we've got to catch the bus," Sue replied. Louise went off to the coffee bar. "David, do you want to go too?" Sue asked. David looked inside.

"No, not really." The three of them walked over to the bus stop and studied the timetable. Michael couldn't remember the times, just knew that they weren't very frequent.

"Well, it looks like 10.35," Michael announced.

"That's another twenty minutes yet," added David. They waited and a few others arrived at the bus stop. Louise ran out from Doc's as the bus arrived.

"We'll have to see what time they come back so we're not carrying too much shopping around for long, especially frozen food," Sue said.

When they got into town they found that there was only one shop selling frozen food in the very small shopping centre. Sue dragged the family around looking at what shops there were before announcing that she didn't think there was much choice.

"There's a Marks which is good, but no decent supermarket," she declared.

"We'll have to make do, darling. We can get what we need from these shops can't we?"

"Yes, I suppose so," said Sue, heading to the market. "We could do with a car, really."

"Yes, I said that before. I need one for work so I'll get some lessons organised." Michael had made up his mind. He was already getting annoyed at the state of the buses, and after shopping, the Riddells came home by taxi.

The weekend had come and gone. Michael left earlier this morning to do some further preparation for the day, so David walked to the bus stop on his own. On the way, he bumped into a girl he'd seen before, and decided there was no harm in speaking, so he waited briefly and approached her.

"Hi. Are you walking down to the bus stop?" David tried to be as polite as he could.

"Yes." The girl gave a short, but not sharp, answer.

"Do you mind if I walk with you?" She didn't answer but allowed him to walk with her. "Do you live far up Station Road?"

"A couple of hundred yards, not far," the girl replied. "Where do you live, Thistle Avenue?"

"No, I live in Rawthorn Drive," David answered.

"Oh, I don't think I've ever been up there, are they houses or bungalows?"

"We live in a bungalow. I'm David, by the way."

"I'm Alice."

"You go to Yarmouth High School, don't you?" David was sure she did.

"Yes."

"I go to Carlton." David paused as the pair reached Doc's. "Are you going into the coffee bar?"

"No, I'm going to meet my friend. She lives down the little back lane." Alice pointed in the general direction.

"Oh, okay. See you later."

David stopped outside the cafe as Alice went off on her own, then went in and up to the counter where Kathy was serving. There were a few people around and she was on her own.

"Doc!" she shouted, needing some help. David ordered a coffee. By now there were two others waiting. Doc heard the call from Kathy and started downstairs as David collected his coffee and walked to a table. As he approached the table he began to feel dizzy. He just managed to get his coffee cup down on the table, and sit down rather than fall, but his head began to throb unpleasantly, the same as last time. 'What is this pain?' he thought to himself. There was very little warning and it came on so quickly. David was struggling and failed to notice that Doc had fallen down the last few stairs and landed in a heap by the doorway. Kathy heard the noise and turned to see what had happened.

"Oh, bloody hell. Brian, quick!" Brian was cooking but came to Doc's aid as quickly as he could. Kathy carried on while Brian helped Doc onto his feet and back upstairs by which time he seemed to have got over his fall. Meanwhile, David stumbled out of the cafe leaving his drink on the table. He needed some air, and made his way towards the oak tree. Within seconds of getting outside, he too started to feel a bit better. Almost as quickly as it had started, his pain went away. He had no idea what the problem was, but by the time he was on the school coach, he had almost forgotten about it.

By Wednesday David was used to his new routine. He walked down the road with Alice, but as usual she went off to meet her friend. He had found out that her friend's name was Suzanne but as yet hadn't seen her. He stood by the bus stop, not wanting to go into Doc's again for now. He noticed another lad about his age, waiting, presumably for the coach, but realised that he hadn't seen him get on it before. Perhaps he was also a new boy, but David thought he had seen him before. When the coach arrived, David got on but the other lad made no move. David guessed he must be waiting for the regular bus. He made his way towards the back seat, trying to spot Mary without making it obvious. In seconds, he recognised her long hair, and thought no one had noticed him noticing her. As he continued up the coach, he could see Arthur watching him.

"Hi, Dave." Phil was the only one to greet him as he sat down.

"Alright, lads." David gave a general hello.

"You got games again today, then?" Mark asked, looking at David's sports bag.

"You could say that." David didn't want to elaborate.

By now, they had established that David was a Spurs fan, and had a big discussion about whether Norwich were the better team. There was no conclusion to the discussion.

When the coach had stopped at the High School, most of the lads got off, leaving David and Phil. As they set off, David turned to Phil.

"I'm just going to have a quick chat with Mary. I'll be back in a while." He got up and walked down to where she was sitting. "Hi," said David.

"Hi. You don't have to keep coming down here you know," replied Mary.

"I want to," David told her. "How's your eye?"

"Better, thanks."

159

"Did Arthur do that to you?" David wanted to know. Mary didn't answer immediately.

"No, it was my fault." She wanted to leave it at that, but David was curious.

"How did you do it, then?"

"Oh, it was stupid, I just wasn't being very careful." David could sense she wasn't happy talking about it, so changed the subject.

David paused before he asked the next question. "I hope you don't mind me asking, but are you Arthur's girlfriend?"

"Who told you that?"

"That's what they said at the back." David indicated with his head that he meant the back seat.

"No, I'm not his girlfriend. Why?"

"That's good. That means I can come and talk to you again."

"I don't think so." Mary turned away. David wasn't sure whether she wanted him to leave her alone or not.

"Are you doing your GCSEs soon?" David changed the subject again.

"No, not until next year." Mary turned back to David, and decided to be a bit chattier. "You live in Somerby?"

"Yes."

"I went to school there. My younger sister goes there now."

"Hey, my sister goes there too."

David wanted to say more but the coach was pulling up at her stop. She got up. "I won't be on the coach tonight but I'll see you tomorrow?" David mad e it a question. Mary smiled at him.

"Maybe." She ran to get off the coach before the others got on. David went back to where Phil was sitting. Jane and Susan joined the boys, but as the coach started to move, David looked out. Mary looked in his direction and waved at him. He waved back.

Carlton Grammar had a football match. David had already made arrangements to get home after the football, as playing meant he would miss the bus. By lunchtime, David felt quite excited about the forthcoming game. He joined Jane and Susan in the dining hall, as he had done most of the other days.

"Jane, what the hell have you got there?" David asked as he put his burger and chips on the table.

"I went for lasagne," Jane replied. "I'm not quite sure what's in it though."

"Perhaps I should have gone for the burger instead," she added uncertainly.

"Can you cook?" David asked her.

"Well I do Food Technology, but I wouldn't say I could cook."

"So how do you know what lasagne is supposed to look like?"

"Don't be daft. I've cooked one in a microwave loads of times," Jane said.

"Yeah, and you burned that," Susan added. They all laughed. Phil joined them. He too had burger and chips.

"Alright." Phil gave a general greeting. "Dave, did you say you weren't catching the coach back tonight?"

"I'm playing football this afternoon, so I'll be getting the bus back."

"What, for the school?" Susan asked.

"Yeah."

"You'll be very late home then." Phil tried to work it out. "You won't get finished till about six."

"No, we should finish about four." David was confused.

"How does that work out then?" Phil thought for a minute. "You're not missing lessons, are you?"

"Yes. All afternoon."

"Bloody hell!" all three replied.

After lunch, David made his way to the changing rooms. These weren't used for normal games, but only for matches between schools or on special occasions, so this was the first time that David had ever used them. Today they were playing Cliff Top in the semi-finals of a regional competition. David was going to be playing right from the start, as he had impressed the coach enough at last week's games. The other school hadn't arrived, so Mr Bowles had the chance to chat to his team.

"Right, lads. You'll see the team I've picked in a moment when I pin it up. I want you all to know that this game is not just about eleven players, it's about all of you. There are likely to be some substitutions so if you're not starting it doesn't mean you won't get to play at some time."

"Is our new boy in?" The question came from the team captain, Nigel Slaughter.

"I'll tell you in a minute. If you win this today, we will go into the regional final."

"What, and play Yarmouth High?" Kevin Jones shouted out.

"Hopefully. But first we've got to beat Cliff Top."

"Are they any good, sir?" David asked.

"Yes, they're okay, but we are better!" Mr Bowles said. "They have Warrener upfront, we all know him, don't we? But if we can stop him, they are just an average side." Mr Bowles finished by clenching his fist in a team salute. In response, the team all did the same, and shouted 'Carlton'. David didn't, because he didn't know what was going on.

"Who's Warrener?" David asked quietly, after the others had hushed a bit.

"He plays up front for Yarmouth Youth, and is being scouted by a couple of professional clubs. He's nippy and shoots well."

"Yeah, but he's only one player, isn't he?" David couldn't see why they should be worried about him. The team seemed to gain strength from David's comments.

"Yes, you're right. He's only one player."

The line-up was then pinned to the board. David was in central midfield with Nigel Slaughter.

"He's taken my place." Nicky Sawyer exclaimed as soon as he saw the team go up.

"You're still playing, Pop." Nigel replied.

"Oh yeah. I'm up front." Pop seemed happy with that. Mr Bowles thought that Pop might be able to do a better job scoring.

As the teams warmed up, Nigel had a little chat with David.

"That's Nobby Warrener," Nigel pointed out a tall athletic lad who was stretching. "He plays for Yarmouth Youth and is pretty good."

"What side does he prefer?" David asked.

"Normally the right side and he'll keep quite wide." Nigel knew him from his matches for Gorleston. "We're a bit weak in our full back positions so we might need to be supportive in midfield when he has the ball." Nigel spoke knowledgably.

"If he's on my side I'll keep an eye out."

The game kicked off and being the strongest side, Carlton kept most of the early possession. David looked around to see where most of his team mates positioned themselves and was happy to see that both of his own wide midfielders seemed to take deeper positions rather than forward ones. As expected, Nobby Warrener took up a position wide on the right half way between midfield and defence. Cliff Top tried all they could to get the ball to him, but in the first ten minutes they hardly strung more than a couple of passes together before a Carlton player got possession again.

Carlton seemed to have the upper hand, and David felt it was just a matter of time before they scored.

The next twenty minutes saw Carlton again doing most of the creating but once more neither Stuart nor Pop could get any decent shots in. Nigel and David pushed forward a bit to look for opportunities as both felt they could shoot better, and as one attack was in progress, Chris Long got caught in possession and lost a tackle. The ball fell just right for Warrener, and again David found himself on the wrong side of him. Again, Warrener went past him like he wasn't there, and this time David wasn't in a position to tackle. One of Carlton's central defenders had to come across to meet Warrener but not before he got another shot in. This time Styles was beaten and the ball went in off the far post. Cliff Top were one up.

David decided that he needed to stay goal side of Warrener all the time, and he indicated what he was going to do to Nigel. Cliff Top were still celebrating as Carlton kicked off, and they were still not in position when the ball was passed out far left for Chris Long who ran forward a few yards before putting in a speculative cross towards Melvin Tennant who was the only player in the area. As he went for the ball he was challenged and beaten in the air but the header wasn't a good one. It fell straight to the feet of Pop Sawyer who controlled it quickly and bent in a shot that left the keeper with no chance. A good way to equalise. That was how it stayed till half time.

The Somerby Tree

The second half saw David staying deeper and this time able to tackle Warrener once or twice. Both tackles were fair, but quite hard, and Warrener moved to the other wing. Cliff Top never got the ball to him again. With half an hour to go, Pop got his second goal of the game. He was waiting to pick up any loose balls on the edge of the area and fired a superb shot right into the top corner. By now Cliff Top were all heads down. Warrener didn't want to know, and David was happy he had him under control. Chris Long scored a third and Melvin Tennant added a fourth to see Carlton cruise into the final. Sawyer was declared man of the match and hailed as the Carlton hero, but Nigel knew that the new boy had played a very big part in winning the game.

It was Friday and the end of quite a stressful week. Sue visited the Post Office which was emptier than she had expected it to be. There were two women ready to serve at the counter and Sue went to the nearest.

"Good morning, how can I help you?"

"I need some stamps please."

"First class?"

"Oh no, second class please."

"Would you like a book of stamps?"

"Yes, I'll take a book of ten please."

Sue felt a bit happier here.

"You're new in Somerby?" The woman seemed interested.

"Yes. We moved up from London just over a week ago."

"Oh! Why did you come to Somerby?"

"Well, my husband has been transferred to a bank in Yarmouth and we thought that Somerby was the best village around."

"Ah, that's nice to hear. Yes, it's a lovely little place, but must be different to what you're used to." The woman at the Post Office seemed keen to find out about them.

"You could say that but we'll get used to it. I'm Mrs Riddell by the way. Sue."

"Are you related to anyone else in the village?"

"No, don't think so. Are there other Riddells here?"

"Yes, just one."

"I don't think we know anyone, I'm afraid."

Sue tried to think who she had got to know since arriving. "Well, we have got to know a few people."

"You will, dear. I'm Betty, by the way, and this is my sister Carol."

"Are you both Somerby people?"

"Depends on what you mean. We were both born here, and our mum was born here, but Dad came from Scotland. He was a fisherman."

"I seem to have found that most people who live in the village don't want anything to do with us."

"Ahh, that'll be Norfolk folk. We're a funny lot to strangers but not that bad once you get to know us. It just takes a bit of time."

"But you seem happy to chat. Some won't say a word."

"We're not as shy as most folk round here."

"So how long have you had the Post Office?"

"For as long as we can remember."

The two ladies laughed.

Sue was happy that at least there were a few nice people around. She made her way home via the butchers but all the way back she saw no more than two other people. It was a quiet village, she thought to herself, but she liked it.

That evening Sue made lamb chops for dinner. After the poor response in the fish and chip shop last week, neither Sue nor Michael were keen to go back, there so fish was off the menu.

"What are we having for tea, Mum?" David was always the first one to worry about his stomach.

"We're having lamb chops with vegetables, potatoes and gravy."

"Lovely."

"Aren't we having fish and chips?" Louise thought it unusual for them not to have fish and chips on a Friday like they had done in London.

"No, not this week darling," Sue told her.

Michael had not been in for long, and he had not yet let Sue know about his plans for the next week. They also had to quickly discuss what they were going to announce this evening. He came in to the kitchen

"Do you feel a bit better now?" she asked.

"Yes, now I can start to relax a bit."

"Perhaps I can come and meet you from work one

afternoon next week and we can go shopping."

"Sounds a good idea, but it can't be Wednesday."

"Oh, all right, not Wednesday then. Thursday would probably be a better day anyway."

"Aren't you going to ask why not Wednesday?"

As Michael asked he realised that Thursday was probably out as well.

"If you want me to. Why not Wednesday?"

"Because I won't be here on Wednesday. Actually, I might not be back in time to go shopping on Thursday either."

"Well, that's very fine." Sue turned to Michael. "We've been here less than two weeks and already you want to leave." She was pulling his leg.

"I know, I know. I've got to interview someone in Reading and I'm travelling up the day before."

Sue and Michael discussed the important subject of the evening whilst getting the table ready for dinner.

"Dinner's ready." Michael called out.

The four of them sat down at the dinner table and began to eat.

"This is fantastic." Michael said. "Have you put something different into the gravy?"

"Might have done."

"What's in it?"

"Do you like it?" Sue teased a little. "In fact, do you all like the gravy?"

Sue looked at David and Louise both of whom seemed to give nods of approval.

"So, what is it?" Michael asked again.

"Nothing really. Just some herbs and cider." "Tastes great, Mum. Good idea."

David thought it tasted fantastic. Sue still laughed to herself as none of them knew the real story - she had put the wrong spices in by mistake. The next few minutes were spent savouring the new taste, but it wasn't long before David had finished.

"While we are all around the table, your mum wants has something to tell you," Michael said.

"Oh, I wasn't expecting an introduction!"

"What is it, Mum?" Louise asked.

"Well, your dad and I have had a discussion, and decided that we have too many children and one of you has to go and live somewhere else."

Louise dropped her knife and her mouth gaped open, while David's attention was grabbed.

"Okay, now I've got your attention, just to tell you that we have made a provisional booking to go to Florida next June for three weeks."

"Wow! Disney!" Louise was already excited.

"Yes, to Orlando."

"Going in June?" David queried the statement.

"Well you'll have finished your first year by then and you don't have exams next year so it should be okay. You'll find getting time off a lot easier next year," Michael explained.

"Great. Three weeks." David was happy. Louise was very happy. The whole family was happy.

Chapter 6
GETTING ON WITH LIFE

Monday 30th January 1995

Monday was of course very busy for Michael and he only had time for a brief chat with John Haylett before the first interview. John had done a lot of work and Michael was pleased with some of his ideas.

"John, this is good," Michael said as he read his report. "You've already identified two or three areas where we can possibly get some new business. Have you covered the points about new things we could offer businesses?"

"Yes. I have had some ideas and have put them in the report. When we get the team together perhaps we can all discuss it?"

"Yes, sounds like a good idea. I would also like a list of things for clerks to look out for."

"What, so they can push customers our way?"

"Yes, that, and pass any customers with problems our way as well."

Michael already had his own ideas but wanted John to come up with some fresh ones.

"I'll be interviewing for the next few days but we can chat again on Thursday."

By lunch time, Michael had completed the first two interviews. He was impressed with both candidates. Christine brought him in a cup of coffee.

"In need of a drink?" She placed the cup down on

his desk.

"Ah thanks Christine, you're an angel."

"I know. And a very poorly paid angel at that."

"I hope you're not looking for a rise." Michael wasn't quite sure what her motives were with that comment.

"Oh, no, sorry I was just talking out loud. I get paid very well thanks. Your next interviewee is already here."

"Who's next?"

"Claire Moffatt."

The last interview finished at just after four thirty. Michael looked at his files on each of the four candidates so far and he knew he was going to have a hard job choosing but for now he could put that problem to one side.

Louise and her friends were again in Doc's after school and by now Louise had got to know most of the kids from Somerby. If they didn't know her, she at least knew their names or whose brother or sister they were.

"Where's your brother then, Louise?" Gillian asked.

"She fancies your brother," Livvy said.

"No, I don't," Gillian protested. "Is he coming in again?"

"Not sure, after what happened last time."

"He doesn't want to worry about them prats." Tina sounded tough.

"I'm not saying he's worried about them, but I don't

think he likes it in here."

As the girls were chatting, Kathy came over to see if they had any drinks left. They didn't.

"Are you girls leaving? I need to clean the table."

"Oh, it's alright Kathy, you don't need to clean the table just for us," Tina replied. The girls laughed.

"Buy a drink or get outside." Kathy wasn't in the mood to discuss the situation.

"I'll buy." Louise stood up

"It's not your turn," Melanie answered. "It's Vanessa's turn."

"I haven't got any money today." Ness showed the palms of her hands to emphasise the problem.

"I'll buy," repeated Louise and went to the counter whilst Kathy watched her. She continued cleaning tables and making sure that everyone was drinking or eating. Louise bought two more cokes and Kathy made a mental note. As Louise returned to the table she pointed out a girl on the far side of the coffee bar who was talking to the older lads.

"Who's that?"

The girls all turned in a synchronised movement, and it was so obvious that the girl in question couldn't help but notice.

"Oh, it's that Maria Bevan," Livvy replied.

"Who's she, then?"

"Her dad owns a lot of the amusements down at Shelby Beach," Livvy explained.

"Is he rich then?"

"What, her dad?" Livvy replied. "Yes, he drives a Mercedes." As Livvy was telling Louise, they all became aware that Maria Bevan was listening to what was being said.

"Hi, Maria." Tina waved to her. Maria turned back and continued chatting with the boys. "She thinks she's so brilliant," said Tina, turning back. They were chatting generally, when Doc walked over to their table.

"All right, Doc?" Tina thought they would be told off for shouting.

"I'm alright, Miss Phillips. How's your dad?"

"Oh, he's okay."

"Still working with the police?"

"Yes. He's moved back to Caister again."

"Oh, I'm sure he prefers that." Doc picked up one of the empty glasses from the table. "Everyone else ok?"

"Yes, Doc."

"Good, keep it that way."

Doc made his way to another table and started chatting.

"I thought we were going to get told off," Livvy said.

"No, Doc wouldn't tell us off. He's too nice," Gillian answered.

David had decided to pop into the coffee bar again to see what Louise was up to. By this time, Doc was upstairs in the office. David didn't want to stay for long, but didn't want to be seen to be avoiding the place. "Hi girls," he said.

"Hello, David," said Tina, the only one to speak.

"Gillian wants to know if you're going to sit next to her again today."

"Shut up, Tina." Gillian went red.

"No, I'm not stopping. Luce, have you remembered Dad's birthday next week?"

"Yes, I've got an idea of what to get him. Are you going to lend me some money?"

"No, I'm not. I'm always giving you money. You need to save some of your pocket money."

"Just asking."

David picked up is school bag and nodded goodbye to the girls. He made his way towards the door.

"Watch your bags, lads, the London hooligan is here."

David looked at the Burgh High lads but said nothing. He opened the door. "That smell is getting a bit better," one of them said. The other lads laughed. David said nothing. He went outside and stopped to think, before turning and coming back in. The Burgh High lads had assumed he was going home, and missed him coming back in. David went back over to Louise's table.

"I've decided to stay."

"Ooh! Gillian it's your lucky day," Livvy teased.

"Shut your gob before I do it for you."

"Louise, can you go and get me a coffee. I'll pay for it," David asked nicely. Louise did.

Thursday had arrived quickly for David, and it was games day at Carlton School. He hadn't spoken to Mary since Monday, knowing that Arthur would notice should he stop and talk to her, but they had waved at each other through the window. David was getting ready for his exams, and lessons were getting harder, as was the homework. Today was one of his better days as he could play football and forget about academic subjects for a while. As usual Mr Bowles picked the school squad to play a better standard of game but added a sprinkle of the other boys to give them a chance. After the teams had been picked, Nigel Slaughter asked Mr Bowles if he could change sides.

"Why do you want to do that?" Mr Bowles asked.

"I just do, please sir."

"Okay."

The switch saw Nigel opposing David. As the game went on, Nigel waited until David had the ball before tackling and he went in hard. David thought the challenges a bit over the top, considering they were supposed to be in the same team, but he didn't let it stop him. He gave as good as he got, and there was one challenge in particular, when Nigel had slinked his way through a melee of players and prepared to shoot, seemingly guaranteed to score, when David flew in and put in a very strong challenge that brought Nigel down in a heap.

"Penalty!" The appeals went up and Mr Bowles considered his decision. Nigel meanwhile lay hurting on the ground.

"Penalty." Mr Bowles wasn't sure but he gave the decision. He pointed to the spot. David couldn't believe it. Nigel by this time had got back to his knees.

"Come on, ref," he said.

"Nigel, I'm not sending him off."

"No, it wasn't a penalty, he got the ball easily." Nigel was impressed with David's timing and honest enough to let Mr Bowles know. Nigel was still on his knees and David came over to help him up.

"Sorry, I didn't think I'd catch you," David apologised.

"Don't be stupid, it was the way I fell that got the decision. You got the ball." Nigel looked at Mr Bowles.

"I've given the penalty, so a penalty it is."

"I'll take it but…" Nigel turned and looked at David. "It wasn't a penalty." Nigel stepped up and the ball flew into the top corner of the net. The game came to an end.

As the teams trudged back to the school changing rooms Nigel came up to David and patted him on the back. "Good game, Dave."

"Thanks, but you still won."

"Yeah, but we shouldn't have." Nigel walked with David for a while. "Do you play football at weekends?"

"No, not at the moment. I still feel a bit new here."

"What are you doing Saturday?"

"Why?"

"Well, can you get to Gorleston Rec for two

o'clock?"

"I think so."

"I play for Gorleston Youth and we could do with another midfielder like you. I'd like to introduce you to the manager. What do you say?"

Nigel was hopeful.

"Yeah I should be able to make it."

The two discussed the finer details and David was happy to try and for a place. He was missing his weekend football.

David had looked forward to Saturday and he was up and ready for breakfast without being asked.

"Wow, couldn't you sleep then?" Sue said as she saw him sitting at the kitchen table.

"Ha, very funny."

"You and Dad going to watch football today?"

"Yes, in Gorleston."

"Are they a good team?"

"Don't really know what their youth team is like, but the senior side is okay."

"So, what are you going to watch them for?"

"One of the lads in the school team asked me to come along."

"Oh!"

"Hopefully he's going to get me a trial."

"Sounds good."

As Sue replied, Louise came into the kitchen and sat down. "Where are you meeting the girls?"

"Down at Doc's." Louise had already had her breakfast and was almost ready to go out. "Do I have to be back at any particular time?"

"Well, I'd like you home before seven."

"That's no problem. I take it I can go out again tonight though?"

"Where?" Sue wasn't sure what Louise had planned.

"You going somewhere, Luce?" David also asked.

"No. It's just that I don't know what everyone does in the evenings."

"Well, we'll see." Sue reserved a final decision. "Do you want eggs and bacon, David?"

"Yes, please, and some tomatoes if you've got any."

"Forgot about tomatoes. I think we've got some." Sue looked in the cupboard and retrieved a tin of tomatoes. Michael came in to the kitchen.

"Breakfast smells almost ready," he said. "Do you know what time kick off is, David?"

"No, but I think he said about two o'clock. That would be right for the time of year."

Louise picked up her bag and said goodbye before making her way down to Doc's. She was meeting the girls before going off into town and had made sure that she collected her pocket money before leaving. When Louise got to Doc's, only Tina and Vanessa were already there.

"Hi, Tina. Hello, Ness," Louise said as she went in and sat down.

"Hi, Louise," both girls replied.

"No Gillian yet?" Louise aimed the question at Tina.

"I called round for her on the way but she wasn't ready. She'll be here soon."

"Let's have some of your coke, Tina." Louise was already thirsty. She looked up at the clock on the wall, it was twenty to ten. "What bus are we getting?"

"The ten o'clock," Tina answered.

"If everyone's here that is," Vanessa added.

"Where are we going in town?"

"Don't panic, Louise, nowhere in particular. Just around the town," Tina answered.

Within ten minutes, Gillian and Melanie turned up, but it wasn't until the bus had arrived that Livvy came along.

"Late again," Vanessa said.

"Not really. I'm in time for the bus."

"Only just."

The girls went off to town.

Michael and David caught the bus later. Michael had seen where the Recreation Ground was during his visit to the Gorleston branch. The bus from Somerby was quite busy, and seemed to stop everywhere. Even when it seemed there was no more room, still people got on. It was a long journey, but by twenty-five minutes past one they were getting off at the town centre.

"We need to get a number eight," David said. Michael didn't answer but knew that was right.

"There's one ready to go, Dad, come on."

David set off at a little trot. Michael quickened his

pace but carried on walking.

"Two returns to Gorleston Rec please."

"That'll be a pound."

"How frequent are the buses back?" Michael asked the driver as he paid him the fare.

"Every fifteen minutes up to six."

"Great."

The bus dropped them off right opposite the Rec, and within a couple of minutes they were inside. The ground was a bit run down but had terracing on two sides and a roofed stand on one. It looked almost like a real ground. Their arrival coincided with the players coming out to warm up. Gorleston played in green and white and David spotted Nigel as he emerged from the dressing room. Nigel kicked a ball around very briefly, then made his way to where David and his dad were stood.

"Dave, you made it then," shouted Nigel. David walked down to the side of the pitch to chat.

"Yeah, I said I would."

"Your dad has come as well. Almost doubled the crowd today!"

"Who are you playing?"

"Bradwell."

"Are they any good?"

"No, not really. Second from bottom, and I think they've only won a couple of games."

"You should win then."

"Yeah, we should, but you never know."

Nigel nodded at a bloke in a black tracksuit who had just emerged from the dressing room.

"That's Scalesy. I'll introduce you when I can. I'd better get back to the lads."

"Good luck, Nige."

Gorleston were on top pretty much all of the way. David wondered to himself where Nigel thought he might fit in, as they seemed quite strong in midfield, but imagined playing for them in a big game. By the end of the match, Gorleston had scored two goals and it was a comfortable victory. Nigel shook hands with the visiting players and then made his way over to David.

"Can you come to the dressing room to meet the boss?"

"Yeah, okay." David turned to Michael. "Are you going to hang on here?"

"I'll make my way round, but you go off now."

"I won't be long." David jumped over the small wall onto the pitch, and made his way back to the dressing room with Nigel. As they neared the entrance, Scalesy appeared.

"There you are." He looked at Nigel. "Poor performance from all quarters today, I don't even think you gave it all."

"Sorry, boss. It was hard to up the performance against them. They weren't that good."

"No, suppose you're right, but these are the games where we get caught out."

"We won, boss."

"Yeah, suppose so. Who's this then?" Scalesy looked at David.

"This is the lad I was telling you about." That was Nigel's introduction.

"Hi, I'm David Riddell."

"And you want to play for Gorleston?"

"Well, I wouldn't mind." David thought the question a bit strange and on reflection his own answer a bit naff.

"Keen then." Scalesy turned to Nigel. "You're recommending him?"

"Yes, boss, I am." Nigel gave nodded emphatically as he answered.

"That'll do. Can you come to training on Tuesday evening?"

"Yes, I think so. Is that here?"

"Yes, Nigel will explain. We'll give you a run out and see what you can do. Where do you play?"

"Midfield usually."

"Are you attacking or defending?"

"A bit of both."

"I'll see you Tuesday then." Scalesy disappeared back into the dressing room.

"Is Tuesday alright?" Nigel sensed an air of uncertainty in David.

"Think so. I've just got to sort out how to get home. What time does training finish?"

"We normally start about six and finish at eightish."

"I'll sort something out. Thanks for putting a word in."

"Don't mention it. You'll be good for the team." Nigel patted David on the back. "I'll see you Monday.

"Okay see you."
David walked over to where Michael was waiting for him and explained what had been organised.

Monday morning was hectic. David was keen to get to school and his trip in was fairly uneventful. He didn't see Nigel till dinner time and spent most of that chatting about the game at the weekend. David already felt part of the team and Nigel knew he would make a good impression at training.
"How long have you been playing for Gorleston, Nige?"
"This is my third season."
"So you were twelve when you started."
"I think I was actually thirteen. My birthday is in September."
"And how did you get to play for them?"
"Well as far as I can remember, I've always been going to play for them. When I was at junior school I was being trained by a Gorleston coach, and it was always assumed that I'd play for their junior side. Strange but it's always been like that. Who did you play for back in London?"
"A local team called Goodmayes United. We weren't part of a senior side, we just grew up as mates from school and we formed a team."
"Were they good?"
"Depends on what you mean. We were one of the top teams in our league."
"But say they were to play against Gorleston Youth, who do you think would win?"

"That's a hard one. I think Goodmayes have some brilliant individual players but Gorleston are far more professional so I'd have to say Gorleston but it would be bloody close."

The two carried on talking about football all dinner time.

Louise had another normal day at school. The six girls spent all day chatting about their weekend, shopping, film and pop stars. Louise had been completely accepted as part of the gang and her academic work was good. When school finished, the girls all went down to Doc's. They took up their usual seats and waited until the last moment before buying anything.

"I see Sally is parading her new phone," Livvy said, pointing over to the crowd of older kids.

"Her new what?" Gillian asked.

"She's got one of those new phones."

"Oh," Tina said, uninterested, and quickly changed the subject. "My dad has promised to take me to a Norwich game."

"Has he got tickets then?" Louise asked.

"I think so."

"You'll be able to see Jeremy Goss playing," Vanessa added.

"Don't say you fancy him," Tina replied.

"He's alright." Vanessa tried not to blush. There was a slight pause.

"I wish my dad would take me to football." Melanie seemed to be almost dreaming as she spoke.

The girls carried on chatting about various things until it was time for Vanessa to go. Quite soon afterwards, David arrived and came over to where Louise was.

"Luce, I'm not staying. Are you alright?"

"Yes. I'll see you later. Tell Mum I'll be in usual time." Louise waved as David made his way back to the door. As he got nearer there were the usual dirty looks from the Burgh High boys but David just ignored them.

Sue spent most of the day doing the washing. It had been quite a busy day. All of the washing had to be put in the tumble dryer and it was quarter past three before she really finished. She looked up at the kitchen clock as she put the kettle on. Now what are we going to eat today, she thought to herself. Beef burgers were the obvious choice. It'll be a quick easy tea with some beans or something, Sue decided. David arrived home first.

"Hello, darling, have you had a good day?"

"Hello, Mum. Yes, not bad."

David made his way straight to his bedroom and got on with his homework. Sue was still taking it easy. She knew that Michael was probably going to be late today and hoped he would ring before leaving for home. David came into the kitchen to look for some biscuits.

"You're going football training tomorrow evening, aren't you?"

"Yes."

"So, what time will you be home?"

"Nigel's dad has apparently offered to give me a lift home, so hopefully about nine." Sue thought about that for a second or two.

"You can have one of those pizza things when you get home."

"Yeah, that'll be good." David looked at the television as he nibbled on a biscuit. "What time is dinner?"

"Depends on when Dad gets home." Sue couldn't be any more precise than that.

As it turned out it was after seven before Michael got home. It had started to rain and he was frozen and most miserable by the time he got in. Sue helped him off with his coat and gave him a hug to help warm him up a bit.

"It's the most useless bus service in the world out here." Michael worked hard not to swear.

"Why's that then?"

"I had to wait twenty minutes for a bus tonight and I won't even mention this morning."

"Perhaps you ought to learn how to drive then. We've discussed it."

"Maybe, but when will I have the time to take lessons?" As Michael replied David came into the kitchen.

"Are you going to take driving lessons, Dad?" Without any real thought Michael replied, "Yes." Sue was stunned.

"You're right, dear. I need to learn how to drive. I

will get some lessons sorted out tomorrow."

Tuesday 7th February 1995
Michael was true to his word and as soon as he had a chance to get out of the bank he found a driving school in town. He found that he would be given a free hour to evaluate how many lessons they thought he would need, and then they would work out a schedule for him, guaranteeing a pass. There was small print which meant he could only fail up to three tests, but it was a fixed price and Michael thought it sounded right for him. His evaluation lesson was scheduled for the coming Friday at two in the afternoon.

David had another normal day at school, but of course this evening he was going to train at Gorleston. Sue had made him a couple of sandwiches for if he got hungry before he got home. As it happened, David threw them away but there was no way he would tell his mum that. He got to the Rec at half past five having wasted some time looking around some of the shops. He was still in his school uniform and felt a bit out of place when the other lads turned up dressed in casual gear. There were four from Carlton Grammar who also played for Gorleston Youth and David was soon able to chat to someone. Paul Baldry got out of a car and spoke to him.
"Hi, Dave. Come on, I'll take you through to the changing rooms."

"Thanks, Paul. I haven't seen anyone I know yet."
"Don't worry, you'll soon get to know everyone."
Paul led David to the dressing rooms that were situated behind the main stand. There were already a couple of lads in there getting changed.
"Hi, Paul," they both said.
"Hi. This is Dave Riddell. That's Mitch, and over there is Peter," said Paul.
"You the lad that Slaughts has been going on about?" asked one of them.
"I guess I am."
"You play in midfield?"
"Yes."
"Well, so do I." Mitch seemed to be making a point. David wasn't quite sure what it was but was certain one had been made.
"Hi, I'm Peter Sutton. Don't worry about Mitch. Slaughts has been winding him up that he's found a better player." Peter laughed as Mitch grumbled under his breath. David felt a bit of pressure from the comments, but nothing he couldn't handle. Another couple of lads came in and in no time the room was full. David didn't start changing as he was waiting to see the man in the black tracksuit first.

Scalesy was next to come in and he said hello to all the lads including David.
"Great, glad you could make it. Have you brought some kit?"
"Yes, but I wasn't sure what you wanted me to do."

"Just get changed and come out on to the pitch."
Scalesy seemed okay.

David did as he was told and they started with a few groups kicking the ball to each other, before some more organised sessions of running and heading and general ball control. There was a match for the last half hour and the twenty or so lads that were training split into teams. Mitch was pitched up against David and it was very much a similar story to when he played against Nigel at school. Mitch went in hard but David went in even harder. By the end of the session, David had won over Mitch's admiration and the two were acting like old friends. Mitch wasn't the only one he'd impressed.

"Dave, can you come along to our game next Saturday?"

"Yes, I think so, where is it?"

"We're playing away at Acle. Do you know where that is?"

"I've heard of it but couldn't say I know where it is, no."

"I'm sure Nigel can tell you. We kick off at two, and I'd like you to come along to see how the team prepares for a game. You won't be playing though, is that alright?"

"Yes, sir."

"Bring your kit as I want you to get changed with the team, and we might find a place for you on the bench. Oh, and call me Scalesy."

"Right, Scalesy. I'll be there."

The Somerby Tree

Wednesday 8th February 1995

David was keen to get to school and talk to Nigel about last night's training session. Having got back late he had only half arranged to go to Acle on Saturday and he still didn't know quite how he would get there, but Michael had told him he would try and help. Nigel gave him directions and told him what time he should be there, and David was ready.

After school, David wanted to visit Doc's. He liked the idea of there being a coffee bar just down the road from where he lived and he was determined to be accepted in there even if it meant a fight.

"Hi, Luce," said David as he walked up to the girls' table. As usual, there were only the five girls left by the time David arrived. "Do you girls want drinks?"

"Are you buying?" Tina was quick to ask.

"Yes, I'll pay." David felt in his pocket for some money. He went to the counter and bought six cokes.

"Thank you, David," Tina said as he returned with them. "We've made a space for you."

Tina pointed to the spare seat next to Gillian. David sat down. He half listened as the girls chatted although Gillian didn't say very much at all. The time passed very quickly and David and Louise soon had to make their way home. They got up and said goodbye, and Louise went off to say cheerio to a few other friends. David waited for her, gradually making his way towards the door. There were a few Burgh boys standing just outside the door, and David knew there was going to be an atmosphere as he left.

"You London boys always chat up little girls, then?" said one of the Burgh boys quite loudly. David ignored it. "They can't chat up big girls, eh?" the lad said, again.

The other Burgh boys laughed. David tried to ignore it but in the end had to respond. He stomped towards them, dropping his school bag on the way.

"Alright, you wankers. Let's get something straight here." David was all ready for a verbal assault but when it came down to it he didn't know what to say. His mouth opened but no words came out.

"Watch out, he wants to eat us." The Burgh boys laughed again. David wasn't quite sure what to do next, then suddenly one of the boys punched him in the face. He was shocked to start with, then felt the pain, but he wasn't afraid. He turned to see who had hit him. There were four of them waiting to see what he was going to do next, and as David clenched his fists two of them took a step back.

"Just stay here lads, he won't take all four of us on," said one of the Burgh boys, but the two who had already started backwards took another step. David took a step towards them.

"Yeah, go on then, London boy, show us how hard you are." There was really only the one who seemed prepared to stand and fight. Louise came and walked between them. She hadn't noticed what was going on, and it was only when she saw David's face that she got some idea.

"This will wait," David said, as he picked up his

bag. David and Louise left. As the two of them walked past the other shops in the block, David looked back to see what the Burgh boys were doing. Only one still stared at him.

David had had a bad night. He managed to persuade Luce to keep quiet about what had happened at Doc's, and explained the bruise under his eye as a football injury at school. Sue didn't know any different and bathed it with some witch hazel, but the pain remained with him all through the night. As he got on the coach the next morning, his eye felt really sore. David was making his way to the back of the coach when he caught sight of Mary sitting near the front. He stopped briefly.

"Hello." David smiled at her as he spoke. Mary turned to look at him. As she did, David was aware that his stomach was feeling funny. He couldn't quite explain it except to say it was weird.

"Ooh," Mary grimaced. "What have you done to your eye?"

"Yes, I got hit." David wanted to say more but was being pushed by someone from behind wanting to get down the coach. He was suddenly aware that he was causing a jam. He looked up and saw what he also feared, that the lads at the back of the coach were watching him. "I'll speak to you later." He started to leave, and Mary smiled. He felt good to see her happy.

"What's happened to you?" Phil was the first to ask. The other lads fired questions at David trying to determine how he had come by the black eye, all except Arthur. David relayed the tale of the incident but was aware that Arthur was staring at him. David turned to look him in the eye. Arthur said nothing.

As the coach pulled up towards the High School, most of the lads were ready to get off. Phil readjusted his position on the back seat, but David stood up and stood in the aisle. He watched as the lads got off and made their way to the school entrance. He turned to Phil.

"I've got to talk to Mary."

Phil didn't answer. He felt it was probably the wrong thing for his friend to get too involved with her, but he said nothing. David walked down the coach, looking out of the window. Nobody was watching, so he felt happy sitting down next to Mary.

"Hello again," David said as he plonked himself down in the seat.

"So, what happened?"

"Just a little bit of a fight."

"Ow! It looks sore." Mary spoke in a sympathetic tone and reached out as if to stroke the bruise.

"Nothing, really. After the initial pain you get used to it. You would know of course."

As David replied, Mary withdrew her hand as if she had been stung then held it into her body in a retiring manner. David was taken by surprise but realised he had possibly said the wrong thing.

"I mean when you had that bruise the other day."

David tried to get Mary to turn back and look at him but she was having none of it. The coach started to pull away and drove slowly past the school entrance. David suddenly became aware that Mary might possibly be looking out to see Arthur.

"I'm sorry if I said the wrong thing." David tried again but Mary kept her gaze on the window. As the coach passed the school, Mary seemed to relax and she turned back to face David.

"Not your fault."

"Well, I'm sorry anyway."

"That does look painful though." Mary again reached out to touch David's bruised eye but this time David said nothing and just let her. As she touched his face, he shivered. Her hand felt gentle and soft.

"Is that any better?" Mary asked as she stroked David's face. David looked at her as the coach halted briefly at the junction with the main road. The pavement was full of kids making their way to the High School.

"That feels nice," David said and he smiled. He had been looking at Mary's brown eyes but the moment was getting a bit intense. David looked away as Mary continued to touch and soothe his bruise. David was looking at nothing in particular, but gradually became aware that not all of the youths on the pavement outside were passing by. The coach was still waiting to turn into the traffic, and David focussed on a group of black-blazered kids who were sitting against a wall looking up at the coach.

David almost froze as he recognised them. Arthur was looking straight at him. David looked at Arthur. He became aware of exactly what Arthur would be looking at as Mary stroked his face. David wanted to stop her from touching him but then on the other hand he didn't want to stop her. He looked again at Arthur whose stare hadn't altered for a second. The coach moved at last, but the two lads kept eye contact.

That evening, Sue baked a cake in honour of Michael's birthday. He was thirty-five. All the family sat round the table to have tea, knowing that there would be a song to sing. David and Louise had bought their dad presents, and as the cake was being cut they gave them to him.

"There you are, Dad. Happy birthday," Louise said, as she handed over her present.

"Thank you, darling."

"Hope you like it, Dad." David gave his father his present as Sue handed cake round. She had a few presents already wrapped for Michael. She brought them over.

"Cor, it's as if it was my birthday," Michael said as he looked at all the presents in front of him. Nobody found the comment at all amusing.

"You say that every year, Dad," David moaned. Michael opened the presents. A silk tie from Louise. A video of sporting funnies from David. Sue had got him a book, an engraved tie pin, a pair of slippers and a new key ring. As he opened the last present, Sue told him that it was because she knew he would be passing his driving test very soon. Michael wasn't quite so confident.

Friday seemed to have come around quickly. The temperature dropped and there was a distinct chill in the air but David waited at the bus stop as usual. Alice and Suzanne arrived and walked over towards where David stood.

"Good morning," David said.

"Oh, hello," Alice replied, but Suzanne just looked in his direction. The two girls continued their conversation, ignoring David.

"Bloody cold this morning!"

"Yes, it is." Alice was again the one to answer. Once more the girls chatted without including David in their conversation. David felt a bit left out. He couldn't help but look over at the two of them. Both looked nice, and Suzanne in particular was a bit posh. It was the clothes she was wearing, expensive gloves and matching hat. Even her tights were expensive looking. Everything about her said money, even though she was only in her school uniform. Alice was similar but seemed a bit more normal. David considered her more approachable. He toyed with the problem of what to say next to try and engage them in conversation, but he was void of ideas.

"What happened to your eye?" Alice asked. David was slow to realise that she was talking to him, and there was a gap before he turned and answered.

"Oh, had a bit of trouble with some lads." David walked nearer to the two girls.

"What, in town?" Alice queried.

"No, there." David pointed over to Doc's.

"Oh, in there," Suzanne said, in a most disapproving tone. "I can't say I'm surprised to hear that there has been trouble in there, what with the yobs that frequent that type of establishment." David wasn't quite sure how to reply. Several responses came to mind. Sorry, I don't understand what you're bloody saying, was his first thought. No, it's not that bad a place, was his second. You bloody stuck up cow was also high on the list. In the end, he settled on "Yes, I agree."

The brief conversation stopped there. The two girls continued to chat and David stood in silence waiting for the coach. He always held back until nearly everyone else had got on, but as the crowd reduced he took his turn in the vague queue. As he neared the door he suddenly became aware of a girl approaching from his right. It was Alice. It was obvious that she wasn't going to wait and David automatically stopped to allow her on in front of him. She grabbed the rail to help herself up the steps but stopped and turned back to David.

"Yes, I agree," she said in a sarcastic tone, and shook her head at the same time. It got her message across immediately. David shrugged his shoulders in embarrassment.

As David walked down the aisle he cagily looked

around to see where Mary was but he failed to spot her. He continued towards the back of the coach to join the other lads. There was the usual chit chat amongst them but David realised that Arthur was again keeping an eye on him. Arthur talked as and when required but always he stared at David. David for his part said very little at all. He was trying to work out exactly what Arthur was doing. As the coach approached the High School, David suddenly remembered what had happened yesterday. Of course, he thought to himself. He's pissed off about Mary. As he thought it, he looked around the coach again to see if he could see her. As the High School lads got ready to leave the coach, David concluded that Mary wasn't on board.

"She's not here this morning." David recognised the voice immediately. It was Arthur's. David looked up at him, standing ready to disembark from the coach. "And she blames you." Arthur seemed quite terrifying as he said it. It was almost like a warning.

Louise went to Doc's after school and met up with her friends. Tina was on her usual form, lording it round the table. Gillian and Melanie talked together whilst Louise chatted to Livvy. Vanessa was quiet.

"What's up with you?" Tina asked.

"Oh, nothing really. I've got to go early this afternoon. My mum will be picking me up early." Vanessa seemed preoccupied as she answered.

"But your mum always picks you up," Gillian reminded her.

"She'll be early today, she had to go to hospital with my sister."

"Oh, why's that?" Tina sounded interested.

"She got beaten up last night, and Mum thinks she's broken her arm."

"Broken her arm?" Louise replied.

"Yes. She's in quite a bad way."

"Who did it?"

"She won't say."

"Did it happen in Leafby?"

"Yeah, she went out last night to do something at the Village Hall and she got jumped on, by all accounts." Vanessa started to tear up as she explained. "She won't say anything or tell me who did it."

"I don't really know your sister that well. Is she a chicken?" Tina asked.

"No, she's not really. I remember her sticking up for herself in the past but there must have been a gang or something."

"She'll be alright." Melanie tried to comfort Vanessa.

"I suppose so. Mary's tough."

Saturday 11th February 1995

David tried to put the events of the week behind him as he was going to watch Gorleston Youth play Acle. David hoped that he might get a place on the bench, but was aware that he had been told that he would have to wait his turn before breaking into the team. Today would be good though, to get to know some of the other players a bit better. As he arrived at the ground, most of them were in the dressing room. Nobody was changing, and wouldn't do so until Scalesy read out the team. David counted the lads in the dressing room and reached eleven. This was good, as it meant they had a team, but it also meant that there was no chance of David grabbing a place by default. Scalesy struggled into the room with his big kit bag, dumped it in the middle of the floor then pinned up the team on the wall. David was a sub. Third on the list, but at least he was named.

"Dave, lad, there should be enough kit for you to get changed. I'd like you on the bench please." Scalesy spoke to him slightly away from the others. "I'm not promising anything, but I'll try and get you on for a bit towards the end. As the game started, David sensed that air of confidence that winning teams strive to get. Acle took a surprise lead within ten minutes, due to a goalkeeping error, but Gorleston never lost their confidence. They had most of the play, but the Acle midfield was strong and battled away hard, so chances were few and far between. All four of the Gorleston midfield took knocks. Mitch Taylor and Nigel were the main force in the middle of the park but the two wider midfielders had to do their own share of tackling. An equaliser was on the cards but it took till nearly half time before it came.

The second half started better for Gorleston, and it

was Taylor who picked up a loose ball to poke home a second goal. Lacey was substituted and Matt Crawley took his place but less than two minutes after the substitution, Nicky Sawyer took a knock and looked to be replaced. Scalesy sent David on.

"Do you want me to play in midfield?"

"No play up front." Scalesy did a straight swap. It didn't really work. While Gorleston were trying to get their positions sorted, Acle equalised. Nigel signalled to Scalesy and moved David into a midfield position. It seemed to work a lot better, and Gorleston pushed for a winner. Ashton came close a couple of times and Nigel also tried a couple of shots. David played more defensively in midfield which allowed the other four a better opportunity to get forward. The number of chances were mounting, but still that third goal was elusive. David eventually got the chance he was hoping for. He put in a really hard tackle, just beating an opponent to the ball as it broke loose, and pushing forward on a run. All the time he looked to play the ball over to the left but challenges kept coming in. David was equal to each one and the momentum pushed him into the penalty area. Just one last defender to beat. David played him a dummy and was through on goal. The keeper came out but it was natural for David to square the ball. He saw Lee Ashton racing in to the box and he faked to play the ball across to him. The keeper fell for it and left the goal at David's mercy. David took the ball on a few more yards past the goalkeeper and just as he was about to stoke home the winning goal, he heard Mitch's voice behind him. David moved aside and Mitch Taylor passed the ball into the empty net. Gorleston won 3-2 with Mitch getting a hat-trick.

After the game, Nigel made a point of talking to David.

"That was bloody unselfish of you."

"He was on for a hat-trick so it seemed the right thing to do. Hopefully one day he'll return the compliment."

"Still unusual to see it done." Nigel was impressed again. He wasn't alone, as both Scalesy and Mitch were quick to congratulate David on a great performance. Mitch in particular thanked David. The two got on well.

"Hopefully you can play next week," Mitch said in earshot of Scalesy.

"Yeah. I hope so too."

"You live in Gorleston?"

"No, in Somerby."

"Oh, I live in Thatcham." Mitch was surprised to hear where David lived. "How are you getting home?"

"Catching a bus."

"My dad will give you a lift."

Mitch and David chatted about the game all the way back to Somerby.

That evening, Louise wanted to go out with her friends. Tina had suggested that Vanessa should come over to Somerby during the afternoon. For all of her tough exterior, Tina had some really caring feelings inside. She knew that Ness was upset about her sister and wanted to try and take her mind off of it. All she could think of was to get her to come over for tea. The rest of the girls were meeting at Doc's that evening. David walked down with Louise but wasn't quite sure whether he was going to go in or not. He wondered about Doc, but nobody knew why he had that nickname, or what his real name was. Louise found her way to the girls' usual table.

"Hi Ness, hi Tina."

"Hello, Louise. Gillian is here, but in the toilet just now," Tina replied.

"Any idea if Livvy and Melanie are coming?"

"Should be," Tina answered. David followed Louise in, and looked around. There were one or two of the Burgh boys in, but neither of them were part of the group who he'd had trouble with earlier in the week. David bought himself a coffee and sat down at the table next to the girls.

"I take it you're staying a little while, then," Louise asked.

"Seems like it."

Another lad of about David's age entered Doc's, and looked around before going up to the counter and getting a cold drink. He had obviously been working somewhere muddy, as his shoes were caked in it, but his clothes were not really that dirty.

He came and sat at a table near David. David watched him out of the corner of his eye until he sat down, then carried on drinking his coffee. Gillian returned to the girls' table.

"Hello, Dave," she shouted across.

"Hi, Gillian." David hadn't actually said hello to any of the girls, but they all took this as a hello to all of them. Tina screwed up one of the napkins and threw it in David's direction. As he looked over she pointed to Gillian.

"It was Gillian."

"Shut up." Gillian shoved Tina. Vanessa laughed a little. David got on with his coffee.

"Gillian wants to know why you're not sitting with us today," Tina shouted.

"I'm sitting with the grownups today."

"Ooh, get you." Tina stuck two fingers up in his direction.

The coffee bar was beginning to fill up and one of the four Burgh boys entered. He looked over in David's direction, but did and said nothing. He was worried in case David was going to come after him.

Tina threw another napkin at David and he threw it back. It landed on some tomato ketchup that had been spilled on the girls' table so Gillian threw it back again. It hit David on the shoulder but fortunately didn't leave a mark. He grabbed two more napkins, scrunched them up to make a bigger bundle, and threw it. It hit Louise on the head. She threw it back even harder, but it missed David's table and landed where the other lad was sitting on his own. David got up to retrieve it. The lad picked it up and handed it to him.

"Sorry about that mate," David tried to sound sincere.

"No problem."

"Do you live in Somerby?"

"Yes. I'm on The Chestnuts."

"Hi, I'm David." David held out a hand in welcome and the lad shook it.

"I'm Pete." David sat down at the lad's table and totally forgot about the girls who by now had started their own conversation.

"Hope you don't mind me asking but where do you go to school?" David hoped the question wouldn't cause any problems. He had never seen the lad before and wondered how old he was.

"Yeah, I go to the High School."

"But you don't get on the coach?"

"No, I'm not allowed to. My dad drives me to school most mornings, or I catch the bus."

"Why aren't you allowed on the coach, then?"

"Oh, it's a bit confusing but my parents live too near the school." Pete gave him a brief explanation, but David didn't understand what the problem was.

"But others get on the coach from Somerby. There's even one who gets on further towards town. Where is The Chestnuts?" David was very confused.

"I live with my grandparents." Pete didn't really want to tell David this but realised he would have to if he was going to explain his situation.

"Oh, I see." David gave up his inquisition although he didn't fully understand the answer. The two chatted more as the coffee bar filled up. All four of the Burgh boys were now in Doc's.

Doc himself was out the back trying to balance the books. Brian was working in the bar, but he knew that Doc would help if he needed him.

The kids were pretty good as they tended not to come up to get served until the counter was free so there was rarely a queue. Brian tried to keep an eye on things in the bar as well as serve, and Doc had got very upset when he heard about the fracas the other day. All the staff had been warned to ensure that nothing like that should ever happen again, and that they should all be on their guard to prevent any fighting or other situations that might get out of hand.

Brian had been a bit offended with Doc's lecture and had discussed it with Kathy. Neither of them had seen the so-called incident and nobody had complained about any fight. Both Brian and Kathy had at first thought that Doc had got it wrong, but on questioning one or two of the regulars it was confirmed that not only was Doc right, but he had been able to name all five who were involved.

Both Kathy and Brian were keeping an eye on the four troublemakers. They had seen that David was in the coffee bar but when the four others came in, they were both on the alert in case of any trouble kicking off. One of the Burgh boys walked towards David, and there were some dirty looks between them but nothing that required any action being taken by Kathy or Brian. David tried to keep himself to himself as he didn't want to cause any problems, so just tried to ignore the Burgh boys. More came into the coffee bar including a lad who was obviously a bit of a gang leader. David paid little attention, but from the way the group all reacted it was obvious someone they all looked up to had arrived. David carried on chatting to Pete.

"How do you get on with the Burgh boys?" David asked.

"Don't, not really."

"I've had a bit of bother with them."

"Was it you who got hit the other day?" Pete said it almost with respect.

"Yeah I got this." He pointed to his eye.

"They don't usually get into too much trouble, but they are very tribal. You're either with them or you're against them. I hate 'em." Pete seemed to be talking from experience. David looked over and saw that the latest bloke who had come in was with his girlfriend. She looked quite nice as well. There were a few other girls in the crowd but this one stood out as being most glamorous. David looked over to the Burgh boys and then he looked again. He couldn't believe his eyes.

"Excuse me a minute," David said to Pete as he stood up. He walked over towards the Burgh boys. He wasn't going to the counter, and it didn't look as if he was going towards the toilet. Kathy nudged Brian and they prepared themselves for a possible intervention. One of the four Burgh boys who had argued with David saw him heading over and brought it to the attention of the one who had actually thrown the punch.

"Oh, watch out, the London pervert is coming over," the Burgh boy said. This made nearly everyone stop and look. "That is, if he's got the little girlies' permission." A couple of lads laughed. David continued over towards the crowd. The new lad with the glamorous girlfriend hadn't really looked before, but with everyone's attention focussed on this new incident he had to. As he turned he walked forward to meet David. David walked up to him and stopped. There was a nervous silence. Kathy moved from behind the counter ready to intervene, and Louise and the girls stood up to watch. The two faced each other. The suddenly embraced one another.

"Dave, how are you?"

"Hey, Mitch, I'm okay."

"Do you know this lot then?" Mitch turned to indicate the Burgh boys.

"We've met."

"So, I don't need to introduce you?"

"No, but I won't stand here as I don't get on with any of them." David looked at the Burgh boy who had hit him. The Burgh boy looked back.

"What, you don't get on with Bob?" Mitch sussed out the situation straightaway. "We'll come and join you then. Come on Jen." Mitch grabbed his girlfriend's hand and followed David back to his table. Bob wasn't happy. From that point on, Mitch and David got on like old friends. Mitch was obviously a bit of an iconic figure at Burgh, so nobody was going to cause any problems at the moment. That wasn't to say that they wouldn't in the future though. David knew that in the long run, Mitch might well have made things worse for him, but he wasn't overly concerned about it.

Doc's on a Saturday was a pretty busy place. It was very much a meeting place for the kids from several villages, before they went out for the evening. The Somerby kids of course would meet in Doc's at any time of day. There wasn't really any quiet time as kids were coming and going all day. Footballers met before and after matches. Afternoon shoppers would have a coffee before catching the bus. Some would just hang around Doc's all afternoon. As the afternoon went on, kids would arrive at Doc's before catching the bus into town for a night out. Doc always stuck to a last serving time of eight o'clock on a Saturday so that the place was empty by half past. Usually the staff would be able to get away by nine.

The café was only one of several shops in the block, but it was by far the biggest, and in the best position. There was no doubting it was the busiest. There were four other shops, two on either side of the cafe. On one side was a Chinese takeaway and a butcher, whilst on the other side was a bakery and a hairdresser's. The baker's shop was busy as it also made cakes and sold confectionery. In many ways, it depended a lot on the café clientele, as they were often the ones buying sweets as well. All in all, the shop staff got on well with each other. Not many people knew that Doc owned all of the shops. He didn't own the businesses, just the buildings. Doc never told anyone they were his, although one or two older locals might have guessed.

Businesses sorted out any leases or rent with a company called Hurst Hattrick Ltd. Nobody knew who was behind it, or indeed why it was called that. It was obvious that it had something to do with England winning the World Cup, but other than that nobody was quite sure why. Doc was often involved in looking after keys for any new businesses, but most people assumed this was because he was the longest serving tenant. Doc would often chuckle to himself when one of the other shopkeepers would take him into their confidence about some aspect of their legal negotiations with the landlords. He didn't often take advantage of it.

A new week started and the Riddells had lived in Somerby for five weeks now and a routine was taking shape. In lots of ways, life was very much how it had always been, with Michael at work and David and Louise at school, but in other ways life was different. The area was very quiet. To Michael it was often a loud silence. On a number of occasions, he had woken up in the middle of the night confused at not being able to hear anything. Transport was of course a big problem. It was slow, irregular, infrequent and finished at a very early hour of the evening. David also found the countryside very dark. There wasn't much street lighting in Somerby, and on a couple of nights he had found himself walking home from the bus stop in the pitch dark. It was surprising just how dark it could get sometimes although, when the moon was full, he could see pretty well.

Sue had tried to get to know the neighbours. On both sides of the bungalow were families of similar ages. To the left were Lance and Dawn, who had three children. They were all younger than David and Louise but not by much. On the right were Greg and Michelle who had a very young daughter. Sue would often see the two wives, and got to know them a bit.

Opposite were newlyweds, Nick and Sharon. Sue had been able to chat to them more than any other neighbours as both were currently unemployed and spent more time at home during the day. Next door to them was another couple who were a little older than Michael and Sue, and Sue had seen both of them. She waved on the first couple of occasions but this failed to raise a response. The next time she saw one of them, Sue made a point of walking towards them and saying 'Hello' but was just ignored. Michael had also waved a couple of times, but it was clear that they were not going to be quick to become friends. Apart from those two, Sue felt the family had settled in well and was starting to get on with the locals.

Sue also made an effort to chat to the postman whenever she could. He was quite willing to discuss almost any subject, but wasn't always quick to start a conversation. Sue had found out that he was called William, and that he had lived in the village almost all of his life. She was sure that he knew most of what was going on, but he would only verify, he would never volunteer information. This morning, there was quite a lot of post for the Riddells. Some junk mail, a few bills and a letter for David. The name and address were handwritten, so it was obviously a personal letter. Sue propped it up on the worktop in the kitchen. David would see it when he came in from school.

As it turned out, David didn't notice the letter when he got home as he was in too much of a rush to get changed and put the telly on.
"Hello, son," Sue shouted.
"Oh, hello," came the response.
"Have you had a good day then, dear?"
"Oh, suppose so."
"Is that a yes?"
"Yes."
David continued to get out of his school uniform

and by now had his turntable on. As the record started, he turned the volume up loud.

"David! Turn that down!" David knew what would be said, so he turned it down a bit.

"Down some more, please." Sue still thought it was too loud. David turned it down a bit more. Sue came to the bedroom door, standing with her hands over her ears. David turned the volume down a bit more.

"Thank you, darling. That's much better." Sue turned back to the kitchen and remembered the letter. She turned back again. "Did you see you had a letter arrive today?"

"A letter?" David got excited. "Where?"

"It's in the kitchen." David followed his mum into the kitchen, and she pointed to where she had left it. He grabbed it and returned to his bedroom.

About twenty minutes later the phone rang and Sue answered it. David kept an ear out to try and ascertain who it was on the phone.

"Hello, Somerby 730825," Sue answered in her usual manner. "Oh, alright. Tea will keep, no problem." From the last response, David assumed it was his dad. "What time do you think you'll be home?"

David only half listened now he knew who was on the other end. He returned to listening to his record but heard the phone being put back.

"Was that Dad?"

"Yes."

"And did I hear tea is going to be late?"

"Yes, your dad's having a driving lesson."
Sue expected some rude comment as a reply but all she got was a stunned silence. Well as silent as the music would allow. David suddenly appeared at the kitchen door.
"Driving lesson?" David asked, open mouthed.
"Yes, you heard right."
Neither said anything else for a few seconds and then Sue continued. "What was the letter?"
"Oh, it was from Rob."
"What, Rob from Goodmayes?" Sue asked, although she had already read the postmark and knew it was from the Ilford area.
"Yes."
"So, any news?"
"No, not really. Goodmayes United lost that replay."
"Oh, did they? That's a shame."
"Yes. Perhaps if I had been playing we might have won it."
"Well, you can't say. If you had played it might have been different, but then it might not have been. You've got to think about your new team now." Sue didn't want David dwelling on what might have been. He didn't.

Michael's first driving lesson was booked for five o'clock after work, and the car was waiting for him in a lay by near the bank. Michael spotted the car immediately and made his way over to it. The instructor had been keeping his eyes open and as

Michael approached the car he wound the window down.

"Hello. Mr Riddell?"

"Yes, that's me."

"Okay. If you'd just like to get in?" The lesson didn't go brilliantly and Michael felt all of his confidence just drain away as it went on. The instructor directed Michael so that his lesson ended in the village, and he eventually pulled up outside the bungalow.

"Thank you," Michael said as he put on the handbrake and turned the engine off.

"No problem. On Friday I can fit you in at half four, will that be alright?"

"Yes. Can you pick me up at the same spot?"

"Of course. Half four on Friday then. And I will have your driving report ready for you then so we can estimate how many lessons we think you need to pass your test."

Michael got out of the car and gave a half wave back to Glen before making his way indoors.

"How did it go?" Sue was there to greet him as he came through the door.

"Yes, Dad, did you have any crashes?" David added.

"No, I didn't crash and the instructor thinks he can get me through the driving test easily." Michael tried to sound as positive as he could even though he had his own doubts. It was enough to convince David anyway. As David went back to his room, Michael talked through his lesson with Sue. He finished by saying he was not as confident as Glen was that he could pass a driving test.

"He'll get you through," Sue said.

Chapter 7
DOC

The coffee bar in the village of Somerby is known as Doc's. It is known to the whole of the village, as well as to many people in neighbouring villages. The establishment is, of course, named after its owner. Very few people know him by any other name apart from Doc, and he is quite happy to answer to that name. In more recent times Doc hasn't really been working in the coffee bar, at least not as much as he used to. This was for a number of reasons, partly because he now had enough trusted staff to run the business for him, but also, he wasn't quite as well as he would like to be. In the past, he had been through a period of strength sapping attacks, but more recently they had got particularly bad again. He was not as fit as he once was, and there was no denying that but these recent spasms had been most irritating. They often kept him away from the friendly side of his business, the talking to the customers, but most of the local kids know him as much by reputation as they do from getting to know him personally, so it isn't quite as necessary for him to mix with his customers. But he rather liked that side of things.

Some of the older members of the village recall that Doc was a Londoner by birth, but nobody knows much about his roots or his early childhood, and having lived in Somerby for nearly thirty years now, he is pretty much accepted as a local, in fact he is a bit of a living legend in Somerby.

When he first arrived, it was a sleepy little village made up of mainly farms and a few cottages, but it was Doc who persuaded people to start their businesses here. Many of those original business owners had by now retired, or passed their businesses down the family and were happily living on the rewards of their hard work, but in most cases, it was Doc who came up with the ideas for their businesses and many were thankful for his suggestions and support.

Doc himself had done very nicely thank you, as he would say. He kept quiet about how he made his money so quickly, but it was fair to say that when he first came to Somerby he had no money at all. Within a couple of years, he had purchased his first piece of land and although he got the land for a slightly undervalued price, it was this purchase that made him. He had the foresight to see that this particular piece of land would be a prime site in the coming years. Not only that, but he seemed to build just what was needed at the right time. As new houses were being built, Doc started to build his shops. As the village grew, so did the number of shops on Doc's site, and it is now the centre of Somerby's shopping, and situated nicely between a hotel and the petrol station and supermarket, so it attracts everybody.

Those that knew him at first wonder at his rise from

homeless child to successful businessman. Doc just tells them that he was lucky.

On his piece of land is the group of shops which are owned by Doc. The land was originally sold as residential, and it was going to be where Doc would build his own home, not that anyone is complaining about its commercial use. Doc does now live onsite above his coffee bar, but in the early days he purchased a small cottage. It's a cottage that he still owns, and not many know but he also owns a few other houses as well. Occasionally he looks back at his time in the children's home, to see just how far he has come. He enjoyed living in the home, and he met some colourful characters of course, but he considers that he owes them something because he learnt so much from them. He never fully explains why, but he often says that had he not been in the children's home, he wouldn't be as rich as he is today.

It wasn't all good fun though. He remembered some horrible things about the home. The cold. The despair. The fighting and crying. There were some kids in there who found it very difficult to survive and Doc felt their pain. He still felt it at times now and often wondered what became of them. He himself was strong enough to stand up against the bullies. Back in those days he was very athletic. It was quite unusual at the time for one to be so fit and strong, and he probably could have been a professional sportsman but he had other intentions.

He did in fact go for a trial at Norwich City, but his mind was made up. His life was going to be spent making the village of Somerby successful. Nobody but Doc ever knew why.

In the early days, Doc worked wherever he could. He was usually able to turn his hand to any labouring task and indeed learnt how to do some bricklaying and how to plaster, and he got jobs working on roads, loading lorries and dock working. He also did some welding which came in very handy. Whatever the task, Doc was up to it. He worked from early morning to last light and whether it was at work or in his home, he never slacked. It was almost an obsession for him. He helped build much of the foundations and the initial building for the shops in Somerby, but it was his innovative ideas that helped him stand out amongst the others. It was as if nothing would stop him from working but that all changed in 1980 on the 9th of July.

It was a day that Doc would never forget. For a start, it was his birthday. Doc never celebrated his birthdays much, but he would have been about thirty on this day. There was a little party arranged for the evening, but around about lunch time that day, Doc went down with the first of many attacks. He is quite used to them now, although they still cause him problems, but they changed his life from that day on. He has never been able to undertake manual work since. He just seemed to lose half his strength from that day, and although he would like to work more than he does, and on occasions has tried, he just can't do anything physical for too long. At least he has made his money, and doesn't need to work too hard.

It was a dreary morning on the first day of March. The early rush in the café had finished and Brian had already cleaned the tables, so there was nothing to do. Doc made himself a coffee and sat down at a table. Brian decided to do the same.

"Not very nice out there today, Doc?"

"No, not really."

"Sometimes that can mean we'll be really slow."

"Yeah, sometimes, but then again it may mean we'll get very busy. You just can't tell." The two of them sat contemplating for a while and occasionally sipping from their coffee cups.

"Which part of London are you from?" Brian asked, rather casually.

"Bloody hell!" Doc almost spilt his coffee. "What made you ask that?"

"Oh, it was just that we were talking about that new lot who have moved up from London."

"What lot?"

"You know, you put the banners out for 'em."

"Oh, them." Doc knew full well who Brian was talking about.

"Well, Kathy mentioned that you came from London, so I just wondered."

"Well, it was really Essex when I lived there, so I lived just out of London."

"Oh!" Brian wasn't quite sure what to make of that answer. He turned it over in his mind a bit and came up with another question. "So why did you move to Somerby then?"

"Seemed like a nice place to move to."

"You lost your parents?"

"Why do you ask that?"

"Oh, I thought you were in a Children's home," Brian said.

"Yes. I lost them before I went into the home." Doc wasn't prepared to reveal any detail. Brian guessed that the affair was probably too difficult for him to talk about and dropped the subject. Coincidentally, a customer came in so Brian got up and took up a position behind the counter. Doc hoped he had fed Brian's curiosity.

That conversation was probably the longest that Doc had had on the subject for ages. Normally he would either change the subject or even just refuse to give any answers. It had been a difficult time for him and it did bring back bad memories when he talked about it. Just thinking about it was hard, and Doc was thinking about it now. A walk was what he needed, so he told Brian he was going out, and he set off for a slow wander round the village. Firstly, he looked back at his café-bar with some pride. Next was a walk to the house where he lodged all those years ago. It was one of about twenty terraced houses on Station Road situated opposite where the railway station used to be and Doc walked past it.

Things had changed quite a bit since he first walked up that road. New houses and bungalows had been built over the years but the old houses were still there. Doc stood and looked at the place before moving on. Next was the cottage where he first lived in his own house. There was a family in there at the moment, renting the place, but a warm feeling came over him whenever he saw his little cottage. He would never sell it. The walk had done him some good and taken his mind off bad things.

Thursday was a fairly busy day and Doc helped out a few times when the queue got too long. It was the time of the afternoon when the local schoolchildren started to arrive. Kathy had managed to get most of the tables clean and now she was needed to work behind the counter. Brian did a lot of the cooking again, so Doc helped out a bit. Louise and Tina made their way to a table as usual. Livvy was the next one to come in and join them and they sat there rather sheepishly looking out for Kathy just in case she came over to see if they had bought anything. The place was filling up fast so Kathy was far too busy to worry about them. Ness was the next one to join them and Melanie the last one to join the table. Gillian had gone home directly from school. She was going out to some family do that evening and had to go and get ready.

"Where's Gillian gone?" Louise asked Tina expecting her to know everything.

"One of her cousins is having an eighteenth

birthday party and she's got to go to it."

"A bit early for a party." Melanie added.

"I think she said it was in Lowestoft somewhere."

"Oh." The other girls replied almost in unison.

"Even Doc is working today." Livvy said as she pointed over at the counter.

"Yeah that's good as they'll never notice we haven't got anything." Melanie replied.

"Oh Doc is alright. He never worries we haven't bought anything." Tina said. "It's just Kathy we have to worry about."

"Yeah you're right. Doc has never thrown us out has he?" Livvy tried to think if her statement was in fact accurate.

"No I don't think he does throw anyone out." Tina replied.

"Oh he does. I've seen him a couple of times get people out because they have just been sitting there but Livvy is right, I don't think he's ever thrown us out."

"No he probably gets Kathy to do it for him." Louise said as they all laughed.

Doc was required as the café was busy. Brian was still doing beef burgers and bacon rolls so both Kathy and Doc were serving. When there was a break in the queue, Kathy started to clear up some tables, mainly collecting dirty cups, glasses and plates but where needed a quick clean as well.

"Oh, oh. Kathy's on the prowl." Livvy caught sight of her.

"Whose turn is it to buy?" Tina asked.

"I think it was Gillian's." Melanie said, hoping to deflect any pressure on her.

"Well, she's not here so it's your turn."

"I haven't got much money."

"I can let you have some if you need any," Louise said as she opened her purse.

"How much have you got?" Tina asked Melanie directly.

"All I've got is forty pence."

"I've got seventy here." Louise handed over some money to Melanie.

"Now go and get some drink." Tina had almost lost patience with her.

"Alright, I'm going." Melanie got up and made her way to the counter. Doc was at the till.

"Can I have a milk shake, please Doc?" Melanie smiled as she asked.

"No problem. What flavour?"

"Ah." Melanie paused "I think strawberry please, or perhaps vanilla."

"So, which one is it?" Doc was quite happy to give Melanie time to decide, but he guessed she was uncertain which flavour would suit everyone.

"No, you're probably right, I think I'll have a Pepsi Max instead."

"Just the one?"

"Yes, just one please. The other girls aren't thirsty."

"So, you won't be wanting any straws then?" Doc was teasing the poor girl.

"Ah." Melanie was a bit stumped. "Your straws

always go soft when you've been sucking on them for a while so it's always best to have some spare." Melanie hoped that did the trick.

"I think you could probably do with two cokes." Doc hadn't finished. Melanie looked at the money in her hand and tried to work out if she had enough for two. She didn't. Doc knew exactly what was going through her mind. "Look here, Miss Huggins, if you buy one coke I'll let you have the second one for free."

"Free?" Melanie almost shouted.

"Yes, but shh. Don't tell everyone. Anyway, you're a friend of Luce's so it's no problem."

Doc took Melanie's money for one coke and passed her two glasses. Melanie looked at Doc with a little confusion but decided to get the drinks back to the table before he changed his mind. As she returned, Tina gave her a serious look.

"Two cokes," she said in a stern deep voice.

"Yes, two cokes," Melanie replied in a cocky tone as she placed the two drinks on the table. Melanie also made a point of returning some money to Louise.

"How did you get two cokes?" Livvy was curious.

"Well, I'm not quite sure but Doc just let me have two for the price of one," Melanie replied.

"You mean you buy one, you get one free," Livvy said in a Yorkshire accent, mimicking an advert on the telly. Almost as if being directed the other girls replied:

"I said you buy one, you get one free."

They all laughed.

"So why did Doc let you have a free coke?" Louise asked after all the merriment had died down.

"Well to be honest I thought it had something to do with you." Melanie replied.

"Me?"

"Yes, you. Doc said that as you were at the table we could have a free coke," Melanie explained. Louise shrugged her shoulders.

"But I don't know him."

"Well, he knows who you are."

"How do you know he knows who I am?"

"He mentioned your name." Melanie had lost interest in the subject.

"What do you mean?" Louise wanted details.

"Well, I think he thinks your name is Lucy, or something like that, but he meant you, I'm sure." Melanie had nothing else to tell her. Louise wasn't sure how Doc knew her, and he obviously didn't know her that well. Regardless, she wondered how Doc had got her name.

The café was really starting to get busy, and there were no tables left to sit at. Not that this worried many of the kids who preferred to stand around the juke box and gaming machines anyway. Doc was busy serving but he kept looking over to where Louise and the girls were sitting. He had decided that today he would try and chat to Louise. He knew he couldn't say much whilst she was with the other girls, but just to speak to her would be enough to start with. As the queue got smaller, Doc turned to Kathy. "Can I leave you serving for a bit, I'm going to collect some glasses."

"Okay, Doc," Kathy replied without looking up from what she was doing. Doc picked up a wet cloth and made his way out to the nearest tables where there were a few empty cups and glasses. He picked these up and returned them to the washing area behind the counter and then went out again. Eventually he made his way over to where the girls were. Everyone said hello to Doc.

"Hi, Doc. Busy today." Tina was the first to speak.

"Yes, Miss Phillips, it is very busy," Doc said as he collected some rubbish that the girls had left. Doc turned to Melanie and spoke to her whilst wiping the table. "Did you need the two cokes then, Miss Huggins?"

"Yeah, thanks Doc. Good of you to let us have it." Melanie looked at Louise and then back to Doc. "Did you say it was for Louise though?" Doc looked hard at Melanie.

"No, not necessarily for her."

"But it's because you know her?"

"Well, I think I know all of you, not only Miss Riddell." Doc winked at Louise as he replied.

"How do you know my name?" Louise asked him. She was still confused about Doc, as although it would probably have been the right reaction to be annoyed that Doc knew her name, she wasn't. He sounded nice and friendly. She couldn't explain it.

"I know a lot of things, Miss Riddell." Doc touched

the side of his nose a couple of times.

"Maybe, but I still don't know how you know my name."

"It's because of your brother."

"You know David?"

"Yes, of course I know him." Doc was starting to feel a little uncomfortable with the seriousness of Louise's questions so he tried to change the subject. "And where is Miss Fortescue today?"

"Oh, she had to go to a party," Livvy answered. Doc didn't answer but moved to another table.

"So, he knows your brother?" Melanie started to quiz Louise.

"Don't think so."

"Well that's what he said, and Doc wouldn't lie would he?"

"I don't know, I'll have to ask David. Does he always call people by their surnames?"

"Yes, I think so," Melanie replied.

"He knew my surname as well." Louise couldn't work it all out. By now Doc had gone back to the counter.

David got off the school coach and crossed the road with Alice and Suzanne. They chatted about how good it was to be home and what had happened at school but quite soon the two girls said their goodbyes and went their separate ways. David stopped and looked around. He considered going to find Luce in Doc's, but as he looked over he could see the Burgh Boys were in there, and he wasn't sure he wanted to cause any trouble today.

The considering lasted only a few seconds and David made his way to the entrance. As he approached, the Burgh Boys saw him, and Bob Packham nudged one of his mates to point him out.

"Come with me, Terry. I want a word with our little cockney."

Bob made his way out of Doc's and approached David. They walked towards each other until they met. David moved to the left to get round him but Bob moved in the same direction to block him again.

"What the bloody hell do you want?" David stared at Bob as he spoke.

"Well, right now I need a nose clip." Bob laughed and Terry joined in. "The smell is just awful."

"Look, if you want to fight, say so. If you don't, just get out of the way." David started to move but Bob pushed him back. David pushed Bob in return and the two of them squared up to each other. Terry took a step back waiting to see what would happen, but neither threw any punches. They just stood up to each other. "What's your problem?"

"I don't like you, that's the problem."

"Well you're just going to have to live with it."

"I don't want to see you around here."

"Well that's just bad luck because I bloody well live here."

"Your buddy Mitch doesn't though, so don't think you're wanted." Bob let David pass. David walked on fully aware that Bob and Terry were following very closely behind. He was now determined to go to Doc's. He didn't want them to think they'd put him off.

After Ness went home, just Livvy and Louise were sitting at the table. Doc decided that this was another opportunity and he started to make his way over. He tried not to make it obvious that it was the girls' table he was making for, so he stopped at a couple of others on the way. Louise and Livvy were still the only two at the table as Doc reached them.

"Hello," Louise said.

"You should call me Doc, for now." Doc replied.

"What do you mean, for now?" Louise questioned.

"Oh, nothing really. How are you settling into Somerby?" Doc asked, but as Louise started to reply he was unable to concentrate on her answer. He was having another one of his attacks. The pain hit him so quickly that his head was suddenly one enormous throbbing pain. He could see Louise mouthing an answer, but the words were not loud enough to break through the whistling in Doc's head. He fell to his knees with the pain. Louise stood up.

"Are you alright, Doc?" She was concerned. She hadn't known him long but already felt a connection with him and she found herself worrying about him. At about the same time there was a bit of a commotion at the entrance to the café bar. The Burgh Boys were creating a bit of a noise. Doc held his head and then his stomach. The pain was terrible. It was as if someone had stuck a fork into him and was twisting it first one way then the other. Kathy saw that Doc had fallen and alerted Brian.

The commotion at the entrance involved David, of course. Having got past Bob and Terry he opened the door to go in and found the rest of the Burgh Boys in his way. Normally they would reluctantly move, but as it was David they didn't. David kicked a bag out of the way and one of the lads pushed David. David stood up to face the lad, who pushed him in the face. It was a nothing push, but David felt a terrific pain in his head. The room started to spin and he felt sick and dizzy. He wanted to walk past the Burgh Boys but he was unable to lift his legs properly, as if they were weighed down. He turned and got back out of the door. The Burgh Boys laughed out loud as David bent down outside the cafe as if he was going to be sick. Terry went up to him and shouted in his ear.

"Go home, London boy." David did nothing but breathed in deeply to compose himself. Bob Packham watched and saw that he was in some pain. He clicked his fingers and Terry left David alone. They went back inside where Brian and Louise were helping Doc back to the counter. As Louise got nearer to the counter, she saw David outside. She could see that he was also having problems.

"Can you manage now Doc, as I have to go?" Louise said to both Doc and Brian.

"Go. I'll be alright now." Doc touched Louise's hand. "Thanks." They looked into each other's eyes for a split second before Louise went to see how David was.

Louise found David leaning with his hands against the wall.

"Are you alright?"

"Oh, Luce, it's you. Yeah I'm alright now"

"Have you been fighting with the Burgh lot again?" Louise assumed this was the case.

"No I haven't been fighting." David sighed. "I just came over a bit dizzy that's all. I'm okay now."

"What's wrong then?"

"It might be migraine, I don't know. I'm better now."

"Are you coming in for a coffee?" Louise asked.

"No, I think I'll go home." David grimaced as if to indicate that he wasn't fully recovered.

"Okay. I'm going back in but I'll be home soon. Tell Mum, won't you?" Louise went back into the café. By the time she got in, Doc had been taken upstairs. Kathy was with him.

"What's actually wrong, Doc? This is the third attack you've had recently."

"Oh, it's nothing."

"Nothing? It knocks you right down. You need to see a doctor."

"I know what it is. It's an illness that I used to have in the old days. I'd forgotten just how bad it could be." Doc just wanted Kathy to leave him.

"Well, I think we should call a doctor."

"No, there's no need. I'll tell doctor when I go for my next check-up." Doc stared at Kathy.

"Okay. But make sure you do."

"You're not my wife, you know." Doc tried to laugh but it hurt.

"No, perhaps not, but I'm the nearest thing you've got to one." Kathy kissed him quickly on the cheek and then made her way back down to the counter.

Tina and Melanie had returned to the table by the time Louise came back in.

"What was going on there?" Tina asked.

"Oh, nothing, he wasn't feeling too well."

"Did somebody hit him?" Melanie asked.

"No, he says not."

"The Burgh lads say he's too frightened to come in because they are here."

"That's crap." Louise stuck up for her brother.

"Okay. That's what they're saying, not me," Tina replied. "Calm down, girl," she added. The girls all laughed. "No, seriously, they say he is scared because everyone keeps picking on him."

"No, I don't think he's frightened at all." Louise was suddenly aware of what her brother might be going through.

"Hey, anyway, I hear you also had Doc collapse over here?" Melanie wanted to know.

"Yeah, he just fell at Louise's feet," Livvy explained. It was more than Louise wanted her to say but she couldn't really deny it was what had happened.

It was another Monday morning, and David waited at the bus stop for the school coach to arrive. He chatted away to Alice until Suzanne turned up. David liked Alice. She was down to earth despite her obviously posh upbringing, and able to converse on subjects that David knew about and understand what he wanted to say. She was nice. When Suzanne turned up the two chatted relentlessly and David took a back seat in the proceedings. As the coach arrived he couldn't help but notice Mary looking out of the window. He could also see Arthur so he didn't make any moves. It was nice just to see her back on the coach after such a long time.

After the coach left the High School, David allowed it a few moments to get away before walking down to chat to Mary. She was sat with another girl but David wasn't going to let that stop him.

"Excuse me, but do you mind if I sit here for a minute." He indicated a free seat on the other side of the aisle, and the girl obliged. Mary said nothing. David sat down next to her. "Are you all right? I've been worried about you."

"You needn't have been," Mary replied curtly. This was progress as far as David was concerned. It wasn't too long ago that Mary wouldn't have even replied.

"Arthur said it was my fault you were off."

"Did he? Are you two talking about me then?" David was amazed at the amount of conversation Mary was coming out with. It was obvious she wasn't relaxed but at least she was talking.

"No, I think he gave me a warning. Has he said anything to you?" David wasn't quite sure what there was between Mary and Arthur, if there was anything.

"None of your business if he has." Mary sounded offended. David assumed the worst.

"Okay. Sorry to ask. I'm glad you're back though." David went back to his mates. As Mary got off the coach, David looked out of the window to try and catch a sight of her. She looked back to see if he was looking. They held their stare for a few seconds as the coach drove off.

The week sped through and in no time it was Friday. David tried to talk to Mary again on the coach but things hadn't improved much since Monday. Although David was certain Mary was looking out for him when it pulled up, as he walked along the corridor on the coach she turned away so that she would see him. David knew she had some problems with Arthur but was confused as to why she let him run her life. He had asked her if they were boyfriend and girlfriend and she had said 'no'. Perhaps they had been in the past although David didn't get that impression. Perhaps Mary fancied him but David didn't think that was the case either. Perhaps Arthur fancied her? No. David was sure that wasn't the situation. From his previous actions, he felt that Arthur wouldn't spit on Mary even if she were on fire. Mary had problems but David just couldn't figure them out.

The days were going fast and it was already Wednesday. In fact, Wednesday 15th March which just happened to be Louise's birthday. Although she still had to go to school it was a day full of excitement as far as Louise was concerned. The girls all wished her a happy birthday when she arrived and she was the centre of attention all day. School just seemed to speed by and in no time Louise was on her way home. She didn't go to Doc's that afternoon but instead went straight home. In fact, none of the girls went to Doc's as they were all off to celebrate Louise's birthday and that meant getting dressed up.

Sue had promised to take them to Pizza Hut in town. It was a great place to be as far as the girls were concerned as you could see all the lads passing the window whilst having a good time eating pizza and salad. Louise was very pleased. It was her twelfth birthday and she was growing up - too fast, if you asked Sue. Michael still thought of her as his little girl and hadn't really noticed how mature she could be but there was no doubt about it, she was already a young lady. There were seven of them at the meal. They had a laugh and generally a great evening, with Louise getting presents from the girls.

She didn't open her family presents until afterwards. It was a tradition in the Riddell household.

The next day, the talk at school was all about their evening at Pizza Hut. It was quite an occasion. Livvy and Vanessa couldn't stop talking about it, as if it was the best thing they had ever done, but Tina wasn't quite so vocal. When school had finished, the girls made their way as usual to Doc's.

They took up a table as usual, and bought a couple of drinks. Louise had treated herself to a vanilla milk shake. They chatted away between themselves, hurling an occasional remark to any passing boy who was silly enough to walk within range. All six were getting on well now. They were a real gang and Louise had never felt happier. Doc had suddenly appeared at the end of the counter and looked over at the girls' table. After a couple of minutes, he made his way over, stopping at a table on the way to put chairs straight. He walked over and looked at Louise.

"I just popped over to say happy birthday, Luce." Doc smiled as he spoke to her, but he also fidgeted with his hair in an embarrassed manner. The girls stopped in mid sentence as he said it. Louise looked up at him and for a few seconds saw that familiar look that she had seen before.

"Thanks, Doc," Louise eventually answered. There was a brief pause until she picked up her milk shake. "It was actually my birthday yesterday."

"Yes, I know but I didn't see you in here yesterday." Doc wiped the table with his cloth, turned and made his way back to the counter. The girls all looked at Louise. Louise continued to suck some more milk shake through the straw as she raised her eyes to look at the others.

"What? What?" she asked, in an accusing tone.

"Doc just came and wished you happy birthday." Gillian was the first to reply.

"Yeah." Louise shrugged her shoulders. "So what?"

"Well, he never wishes us happy birthday." Gillian sounded offended and she pulled a grumpy face. "Anyway, how did he know it was your birthday?"

"Well, I don't know. Perhaps he overheard us talking." Louise didn't think it was a big thing to create any fuss over.

Thursday was quite an important day for David. He was playing football that afternoon and it was a game he had been rather looking forward to, against Yarmouth High School. It was a match of hidden importance as far as David was concerned. He knew it was being referred to as a Cup Final but when he asked Mr Bowles about the game, he confirmed that in fact it was just a round in the County Cup competition and that they were still playing in the last sixteen. For the rest of the team though, they felt the local rivalry more than David and knew that if they won this game they could boast of being the best side in Great Yarmouth. Everything was regional to start with, so technically it *was* a cup final. It was obvious when David got to school that morning that it wasn't only the team who were feeling the excitement of that afternoon's game. One or two of the school kids had also asked what time kick off was and wished him good luck. It all seemed a bit over the top to David.

Eventually the team were getting changed in the dressing room and the talk was all about how good the Yarmouth High team were. They had Davison. They had Lacey. We'll never get past Williams. David found it all quite depressing. When Mr Bowles came in for his pep talk, he too talked more about how to stop Yarmouth than anything else.
"But boss, we have a bloody good team as well," David said. It stopped Mr Bowles with a jaw dropping blow. He didn't reply but just looked around at the team. They too had stopped talking, more in fear of the opposition than anything else.
"Our midfield is probably better than theirs," David added. Still Mr Bowles did nothing but look down at his notes. "Our defence is bloody difficult to beat and we can always score goals." David sat back down as he reached the end.
"Yes, you're right." Mr Bowles replied. "We've got a team that can beat anybody. We can beat this lot. Just go and show 'em how good you are." Mr Bowles completed his team talk.
"Right, Carlton. This is our game, our day. You're all going to be heroes." Nigel spoke as the team captain. The team let out one mighty roar and

everyone felt good.

As they made their way out to the pitch, the Yarmouth High team had already started to make their way out. They looked really professional in their red shirts and black shorts and socks but Carlton were proud of their colours as well. They played in sky blue and the kit looked good. David walked out and as he turned the corner of the school building and was shocked to see about twenty or thirty people stood around the pitch waiting to watch the game. There were a couple of newspaper reporters and photographers, and David also spotted Scalesy. As he made it on to the pitch it was like a real game with the crowd clapping. It got worse when a large number of Carlton school kids were allowed to come out of lessons early and watch. They chanted the usual naff songs as if it was a hockey international. But it got the Carlton team going.

In many ways, the match was a bit of an anticlimax. Nigel and David had concocted a plan to pick up on Arthur all the time. They didn't man-to-man mark, but made sure that one of them was on him at all times. This meant that at various times, both could start attacks and be there to support the front players and Carlton had most of the game in the first half. Nicky Sawyer, Pop, as most of the lads called him, managed to squeeze free of the defence half way through the first half and although he sliced his shot a little it still had enough power to go past Steven Williams in the Yarmouth High goal. The crowd were ecstatic and the chanting continued right through the break.

Mr Bowles had warned the Carlton lads to be prepared of a bit of an onslaught in the opening part of the second half but with Arthur Davison never really getting into the game, it didn't materialise. Nigel and David had run the midfield both in respect of defending and attacking and a headed goal from Chris Long in the second half was enough to see Carlton through. As the final whistle blew, the team jumped to celebrate a most gratifying win. A lot of the kids who had been watching had left to go home by now but those who remained shouted the name 'Carlton' at the top of their voices. Carlton were the winners.

Friday afternoon and Michael arrived home after another driving lesson.
"How did it go?" Sue asked as soon as Michael got in.
"Glen said it went well. He's proud of me." Michael was almost beaming with confidence. "But he did say it would probably take about six months to get me through the test."
"But he'll get you through, that's great." Sue dried her hands. She walked over to her husband and gave him a hug. "What's that in your pocket?" She wasn't being rude, but ran her hand down Michael's

trousers to a lump quite obviously sticking out.

"Oh, that," Michael replied. "That's my new mobile phone." Michael retrieved it from his trouser pocket and placed it firmly down on the table.

"Mobile phone!" Sue exclaimed. This signalled an onslaught of curiosity. David was the first one to come into the kitchen.

"You got a mobile phone, Dad?"

"Yes." Michael had hardly got the reply out when Louise appeared.

"Cor, Mum, I want a mobile phone," Louise said with some certainty.

"I don't think so, darling." Sue tried to nip this in the bud.

"But, Mum, all the girls at school have phones."

"I haven't seen them with any phones."

"Honest, Mum," David interrupted. "It's the new accessory that everyone wants."

"Who are you going to call on it?" Sue couldn't think of any valid reason why David or Louise might possibly need a mobile phone.

"I can keep in touch with Tina," Louise said.

"You can phone her now anyway."

"Not when we're out, though." Louise knew what she meant.

"And if you want to know where Louise is when she's late home you can ring her." David hoped this would be a more desirable reason.

"We'll have to see."

David and Louise finished saying their hellos to

Michael and shot off back to what they had been doing before he came in.

"Have you gone and bought this?" Sue was concerned.

"No. It's given to me by the bank."

"How much are they?"

"Don't really know. Are you thinking about the kids then?"

"I doubt it'll go away."

"I'll try and find out."

Tuesday was quite a wet morning. David waited for the coach wondering what the day would bring. It wasn't a particularly brilliant day today, it was double science for a start. The crowd of kids started to move so David knew that the coach was in sight. He took up his normal position, away from the crowd, and waited his turn to get on. As he looked up at the coach he was surprised to see Mary not only looking at him but also giving him a little wave. He waved back and she smiled. It was one of those magic moments. David's heart fluttered and he thought he was in love. It was a strange feeling. He'd fancied a number of older women, models and film stars, and there were also a couple of girls at school who had showed some interest in him, but none that interested him. Mary was different. He couldn't explain why, she just was.

As he got on the coach, David looked over in Mary's direction expecting her to be looking the other way, but to his surprise she was watching him. As he got nearer she waved again, and even mouthed "Hello." David was flabbergasted. As he got to the back of the coach he said his usual welcomes to the lads but realised that Arthur was not on the coach. It explained everything. After the coach left the High School, David went and joined Mary.

"Morning. How are you?" David asked.

"I'm well, and you?"

"Yeah I'm okay." David wanted to ask why she was so friendly today but feared asking might change the mood. "It's a shame that I never get enough time to really talk to you."

"Is it?" Mary's answer was just a little aloof.

"Yes, of course it is. I like chatting with you." As David spoke, Mary started to blush a little. "I like seeing you on the coach." David thought he might have gone just a little too far.

"Don't be silly."

"Hey, what do you do at weekends?"

"What do you mean?"

"Do you go shopping? Or into town, or perhaps to Norwich?" David just wanted to get to know Mary a bit better.

"Usually I spend most weekends at home."

"At home. Oh. Well, do you watch the telly or listen to music?"

"I do both of those. We usually have the radio on in the mornings." Mary answered.

"No, I mean at weekends."

"Oh, I haven't got time at weekends. I have to help with the housework." Mary seemed a bit surprised with the question.

"What, all weekend?"

"Yes, usually." Mary started to get to her feet. "I've got to get off."

"Okay." David smiled at her and she smiled back in return. "Have a good day, and hopefully I'll see you on the coach tonight."

David would have liked to have talked more but their time was brief.

On the way home they had even less time as the route between the two schools was different and took a lot less time. David waited for Mary to sit down, then he walked up to see her. She was with one of her school friends, so the chance for him and her to chat wasn't there. As he approached though, she turned to look at him.

"Did you have a good day?"

"Yes thanks," Mary answered. There was an awkward silence and David concluded that this was not a good time to talk.

"Okay, I'll see you tomorrow," David said, as a form of goodbye. Mary waved a little wave and mouthed "Sorry."

David decided to pop into Doc's to see if Luce was there. As he expected, some of the Burgh boys were in and there was a general groan from them as he walked past. He was able to ignore them most of the time, and today he just made his way over to Luce and the girls. He didn't stay too long, as after fifteen minutes or so he started to have one of his migraine attacks.

The pain came on suddenly, and it was too much for him to bear whilst sitting in a noisy coffee bar.

"I'm going to have to go home Luce. The noise is hurting me."

"Will you be alright?" Louise wanted to help her brother but didn't want to leave her friends.

"I'll be all right." David stood up and gave a cautious nod. As he got to the door one of the Burgh boys threw a paper cup in his direction but it missed by miles. David saw it, and thought about making something of it but under the circumstances he decided to continue on his way home. Just a lie down on his bed would be good, he thought, but by the time he got home, he was already starting to feel better.

David hadn't managed to chat with Mary again all of last week but today he got a chance. He noticed she had an empty seat next to her, and when the time was right he sat in it.

"Hello, you," Mary said, in a very friendly tone.

"Hello you, back." David was pleased with the way the two of them seemed to be getting on.

"I hear you play football."

"Well, yeah, I suppose I do."

"And you're quite good."

"I do all right. There are loads of players better than me but then loads who are worse." David didn't want to sound conceited.

"Where do you play?"

"Midfield."

"Where's that?"

"Well, it's a position in the middle of the field."

"No, I mean where do you play football?" Mary laughed as she realised the mistake David had made. It was a beautiful infectious laugh that got David laughing with her.

"Oh. I play in Gorleston."

"I'd love to go and watch a football game one day."

"Come with me." David took his opportunity quickly.

"I'd have to ask my mum. Would it be after school?" Mary seemed totally oblivious to half of what was going on in the world.

"No, we play at weekends. On Saturday afternoons." David hoped that would be more convenient than after school.

"Ah, well, I wouldn't be able to come then. My uncle would be expecting me."

"Well if not this Saturday, perhaps another Saturday?" David asked hopefully.

"No, I don't think I'd be able to get away on Saturdays. It's cleaning day." They were getting very near to Mary's school so David knew their conversation would be ending. "I'd love you to come and watch. Please ask and see if you can get an afternoon off."

"I doubt I will." Mary spoke as she was walking to get off the coach. "Bye".

Wednesday was soon here and David wanted to see if Mary could come with him to football on Saturday. He couldn't sit next to her, but still had to ask.

"Did you ask your mum?"

"Ask her what?"

"About coming to the football with me."

"What, on Saturday? No, I can't."

"Your mum said no?"

"No, I just can't." Mary wouldn't give any reasons and wouldn't answer any other questions, so David accepted it and sat back down.

Yet another Thursday, and David was due to play football again for Carlton Grammar. They were now in the last eight of the County Cup, and after the game a fortnight ago they were being referred to as the Yarmouth champions. The county was split into eight regions, and Carlton were representing the Yarmouth area. Their opponents were not to be dismissed as just another team to play, though, as they were from Bishop's Grammar in Kings Lynn, and the current holders of the cup. This didn't necessarily mean that it was the same team, as the cup was won last year by boys who had left the school, but it did show that they had some pedigree and were not to be underestimated.

Carlton were in buoyant mood after the last round and all feeling confident. Mr Bowles gave a much more positive team talk this afternoon and Nigel said his usual bit to get the team ready but confessed his more private fears to David.

"I cannot find out anything about this team so I have no idea how good or bad they are."

The game started well for Carlton with Nigel scoring from a free kick in less than ten minutes. It put Bishop's on the back foot and they didn't really create any chances until ten minutes from half time. On their first attack, one of the Bishop's forwards dribbled between two defenders and slotted home an equaliser from just inside the area. It was what Bishop's needed as they were just beginning to drop their heads. From the restart, Paul Baldry took on the Bishop's full back, crossed a ball in to the area and Nicky sawyer headed in at the near post. The Carlton lead had been restored in less than a minute. Bishop's never looked to be in the game again and Carlton were the eventual winners by 4-1.

Chapter 8
MEETING THE RIDDELLS

Sunday 2nd April 1995
It was a bright crisp Sunday morning and Sue was
up early. It was her birthday, her thirty-fourth. She
couldn't understand why, but for some reason she
was particularly excited about her birthday this
year. It wasn't any special year, like a fortieth, but
things just felt right. She busied herself in the
kitchen while checking the clock. Just before seven
thirty, far too early for any of the other members of
the family to be waking up but there was a surprise
this morning.
Sue heard a gentle noise at the kitchen door and
turned to see Louise standing there half awake in
her nightdress.
"Happy birthday, Mummy." Louise handed Sue a
card and a small brightly wrapped box.
"Thank you, darling." Sue took the card and the box
and hugged Louise close. "You didn't need to get
up so early."
"I heard you," Louise yawned.
"Go on darling, get back to bed for a while." Louise
looked up and smiled.
"Are you going to open your present?"
"Yes, of course I will."
"Open it now, and then I'll get back to bed."

Sue removed the ribbon and with only a brief
difficulty, the wrapping paper. It was a bottle of

perfume. "Thank you, darling." Sue gave Louise a kiss. Louise was happy enough, and returned to her bedroom, passing Michael on the way.

"You all right, Louise?" Michael asked.

"Yes, Dad, just gave Mum her present."

"Good girl."

"I'm going back to bed for a little while."

"Okay, darling." Michael gave Louise a pat on her head, and made his way into the kitchen.

"Happy birthday my lovely wife." Michael walked towards Sue with his arms wide open. Sue turned and reciprocated. They hugged briefly.

"Where's my present, then?"

"I've only just found out from our daughter that it was your birthday," Michael joked.

"Ah, well, if it was her fault then I forgive you," Sue laughed.

By nine o'clock, Louise had got up again and David had also surfaced. The family sat down to a fried breakfast, which Sue had cooked for them. Michael had of course got Sue a couple of presents and David brought in his card and present to give to his mum.

"Happy birthday, Mum," said David, looking around to see what was for breakfast.

"Thank you, son," Sue replied, opening the last of her presents.

"Do you fancy a walk today?" Michael spoke in between eating.

"Did you have somewhere in mind?" Sue replied. Michael did, but he wasn't going to tell Sue that.

"No not really." Michael shrugged in denial of any preconceived ideas. "I just thought that if the weather was fine we could go for a walk somewhere."

"Yes, okay," Sue replied, suspecting a plot.

As it happened, Michael did get Sue out for a walk. They didn't go far but she enjoyed it. She held on to Michael's arm which made Michael feel good.

"It's nice to be able to get out into the country, isn't it?" Sue said.

"Well, yes, but we used to do this in London."

"Yes, I know, but it's not the same if you've got to get a bus. And anyway, it was more crowded in London, even in the parks. Around here you can walk for ages and not see anyone. It's brilliant."

"Yes, I suppose so," Michael replied as he glanced at his watch. "It's getting on for half past four, you know."

"Yes, I suppose we ought to start heading back." Sue and Michael looked at a row of old country cottages as they made their way round a bend. "I'd love to live in a cottage."

"Would you?" Michael was surprised. "Perhaps we should have a look if one comes up for sale."

"Yes, that would be good," Sue replied. The conversation continued as they made their way back home. When they got in, David and Louise were standing in the kitchen waiting for them.

"What's been going on here, then?" Sue assumed that the two of them were trying to hide something.

They both looked very suspicious but she couldn't see what they had done. Michael knew exactly what they had done, as less than half an hour later, a Chinese meal was delivered. It meant that Sue didn't have to cook, and the kids were happy with the food. Sue agreed it had been a very nice day.

Monday 3rd April 1995
The next day everything was back to normal. Michael went off to work and David and Louise to school. Sue was left on her own at home, not that she was worried about that. In fact, in many ways she was quite happy to have her space and uninterrupted peace. She got on with cleaning up a bit and doing some washing.

Doc was also doing his washing. The coffee bar had got over its early morning rush, and was quietly ticking over. Brian was in charge and Doc was quite happy leaving him to it.

"I'm popping out for a while, Brian."

"Okay, boss," replied Brian, as he wiped down the worktop behind the counter. Brian was used to Doc nipping off every now and then. It was the privilege of being the boss, he thought.

Doc left through the front entrance, and walked a few paces to the car park in front of the pub. He looked around at the village. His village. The green had a few people on it playing games, and there were a couple of mothers with their young children on the playground. It was almost idyllic. The sun was shining, everything seemed great. Doc walked on past the pub towards the crossroads. Coming the other way was Mrs Abington.

"Hello, Doc, how are you?" she said, as she stopped and put her shopping bag down.

"Very well, Mrs Abington, thanks. Have you been shopping then?" Doc pointed to the bag.

"Oh no. I've been up to the nursing home and taken some of their old books." Doc didn't reply. "I take them into town and change them every now and then, so they get a chance to read something different."

"Oh, right. Do you have to buy new ones, then?" Doc asked.

"Oh, no. I just swap them in the charity shop."

"Ah, I see." Doc searched around in his pocket and produced a fold of notes. He slowly unfolded them and withdrew a fiver. Handing it to Mrs Abington he gave her a quick smile. "If you can find some other books as well, please do."

"Oh, Doc, that's very nice of you." Mrs Abington stuck the note in her jacket pocket and then picked up her shopping bag again. "Thank you very much Doc. I must be on my way now."

"Look after yourself, Mrs Abington."

Doc got to the crossroads and then turned right. Cooper's shop was about fifty yards from the junction, and Doc made his way there. Cooper's had a little launderette next to their shop, but it was hardly ever used. Doc couldn't remember the last time he saw anyone other than Mr Cooper in there.

Doc entered the shop. There was a customer

looking at newspapers and magazines whilst Mr
Cooper stood behind the counter waiting to take as
much money as he could. "Hello, Mr Cooper," Doc
said, as he shut the door behind him.

"Oh, Doc. Good to see you, are you okay?"

"Yes, thanks. I'm just having a little stroll around
the village, and couldn't do that without coming in
to see you."

"Ah, thanks Doc. Did you want anything?"

"No thanks, Mr Cooper. How's business?"

"Ticking over, I suppose. We need another one of
those fantastic ideas of yours Doc. I don't suppose
you have any, do you?"

"No, sorry Mr Cooper. You know I'll let you know
if I do."

As the conversation continued, the customer in the
shop was waiting to be served. Mr Cooper did not
attend to her though until Doc was finished.

"Did you find everything you wanted?" Mr Cooper
asked, as Doc took a step back and watched him
working. The customer was a middle-aged woman
but not anyone who Doc knew.

"Yes, thank you." The woman handed a magazine
to Mr Cooper.

"That'll be one pound twenty-five please." Mr
Cooper stood waiting for the woman to sort out
some change from her purse. "Do you know our
Doc?" As Mr Cooper asked, the woman stopped
and looked at Doc.

"No, sorry, I don't know you. I'm not with the local

surgery." Both Mr Cooper and Doc laughed.

"Sorry, Madam, I'm not a doctor. It's just what people call me round here. Doc."

"Oh, I didn't realise." The woman was a little flustered at the embarrassment.

"Hey, he may not be a doctor but he comes out with lots of great ideas." Mr Cooper tried to impress the woman while Doc began to blush a little. There was a pause. "In fact, when he was only a little lad he came into my shop with a new idea."

"What are you talking about?" Doc was confused.

"Don't you remember coming in here with that little advert?" Mr Cooper recalled.

"Yes, about looking for lodgings, you mean?"

"I think that was it."

"So, what was the idea?"

"Well before you came in with the idea of putting an advert in the window, nobody had thought of it." Mr Cooper had been impressed with Doc from an early age. Doc hadn't even realised it had been such a revolutionary idea. As far as he was concerned, people had been advertising in windows for years.

"Oh, it was nothing."

Doc continued around the village and soon found himself at the bottom of Rawthorn Drive. He stood there for a few minutes and looked around the area. Not much had changed from the way that Doc remembered it all. In one way or another he had spent a lot of his life on this road. He knew the bungalow the Riddells had moved into, and considered calling in on them just to see how they were settling in. He made his way up the slight hill and with every step his stomach seemed to float higher and higher into the air. It was a strange sensation that he didn't ever feel anywhere else. His head was light and his palms were sweating. It was the anticipation.

Doc went to the door of number twenty-six and rang the bell. He felt a bit exposed waiting, as if all the neighbours were at their windows looking at him. Sue was in the bedroom sorting out ironing when she heard the bell. She wasn't expecting anyone at this time so guessed it would be some salesman. She got to the door and saw a man standing there, and she looked him up and down. He seemed okay.

"Can I help you?" Sue said as she opened the door.

"Well, I'm sorry to interrupt you, I hope I haven't disturbed you?" Doc tried to hold back the urge to grab her and give her a great big kiss. It was all he could do to call her Mrs Riddell but he coped. Sue wondered what the man wanted and seemed to feel his discomfort but had no idea what was causing it or what might have been going through his mind. She could see that he was happy, and had a big smile.

"Er, no, not really, but I am busy. Are you collecting?"

"Oh, no." Doc laughed at her response until it dawned on him that she didn't have the slightest idea who he was. This was going to be a bit of a problem. "Sorry, I'm Doc."

"Well I think you have the wrong address as we haven't called you." Sue started to close the door.

"No Mrs Riddell, I have the correct address." This made Sue stop closing the door and look at the man a bit closer. Ordinarily she would have just slammed the door shut in his face but his voice was nice and she didn't feel that he was there to do her any harm. Regardless of the warm feeling she got from him, she kept him there at the door step.

"You know my name?"

"Yes, I'm sorry, I just want a chat. I'm called Doc and I run the café in the village." Sue immediately guessed that there had been some trouble involving David.

"Is there a problem?"

"No, no problem. It's just that on behalf of the village I wanted to welcome you and your family to Somerby. Are you settling in okay?" Doc made a move towards the door as if to enter but Sue was having none of it and he moved back.

"Yes, thanks, we're doing okay. Was there anything else?"

"How's your husband finding the bus service?" Doc almost choked again at the beginning of the sentence. Sue was surprised at the question. Not because there was no problem, in fact as she well knew, Michael was finding the public transport very inconvenient but she was shocked to think that he had discussed it with the bloke who ran the coffee bar.

"Er, well," she took a deep breath. "He's finding it very hard."

"Yes, I know. Having come from London it's very difficult to get used to the slow ways down here." Doc was still hoping to get in through the door but Sue wanted him to go away. Just then, Mrs Armstrong, the next-door neighbour, walked up her drive.

"Hello, Sue," Dawn shouted out.

"Hello," Sue replied.

"Hello, Doc. How are you feeling today?" Dawn continued.

"Not too bad today, Mrs Armstrong, thank you." Doc looked at Sue and raised his eyebrows. Sue found this quite funny and along the same thinking as her own. After Mrs Armstrong had gone inside Doc continued. "Nice woman but always a bit nosey."

"Yes, I agree. Do you know her then?" Sue asked. This caused Doc to swallow hard as he thought about how to answer the question.

"I've known her for a few years, yes."

Sue relaxed a little bit after her neighbour had clearly identified the man at the door as Doc.

"Dawn said you weren't feeling too well."

"Oh, it's nothing, I just get a bit weak every now and then. Go dizzy and faint, you know?"

"Would you like to come in and have a seat for a while?" Sue had by now got to feel better in Doc's presence,

"That would be great, thanks." Doc stepped into the kitchen and the sight of it almost knocked him over. His head spun and his knees gave way. Sue saw him clutch at the kitchen table to stop himself from falling over.

"Quickly, sit down." She pulled a chair out for him. "Would you like a cup of tea?"

"Oh, yes, that would be lovely."

Sue put the kettle on and got a couple of mugs ready. She looked over her shoulder at the man she had let into her home, and was surprised to find him smiling so brightly as he looked around the kitchen. The smile was warm and friendly and one that made her feel comfortable, but she didn't really know the stranger, so she was still very much on her guard.

"Do you take sugar?"

"No, thank you. I used to but I stopped," Doc replied as he took in all the different things in the kitchen.

"Yes, my kids take lots of sugar in their tea, I'd like to see them cut down a bit."

"They will, they will."

"So, can I ask you something?"

"Of course you can." Doc wasn't quite sure what to expect next.

"Well, I just don't understand why you are here seeing how well we are getting on."

"It's the neighbourly thing to do. I'm part of the village that you have chosen to move to and the village is pleased to see you move in."

"That's just the point though."

"What do you mean?" Doc was aware that he would have to concentrate a bit more on what he was saying, as up until now he just wanted to watch Sue talk. He was almost in a dream.

"The local people aren't pleased to see us."

"Has anyone in the village been rude to you? Let me know who and I'll sort it out."

"No, nobody has been outright rude but none of them have shown any indications that they welcome outsiders to the village."

"Just give them time…" Doc wanted to say that word but stopped himself. There was no way he was ready to get into that conversation.

"Yes, that's okay, so why are you so keen to say hello?" Sue was still not entirely happy with everything.

"I suppose it's because I know what you've gone through moving from a big city, that it makes me that little bit closer to you and your family." Doc realised he hadn't prepared himself for any interrogation.

"So, haven't there been lots of other families that have moved in from the city?"

"Yes, there are a few."

"And do you greet them all?"

"I try to get to see all the new people that move into the village but I don't always get the time."

"So, we're one of the families at the top of your list?"

"Yes, I suppose you could say that," Doc answered as Sue poured out two mugs of tea and brought them over to the kitchen table. She placed one in front of Doc and sat down opposite him at the table, clutching the other mug.

"I find it all quite strange." Sue wasn't sure what to make of it all but liked the man, so just allowed things to carry on. She still suspected that there was some ulterior motive to his visit, and awaited the sting. It would be a request for money or involvement in some scheme, she was certain.

"How's your dad, sorry, I mean husband, getting on with the buses?" Doc shook his head with embarrassment at saying the word dad. Sue just laughed.

"Yeah, he's finding it hard. He's started learning to drive."

"What, so soon?"

"What do you mean, soon?" Sue was confused. Doc had to think quickly.

"It's unusual for people in moving here to come to the decision to drive so quickly. It's normally at least a year." Doc thought on his feet.

"Oh right." Sue was surprised to hear that. "No, he's taking driving lessons with a school in town somewhere."

"That's good. And Luce. How is she settling in?"

"Luce?" Sue gave Doc a funny look. "You mean Louise?"

"Sorry, yes, of course I do, Louise." Doc rebuked

himself for being so slack.

"Oh, she's doing really well. I think she goes into your café most days."

"Yes, I've seen her." There was a brief pause as both sipped from their mugs of tea. Doc spent the time taking in as much of his surroundings as he could, and that included Sue. Sue thought he looked like he was casing the joint ready to burgle it at some later stage. She broke the silence quite quickly.

"You haven't asked about David, my son?"

"No, I was getting to that. How is he settling in?"

"Oh, he's settling in, just about, but I thought you were going to ask how he was recovering from his fainting attacks?" Sue was a bit annoyed that Doc hadn't asked. "You seem to suffer from very similar problems."

"I did know. I just wasn't sure if it was okay to talk about it?" Doc got the last part of his reply in over the sound of the telephone ringing.

"Excuse me." Sue stood up to go and answer the phone.

Sue answered the phone. It was Michael, just letting her know that he would probably be a bit late that evening. She told him that Doc had called round to say hello to them all, and Michael seemed a bit surprised but not too concerned. As Sue returned to the kitchen she saw Doc had got up and was looking at some of the family photos that were placed on the window sill.

"Ah, you don't want to look at those, do you?" Sue

found it a bit imposing that he was looking at her family photos even if they were on show in the kitchen. Doc turned, like a burglar caught in torchlight.

"Sorry, I just got up to put my cup on the draining board and noticed the photos."

"Oh, no worries, I just wouldn't have thought you'd be interested in looking at them."

"No, they are lovely photos. You will need to look after them." Sue was again confused at Doc's comments.

"Look after them?"

"I mean to be able to look at them in the years to come." Doc smiled again and Sue nodded in agreement even though she didn't really think the caution was justified.

"I like that one of the whole family." Sue indicated with her eyes at the main photo.

"What, the one in Hainault Park?"

"Yes." Sue thought back to the great day the family had there. It was a place that they had gone to quite regularly on a Sunday. The kids were young enough to enjoy just running around in the woods and Michael and she could spend some time together. Sue had a sudden thought. "How did you recognise that as being Hainault Park?"

"Oh, I often used to go there, and that's a popular spot." Doc tried to sound genuine. Sue wasn't absolutely convinced but she had to accept his explanation.

There was another brief pause as Doc devised his next move. "Sorry, but do you mind if I use your toilet?"

"No. That's okay." Sue was taken aback by the request. "It's down the hall straight in front of you." Sue shouted the last part as Doc had already got up and started down the hall. Sue looked at the photo of the four of them in the park again. The kids were smiling and seemed so obviously happy. It would be nice to get a picture of the four of us in Great Yarmouth soon, she thought to herself. She considered various places where they could get a good photo. She heard the toilet flush and expected to see Doc reappear in the kitchen but he hadn't. She moved to the hall to see him in David's room.

"It's this way," Sue said. Doc turned around and smiled again.

"Yes, silly mistake to make."

"That's my son's bedroom." Sue felt a brief explanation was required but didn't know why. She looked at Doc and saw him wipe away what seemed like a tear from his left eye. "Are you alright?"

"Yes, I'm okay thanks." Doc couldn't explain to Sue what the emotion was all about. They made their way back to the kitchen and sat down again.

"Did you have another one of your fainting attacks?" Sue asked quite concerned.

"No." Doc shook his head. "No, I'm fine, believe me."

"If you're sure." Sue sat and drank the rest of her tea. "So, when did you move to Somerby?"

"Oh, many years ago." Doc replied.

"Yes, but when exactly?"

"In 1966, I think it was." Doc muddled over it a bit.

"And how old were you at the time?" Sue was getting interested.

"Just fifteen and a half."

"So, did your parents decide to move to Somerby for work purposes? Surely there wasn't much work in those days around here. Just farm labouring. Was your father a farmer?" The questions spilt out as Sue thought of more things to ask.

"No, he wasn't a farmer." Doc laughed at the thought of it.

"What did he do?" Sue followed up with a more direct question this time. Doc thought for a second before answering.

"I don't really know what my father did." This brought on another few seconds of silence.

"Oh." Sue didn't know what to make of the answer.

"So, if you've been to Hainault Park before, that must have been in the early sixties."

"Er, yeah, I suppose so." Doc felt he was getting into difficult territory. He looked at his watch and realised it was getting on for the end of school. "I ought to be on my way." They both made their way back into the kitchen. "Thank you for the tea."

"Anytime. Thank you for welcoming us to Somerby."

"Well, if you have any problems, you know where I am." Doc wanted to kiss her and give her a big hug but he stopped himself. He walked out of the bungalow as Sue held the door open. Doc took a few steps down the drive and then stopped and turned around again. "By the way, I forgot to say happy birthday for yesterday." Doc turned and went on his way.

"Thank you!" Sue half shouted after him. How the hell did he know it was my birthday yesterday she thought. Then it dawned on her that there were some birthday cards in the living room that he must have seen.

When David got off the school coach Tuesday afternoon he made his way past Doc's with absolutely no intention of going in there at all. Louise was already at one of the tables and she saw David so she knocked on the window. David stopped and turned to look. Louise beckoned him to come in.

David made his way through the door and was pleasantly surprised to find that most people didn't seem to take any notice of him. He walked over to the girls and said hello. Louise asked him for some money, which he gave her, and then he turned to leave. As he did, the lad he had met before, Pete nodded and caught his eye. Pete was sat at a table on his own again so David thought he'd just go over and have a quick chat with him. After about five minutes, it was obvious that he was going to stay for a little while so he bought a cup of coffee.

The two of them chatted about various things and David was happy that at last he could feel a bit more comfortable in there. None of the Burgh Boys seemed to be concerned, not even Bob, and it was almost as if he had been accepted. Even Maria Bevan had stopped and chatted to both Pete and David. This annoyed Tina and Gillian no end but they would never say so. Maria was a good looking girl and knew it, but she was also pretty rich. It wasn't that she flaunted her money but she had that inner confidence that many kids didn't have.

The café was at its fullest and Kathy and Brian were very busy. Doc had gone into town to pick up some supplies and he returned just as the coffee bar was at its busiest. He parked the car round the back and carried a few boxes through to the counter, things like napkins and straws, nothing really heavy. But as he stood holding them, there was a little slip and Doc fell. Straws went all over the place and many of the kids laughed, but Doc wasn't amused. He had hit his head and was feeling quite poorly. Whilst all this was going on, David also started to have another migraine attack so he gave his apologies to Pete and left for home.

It was Thursday afternoon just after two and Doc found himself walking up Rawthorn Drive again. He looked at all the bungalows and tried to work out who lived in each one. There were just about more he didn't know than he did, which Doc felt was good, as he believed that would make him less of a know it all than perhaps some people might accuse him of. As he made his way up the hill he looked towards the window of number twenty-six and saw Sue through the window. He waved. She waved back. That's good, he thought.

Sue came to the front door as Doc walked up level with the house. "Afternoon, Doc, all right?" Sue thought it a bit strange asking someone she barely knew how he was, and even stranger using his nickname.

"Thank you, Mrs Riddell, yes, I'm okay today." Doc walked up the drive towards her.

"Call me Sue, please."

"Yes of course, Sue." Doc complied. Sue felt that Doc had wanted to call her by her first name during their first meeting. She sensed that at times he was uncomfortable calling her Mrs Riddell so she was pleased to ease any tension.

"So, how are things at the coffee bar?"

"Usual." Doc said very little.

"You're not closed today are you?"

"No. I've got two great people who look after the place for me and it gives me the freedom to walk around a bit whenever I want. It helps to build up my strength."

"Oh, I see." Sue didn't really but felt it was the right reply to give. "So, whereabouts in London did you live?" Sue wanted to find out a bit more about Doc.

"Oh, well most of my time was around the Dagenham area." Doc tried to generalise.

"And you moved up here in 1966?"

"Er, yes, I suppose you could say that." Doc wondered where this was going.

"So, you'll remember the smogs?" Sue had often heard about the thick smoky fogs that London had in the sixties but had never witnessed one herself.

"Was that a television programme?" Doc thought it sounded a bit like one of those puppet series.

"No, you know, the thick fogs."

"Oh, those. Yes, I read about them." Doc had a vague recollection.

"Well surely you would have seen them?"

"Can't remember them. Perhaps they never got them in Dagenham." Doc wasn't quite sure when and where these fogs were found. Sue wasn't quite sure herself either, so was reasonably happy about the reply.

"Do you remember the swinging sixties then? You must have been right in the middle of it in London?" Sue asked. Doc thought about it for a while.

"It wasn't all it was cracked up to be really." Doc had heard that answer before and guessed Sue may well have done too. She had.

"Shame. What was your childhood like?"

"Well I remember England winning the World Cup. The Beatles. Doctor Who." Doc hoped that was enough. "Apart from that, just a normal childhood."

"Why did you move up to Somerby?" Sue was generally just trying to be chatty but the question caused Doc some pain. He showed the signs of it briefly.

"My dad wanted to move to the country." As Doc replied, there was a movement outside the kitchen window as someone walked past it. The sound of the front door opening could be heard and Sue leapt to her feet. It was Michael. He appeared in the kitchen.

"Hello, darling," Sue said, as she gave Michael a hug.

"Hello. Who's this?" Michael looked at Doc. Doc stood up. He felt that pang of emotion getting ready to hit him again.

"Oh, sorry. I'm Doc." Doc stood up and reached out his hand to shake Michael's.

"Oh, yes. The bloke who owns the coffee bar. Nice to meet you." Doc sat back down again. "What brings you around then?" Michael asked without thinking.

"I was just passing and saw Sue, err, sorry, your wife outside and we just chatted." Michael looked at him and then looked at Sue.

"Yes. She does things like that." Michael made his way through the kitchen to the hall and off towards the bedroom. Sue sat back down again.

"So how long have you owned the coffee bar?" Sue continued her questioning.

"Quite a few years now. I actually had it built." Doc sounded proud of his achievements.

"You must have had some money! Do your parents own a big place somewhere?" Sue looked at him as she posed this next question. Doc half laughed.

"No, they don't own anything big. A place this size really."

"Are they local?"

"Yes, pretty close." Doc turned as he answered to see Michael come back into the kitchen.

"So, you're Doc. I've heard a lot about you from my daughter." Michael remained standing near the fridge freezer.

"What Lu-" Doc stopped himself. "Louise, you mean?"

"Yes." Michael nodded.

"She's a great girl."

"Bloody hell. You must see a side of her I don't then." Michael joked. "No honestly she is a good girl." Michael walked over and put his arm around Sue. "I'm proud of both my girls." Sue looked up at him and smiled. Doc thought they looked just great.

"I must be getting back to the café. They'll be having the school kids in soon." Doc stood up and held his hand out to shake Michaels hand again. As they shook hands, Michael felt Doc holding tighter than he expected to. He didn't comment. "Right, nice chatting to you both, I'll call round again if I'm passing."

"Yes, please do," Sue answered. Doc left and started to make his way back to the coffee bar.

"What was he doing here again?" Michael asked as soon as Doc was far enough away.

"I don't know. He just walked past."

"What, and you invited him in?"

"It wasn't quite like that, but yes, I did."

"Well, I don't like him. He's funny." Michael couldn't quite explain. "Something about him. I don't know what it is."
"Oh, he's alright. When you get to know him." Sue argued.
"Well, I don't like him."

Doc got back to the café just as the first lot of school kids were arriving. Brian and Kathy were ready for the onslaught.
"There you are, Doc. Wondered what had happened to you." Kathy shouted across as he entered the café.
"Everything okay?"
"Yes, no problems." Kathy was busy taking drinks orders whilst Brian was beginning to get burgers and bacon cooked. Doc walked over to the counter to see for himself how things were.
"You seem to have things under control. I'm popping up to the office for a little while." Doc made off.

As time went on, the place got busier, and Doc came back down from the office. It was noisy and everyone seemed to be having a good time. He was happy. Kids were buying drinks and crisps and only at a few of the tables nobody had bought anything. Louise and the girls were in, and Louise was getting ready to buy a drink or two. As she got to the counter Doc moved towards her to serve. "And what can I do for you, Luce?" Doc asked.

"My name's Louise." Louise sounded a bit put out that Doc got her name wrong.

"Oh, sorry. I thought I'd heard someone calling you Luce before."

"No nobody calls me Luce," she replied.

"Not even your brother?"

"Oh, David. Well, he might, but my friends call me Louise." She was adamant and nodded her head sharply at the end of her reply.

"In that case then, what can I get for you, Louise?"

"Two cokes, please." Louise fiddled with the change she held in her hand whilst Doc went off to get a couple of glasses.

"Bottles or tap?"

"Tap, please." Louise went for the cheaper option.

"Don't you think bottles are better?"

"Yes, but they cost too much." Louise smiled. "Tap please."

"I'll give you two bottles but charge you for tap."

"Bottles, please." Louise smiled again. As Doc opened the bottles he continued to chat.

"So, are you settling in okay?"

"Yes, I think so. You know I'm new around here then?"

"Of course I do." Doc handed her the two glasses. Louise paid and made her way back to the table. She was beginning to feel more a part of things in the village and she was happy.

Sunday was quite a special day in the Riddell household as the whole day was going to revolve around football. It was the FA Cup semi-finals this weekend and that would normally cause some excitement for Michael and David, but more than that this weekend, Spurs were in one of them. That alone would normally mean that the whole house was breathing football but this year, Spurs were playing Everton and that meant not just football all around the house but football rivalry as of course Sue had declared her loyalty to the Merseyside club.

Michael and David had long been planning what they were going to wear that afternoon. Spurs shirts. Spurs scarves. Spurs hats. The whole ten yards in fact. Michael had found his old rosette and a large wooden rattle that many years ago he had taken to football matches. It was painted in a glossy blue and white and made the most dreadful noise.

"Did you really take that to football?" David asked.

"Yes. In the old days, before my time you realise, every kid had a rattle."

"What, and they all swung them round and made that noise?"

"Yes, most of them." Michael couldn't exactly recall the noise being that bad when he went to football but then only a few rattles were really used when he went. "Hey and everyone had wooden stools or boxes so you could see better."

"Get out of here." David exclaimed, finding it hard to imagine his dad standing on a box at a football match.

Sue entered the room listening to the two of them talking football.

"Okay boys, make way for another supporter who hasn't got a stool," Sue said, as they both turned.

"Oh, Mum," David moaned as he saw what she was wearing. She had found an old Everton shirt and put it on over one of her t-shirts. She then had a blue and white scarf around her neck.

"Hey, excuse me," Michael said. "I think you should be in the away end." He pointed to the kitchen.

"Didn't think they had away ends at semi-finals?" said Sue. Michael and David looked at each other, and pulled funny faces knowing she was right. As they were looking at each other, Louise entered the lounge.

"Come on, Everton." Louise shouted. She was wearing a blue top, and had a white bobble hat on.

"You don't support Everton, Luce?" David wasn't sure if he was more annoyed or surprised.

"No, but I'm on Mum's side," Louise answered.

The match was waiting to start as the whole family threw mock insults at each other and had a friendly slanging match. Louise continued with the fun for a little while before making sure that the men were fully engrossed in the game, and then she went off back to her bedroom to get changed. Sue made some tea and the four of them sat down watching the game, gasping and groaning as the action took over. As Spurs mounted an attack both Michael and

David sat there kicking an imaginary ball as if they were playing themselves. Sue found it all quite funny watching them both. Before too long a goal was scored but the men weren't cheering as indeed it was the underdogs, Everton who took the lead.

"Lucky goal." Michael shouted as Sue came into the room cheering at the news that her team had taken the lead. Spurs would probably be back on level terms by half-time but she knew enough to know that her team were playing well and she wasn't going to let the boys off that easily.

"Come on, you Toffees," Sue shouted.

"Don't, Mum." David was already feeling the pressure. His team were one down and Everton playing well.

"We'll get a goal soon, hopefully." Michael tried to reassure his son. He knew he wouldn't be calm until they equalised as they both got worried if Spurs were losing especially in a big game like this.

"Yeah, Jurgen will show 'em soon." David said in hope. Sue felt the tension and decided to leave them to it. She went back out to the kitchen and put the radio on. If Everton could possibly score another goal, she would pop back in and wind them up a bit.

The score remained 1-0 at half time and both Michael and David walked around the house in tense concern during the interval.

"Everton are playing really well," David said to his mum. "I've been impressed with them so far." David couldn't hide the tearful tone of his voice as he tried to sound sincere. Sue gave him a hug.

"Don't fret. The second half will all be different."
Sue hated it when football got to her boys like this.
She knew that Michael would be feeling the same
but he was big and ugly enough to cope with it
himself. Her little boy needed her support.

The second half soon brought another goal but it
wasn't one that Michael and David had been hoping
for. An error by the Spurs keeper had presented
Everton with a golden opportunity and they weren't
in the mood to give it up so took a two-nil lead. Sue
was quietly pleased at seeing her team take a bigger
lead but when Spurs got a penalty to pull a goal
back, she guessed the game was up. She went
through to the lounge.

"That was never a penalty," she joked hearing that it
was considered a bit dubious.

"Of course it was a penalty." David was laying on
the carpet and getting more and more excited as
Tottenham tried to get going again. Sue waited for
the equaliser to come but it was Everton who scored
again. A third goal, then a fourth. It was too much
for David. As the end of the game approached, he
threw his hat in the corner and stormed back to his
bedroom. Everton had thrashed Spurs 4-1 and it was
going to take him a while to get over it. Sue got out
of her blue and white Everton clothes and got on
with doing dinner. It was going to be a quiet
evening.

The Somerby Tree

Tuesday 11th April 1995

It was Tuesday and the evening was just beginning to start to take a hold. Doc had not had too busy a day and things were fairly quiet. It was quite an unusual move for him but he asked Brian to look after the place whilst he went out for another walk around the village. Doc had not had any fainting problems for a while so he enjoyed being able to go out for a walk. He did it almost without thinking but within minutes he was striding up Rawthorn Drive as if he was making his way home. The Riddell house came within view and Doc stopped in his tracks. He deliberated with himself about the pros and cons of calling at the house again but it didn't last long and he continued on his way.

After only a minute or so he was at the end of the drive. Although it was still relatively light out, the kitchen light was on and Doc could see Sue moving backwards and forwards through the window. He watched her for a while until he remembered exactly where he was. He started to walk up the drive and noticed that Sue had caught sight of him and moved to the front door. It was only then that it struck Doc that he had no real reason to come up and see them. Sue appeared at the door. "Hi Doc. Everything okay?" She wondered what the purpose of his visit could be. Doc found her welcome most soothing. He looked at every feature on her face whilst hurriedly trying to think of what he could say.

"Yes, nothing wrong." Doc walked up to the door.

"Just wanted to ask you a little question."

Doc had suddenly thought about offering Louise a job. He expected that David would find something, but he didn't think that Louise would be able to that easily. Sue stepped back to invite Doc in and they made their way into the kitchen.

"Take a seat Doc." Sue pulled a chair from the table. "So what can we do for you?" Sue asked.

"Well actually it may be more what I can do for you." As Doc answered, Michael entered the kitchen.

"Hello, err…" Michael wasn't quite sure what to call him. "Sorry, I don't know your name." Michael was a bit embarrassed.

"You can call me Doc. Everyone else does."

"Oh right. But what is your name?" Michael felt he ought to try and find out.

"I don't tend to tell people what my real name is."

"Oh, is it a secret?" Sue was interested.

"No, it's not a secret, it's just I don't ever use it." Doc hoped they wouldn't pursue the point.

"Ah, right." Michael answered. He looked at Sue. They were both anticipating an answer but there was nothing. Doc didn't even look as if he was thinking about answering. "So how did you get the name Doc?"

"Well, it was a nickname I picked up as a boy. Came from my initials." Doc replied. Michael thought for a minute. D, O, C he thought to himself. The D was quite easy. It could be David or Dennis or Duncan. Surname beginning with C and a middle

name beginning with O. Dennis Oliver Charlton?
Michael thought all of this in a split second. Then it
dawned on him that the O and the C might both be
his surname. That would have to be O'C.
Something like O'Connell. That might explain
things a bit. Doc was Irish. Not that that really
explained anything at all, but it helped Michael put
some things in his mind into order. Doc must have
been quite alone when he first came to Somerby, all
the way from Ireland. Well that was Michael's
assumption anyway.

As the three were thinking, Louise poked her head
around the door. "Mum, I think David's a bit funny
again." She had a worried look on her face, and had
heard the conversation coming from the kitchen.
Louise looked across at Doc. "Oh, hello."
"Hello, Louise." Doc replied. He too was beginning
to feel a bit of a headache coming on. Sue got up
and hurriedly made her way to David's bedroom.
David was sweating and almost in a trance. His eyes
were staring into nothing and although she tried
desperately to communicate, it was impossible.
Fortunately, Sue was quite calm in an emergency
and she got over the initial shock of seeing her son
in this state. She could get on with things and keep
David cool and dry as well as comfortable. David
was totally unaware of anyone else being with him.
His head hurt and although he wanted to rub it, he
was unable to do anything. He had no control over
his limbs. He just saw objects moving. David tried

to concentrate on one item at a time, any item. The room was beginning to spin, and he was feeling sick. "Michael!" Sue shouted from the bedroom.

Michael was relieved to get the call; he found that any conversation with Doc was difficult. He couldn't put his finger on it, but there was something not right about him. Michael rushed to the bedroom where David was sick all over the carpet.

"I'll go and get a bucket." Michael went back to the kitchen to look for a bucket. He rushed straight over to the cupboard under the sink and searched around inside. Moving a number of other cleaning implements and half used bottles of liquid he retrieved a good sized plastic bucket. Trying to be polite, he turned to Doc as he made his way quickly back to David's bedroom. "Look, I'm sorry, Doc, but we've got…" As he looked closer it seemed that Doc was also not too well but considering David's plight to be the priority he only glanced briefly in Doc's direction. He didn't take it all in but thought things didn't look too good. Michael thought about stopping but Sue was calling out from David's bedroom and there was really no other choice.

Doc tried to get to his feet but he was also feeling rather poorly. It wasn't just a pain, it was a more pressurised feeling inside, as if there were memories trying to break free from his mind. Doc had experienced these attacks before and was quite used to dealing with their effects, but this one came on quickly and took him by surprise. He stood up and used the kitchen table for support. When he felt steady enough, he made for the front door. As he opened it, Michael returned to the kitchen.

"Are you alright, Doc?" Michael asked. Doc gave a gesture with his arm to suggest he didn't need any help and continued to make his way out of the kitchen. The front step was quite steep and he stumbled a little but found his feet again and made his way down the street. Michael watched but kept an ear on how things were going with his son.

After another couple of minutes, David was able to talk again and Sue felt happier with the situation. It was nearly half an hour later before everyone was back to normal. David went to bed. Although he was feeling a lot better, the whole incident had drained his strength and he was quite tired. Michael, Sue and Louise were all sat around the kitchen table again. Nobody was really saying anything.

"What happened to Doc?" Louise asked.

"Oh, he went back home." Michael replied. He looked at Sue and she smiled.

"Hope you apologised?" Sue said.

"What for?" Michael gave her a strange look as he replied. "He just got up and went."

"Well it wasn't good that David was ill and we all left him alone in the kitchen."

"Oh, I think he knew what was going on. Anyway, I don't know what it is but there's something about him I don't like."

"Don't like?" Sue questioned that phrase.

"Well, you know." Michael scratched his head and paused. "He's weird."

"Oh, Dad, he's not." Louise added.

"And how would you know, my girl?"

"I see him more than you do." Louise sounded quite offended at her Dad's remarks.

"Well, I don't like him." Michael gave an indignant reply. He looked for some support from his wife, but none was apparent. "I don't think you should go to that coffee bar."

"Oh, Mum, that's not fair." Louise was now looking to Sue for support. "Dad, all my friends go in there."

"I just don't think you should. He's a bit strange and seems to be taking too much interest in you."

"He's not." Louise slammed her palm on the table as she replied. It was time for Sue to intervene.

"Your father is right. Doc is getting a little bit too close." Sue then looked at Michael and placed her hand on his. "But I think he means well."

Michael didn't reply immediately so Sue backed up her previous statement. "I'm sure he only wants to make sure we're alright and he's not done anything to suggest otherwise has he?" Sue posed the question to Michael directly by moving her head so that her face was directly in his. There was a brief pause.

"Well, maybe not, but I still don't think Louise should have anything to do with him. Nor David for that matter." Michael stood up having made his declaration. "That's just what I think." Michael left the kitchen and went into the bathroom.

"Don't worry, darling. You can still go to Doc's. Just don't get too friendly with him."

Sue knew that Louise was a friendly talkative girl and would probably find it hard to not talk to him but hopefully time would pass before the subject came up again, and Michael wouldn't feel quite so strongly about it.

It was Saturday morning and David was due to play football that afternoon at Gorleston Rec. It was going to be a reasonably tough game against Wymondham Youth but a game that David relished. Louise was going into town with the girls and she had already left to meet them down at Doc's. Louise knew that David was being picked up about twelve thirty and she told him to come and see her on his way to the bus stop.

Louise was sat at a table with Tina, Melanie and Livvy. They were still waiting for Gillian, and Ness, who was certain to be the last one to arrive. They all had money today so they bought their own drinks.

"I want to have a look in Top Girl today," Livvy announced.

"Oh, yeah, they've got some lovely tops in there," Louise added.

"I take it we're going down Regent Road?" Tina asked.

"You always want to go down Regent Road. We

can go along the front as well." Melanie replied. Just then David entered. Gillian wasn't far behind him. They both made their way over to the table.

"Hello, David." Louise said.

"Hello, girls. Can I join you?" David slid in next to Tina. Gillian reached the table.

"Hello everyone."

"Hello Gillian," all the girls replied.

"Hey Gillian, are you going to buy me a coffee?" David asked, as much to embarrass Gillian as to actually get a drink. Gillian went red.

"Only if you pay." She nervously asked for the money. David obliged.

Doc was not in the coffee bar. He was in the Chinese take-away talking to Ken.

"How is business then, Ken?"

"It is okay, Doc," replied Ken.

"Last night was busy?"

"It was a good night. Fridays and Saturdays always good." Ken told him.

"I think I might come and visit you this evening."

"You have company tonight, Doc?"

"No. Just fancy Chinese for a change. I'll pop round when we've closed."

"Okay, Doc, see later."

Ken carried on unloading some goods while Doc went next door. A woman called Doris ran the baker's shop, Doris Nichols. She had her own little oven at the back of the shop, but most of her bread and rolls were delivered from Gorleston. She had the only bakery for quite a distance and in summer she got a lot of custom from holidaymakers. Doc had again been instrumental in persuading Doris to open the place, and she was very much against the idea at first suggested, but she would have to admit that she had never regretted it.

"Hello, Doc." Doris shouted as he entered. There were at least four people waiting to be served but Doris went straight to Doc to ask what he wanted.

"All I want really is one of your uncut bloomers please, Doris." Doc looked around to see if there were any customers he knew. Nearly all of them knew him and not one was unhappy that he had been served before them. Although he recognised most of the people in the bakery, none were people he knew well.

"Is there anything else?"

"No thanks, Doris, this'll do. How much?"

"Oh, Doc. It's on the house." Doris handed the loaf to him and then got on with serving other customers. Just as Doc was getting ready to leave he caught sight one of the customers and recognised them as someone he hadn't seen for ages. Doc recognised her quite quickly though.

"Harriet?" Doc said it almost as much as a question than as a statement. The woman turned to look at him.

"Bloody hell. It's, it's…"

"Doc. Call me Doc," he chipped in.

"Oh, Doc." The woman obviously didn't recognise the name.

"It's Harriet. Harriet…?" Doc never did know Harriet's name.

"Harriet Matthews."

"Yes, of course, Harriet Matthews. You probably remember me by another name from when we were together in the home," Doc said quietly, in case Harriet didn't want anyone else to know. "So, how are you?"

"Oh, doing fine thanks."

"You live in Somerby now?"

"No, in Leafby. I moved there when I got married."

"Oh right. Sorry, I didn't know you were married. Have you got children?"

"Yes, two girls thank God."

"I thought girls were supposed to be more difficult."

"Oh no, boys are much worse."

"What are their names?"

"What, my girls? Mary and Vanessa."

"Mary?" Doc exclaimed, but almost coughed in surprise. He tried to hide his response. All sorts of thoughts were flying through his mind as he tried to think of what to say next but Harriet continued.

"Yes, lovely girls they are and both Capricorn. Such a lovely sign, Capricorn."

"That's a lovely name." Doc seemed to be repeating the name Mary over and over as both he and Harriet were thinking.

Harriet finally remembered exactly who Doc was.

"Did you change your name, then?"

"No. It's just that everyone knows me as Doc. In fact, it was George who first came up with the name."

"What, George? Surely not. Was it?"

"How is George?" Doc asked. Their conversation caused Harriet to take longer than she wanted but she wasn't too put out. Doc walked out of the bakery and stood outside, stunned. He seemed to be repeating the word Mary. He felt a bit of a headache coming on again. He tried to sort out all the information he had just gained. It would explain a lot. He stood there gazing at nothing.

David had just about finished his coffee and was checking the time Ness arrived.

"Hello, all!" Ness waved as she called out.

"Hello, Ness," nearly everyone replied.

"Are you getting a drink?" Melanie asked her.

"No, I don't think so. Not today." Ness looked around the table. "There's nowhere for me to sit."

"Oh don't worry, I'm just about to go." David got up to let Ness in. "I'll see you this evening, Luce." David picked up his kit bag and made his way out of Doc's. As he left he noticed an old estate car parked outside. It was a bit of a wreck. It wasn't parked in a normal parking place and was in his way, which meant he would have to walk around it. He saw someone in the passenger seat but didn't really pay much attention till he was right up to the car. He walked past and then did a double take at the passenger. It was Mary. David went back to the passenger window and knocked. Mary saw who it was and wound the window down. David hadn't spoken to her for at least a couple of weeks.

"Mary, fancy seeing you here."

"Hello."

"What are you doing here then?"

"Oh, my mum is in the shop." Mary seemed a little more relaxed for a change. She was happy and smiling.

"I thought you weren't able to get out on a Saturday."

"What do you mean?"

"Well, you said you cleaned all day Saturday."

"Usually I do but Mum needs me to go shopping with her so she's got me out of doing it."

"That's good then?"

"I still have to do it tomorrow."

"I just wondered if you could come to watch me play football." David said as he leant further into the car. Mary touched his hand.

"I'd love to, but she won't let me."

"Your mum sounds horrible."

"Well, it's not really her. It's more Uncle…" Mary didn't finish the sentence.

"What if I asked her?"

"No, it wouldn't be worth it, she wouldn't say yes." Mary held David's hand. "Are you going to play football now?"

"Yes, I'm waiting to be picked up."

David wanted to make the most of this opportunity to talk to Mary. "Why is it that sometimes I feel that you want to talk to me and then other times you don't?"

"I always want to talk to you. You know that."

"No, not really, because often you ignore me. Why?"

"Sometimes it is easier."

"Is it about Arthur?" David went for the jugular.

"I can't say."

"Do you love him?"

"No. No way. In fact, I hate him," Mary replied, the answer that David was hoping to hear, but perhaps more emphatically than he expected.

"So, why are you so afraid of him?" David hoped to find out the reason but just as he asked his question, he became aware of someone getting into the driving seat of the car.

"Who's this then, Mary?" asked her mum.

"This is David. He goes to school on the same coach as me."

"Hello, David. Nice to meet you, but we have to go shopping now. Bye."

"Oh, hello. And bye." David was taken aback by the abruptness of it. He waved at Mary as the engine started up. She waved back to him as the car moved away.

"Sorry I'm late, darling. I was chatting to an old friend," Mary's mum said as they made their way to Norwich. Mary was only half listening while looking back at David. David waved again as the car disappeared. He was sure that Arthur was the reason she wouldn't always talk to him on the coach.

It was Monday morning, and David waited for the school coach as usual. Alice had been chatting about the state of the village and how they should all do more to keep it clean, and David was quite pleased to see Suzanne for once.
As the coach arrived he looked, but couldn't see Mary. She didn't always sit in the same place, so it didn't mean she wasn't on there. After their meeting on Saturday he just wanted to make sure he said hello to her, if nothing else. He thought about the Arthur situation. He decided not to just get on and talk to Mary, but wait until after the High School before talking to her. They chatted a little bit. David was happy. Mary seemed to be okay with it.

By Thursday David was again preparing to play for Carlton Grammar. Mr Bowles had found out on Monday who they were playing in the county semi-finals; he was pleased that they had drawn London Road High School from Thetford. The team that they wanted to avoid, Bowthorpe, had somehow managed to get knocked out by a school considered to be the weakest in the competition. When the Carlton lads heard the news, they were almost in shock. It was a giant killing. They knew that they were now the favourites to win the County Cup.
Once again, Carlton had been lucky enough to get a home draw in the semi-finals. London Road had to travel and it was a big day out for them. Mr Bowles knew that Carlton only had to win this one and they would be playing at Carrow Road. The County final

was always played there and he was looking forward to it because he had never had the pleasure of going there as part of a playing team. Nigel had played on the pitch two or three times but apart from him, everyone else was waiting for their dream day.

The game started as usual, with both David and Nigel controlling most of the play in midfield. The two had begun to strike up a real understanding and they would usually know what each other was thinking. This helped the defence no end as they could rely on the midfield stopping most attacks and never letting them take too much pressure. Chris Long turned his ankle quite early on, and Richard Kruber went on in his place. Nicky Sawyer had a couple of shots and Stuart Tennant hit one wide but nothing seemed to be going Carlton's way in the first half, and the teams turned round all level at half time.

The second half was a similar story but London Road created one or two more chances, though nothing to be really worried about. They were limited to long shots and crosses from well outside the box. One such cross was heading to complete safety as there were no London Road players in the area, but confusion struck between the Carlton keeper, Trevor Styles, and the defence, with both leaving it for the other to cope with. As the ball bounced in the box, Styles decided to come and claim it, but slipped as he tried to move forward. The ball bounced higher than he'd expected and straight into the empty net. London Road were one up. The Carlton boys just looked at each other in complete astonishment, but Nigel got them going again and soon enough they were working to get the equaliser. Move after move saw Carlton split right through the opposition midfield, and the ball got through to the forwards pretty well, but shots were either wide or soft and the equalising goal never came. Carlton were out.

Chapter 9
THE TREE

So, what to say about Somerby? There's quite a lot to know about it. It's a small village which has in recent years started to expand. This has meant new housing which in turn this has resulted in the demolition or removal of some of the old and established parts of the village. Some say it is modernisation and needs to happen, but others say it is part of the heritage of the village and is a travesty that any of it is being removed at all. One main structure in the village isn't being removed and the locals are pleased about that. Their large old oak tree is staying. It's not just any old tree, mind you, but The Tree. It has played a very prominent part in the history of Somerby.

According to old stories, the tree was the main reason why the village was established in the first place. Very little detail has been recorded properly about how the village started, or even got its name, but the story goes that the area was invaded by a number of Viking warriors who landed on the east coast and then prepared themselves for a march inland to raid and plunder the big towns that were establishing themselves. The Vikings were led by a few battle-hardened and well respected chiefs, and one of them was called Somer. It is said that this great chief saw a very large tree from the sea, and made his way to it. His warriors would have made camp around the tree while preparing for their incursion, and naturally, when they returned with their plunder, they made their way back to the tree. Quite soon, a small settlement was established in the area.

Other stories tell of the same Vikings landing on the coast but then being drawn to the big oak tree because it held magical powers for them. The Vikings held beliefs that many of the trees around held magical powers as most of the area would have been forested when the Vikings first arrived, and indeed the whole area that covers Somerby and Leafby would have been part of the same forest, which now has been cut down and built on. Some thought that the whole wood was magical, and that many of the trees could produce some special power if needed.

The Danish word for settlement was 'by' and it was only natural that the settlement around the tree should become known as the Somer's settlement or Somer's By in Danish, and from there the village of Somerby was born.

By the time the Vikings returned home, the village was occupied by not only Vikings but also by Anglo Saxon people who had integrated with them. Somerby seems to have been the only village established around a tree. It is believed that back in history, Somer would perform rituals and ceremonies around the oak tree and as the Anglo-Saxon way of life took hold, there were properly recorded annual festivals around the tree. It was the centre spot of the village. No festivals are held in Somerby anymore, but the tree is still there. Even the pub is called The Oak, and is situated within a very short distance of the tree. The tree is central to the village's growth.

It was fitting that when the Riddells arrived in Somerby there were some lights placed in the old oak tree to greet them. It may have been a regular way of greeting the old warriors back to Somerby in the past. Doc had climbed up into the tree in his younger days, before he became weak with illness. He found a private hideaway up there, a seat where he could survey everything that was going on around the village, and a place where very few people could see him. He loved climbing up into the tree but if he were to do it now, he would have to get himself a ladder. It wasn't something that he felt he needed to do now, so he hadn't been up there tree for years but he remembered his little place. He had spent many an hour carving away at the bark of the tree. He had never told anyone about those days. He was a lonely kid back then with no friends, nobody to turn to. He would sit in the tree and ponder his life, what it had delivered to him and how he would deal with the blows he had been given. In many ways, he became a very much stronger person because of the tree. It represented strength, age, wisdom. Doc would talk to it and imagine it answering him with worldly advice.

Doc fell in love with Somerby. Having moved from

a big city when he was younger, it was a bit of a culture shock at first, trying to fit in with a very quiet and slow way of life but it grew on him and he began to appreciate what Somerby had to offer. He thought back to when he first came to the village and how he had no idea just what an important part the village would play in his life. Certainly, he couldn't properly recall if he had seen the tree when he first arrived in Somerby, but on reflection, taking into consideration what went on when he got here, it didn't take him long to see it. When he arrived, back in 1966, Somerby was quite small, but he had a vision of how it could be, how it would grow into a bigger village one day. Now, about thirty years on, he was part of the village. The village was part of him. The tree was part of him really. It had been his friend in times of need. He would never want to see the tree harmed in anyway.

Doc thought about how the village had been even a few months ago, but of course this was very difficult. He had seen many of the buildings around being built, and quite a few of them at his behest. Even those that were already here in 1966 had changed. The garage for instance: it was just a little independent petrol station in the old days, but the major oil companies had come in and made an offer the old man couldn't resist. Doc was pleased to see that he hadn't sold up completely and had kept the repair part of the business going, which of course by now was being run by his son Neil. It was another place that kept the village together. Doc carried on and considered how much had changed in thirty years. This house had gone, that shop had gone, and he got round to wishing he was back in 1966. When times were good, he thought to himself. But then he remembered that times hadn't exactly been that good.

Things weren't always good, Doc thought. Back in 1966 he was alone with nowhere to call his home. He had just got out of temporary accommodation but then he made his way back to Somerby and took up lodgings. He didn't realise at the time how unusual it was, or how lucky he was to get lodgings, as there had never been any before in the village. Even The Oak hadn't started taking in guests. Doc was adamant that he wanted to live in Somerby and he had written out an advert that had been displayed in the local shop. It was the start of a new chapter in his life. He was surprised when he received an answer to his advert, but Helen Bailey saw it and decided almost there and then that she wanted to take in a lodger. Her husband John wasn't quite so sure to start off, with but Doc won him round quite soon. They had a grown-up son called Phillip who had left home only a few months earlier and Helen was happy for some more company. Doc had his own bedroom in their house on Station Road. It was just opposite the railway station, and from his window he could see the trains moving by every now and then. Steam trains were strange to him, having only ever seen them in books before.

Nearly three years he stayed in there, until he was able to buy his first home. Doc had become quite well known around the village even at that young age, although of course he wasn't always known as Doc then, but the nickname had already been created and he encouraged its use. He would sometimes meet two or three of the local lads in the village, and they would go off across the fields, scrumping, or just generally playing. One of those friends was Pete, Peter Phillips. When they played, he would always want to be the one in authority. A policeman, a soldier or something very similar. Doc wasn't surprised to find Pete finishing up in the police.

Monday morning brought the start of a new week and when David got on the coach, he said hello to Mary as he was walking up the gangway. There was nobody next to her, so in an effort to try and avoid a hold up for anyone behind him, he sat down in the empty seat to allow them past.

"Hello Mary. You look beautiful this morning," David said.

"What? Don't say things like that," Mary said as she shook her head. She seemed offended.

"Sorry, I didn't mean to upset you." After how well the two of them had been getting on, this was a bit of a blow. "It's not because Arthur's on the coach, is it?" David looked towards the back of the coach as he asked.

"No." Mary turned away and looked out of the

window. David gave up and made his way to the back seats. He was annoyed though. As he approached the back seats he saw Phil who gave him a little nod.

"I didn't think you wanted to sit with us anymore," Arthur said. David turned to him. "I'm here aren't I?"

"Perhaps you prefer sitting nearer the front of the coach."

"And why would you think that?" David wasn't quite sure what to say next and it didn't look as if Arthur was going to reply. There was still tension but nobody seemed to be saying anything, so David just took his place on one of the back seats.

"Hi, Dave," Phil said.

"Hi," David replied. The rest started chatting and the tension was relieved. Arthur wasn't talking to anyone. He was in one of those moods again where all he wanted to do was stare at David. David knew what he was doing but took no notice.

As the coach turned towards the High School, half of the kids started getting ready to get off, including the lads on the back seats.

"Arthur," David said aloud. Arthur turned to stare at him. "If you've got any problems with me talking to anyone on this coach then perhaps you'd better tell me." As he said it, he was telling himself 'Oh for Christ's sake shut up,' but he just kept on talking. "You know, if there's a girl here that you feel you own, just say."

Arthur refused to reply but David could see the hate in his eyes. The other lads were watching with great interest. There was no response but Arthur stood still so David added, "If you've got a problem with it, sort it out with me, not her." The lads looked at Arthur again, as they wanted to know what had been going on. It was obviously something out of school, and nothing they knew anything about. Arthur knew exactly what David was talking about. He thought long and hard about his reply.

"I don't know what you're talking about, London boy. I think you must have the wrong man."

The lads laughed. David sat back down. Arthur and the rest started to get off the coach. Just as they were about to get off, Arthur stopped. He made his way back up the coach. "I don't really think there is anything to sort out, is there? You just keep your nose out," he said directly at David.

"I'm going to keep on talking to her. If you don't like it then we'll meet."

"I wouldn't waste my time meeting about nothing."

Arthur looked up the coach towards Mary as he said the word 'nothing'.

"If I hear you've taken it out on her, we'll meet anyway." David was a mixture of nerves and annoyance. Even he couldn't believe what he had just said. Arthur turned to get off the coach but then quickly turned back.

"Do you think she's going to tell you anything?" Arthur laughed. "You know nothing." Arthur turned and made his way off of the coach only stopping briefly to look at Mary.

As the coach started to drive away, Phil moved nearer to David.

"Bloody hell, Dave. What was that all about?"

"You know who it was about."

"What, her down the front there." Phil knew which girl but didn't know her name.

"Yes, Mary."

"Oh, Mary." Phil couldn't understand what all the fuss was about. David went down to sit next to Mary.

"Sorry about all that."

"What was going on then?" Mary had seen the commotion but didn't know what was being said.

"Oh, it was nothing really."

"But it involved Arthur, I suppose?" Mary seemed worried.

"Well, yes."

"And me?" Mary was beginning to realise what might have been going on.

"He told me more or less that I couldn't talk to you. He's got no right to say that." David hoped that Mary would reply and agree with him, but she said nothing.

"Do you think he's right, then?" David tried to push her a bit for an answer.

"Right about what?"

"Me being able to talk to you."

"Oh, I don't know." Mary's reply wasn't quite what David had hoped for. To make matters worse, the coach was now arriving at St. Nicholas' where

Mary got off. She got ready to disembark but was clearly annoyed. David assumed it was he who she was annoyed with.

"If Arthur does anything to you, you let me know and I'll sort it out." David thought this was the least he could do. Mary didn't reply. She just looked at him and shook her head. She got off the coach and didn't look back once.

It was Tuesday and the Doc had been pretty busy most of yesterday so today was the first chance he had to look at all of the kids in his café and decide which one was Vanessa or Ness.

"Kathy, you say that Ness Matthews comes in here?"

"Yes. There she is, over there," Kathy said, pointing to a table near to the door. It was occupied with a mixture of boys and girls, and when Kathy pointed her out he could see immediately just exactly which one she was. She had Mary's looks, but wasn't quite as thin as her sister. Her hair wasn't as dark or as long, but it had those characteristics that Doc recognised. His mind wandered back to when he was a young lad and times were good. Yes, he thought to himself, there's nothing wrong with the 1990s. As he snapped back to exactly where he was, he walked over to the kids collecting plates and rubbish as he went. Soon he was by the table where Vanessa was sitting.

"So, you're Vanessa Matthews." His opening statement caused most of the kids to stop talking instantly and Ness to go a little red.

"Yes, I'm Ness. Have I done something wrong?"

"No, nothing." Doc looked at her young face. He could see more similarities between her and Mary, but only occasionally. "No, sorry, don't worry. I know your mother."

"Oh, do you?" Ness replied. There was a brief pause and then everyone got on with their own conversations. Doc went back to the bar. He looked out for Ness whenever he was in the café after that.

Doc tried to remember when he had first met Vanessa's mother. Although he got on very well with Harriet and associated her with some good times, he had to admit that he had first met her whilst going through probably the worst time of his life. He had found himself all alone in the world, nobody to talk to. There wasn't anyone he could discuss his problems with back then. Somerby was a completely new place to him and he often wished he were dead.

This may sound a bit dramatic and indeed now that time had moved on for Doc he recalled back to those days when he had regularly considered suicide and thought of how silly he was. He had achieved so much since then. All he had had to do at the time was to think of the positive things in his life. It sounded easy but it hadn't been.

Doc looked out through the big glass windows to the big oak tree that stood tall and magnificent in the middle of the green. He couldn't recall how or why he had first decided to climb the tree. He just remembered that once up there he would spend hours watching the world around him and the people walking around the village. He could see the sea if he climbed up a bit higher. This brought him some solace when he needed it most. The sea would take his mind off everything. He would dream of the past and the future, strange dreams indeed.

Doc remembered the little items he had kept in his tree, precious things to him, even if they had no real value. There was a piece of metal he retrieved from the crash site. It was nothing but an old bolt from the engine but he kept it for years. There was the postcard he had first managed to get, and of course his penknife which he still had, somewhere. He used it quite regularly in the tree. He had started to carve his initials up there. He hoped that maybe one day someone else would see what he had carved. He hoped that very soon things would get back to normal for him. It was a silly thought as he knew full well that things could never get back to normal, not anymore. He was who he was and nothing was going to change it. Things had got in a real mess, he thought. His mind wandered back to when he lived in London as a boy. His mum and dad would give him a cuddle when he was upset. He had missed that. He missed that very much.

Chapter 10
TALKING TO LOUISE

Thursday 5th May 1995

Louise had had a good day at school and she was bursting with self-confidence as the girls sat around their usual table at Doc's. All six of the gang were there and Tina was full of herself as always, but Louise wasn't far behind.

"Hey, Eddie," Tina shouted out. "I hear you fancy Hilda Haylett." The whole café bar listened and looked at Eddie.

"I've heard you two were kissing in the playground this afternoon," Louise added. The whole place seemed to be staring at Eddie. He didn't know what to do or say.

"Are you her boyfriend then?" Tina continued to add to the embarrassment she had already caused him. She regretted doing it to some extent as she quite liked Eddie but the feeling of regret only lasted a split second. Eddie said nothing but cowered in a corner, and the rest of the kids had already started to get on with their own conversations, so the interest waned. Tina turned to Louise. "You're in a good mood today."

"Am I?"

"Yes, you bloody well are," Tina told her.

"We're all happy, aren't we?" Gillian added. Nobody said anything but everyone nodded.

"You see it's not just me, we're all happy," Louise answered.

"Whose turn to buy a drink?" Tina looked around the table as she asked.

"Not mine," Melanie replied, quietly, so as not to cause an argument. All the girls kept quiet.

"I think -" Louise started to talk. This was a relief to all the other girls as at least someone was going to volunteer. "I think it's your turn," Louise said.

"Hope she's not looking at me," thought most of the other girls as they slowly looked up, in the hope that Louise wasn't looking at them. As they did and found she was looking at someone else a feeling of even greater relief went through them. Louise looked directly at Tina. "Yeah, it's your turn," Louise said, indignantly. The other girls were already at amber as nobody ever asked Tina to buy the drinks. There was a calm before the storm as Tina took in what Louise had said. Was she going to hit her? What would she say?

"Okay, then. It's my turn." Tina got up and went off to the counter. As she got out of earshot, there was almost a group sigh of relief.

"I see Doc is behind the counter today," Livvy said.

"He'll probably come over and have a chat with us," Ness added. Louise knew she had been told by her father not to get too involved with him, but she found him friendly, and knew that her mum thought he was okay. She guessed it was something her dad had overreacted to and it wasn't going to stop her from enjoying her time in the coffee bar.

"What do you make of him?" Louise asked.

"Make of him?" Tina thought it a weird question. It was more what you would ask if you were thinking of getting a boy to go out with you, Tina thought.

"He's okay. Why do you ask?"

"Oh, nothing really. It's just that my dad seems to think he's a bit strange."

"Your dad?" Tina was even more confused. Louise was rather slow in explaining and Tina had no real interest in the conversation, which just stopped. Livvy had been listening without joining in, but saw an opportunity to get involved.

"Why does your dad think he's strange, then?"

"Oh, nothing really, Livvy," Louise replied as she picked up her glass. She had noticed that Doc had come out from behind the counter and was slowly making his way round the tables. She wished she hadn't said anything now, but hopefully Livvy wouldn't continue and the topic would change to something else. She wasn't going to be that lucky.

"So, does your dad know Doc?" Livvy asked. Louise shrugged, hoping that would be enough to answer her, but it wasn't. "Your dad has never been in here, has he?"

"No."

"So, how does he know Doc, then?" Livvy had really done it now, her question coincided with Tina and Melanie listening and her question caused them to turn and look straight at Louise for a reply.

"I don't know," Louise lied.

"Oh!" None of the girls knew what to say after that.

About fifteen minutes passed before Doc reached the girl's table. As soon as he was in earshot, Tina tried to embarrass Louise with a few well-chosen words. She was still a bit miffed at being told to get a drink, and saw this as a bit of revenge.

"Hey Louise, it's your man," Tina said as she caught Doc's eye. The idea was to embarrass Louise but Doc turned red almost immediately. This wasn't what Tina had intended to happen but she was excited at the impact her line had had on him and she wasn't going to miss the opportunity to get the most out of any situation.

"Hello, girls," Doc felt himself burning up but tried his best to keep his composure.

"Hello, Doc." Nearly all the girls replied but not Tina or Louise. Louise did everything she could to not look at him, or she felt she would also go red. Tina on the other hand was really enjoying it all and kept eye contact with Doc. She was aware that he was uncomfortable about it and this made her want to do it all the more. She never quite realised before that there was this side to Doc.

Doc could feel Tina's eyes burning into him and he wanted to confront her, but felt that if he did it would only make things worse. There was a small pregnant pause until Doc spoke again.

"I see you girls are trying to cause trouble again in here."

"What do you mean, Doc? We're not doing anything." Tina was first to respond. She had assumed he said it to try and divert away attention.

Louise still couldn't risk looking at Doc in case the other girls were watching her, but she thought exactly the same as Tina and started to feel concerned about what Doc might say next.

"Upsetting little Eddie." Doc looked over to where Eddie was standing. Tina had almost forgotten what she had shouted out earlier but soon remembered.

"Oh, he's alright," Tina replied.

"Yeah, we're all friends with Eddie," Melanie answered. The tension had left Doc and his blushes disappeared. Louise looked in his direction and they caught each other's eye and there was a moment that more or less said everything. Both knew that they had each felt the awkwardness, and were quite relieved for the moment to have passed. It was quite strange but from that moment on, Louise knew she liked Doc. She could never explain it, not even to herself, but they had communicated on a level that they both understood. Doc wiped the table with his wet cloth and picked up the litter that was there, and swiftly made his way to the safety of the counter. He almost breathed a sigh of relief when he got back.

A little while later, most of the girls had started for home. Louise had left the coffee bar but stood around outside for a while chatting to a number of other school friends. When Tina and Melanie had gone, she returned to the coffee bar. She couldn't think why, but she just knew that she must go and speak to Doc again. As she went back in she looked over towards the counter, but only Kathy and Brian were there. 'Damn,' she thought to herself, as she turned to leave the place again, then she noticed Doc cleaning one of the tables in the far corner. She stopped twisting around and remained poised for a second before heading over towards him.

"Hello, Luce," Doc said as she reached the table. "Have you left something behind?"

"No, I just wanted to apologise for what Tina said." Doc stopped what he was doing and turned to face her.

"You haven't got to apologise for her. Anyway, it was nothing."

"But you were embarrassed?" Louise asked a question as much as stated a fact. Doc smiled and rubbed under his nose with his hand.

"Er, yes, I was, a bit." Doc felt he might blush again but he didn't.

"Well, I'm sorry anyway." Louise turned to leave having said what she had come back to say.

"Is everything okay at home?" Doc asked quickly. Louise turned back and bowed her head as she answered.

"Yes, but Dad doesn't like me talking to you too much." Louise replied. Doc was quite taken aback at her reply. His body language was obvious, even to Louise, and she was quite surprised at the way he took it. "It's no problem though, Mum thinks you're alright." Louise wasn't quite sure if that was the right thing to say or not, but she had already said it.

"That's not why David hasn't been in much, is it?"

Doc asked. "Or is he seeing Mary?"

"Seeing who?"

"Oh, I'm not sure." Doc guessed that Louise didn't know about Mary. "I might have got that wrong then. Just wondered why David hadn't been in much lately."

"I think he's a bit scared."

"Scared. Scared of what?"

"He gets picked on by the Burgh Boys." Louise thought Doc already knew that.

"But that doesn't worry him." Doc was quick to reply.

"Well, he hasn't really shown his face in here much, has he?" Louise had only assumed that David was afraid of being picked on but hadn't asked him.

"No, honestly, if you ask him he'll tell you. He's not frightened of them at all." Doc sounded almost like he was talking as a proud father. Louise looked at him strangely then shook her head a little. She turned towards the door.

"I'd better get home."

"Don't do your brother down, will you?" Doc said as she walked away. He couldn't be sure if she had heard him or not, but she never replied.

As Louise made her way back home she went over in her head what she had said to Doc. 'My mum thinks you're all right', she said over to herself in a self-mocking way. What on earth did she say that for? There was no way she would tell her mum what she had said. Apart from that she was quite pleased with the way their little conversation had gone. She was surprised how he seemed to defend David, but guessed it was probably a bloke thing.

It was Friday morning and David chatted to Mary quite a bit on the coach. To not cause her any problems, he went straight to the back of the coach when he got on and made a point of not looking over in her direction, although he had quite easily been able to spot where she was sitting. Having said hello to the lads on the back seat and chatted a bit, he went and sat with Mary before the coach got to the High School. Mary was still quite reluctant to chat much when Arthur was still on the coach but since the incident, Arthur didn't really seem to take any notice. This was the first time, though, that David had gone and sat with Mary before the High School kids had got off, which before would have been a very brave move, but David felt the atmosphere was okay to be so bold.

The day went pretty much as usual for everyone this Friday. Being the weekend tomorrow it seemed that practically everybody was helping to make the day go quicker. Doc felt as if he had missed most of the day as he busied himself around the coffee bar. In his mind, he was going over his conversation with Louise and smiling inwardly at how well it had all gone. He felt very much as if they were friends.
As the afternoon busy session approached, Brian, Kathy and Doc sat down to take a very quick break.

Brian had made them all bacon sandwiches which was something Doc was quite happy for him to do. His policy was to make sure that his staff were happy when they were working, and if they needed food and drink he'd rather they took things with his knowledge than him finish up with no stock. So, they sat there drinking tea and eating sandwiches, chatting about the weather. Brian suddenly changed the subject.

"We seem to be getting more kids in, Doc."

"Do you think so?"

"Yeah, I thought as much too." Kathy added. "Aren't your takings going up?"

"Well, yes, but that could be because the kids are drinking more. Those new canned drinks they are buying cost a lot more than the old colas, you know."

"What, the Red Bulls?" Kathy half laughed at Doc as she asked. She thought he sounded like an old woman talking as he was.

"Yes, and those Irn-bru things." Doc stopped to sip some tea. "I just assumed that as things were costing more, we were taking more in."

"Surely you know from your stock orders, boss?" Brian always believed that Doc was right on top of the numbers.

"I haven't done a full stock check for a couple of months, Brian," Doc answered as he watched Brian cover his bacon sandwich with ketchup. "Anyway, we'll have to order more ketchup." Kathy laughed, Brian just looked at him.

Doc stood up, walked back to the counter and pulled a couple of napkins out of the holder. Returning to the table he placed them on the table in front of Brian. While he was doing this he continued talking. "So, we've established that we are getting busier. Are you two after more money?"

"No, that wasn't the reason, but if you're offering?" Kathy didn't want Doc to think they were asking, but she didn't want to drop the subject if there was any chance of getting a raise.

"I'll have to see. I have to admit that you two are worth your weight in gold," Doc said.

"So, we should be paid a bit more then?" Brian asked, in a half-joking way.

"Well, no, not really, as the price of gold has gone down." Doc laughed at his own little joke.

"Ha, ha," Kathy replied. "Seriously though Doc, you seem to be spending more time helping out at busy times, don't you?" Kathy looked at him. Doc looked thoughtful before nodding.

"Yeah, you're right." As he replied the door opened and a couple of Somerby kids came in. "Looks like they've started." All three got up and made their way back to the counter, with Kathy collecting the empty cups and plates.

Louise and the girls were quick to get to Doc's, having run down the road after school, and as always on a Friday they were in a giggly mood, ready for the weekend. It was quite a normal afternoon for them, coke, a couple of rolls and perhaps a bag of crisps, nothing that was going to spoil their teas when they got home.

Doc was helping out again very soon, and this time he tried to pay a little bit more attention at looking at exactly how many kids there were in the place. He started to count them but before he had got very far, he would get asked for something and lose his place. He just had to admit that there were a lot more kids in that he had first realised. It was quite strange as he probably wouldn't have noticed, had he not had the chat with Kathy earlier. Doc stood and watched for a few minutes and then focussed on just how busy Kathy and Brian were. Kathy caught sight of him watching and shouted over. "Doc, can you give us a hand?" It was enough to pinch Doc back to reality.

"Yeah, sorry Kath."

"No problem, but we are getting a bit of a queue."

Kathy and Doc both moved to look at the queue.

"I've never really noticed just how many are in here recently." Doc shook his head, wiped his hands clean on a tea towel, threw it behind the counter and got himself ready to serve.

As Doc served, he thought more and more about what Kathy and Brian had said that afternoon. They were right. They did deserve more, and he would calculate what he could afford to give them. He knew it wouldn't be that difficult to make a few changes and free some money to pay them a bit extra. He then decided whether to give them a raise, or perhaps a bonus instead. As he tossed over the ideas in his head he continued to work through the customers who were still queuing for Coke like it was going out of fashion. This continued for almost an hour until the queue suddenly diminished. Doc slumped down on a seat out the back behind the counter. He slapped his hands down on his knees, indicating that he had made up his mind. He would give them both a bonus and a raise. Doc was pleased with himself but then it dawned on him that it didn't really solve the problem of them being rushed off their feet. It was likely that the same rush would meet them every day of the week at around the same time. Doc went upstairs to rethink.

It wasn't long before the idea entered Doc's head. He didn't know why he hadn't thought of it sooner. He stood up quickly and made his way down to the coffee bar. Looking quickly to his left he saw that the cafe had quietened down a bit and Kathy and Brian were calmly getting on with things. He looked over to where he knew that Louise and Tina and her mob usually sat but the tables were mainly empty. Doc's disappointment could be seen by anyone who was looking at his face at that very moment. He prepared to make his way back to the counter when he saw Louise stood outside. She was talking to one of the girls. Doc couldn't see exactly which one it was, but he didn't want to go out there whilst they were talking. He waited briefly inside the café until they parted then he made his way outside.

"Louise! Louise!" he called out, without shouting. Louise turned to see who it was calling her and was a bit surprised to see Doc walking towards her.

"Hi, Doc. Everything okay?"

"Yes, nothing is wrong." Doc was getting excited at the thought of what he was going to do next. It almost left him breathless.

"What is it?" Louise needed to get home so didn't want to waste any more time.

"Well, I hope you don't mind, but I just wanted to ask you if you were interested in a little job?"

"Job?" Louise was surprised. "What job?"

"Nothing too much, but for about an hour every week day, I need someone to help Brian and Kathy. What do you say?"

"What would I have to do?" Louise was interested.

"Not a lot. Collect some glasses and plates, a bit of washing up. Just to help them out during the busy times." Doc waited for Louise to say yes. Then he realised she was possibly thinking about her answer. He knew she would say yes, and had planned that she would say yes, but it had never crossed his mind until just then that she might not want the job.

"How much would I get?" Louise didn't want to sound too keen and believed that it was the correct thing to do to ask a question or two about exactly what Doc was proposing. She couldn't think what she needed to know, but automatically was straight on to the important things. Doc thought about it quickly. Five pounds an hour, that'll be twenty-five pounds.

"Thirty pounds a week." He was of course keen for her to work with him so he added on a little extra so that she wouldn't turn the job down because he had been too tight. Louise wanted to say yes immediately, but knew that it wouldn't be cool to agree straightaway. She tried to think of what else she could ask. A number of questions went through her head that perhaps gave the impression that she was thinking about the offer.

"Yes, please," was her only response.

"Well, that's good." Doc beamed. Louise tried to stop herself from jumping up and down. "If you can call in and see me sometime over the weekend, we'll just run through what you'll be doing.

"Yes, of course." Louise did jump excitedly a little bit and then grabbed Doc by the arms and kissed him on the cheek. "I'll see you tomorrow." Louise turned and walked off as nonchalantly as she could. After walking about twenty yards she started skipping which she did nearly all the way home. Doc felt like skipping as well but he didn't. He felt good about what he had just done but thought the kiss was a bit over the top. Having said that, it gave him a nice feeling.

Louise came skipping home and Sue could see straightaway that she was happy about something.

"Hello, darling. What are you so happy about?" Sue was washing a few things up at the kitchen sink as she spoke.

"What do you mean? Why shouldn't I be happy about something?" Louise was stunned that her mum asked such a question.

"I watched you walking along the road and I know that something has made you happy."

"Oh, it's nothing," Louise lied. She wanted to wait for the right moment before telling Sue her news. Sue knew that there was something, but wasn't upset that Louise wasn't ready to tell her yet. She knew she would find out sooner or later and she was just pleased that her daughter was so happy. She pulled the plug out of the sink and wiped her hands. Throwing the towel back down on the work-top, she made her way over towards Louise who was sitting at the kitchen table.

"Did you have a good day at school today?" Sue guessed that a change of subject was the best way forward.

"Yes. We learnt some French." Louise had dumped her school bag down on the floor and she picked it up to try and retrieve her French book. "Oh, I remember a little French." Sue sat down beside her. "Je suis Susan." Sue said with a very phoney and over the top French accent.

"You mean 'je m'appelle Susan'," Louise corrected her in a similar accent.

"Well, it was a long time ago that I learnt how to speak French."

"Don't worry, Mum. Everyone in Somerby speaks English so you don't need to know how to speak French." Louise smiled as she replied, and Sue gave her a hug and stroked her hair. It was a loving hug and the stroking was nice for a while until Sue turned it into an examination for nits. "Oh, get off Mum!" Louise shrugged off.

David appeared at the kitchen door from his bedroom. "Mum, when are we having tea?" Sue got up and walked over towards the oven.
"Probably not for another hour yet." Sue looked at the clock on the oven. "Your father should be home just after six, so hopefully about half past."
"And what are we having?" David was starving.
"Quiche and salad."
   David walked over to the fridge and opened it. He looked around inside.
"Can I have some cheese?"
"What do you say?" Sue reminded him of his manners.
"Please."
"Yes, cut a little bit, don't have too much."
"Ooh, can I have some too please?" Louise asked.
"Get your own," David replied as he searched for a sharp knife.
"Cut a piece for your sister," Sue demanded. David gave his mum one of those looks, and then proceeded to cut the smallest bit of cheese he possibly could before handing it to his sister.
"Oy! Mum! That's not fair," Louise moaned. David laughed and made his way back to his bedroom.

It was nearly seven before Michael got home and

changed and the family were sitting around the table ready for their dinner. Sue served up the quiche and each took it in turn to help themselves from the large salad bowl.

"Can I have the vinegar, please?" David asked as Michael passed it to him. All helped themselves to some boiled potatoes which were also in a large bowl on the table before tucking into their dinner. There was silence for a couple of minutes.

"Who are you playing tomorrow David?" Michael asked.

"You know who we've got, Dad," David replied with a moan. Michael shrugged his shoulders so David told him again. "We're playing Yarmouth tomorrow."

"Oh, of course. What team are they likely to field?"

"Oh, it'll be their strongest. Maybe even one of the reserve players might get used."

"Does Scalesy do that at Gorleston?" Michael wasn't sure if he did or not.

"He will use reserve players every now and then. Sometimes they are getting a bit of match fitness in so we have to let them but he wouldn't ask the reserves for players."

The family continued to munch their way through their dinner and the conversation was brief and sporadic. Louise thought the time was right for her to tell the family her news.

"By the way, I've got a job," she said, and then carried on eating. Michael and Sue looked at her, and then each other, in amazement.

"A job?" Sue asked.

"Yes, I've got a job. You're always saying I need to earn some money, so I've gone and got a job." Louise sounded very proud of what she had done.

"And what job is it? A paper round?" Michael asked.

"No, that means getting up early in the morning."

"So, what job then, Luce?" David was also curious.

"I'm working in a shop." Louise was going to come straight out with it but then changed her mind just at the end of the sentence.

"Doing what work?" Sue needed to know.

"Collecting things up."

"What things?" Michael asked, for further clarification.

"Plates, cups and glasses."

"Oh, what, at the café?" Sue had more or less put things into place. It sounded like quite a nice little job.

"Yes. I work for an hour every day, Monday to Friday." Louise was pretty sure that was what Doc had said to her. Michael started to eat again whilst taking in what his daughter had just announced. He was quite proud of her.

"So how much do you get paid?" David was starting to get a little envious.

"Thirty pounds a week." Louise exclaimed proudly. David's head dropped.

"Thirty pounds?" Sue was greatly surprised. There was another short pause whilst everyone took in the news.

"There you are, David, why couldn't you go out and get a job like your sister?"

Michael was pleased for his daughter but had hoped that his son would have had similar initiative to go and do something like this first. David was annoyed. Not only had his sister got some money coming in but now his parents were going to have a go at him. He had no answer.

"I wouldn't want to work for Doc anyway," David said.

Not realising what he had done, his reply caused more trouble than he expected. First, Louise gave David a nasty look just before she glanced quickly at her dad and then hopefully at her mum. Sue looked out of the corner of her eye at Michael to see how he would react. Michael took a few seconds before realising that everyone was looking at him. It then dawned on him what David had said.

"I thought I'd made it clear the other night that you were to have nothing further to do with that Doc and now you are going to work with him." Michael got louder as the sentence neared its end. "Well young lady, what exactly do you think you're doing?" Michael wanted to make sure that Louise had not done this on purpose just to spite him. Louise had totally forgotten already what her dad had said the other evening.

"But I won't be working with him, just for him." She hoped this would make it better.

"No, I'm not happy with that." Michael was

beginning to feel that this had been done on purpose. "You go down there tomorrow and tell him you don't want the job."

"Why should I?"

"Because I've told you to." Both Michael and Louise were getting carried away and Sue could see that this might well get out of hand.

"Hang on a minute, Michael. Louise hasn't done anything wrong here." Sue tried to calm the situation a bit.

"She should have asked us first before applying for a job." Michael was adamant. "Especially a job there."

"I didn't apply for the job." Louise was getting upset and her voice was starting to sound a bit tearful.

"What do you mean you didn't apply for the job? What you expect me to believe that they just came up to you and asked you if you wanted to work there." Michael was getting annoyed.

"Well, yes, they did." Louise was already croaking.

"Well, you can just go and tell them to take their job back." Michael tried not to shout. Louise slammed her knife and fork down on her plate and they made a loud noise. She burst into tears.

"It's not fair." Louise blubbed a few words. "I get a job and you make me give it back."

She was ready to burst into a real cry but it never quite came. David couldn't believe what was happening. Sue walked round and cuddled Louise.

"Don't cry darling. We'll discuss this properly. Like

adults." Sue looked at Michael as if she would kill him if he didn't agree. He didn't object.

Michael and Sue said no more on the subject until after dinner. David and Louise were allowed to leave the table whilst Sue and Michael cleared away dinner.

"I need to find out how Spurs are getting on." David exclaimed as he got up.

"Oh, yeah, they're playing QPR tonight aren't they?" Michael answered. The kids left the kitchen. Almost immediately Sue laid into Michael verbally.

"What do you think you were doing?"

"What do you mean? She's done this on purpose."

"No, she hasn't."

"Well you know I'm not happy about that guy."

"What, Doc? He's all right."

Sue managed to get Michael to see things a bit differently and eventually got him to agree that Louise could take the job. When Louise had calmed down she was pleased to hear that her dad had changed his mind. She wasn't happy with him but she gave him a hug anyway.

As everyone was sat together in the lounge and Michael and Louise had got over their little difference, Sue knew that the moment was right to bring up the next subject.

"Right. As we are all here, there's something else we need to talk about." Sue spoke as formally as she could, not wanting to give away any sense of the excitement she was feeling just anticipating what she was going to tell them all.

Louise was the first to sit up and start paying attention but she remained sat with her dad. David turned away from the television, and Michael looked confused as he wasn't sure what Sue was going to say next.

"Now, your Father and I have done some talking." Sue took a pause. Michael didn't have a clue what she was talking about, but Louise and David were listening intently. "And we have had a look at how much money we have." Michael still hadn't got a clue what was coming next. "And we have decided that we can afford to go on holiday next summer." Sue clapped her hands in excitement. David and Louise just looked at each other whilst Michael began to catch on with what his wife was about to announce.

"But we go on holiday every year," David added.

"Yeah, we do," Louise chipped in.

"So, aren't we going on holiday this year?" David said in a depressed voice.

"Yes, we're going away in August this year," Sue replied

"So why is it so special that we're going on holiday next year?"

"Ah, where do we normally go?" Sue hadn't intended it as a question but it was clearly taken as one.

"Isle of Wight." David answered.

"Yes." Sue gave them all time to take that thought in. "And where else do we go?" Louise couldn't remember more than three holidays.

"Butlins!" she exclaimed, not being able to recall exactly where the holiday camp was that they had gone to.

"Well, yes, we went to Bognor Regis," Sue replied.

"That was a good holiday, are we going back there?" Louise asked.

"No." It was a short response from Sue that almost made Louise jump back. "We're going somewhere else."

"I thought you said we were going to York?" David had suddenly remembered overhearing his parents discussing it. He thought it was quite a naff place to go.

"Yes, we're going to York this year, but next year we're going somewhere better."

"Where, where?" Louise was getting excited.

"Somewhere a little bit further away."

"Ah, now Dad's learning to drive we're going to drive somewhere," David said.

"No, we can't drive there." Sue teased. "It's a bit too far to drive there."

"So how are we going to get there?" Louise asked.

"By plane."

"Plane!" The reply came from both Louise and David. They looked at each other and repeated their statement. "Plane!" This was great news as neither of them had ever flown anywhere before and it was a holiday in itself just to be flying.

"Are we flying from a big airport?" David asked.

"A big airport?" Michael joined in. "What do you mean by a big airport?"

"Well, Gatwick, as opposed to Norwich," David explained.

"Ah. I'm not sure." Sue looked at Michael.

"I think it would be Heathrow," he replied. Sue was happy that this was probably correct and was pleased to see the kids excited about the news when she realised she hadn't actually told them yet. Well at least not where they were going.

"But you don't know where we're going yet."

"Doesn't matter, if we're flying there. That's great," David replied.

"Well, we're going to Disney in Florida." Sue said it. It was a bit of an anti-climax as neither David nor Louise said anything. It hadn't quite sunk in to be honest, but it was beginning to. The rest of the evening was full of unanswerable questions about what it would be like, what rides they could go on, would the hotel have a swimming pool. The family was full of it for many days to come as well.

It was Saturday and the weekend had begun again. David still had Disney on his mind as he waited to be picked up by Mitch to go off to football. Today was a very important game for the team as not only was it against their local rivals, Yarmouth, but it would be the decider as to which team finished above the other in the league tables at the end of the season. Both teams had very similar records with

Yarmouth a single point ahead of Gorleston going into this game so a win for David's team would see them leapfrog their rivals.

As Mitch's dad drove them to the ground, David was deep in thought about loads of things. Disney. Mary. Arthur. He had managed to forget about the forthcoming battle against Arthur Davison but now it was filling his mind.

"You're quiet today," Mitch said.

"Thinking about things," David replied. "It's a big game today."

"You don't say," Mitch laughed. "We can beat them easily if we play our game but if we don't, they've got the players who can hurt us."

"Well, we'll just have to play our game then." The two slapped hands in a high five.

As the lads got themselves changed in the dressing room, Scalesy walked around shouting out bits of information to various members of the team. Reminding the defenders which foot their intended opponents prefer to kick with. Reminding Pop and Ash to switch sides when he tells them to. Nigel was then given a big lecture about what he should try in various dead ball situations. There was no doubt about it, this game meant everything to them.

The referee came in and gave the lads his little speech about what he would clamp down on and how he would try and let the game flow if they were all grown up about it. Scalesy stood listening intently and nodding in agreement. As the ref wished them luck, Scalesy walked with him out of the dressing room, shutting the door behind them. When he re-entered the dressing room, all the lads looked up at him.

"What a wanker!" Scalesy said. It had the effect he'd hoped, as all the team laughed and looked far more relaxed. "Go on out there and let's show 'em!" Scalesy shouted. The whole team shouted back as they began to line up behind Nigel. After a couple of minutes' wait, they made their way on to the field and the game was ready to start. David had seen Arthur, and he had given him the stare as he juggled with the ball. David guessed this was going to be a hard battle between the two of them but he knew he would do his best and try to get the better of him.

As the game started, Arthur and David found themselves almost face to face and Arthur took the first opportunity he could to push David over when the play was going on elsewhere and give him a little kick. David expected it and was ready to give back what he had taken when he could. The first ten minutes or so was quite scrappy and neither team seemed able to put more than three or four passes together before losing possession. As always, when Yarmouth had the ball in defence they looked to play it to Arthur so he could look for that telling pass but David never let him settle on it and he would be forced to play shorter passes before being caught in possession himself. Arthur guessed he would be marked tightly and was ready to get rid of the ball quickly if he was going to be tackled.

David found it hard to get much of the ball early on but by dropping deeper into defence he got the ball and started to try and build some attacks. On one such occasion, he found himself being tackled by another Yarmouth midfielder and as he passed it out wide a challenge came in from behind which felled him quite heavily. The referee heard the bump but hadn't seen the incident properly so just kept an eye for any off the ball indiscipline. David felt the challenge and without even looking knew exactly who had put the foul in.

"You're a bit of a softy," Arthur said with a laugh as he ran past David still down on the floor. David rubbed his calf as he gingerly got back to his feet. The referee ran near to him. "Are you okay, son?"

"Yeah, I'll live," David answered. He tried to run off the ache but only a couple of minutes later found the ball at his feet and himself being challenged and kicked in the shins in the process. The ball moved on and David was left trying to get himself back into the game by running off his pain but he was called back into action almost straightaway as he tried to tackle Arthur. The ball bounced loose and David thought he would be the one to get control of it when Arthur slid in from his side, taking him down just before getting the ball. The referee blew for a foul but David stayed down longer than he would have normally. This second challenge was on the same calf he had been hit on earlier and it hurt.

David struggled for the next ten minutes and it was crucial as Arthur started to run things in the middle of the field. He sprayed passes far and wide both to the left and right. David couldn't keep up with him as he struggled to run properly. Yarmouth scored a cracking goal during this period to go one up and Scalesy shouted at Nigel to get the midfield sorted. David also noticed that the manager sent one of the substitutes to have a little run. He took that as a sign that if things didn't improve, Scalesy would make a change and he guessed he was the one who would come off. He knew he should have been tackling better to stop these Yarmouth attacks but it had taken a good ten minutes for him to feel capable of running again. Eventually, David began to feel better and he should be capable of getting a grip on the game.

As Arthur put another high challenge in, David felt it was also time to get a bit of his own back. Arthur dribbled past one challenge and ran with the ball towards David. It was the perfect chance and as Arthur swerved his body and the ball to David's right, David just took one almighty swipe at Arthur's left knee. Arthur was sent tumbling as the referee blew for a foul. The Yarmouth officials shouted and the referee gave David a yellow card.

The Somerby Tree

Scalesy was tearing his hair out.

Nigel came and had a little word.
"David, you're better than that."
"What do you mean? This is a battle out here."
David was annoyed with Nigel's advice.
"Don't let him bring you down to his level. Beat him at football." Nigel patted David on the back and David considered what had been said. For the rest of the first half, Arthur hardly got the ball with David tackling and intercepting everything. Gorleston finished the half by far the better team but still one goal down.

The second half continued in the same way with David stopping everything in midfield and Nigel and Mitch creating attack after attack. Arthur had almost given up but he wasn't going to let David get the better of him so when the chance appeared and David was on the ground with the ball popping around, Arthur made sure he put his foot in and caught David clear on the ankle. He put his studs in and twisted his boot to cause more pain. David felt it alright as it shot up his leg but adrenalin allowed him to jump to his feet and he aimed a kick at Arthur. He missed completely but the referee saw the incident and David was sent off. Scalesy saw all of what had happened and wasn't annoyed with his player this time, but disappointed with the referee who only saw the retaliation. It put Gorleston down to ten men but they continued to pile on the pressure. They just couldn't score. Yarmouth did though. The game finished two-nil.

As the Gorleston lads trudged back to the dressing room, David had already got changed and was on his way out. Nobody said anything. The Yarmouth lads in contrast were full of it. They had finished a couple of places above Gorleston because of this result and it was almost as if they had won a cup final. Mitch was one of the last to make it back to the dressing room.

"You alright?" Mitch asked David.

"Yeah. A bit sore but nothing broken."

"It was a bit of a nasty one. Surprised he didn't get sent off as well."

"Bloody ref. Anyway, it was personal." David swung his bag over his shoulder. "I'll be waiting out here."

"Okay." Mitch continued into the dressing room.

David walked around waiting for his lift home and a couple of times felt the pain shooting through his knee where he had suffered the injury whilst playing. He would occasionally shout out a swear word as he felt the pain. He found himself at the back of the dressing room. The noise of lads shouting at each other whilst in the showers could be heard through an open window. David listened to see if he could hear any voices that he might recognise. 'I wonder if they're blaming me' David thought to himself. He was annoyed at having got himself sent off but felt that by then the game had probably already been lost. He could make out Dave Kings voice but all that was being talked about was when training would be starting for next season. It was all quite boring really. David suddenly became aware that he was being watched. There was a noise that he couldn't really explain but it made him turn sharply.

"Oh, it's you." David stiffened at the sight of Arthur. "And what the hell do you want?" David wasn't going to be seen to be afraid of him but the fact hit him quite quickly that here he was, with Arthur, and nobody else was about.

"I just wanted to fucking remind you." Arthur moved closer to David and looked him straight in the eye.

"Oh, yeah. Remind me what?" David tried to sound brave but inside he was shaking. What was Arthur going to do? There was probably no way he'd come out best if Arthur chose to fight.

"You keep poking your fucking nose in my business." As Arthur finished the sentence, he hit David in the stomach with one big punch. David doubled over but refused to go down. Arthur placed a kick to the side of David's injured knee and he fell immediately. David wasn't sure which hurt the most, his knee or his stomach. It was probably his pride that was hurting just as much. Arthur clenched his fist as if he was going to hit him again but then stopped. "I won't tell you again. You leave that little slag alone."

David knew who he meant of course. There was a noise as if someone else was about to walk around the corner and both Arthur and David looked to see who it might be. It was Scalesy, the Gorleston boss and as David saw him his pain almost went completely. Arthur looked at the man as he stopped to try and take in what was happening and then looked back at David. Arthur said nothing but just walked away.

"Are you all right?" Scalesy asked.
"Yes, it's nothing." David gingerly made it back to his feet. "My bloody knee went or I'd have killed him." As David spoke, Mitch arrived on the scene.
"What's happening?"
"Davison was here."
"You two fighting?"
"I think they were." The boss said. "All this because of football." As the boss spoke, Mitch looked at David. He knew it was over more than football. David shook his head. Mitch said nothing.

Louise made her way to Doc's that afternoon. She had originally intended to go and call in sometime during the morning but she didn't want to appear too keen and it would have been unusual for her to have gone out of the house too early and may have started her dad asking questions. She didn't want to cause any more problems over this job.

As she walked in, she had a quick look around to

see who else was in there who might know her. None of the gang were in but then Louise wasn't expecting them in much before half past two. The place was still quite busy though, with a good half of the tables occupied. She looked to see if she could see Doc but he wasn't about so she made her way casually up to the counter and spoke to Kathy.

"Hi, Louise. Are you okay?" Kathy asked, as she would ask nearly all the customers.

"Yeah, quite well, thanks Kathy."

"What would you like?" Kathy assumed Louise was ready to buy something.

"Is Doc in?"

"Well yes but he's pretty busy. What would you like?"

"Oh, I don't want anything," Louise replied. Kathy looked at her strangely. "No, I've just come to see Doc." Kathy looked at her again. She thought the comment peculiar.

"Have you got a complaint?"

"No, I've come about the job."

"Oh, sorry Louise. There's no job vacancy." Kathy replied. Louise felt she had possibly been given the sack before she'd even started.

"Oh, right." Louise considered what to do next when Doc appeared through the door behind the counter.

"Hello, Miss Riddell, you've come about that job then." Doc clapped his hands as he spoke. Kathy's jaw dropped and she turned to make sure she had really heard what she had heard. "Come through."

Doc beckoned Louise through. "Oh, Kathy."

"Yes, Doc?" Kathy replied still looking astonished.
"I think we may have an answer to our problems."
Doc moved his eyes in Louise's direction to
indicate her.

"Oh, right," Kathy replied. It took her almost a
minute to regain herself and get back to work.

Louise followed Doc up the stairs. She looked at the
bare white walls and the threadbare carpet on the
stairs. It wasn't dirty, but more a well-used look. At
the top of the stairs there was a small landing with a
closed door to the left and an open one to the right.
Doc walked through the open one and she followed
him into a small office.

Doc pulled out a chair and placed it down on the far
side of the office away from the desk.

"Please take a seat, young lady." Doc stretched out
his arm. Louise sat down. Doc went off through
another door and she looked around the room.
There was a computer on the desk piles of papers
and books next to it. There was a calendar propped
up at the back of the desk and a few post-its stuck
on the pale yellow wall. Louise recognised a badge
which was stuck at the back of the desk. It looked
like the Spurs logo but she couldn't quite see it
properly. She thought about getting up and taking a
closer look but she heard a sound coming from the
next room. Doc returned with a chair and sat down
facing Louise.

"Right. Let's go through what I want you to do,"

Doc said as he picked up a writing pad and flipped over the front cover. "Are you okay working Monday to Friday?" Doc asked Louise. She hadn't really given it any thought.

"Yes, I'm happy."

"Good." Doc scribbled some notes on the pad. "And what time do you finish school?"

"Oh, we are usually out at three-fifteen," Louise replied. Doc wrote some more things down and every now and then tapped the pencil on his nose. Louise watched him and felt quite comfortable in his company. She just didn't know why but he obviously made her feel relaxed.

"So, would you be able to start work at four?"

"Yes." Louise answered without giving it any thought but after consideration knew it was the right answer.

"I'd like you to work between four and five to start with but I may change that to half past four to half past five." Doc wrote some more notes and then placed both the pad and pencil down on the desk. "You'll get paid thirty pounds at the end of your Friday hour if that's alright with you?"

"Err, yes." Again, Louise wasn't quite sure what other options she had.

"And now we'll discuss what you're going to be doing." Doc pulled the chair nearer to Louise and looked her in the eye. The contact probably lasted a bit longer than it should, but both felt okay about it even if Doc was a little embarrassed. "I need you to collect plates, cups and glasses from the tables, do some washing up and make sure there are enough clean ones for Kathy and Brian to use for serving." Doc waited for some acknowledgement that Louise had understood but it never came. "If the tables have lots of rubbish on them, you will need to get a bin and go round clearing." Again, Doc waited for Louise to take that in. She seemed ready for the next instruction. "I will generally expect you to do anything else asked of you by Kathy." Doc thought for a second. "Or Brian, of course."

"Like what?"

"Well to be honest, I don't know. Perhaps you may need to go and get some stock from the store room."

"Where's that?"

"Kathy will show you. You won't be going anywhere near the hot plate though. Is that understood?" Doc thought that might be a bit dangerous.

"Yeah, understood," Louise replied.

Doc stood up and took Louise back down to the front of the café to introduce her to Kathy. He allowed Louise to help herself to a coke and a bag of crisps and she went and sat down at one of the tables whilst he chatted with Kathy to explain what he wanted her to tell Louise. It took Kathy nearly forty minutes to show Louise around but by two o'clock, Louise was an employee. It was agreed she would start the following Monday and take it from there. Louise decided she would walk back home and tell her mum how it had gone, and then return to the café to meet up with the rest of the gang.

Louise couldn't wait to tell her mum about her new job.

"Mum, guess what? The job is brilliant."

"Brilliant. What do you mean?"

"My job working at Doc's."

"Doc's?" Sue carried on doing some washing up whilst talking. "Oh, you mean that coffee bar."

"Yes, Doc's."

"And what work will you be doing then?" Sue was probably as excited as Louise about it all but wanted to sound only moderately so about it all.

"I'm going to be working, serving behind the counter a little bit. Oh, and collecting plates and washing them up." Louise almost jumped up and down as she told her about it all.

"Oh, darling that's good. You'll be able to do that no problem. You know you should have come and asked us first before you got the job."

"Yes, I know but it's alright. Doc said so."

"Well, excuse me, but Doc doesn't run this household, and it's up to me and your father whether or not you can work there. We haven't actually said you can."

Louise was deflated. She stamped her left foot down on the carpet but it didn't make much noise. Sue noticed it though. She knew Louise's little habits. Her daughter was angry.

"I'll have a word with your father and make sure it's all right."

"I start on Monday."

"On a school day? That's not so good." Sue wasn't so happy about that.

"It's only for an hour."

"But you'll have your homework to do."

"I don't usually get home till six anyway."

"But you might be too tired." Sue didn't want Louise to think she would get her own way so easily. "Let's just wait and see." The conversation ended.

As it happened, Sue managed to discuss Louise's new job with Michael during the day and kept putting in lots of comments to the effect that Louise would probably start to help out more around the house if she was given this responsibility. Do some washing up and clearing up etcetera. By the time Michael got round to mentioning about Louise and her new job, he had already made so many comments on how good it would be to see Louise doing just exactly the thing she was going to be employed doing. He wasn't happy but was unable to provide any argument that Sue didn't just shoot down immediately afterwards. Louise was totally unaware of how much work her mum had done behind the scenes.

David had done very little yesterday and as it had been a Sunday he spent most of it in bed. His pride was probably more battered than his body but it was his body that ached and reminded him of the beating he had received. He was quite surprised that his mum and dad had accepted so easily that all of his injuries were received through football, but he had to admit that it had been quite a bruising game as well. It had been difficult to start with but he had managed to persuade his mum to allow him the day off school and that in itself made him feel a bit better. It was quite funny really how the body works but in that brief few seconds where his mum had agreed that he could have the day off, David's aches and pains got slightly better.

The day dragged as far as David was concerned. His dad had already gone off to work by the time he woke up properly, and Louise was just about to leave for school, so it was just him and his mum. Sue came in and checked that he was all right.

"How are you feeling this morning?" Sue asked him.

"Ooh, a little better," he replied whilst groaning and pulling a pained face.

"You get back into bed for a while longer."

"Okay." David did as he was told immediately. Sue didn't see that very often.

David went back to sleep and didn't wake up till lunch time. He looked at his watch saw that it was just five past twelve. David moved his legs about under the sheets and they ached with every twist and turn. Sue brought him in a cup of hot milk.

"Here you are, dear, sit yourself up a bit and drink

this." Sue placed the cup down and helped David sit up. "There, that's a bit better."

"Thanks, Mum."

"So, are you going to tell me who you had a fight with?" David was taken by surprise and the look he gave his mum said everything.

"Fight? What fight?" David replied.

"It's okay, you don't have to tell me." Sue shrugged her shoulders and gave a look of uncertainty. "It just helps sometimes to talk these things over." David made a reach for his drink. Sue touched his hand. "It'll be too hot. Leave it for a bit."

"Mum," David said as Sue got up to walk out of his room. She stopped and turned back to look at him. "It's a problem I need to sort out on my own."

"Yes, I know it is. Talking about it doesn't mean you're not sorting it out yourself though."

"Maybe not."

"Don't forget, your dad and I are here if you need us. We're not going to tell you off and we won't interfere." Sue turned again and made off for the kitchen.

"Thanks, Mum," David shouted.

Before long, Louise was home from school. She didn't stay too long as it was her first day at work so she changed into some proper clothes and gave her mum a kiss before shooting back out of the front door and to Doc's. She had totally forgotten that David was at home. Within minutes she was at the café.

"Hello, Louise," Kathy said as Louise walked up to the counter.

"Hi, Kathy." Louise leaned on the counter. "Hello Brian."

"No good you leaning on that side of the fence, my dear, you've got work to do." Kathy beckoned her through. Louise looked at her watch. It was still only ten to four but she followed Kathy behind the counter and to the far end. "Right, we need to sort you out an apron."

"Apron!" Louise almost shrieked. "Apron!" Kathy just laughed.

"Yes, apron!" Kathy imitated Louise's alarm at the thought of having to wear an apron. "If you don't wear one, you'll spoil all of your clothes. At least you had the sense to put some jeans on."

"Well, I had to get out of school uniform." Louise looked up as she replied and spotted Livvy and Ness making their way to their usual table. Louise was quite excited at the thought of presenting herself as one of the staff. "Okay I'll wear an apron." Louise gave in. Kathy sorted out the smallest apron she could find and helped Louise tie it up.

"Right, you're ready to roll."

"What do you want me to do?"

"Just go out there and collect up some of the things off the tables." Kathy saw that a queue had already started to form and she needed to go and help Brian. "And not too much chatting."

Louise made her way out to the nearby tables and collected a few glasses. There weren't that many, but she took what she could find back to the sink to be washed up. The rest of the gang had sat themselves around the table and they were all wondering what had happened to Louise when she made her way over.

"Oh. You've been home and got changed," Tina noticed. Livvy and Melanie moved across to let Louise in beside them but she didn't sit down.

"Aren't you sitting down?" Livvy asked.

"Got somewhere else to go?" Tina added.

"No, I'm not sitting down. I'm busy working," Louise replied as she grabbed the one glass and plate on the table and walked directly back to behind the counter. The girls were astonished.

Louise came back a few times and had little chats but as it was her first day she didn't want to upset Kathy or Brian so she made sure she wasn't chatting too long and got all the glasses and plates collected and washed. Tina and Gillian were the last of the gang to leave all saying goodbye to Louise before leaving the café. Louise was worn out by five and the place was still very busy.

"Time you packed up, girl," Kathy told her.

"Yes, I suppose so. Have you got enough plates?"

"Yes, thanks. You've worked well today. I'll let Doc know how well you did."

"Oh, that'll be nice."

"You seem to get on quite well with him, don't

you?" Kathy leaned against the sink as Louise started to take off her apron.

"Yeah, I suppose so. He's all right."

"Oh, he is. Very friendly, if a bit weird. He doesn't really think badly of anyone."

"Have you known him long then?"

"Quite a while." Kathy thought. "Must be about twenty years now, perhaps more." Kathy scratched her head. "It's hard to think back."

"So, were you school friends?" Louise asked.

"No, we didn't go to school together. In fact, I don't know where Doc went to school. He's lived in this village all of his life I think." Kathy was still thinking hard. "So he must have gone to the local school, but I'm not sure."

"Why do you call him Doc?"

"I don't really know. He's always been Doc." Kathy suddenly realised that she had left Brian on his own. "Must be getting back. See you tomorrow Louise."

"Yeah, okay. Bye." Louise had enjoyed her first day at work. She liked Kathy and liked being able to feel important. Life was good.

Tuesday arrived and David was back to school. His eye still had some bruising but apart from that he didn't look too bad. He was still a bit stiff from the bruising around his ribs but when he got on the coach and made his way towards the back he walked as well as he could. He looked to see if Mary was on the coach but she wasn't. As he reached the back seats Arthur was first to speak.

"Make way lads, cripple coming through."

"Ha, ha! Very funny," David replied.

"Bloody hell, mate, what happened to you?" Phil asked.

"Oh, I got jumped on by some wanker."

"Looks like the wanker got the better of you," Arthur said, as he chuckled.

"Yeah, maybe this time, but he won't next time."

"I'd be careful if I were you, looks like you were whipped good!"

"Oh, don't you believe it. He took me by surprise and by the time I was able to react there were too many witnesses."

"So, did you actually hit 'im then?" Arthur asked teasingly.

"I'll hit him, don't you worry. When he's not ready." David felt the pain in his ribs as he raised his voice.

"Seems to me this bloke's got the better of you." Arthur turned away to chat to someone else almost as soon as he had finished the sentence. "It was a bloke, wasn't it? Not a girl?"

"I don't fight with girls. This wanker practices on young girls though." David ignored Arthur as he turned to Phil. "What lessons you got today?"

Arthur kept calm on the surface, although inside he was absolutely seething. He wanted to hit David again there and then. Have it out to see who was in fact the strongest. He felt though that if he reacted to David's comments, he was letting himself down so he tried to ignore it. Everyone continued chatting away. The rest of the journey to school was uneventful. Arthur wasn't really listening to anyone else. He was punching David in the face in his mind. David meanwhile wondered where Mary might be but he didn't see her on the coach for the rest of the week.

***

Louise sat down at one of the tables in Doc's drinking flavoured fizzy water straight from the bottle. Tina was sat on the opposite seat playing with a salt container whilst watching everyone else in the coffee bar.

"Where's Livvy?" Tina suddenly asked.

"Oh, she's had to go home early today."

"Why, what's she doing?"

"Don't know." Louise shrugged her shoulders. She looked up at the clock. Nearly quarter to four. "I thought Gillian would have been here by now."

"She's outside chatting. Melanie's out there too." Tina seemed totally uninterested but was obviously quite aware of most things that were going on around the place.

"Do you want to go and join them?"

"No. They'll be in, in a moment. You'll see."

Almost as if by magic, Melanie and Gillian walked through the door. Gillian went directly to the counter whilst Melanie joined the girls.

"So, what's kept you?" Tina asked, as if she was telling Melanie off.

"Oh, nothing. Gillian was trying to get some money

from her cousin."

"Is she buying then?"

"Don't know. I couldn't make out how much she got from him."

The three of them looked up to see what Gillian was doing at the counter. She was talking to Kathy and seemed to have at least two bottles of drink. Kathy handed her some change and Gillian tucked the drinks under her arm as she made her way to the table.

"Two drinks. And some straws." Gillian announced as if she was buying lots of drinks.

"I should think so too." Tina grabbed at one of the bottles and threw a straw into the top of it. As she sucked up some drink she almost dismissively looked around the place before returning her eyes to the girls at the table.

"Thanks Gillian," Melanie said.

"Okay."

"It was her turn to buy the drinks anyway," Tina added. Gillian ignored the remark.

"Are you having any?" Gillian asked Louise.

"No, thanks. I've got to start work in a few minutes."

"Perhaps you can get us some more free drinks then?" Tina added.

At five to four, Louise made her way behind the counter and put on her apron. The café was already quite busy and both Brian and Kathy were only able to give her a quick nod as she arrived.

"Do you want me to collect anything in particular?" Louise asked.

"Be a darling and wash some little plates up please," Brian replied, "We're running a bit short."

"Okay." Louise duly obliged. She walked over to the sink and filled up a bowl with some hot water. She added washing up liquid from the plastic bottle at the back of the sink, ploughed through the masses of washing up piled on the side and found a number of small plates. These she washed and laid down on a large draining board to dry. "I'll go and see if there are anymore out there." Louise spoke as a statement rather than a question. Neither Kathy nor Brian replied. They were too busy.

Fairly soon, Louise was back behind the counter washing and drying up again. Almost as soon as she dried the plates and got them back on the shelves, Brian or Kathy were grabbing them to use again. Every couple of minutes there would be a shout for more glasses or more forks and Louise quickly went out to collect whatever was needed, washed and dried it ready for use. The place seemed a lot busier than it used to be and even Doc had come down to help out with serving.

The time rushed past very quickly and Louise didn't even notice when the girls got up to leave. Tina just left, but Melanie and Gillian made sure to say goodbye before they went. Louise looked up at the clock and Doc noticed.

"Looks like we've been working you too hard," Doc said, as he realised it was nearly a quarter past five. He looked at the queue still waiting to be served. "Are you happy to stay till half past?"

"Yeah." Louise nodded approvingly.

Within five minutes the queue had diminished and some normality had returned to the coffee bar. Kathy automatically went off to clear the tables leaving Brian to serve the last few customers.

"I think you can go home now." Doc almost called Louise by her pet name but stopped himself just in time.

"Thanks, Doc."

"Thanks for staying on."

"Oh, no problem," Louise said as she undid her apron.

"Do you need to ring Mum to let her know you'll be late?" Doc asked concerned.

"No. She's not expecting me in till sixish anyway."

"You know how special your mum is?" Doc had his eyes closed as he said it.

"All mums are special, aren't they, Doc?"

"Yes, I know, but your own mum is always the best."

"Yeah, all right." Louise looked at Doc strangely. What a weird thing to say she thought. "So, where's your mum?" Louise asked.

"Well, I lost her when I was a teenager."

"Lost her?" Louise didn't quite understand what he

meant.

"Oh, it's a long and complicated story."

"So, did you find her again?"

"Yes and no." Doc shook his head.

"Ah, that sounds sad." Louise patted Doc on his shoulder. Doc forgot where he was for a moment and almost automatically put his arm on her shoulder.

"Thanks L…" Doc removed his arm almost as soon as it had touched her. He cut his reply short and stood upright again as if he had been told to stand to attention.

Doc's mood changed very quickly.

"You know, when I was a young lad I had a special place to go when I was sad."

"Did you?"

"Yes. Do you have a place?" Doc asked her. Louise thought for a few seconds.

"I suppose I do."

"And where's that then?"

"I'm not telling you." Louise sounded quite indignant.

"I won't tell you where my place is then."

"Oh, go on. Where do you go?"

"I go and sit in my tree." Doc said it with pride as if Louise should have been impressed with what he had just told her.

"In a tree?" Louise thought it sounded a typical boy place. "That's a daft place."

"No, really, it's a place you could also go to."

"Why would I want to go and sit in a tree?"

"It'll hopefully be a special place to you as well, sometime." Doc saw the look on Louise's face and guessed she had no idea of the relevance of what he had just said to her. "It's the big oak tree out there in the middle of the green." Doc pointed but Louise was not paying attention. "It would be good if you could tell Mum and Dad as well." Doc added. "I mean your mum and dad of course, Louise. They might find it has a special meaning to them as well."

"My dad up in a tree! Now you really are joking. Not even David would climb a tree." Louise picked up her bag. "Right, I'll see you tomorrow." She went through to the front of the coffee bar. "Bye Kathy." Kathy waved back. "Bye Brian." Brian raised his hand in acknowledgement.

Friday was soon here and Louise and Doc chatted again after she had finished work. It was her first pay day, and she had gone upstairs to his little office to get her money. She was pretty excited. Doc went on again about her mum and dad and how much she should appreciate them and look after them when she got older, and also went on about this bloody oak tree he used to sit in as a boy. Normally she would have listened to him more, but her eyes were fixed on all the money lying on the table, and particularly on the money Doc was putting in a little brown envelope for her.

"So, will you tell your mum and dad about the oak tree?"

"If you want me to," Louise replied with little idea exactly what Doc was on about.

"I would like them to know but it would be better coming from you."

"Oh, right."

"It will become a very important place in the future."

"Will it?" Louise had heard similar sorts of things from her teachers talking about other famous buildings. She couldn't remember any of them at the moment. One of them might have even already mentioned the village oak tree but she didn't think so. "I'll tell my dad."

"That'll be good." Doc hoped she would keep her word.

As Louise got home, Michael was just a few yards behind her having walked from the bus stop. She saw him as she opened the door so left it ajar for him.

"Hello, Dad."

"Hello, Louise. Are you ok?"

"Yes, Dad."

"Not too tired after a hard day at school?" Michael half teased her but was also half serious about the question. Louise knew he wasn't happy about her working at Doc's and guessed he was referring to the coffee bar rather than school.

"No, Dad. Not too tired."

Michael said hello to Sue, and then shouted a

greeting to David as he made his way to the bedroom. David had headphones on and was listening to music so Michael never got a reply. Louise stayed in the kitchen with Sue.

"Busy tonight?" Sue asked.

"Yes, it was." Louise dropped herself down on to one of the kitchen chairs and dropped her arms on the table resting her head on them as if to sleep.

"Don't worry. You can have a lie in tomorrow morning."

"Yeah, suppose so." Louise sat up again and started to open her little brown envelope.

"Ooh. How much did you get?"

"Loads." Louise counted each note out on to the table but silently in her head so her mum couldn't find out. "And it's all mine." Louise hugged the notes.

"Well, don't go and spend it all." Sue tried to give her some wise advice.

"Of course I won't."

There was a short pause whilst Louise put the money back into the envelope.

"Do you know anything about the big oak tree on the green?" Louise asked.

"Is that a book?"

"No. I mean the tree in our village. In Somerby."

"What about it?"

"Do you know if it's famous?"

"No I don't think so. Why?"

"Oh, Doc keeps going on about it."

"Well perhaps it is then. You'll have to ask one of your teachers at school. They should know." Louise nodded in reply to Sue's idea but had very little intention of asking.

A little bit later Sue and Michael got talking about Louise and her new job again. Sue knew it was still a touchy subject with Michael and tried to steer the subject away from him as much as possible but it was difficult when he raised the subject himself.

"Is Louise looking tired to you?" Michael thought he was being incredibly subtle with this question. Sue knew otherwise.

"No, not really. She seems very grown up just lately."

"Ah, yes. She's my girl." Michael beamed with pride. "But this job she's doing, it's surely too much for a girl of her age."

"I was doing a paper round every morning when I was her age and that meant getting up early in the morning," Sue replied. Michael though about how much he hated doing his paper round when he was a boy.

"Yes, but that's a much easier job."

"Can be quite dangerous out on their own nowadays."

"Yeah, you've got a point. I'm just thinking that she's being given too much work to do and her education might be the worse for it."

"Don't be daft. It's all part of growing up. She'll be fine." Sue tried to convince Michael. Even she wasn't completely convinced but understood how important that little bit of independence was. Michael said no more. He pondered over Sue's words. He still wasn't convinced.

It was Monday morning and David stood waiting for the school coach. For some completely unknown reason Mary popped up in his thoughts. He hadn't really spoken to her much since the fight with Arthur and he was uncertain how she was. The fact that she had not been on the coach herself for a few days after the event had him quite concerned. He imagined that Arthur wouldn't have thought twice about taking his frustrations out on Mary if the opportunity arose but then he assumed that it was pretty unlikely that such an opportunity would arise. He tried to keep that thought.

As the coach arrived, David saw Mary through the window. He waved but she didn't respond. David wasn't sure whether she had seen him so couldn't be sure if she was ignoring him or not.
"Hello, Mary," David said as he approached her seat. She had another girl sat next to her. Mary looked up at him briefly and smiled, but didn't reply. David continued to the back of the coach fully aware that Arthur was watching both him and Mary.

After Arthur got off the coach, David made straight for Mary. The seat behind her was empty so he sat there. Leaning over the seat, he poked his head into Mary's view.

"Well, hello then."

"Hello." Mary was obviously not happy about him being there.

"Are you ok?"

"Yes, thanks."

"Can I come and sit next to you?" David was quite surprised at the strength of his request.

"I don't think it would be a good idea," Mary answered as she turned her head away, so he couldn't look at her. David assumed that Arthur was probably the reason for this but wished that she could talk to him more.

"I'll see you on the way home."

"Maybe." Mary was not very inviting.

The conversation on the school coach on the way home was pretty much the same, and David eventually got the message. Mary didn't want him sitting next to her, was uncomfortable with him talking to her and generally seemed not to want to know him at all. He felt unhappy. He guessed this was what heartbreak felt like. Not wishing to make a fool of himself though, he accepted the situation as far as he understood it and left her alone. 'Maybe one day' he thought to himself.

Monday at the coffee bar was fairly quiet. Louise wanted to be sat back down with the rest of the girls. Ness and Livvy waved regularly. Melanie and Gillian had come over to say hello. Louise missed sitting with them. But she was glad of the money. It was much better than getting pocket money, as she felt she was able to spend it on whatever she wanted. But she did miss her friends.

Kathy came over and chatted to Louise as she stood by the draining board wiping up a few things.

"How are you finding it then, my love?" Kathy leant against the sink.

"All right I suppose, Kathy."

"Are your parents okay with you working so much?"

"Er, yes." The slight doubting tone in her answer said so much.

"They'll have to come in and see how good a worker you are. They'd be proud of you, you know."

"Would they?" Louise wasn't so sure.

"You know Doc quite well?"

"Yes, I suppose so."

"Is he an uncle or something?" Kathy looked for some sign that they were related in some way.

"Uncle? I don't think so."

"I just wondered, as he seems to look out for you, and of course you live in his house."

"His house?" Louise was really confused now. "It's not Doc's house. He lives here doesn't he?"

"No. He actually lives in a little cottage around the corner, but I know he doesn't live in your house."

"So, it's not his house then?"

"I just know it as Doc's place. Or bungalow really."

Kathy tried to recall what she had seen and been told. "I know he can be a bit weird but he's had a lonely upbringing you know." Kathy was already defending him. "He used to just sit around on that building site and watch every brick being laid for that place. Only that bungalow."

"Oh, right." Again, Louise wasn't taking too much in.

"Nobody knows why. He just kept an eye on that bungalow. Everyone assumed he was going to buy it but he didn't."

"Perhaps he couldn't afford it." Louise had heard her mum and dad talking about the price of houses.

"No, dear. He could have bought the whole bloody estate if he'd wanted to."

Thursday was soon here and Louise was working her usual duties. It was quite busy again and she found herself rushed off of her feet trying to keep up with all the requests for clean glasses or plates. Doc was around again, and he would chat to her briefly during her hour working at the coffee bar. As usual he talked about her parents. He would then go on about the tree. Louise knew where this bloody tree was now he'd gone on about it so much.

"I know Doc. The big oak tree on the green." Louise would say.

"And don't forget to tell your mum and dad," Doc would always add.

They had had this conversation so many times that

Louise practically knew it off by heart. Doc also went on about her looking after her mum and dad. It was a strange thing for Doc to mention but he did. To be honest, Louise was beginning to get absolutely fed up with it.

Friday was as busy as ever and Doc wasn't around. He was dealing with some paperwork upstairs in his office and Louise was quite glad he was out of the way. Kathy and Brian were very busy and Louise was ordered here and then there and Brian shouted at her when she brought him big plates instead of little plates. Louise wanted to cry but she composed herself very well and even fought against the urge to just drop the plates where she was standing. She managed to put the plates down and go back to the sink to wash some small ones. The tears were welling up in her eyes and they started to sting as she held them back. It couldn't last. The first tear dripped down her cheek and then she just cried.

It probably only lasted a couple of seconds but Louise imagined she was crying for ages. She composed herself and then sheepishly looked around to see if everyone was staring at her. She expected that the whole café would be looking but initially she couldn't see anyone. She rubbed her eyes a little bit and looked a bit closer. Nobody. Surely Kathy would have noticed but no, she was busy serving. It would appear that not a single person had really noticed.

Louise pulled herself together and continued working up until nearly five o'clock when she took off her apron and made her way to Doc's office. He was busy fingering through some accounting books so she tapped on the door.

"Come in," Doc shouted out without looking up. Louise pushed the door fully open and made her way towards the edge of the desk. Doc raised his head still tapping his pencil on the side of his nose as he did so. "Ah, Louise. Come in. Ready for your money?"

"Yes, please." Louise replied still using a sorry tone.

"Everything all right?"

"No, not really."

"What is it?"

"Well my mum and dad aren't particularly happy about me working." Louise thought this was the perfect way to get out of working without making it known that she didn't really want to.

"Oh. I'm sorry to hear that but perhaps not completely unexpected."

"I think I ought to stop working to stop them from arguing." Louise wasn't quite sure how thick to lay it on.

"No, you're quite right. Look if they want to come and visit, perhaps I can put their minds at rest."

"I'll see." Louise wasn't overly happy with the answer but at least she had mentioned something. She wasn't working over the weekend so had a couple of days to try and sort out what to do next.

"There's your money." Doc handed her the small brown envelope. Louise took it and made her way straight home.

As Louise got home she gave her mum a big hug. "Hello, mum."
"What's all this then?"
"I got shouted at tonight." Louise started her sorrowful story.
"What, by Doc?"
"No by Brian. He made me cry."
"The beast. What happened then?" Sue gave Louise a big strong comforting hug to help the bad feelings disappear and happy thoughts come back.
"He just shouted at me when I gave him some plates."
"Did you tell Doc?" Sue was angry. "Did he make him apologise?"
"No." The tone of Louise's answer suggested that she had not received an apology. "And they make me work so hard."
"Did you get paid?" Sue wondered if her daughter may have got sacked.
"Yes." Louise held up the envelope. "I don't want to work there anymore." Louise pretended to cry again. Sue hugged her once more.
"It's all right darling. You don't have to if you don't want to." Sue tried to reassure Louise but she was surprised at just how quickly she changed.
"Good." Louise withdrew from the hug and opened her wage packet. "I want to go into town tomorrow,

Mum."

"Do you, darling." Sue guessed that Louise wasn't half as upset as she was making out.

"Yes. What's for dinner?" Louise didn't wait for a reply as she skipped off to her bedroom. Sue had an inkling of what that little conversation was all about.

Sue hadn't had the opportunity last night to talk to Michael about Louise and her job. She would have preferred to discuss the situation with her husband privately as she was quite conscious of the fact that Michael and Louise were coming from different directions on the subject. As she cleared away the breakfast things, Louise was getting ready to go out, David was doing something in his bedroom and Michael was pottering around in the back garden. It was a typical Saturday morning.

"Mum, what time have I got to be back?"

"I'll be getting tea ready for half six. I take it you're not going to be in for lunch?"

"No, we'll get something in town."

"Make sure you do." Sue hoped the girls would eat something but guessed they probably wouldn't. Louise looked at the clock. She had loads of time to finish getting ready.

Michael walked towards the kitchen from the garden.

"Are you going out?" he asked Louise as she rushed past him in the direction of the bathroom.

"Yes, Dad. I haven't got much time."

"Have you done your homework?" Michael looked at Sue for some indication whether their daughter had done her homework or not. Sue half shrugged. "Louise." Michael raised his voice.

"What?"

"Have you finished your homework?"

"Not all of it. I'll finish it off later today." Louise locked the bathroom door as she shouted her answer. Michael walked into the kitchen.

"All right with you?" he asked Sue. She nodded. "Is she alright?"

"I think she's having one or two problems with her job."

"What?" Michael seemed to overreact. Sue regretted the way she had mentioned it but at least she had brought up the subject.

"Nothing serious." Sue tried to bring the problem into perspective. Louise came back into the kitchen having applied some make-up.

"What problems are you having at work?" Michael was straight in with the question.

"They keep shouting at me when I haven't done anything wrong." Louise was quite unaware of the effect her answer was to have on her dad. He looked across at Sue.

"It's not that bad." Sue added to try and calm the potential eruption.

"You weren't there, Mum. You don't know." Louise believed she had to enhance the problem to get the support of her parents should she decide to leave, so considered adding a little bit more. "And they make me do all the work, and Doc keeps asking me stupid questions."

That was pretty much the last straw for Michael. He was annoyed that neither Louise nor Sue had been prepared to listen to his original concerns over the notorious Doc. Both were keen to defend this man they didn't really know, and that annoyed him even more. Louise returned to the bathroom leaving Michael and Sue in the kitchen.

"I'm going to let him know just what a tyrant he is."

"Don't be stupid, Michael." Sue knew he was annoyed. "He's trying to run a business just like you do."

"He's got no right employing young girls." Michael began to pace around the kitchen. "And then force them to work harder than his full-time staff."

"He's not doing that at all, dear. Louise is just not used to working hard and she's finding it difficult. Doc isn't doing anything wrong or illegal." Sue was surprised at her own support for Doc. There was something about him she liked. It wasn't sexual at all. Just nice.

"I think we need to come to some arrangement with him though." Michael wouldn't let the subject drop.

"Yeah, maybe." Sue brought the subject to a close.

It was nearly an hour later that Michael managed to find an excuse to get out of the house. They had run out of butter and Sue needed some for tea.

"I'll pop down the shop and get some, darling." Michael volunteered.

"Ah, that's nice of you."

"Do you need anything else at all?"

"No, I don't think so." Sue couldn't think of anything else that wouldn't wait for the weekly shop. "No, just the butter, dear."

Michael almost ran down to the shop, or at least looked as if he was competing in a walking race. He was quite ungainly when he ran but he was on a mission. His mind was running through just exactly what he was going to say to this Doc when he got there. He guessed he would forget the butter if he didn't buy that first so that was what he did. With the butter safely in a shopping bag he made his way round to Doc's. It was full of teenagers, all standing around as if they were looking for trouble.

As he entered it seemed as if everyone turned to look at him. It lasted only a split second before everyone continued with whatever it was they had been doing previously. Michael made his way to the till where Brian was serving coffees.

"What can I get you?"

"I want to see Doc. Is he in?" Michael was ready to get straight to the point.

"Yeah, I think so. Who can I say it is?"

"Say it's Louise's dad."

Just then, Doc appeared through the door behind the counter.

"Dad." Doc repeated the word. "Hello, Louise's

Dad." Doc held out a hand as if to shake Michael's, but Michael didn't take up the offer.

"I want to have a word with you." Michael made it clear. Doc was strangely excited about the whole thing, but he quickly realised that Michael was annoyed.

"Ah, all right. Will you come up to the office?"

The two made their way up the stairs and Doc pulled a chair out for Michael to sit down.

"I'm going to make this quick." Michael was holding the plastic shopping bag extra tightly. Doc waited. "My daughter Louise isn't happy working here and you're the main reason."

Michael expected Doc to protest or at least defend himself and was ready to launch into a verbal attack but Doc surprised him.

"Oh, right." Doc scratched and rubbed the side of his face uncertainly.

"Yes." Michael almost had his breath taken away from him as he didn't get the answer he had expected. "And she is being worked too hard."

"Right." Doc nodded in agreement. There was a short pause. "Has she mentioned the big oak tree to you?"

"What?" Michael thought this might have been some incident that Louise had got into trouble for that he had not been told about.

"The big oak tree on the green."

"What has she done?"

"No. I need you to know that the big oak tree will

be important to you one day."

"What?" Michael was confused. "What are you going on about?"

"I asked Luce to tell you about the tree."

"Look I don't think my daughter will be that happy working here anymore and if you want to keep your staff you need to be more thoughtful about your younger staff."

"Oh, yes I will." Doc stood up as Michael stood and turned to leave. "Look Da…n," Doc appeared to be having trouble remembering what Michael's name was.

"The name's Michael."

"Yes, sorry, Michael. Try and remember about the tree."

"I haven't got a clue what the hell you're going on about." Michael left the office. He was happy he'd delivered his feelings. As he made his way down the stairs he could hear Doc still chattering on about a bloody tree. 'The man's a fool' he thought to himself. Hope my son doesn't grow up to be like him.

Michael was in a pretty confused state, as he wasn't quite sure if Doc had realised he had just been told off. The more he thought about it, the more he was uncertain himself whether he had told Doc off. He started to calm down a little as he walked up Rawthorn Drive. By the time he reached home, he considered the matter dealt with.

"Thanks, darling." Sue grabbed the bag with the

butter in and gave Michael a little kiss. He put his arm around her waist and gave her a little squeeze. "Ooh. That's nice."

"So, what have you told Louise about her job?"

"That we'll support her whatever she wants to do." Sue knew that this might be the right time to get this sorted. "She's just finding it hard. Having to actually do some work."

"But if she's being mistreated down there, I don't want her working for Doc."

"Yes, I know dear but don't blame him for Louise's situation."

"Well who else do I blame?" Michael wasn't quite as annoyed as he had been.

"He's running a business. He needs staff that are happy to work. I'm not sure that Louise realises that."

"Well, I'd rather pay her myself than have her working there," Michael said, without really thinking.

"You'll do nothing of the sort! She'll never grow up realising what life is all about if you just spoil her like that." Even before Sue had finished her reply, Michael knew she was right. At last the two of them were on the same track over this.

"Okay. You're right." Michael smiled. He almost laughed at the way he had been so stupid over it all.

"Look, she'll be told again that you're not happy, but she if she decides to carry on working, you'll support her." Sue told him.

"Yes. I will."

Sue managed to get Louise alone in the kitchen that evening to let her know what decision she and Michael had made. It was quite an adult moment really, and one that Sue was extremely proud of afterwards. Louise listened, made comments back and in the end seemed to fully understand where everybody stood on the point. Sue found it quite a magical moment.

Louise had a pretty good day at school. Monday was a strange day as it started with maths, which Louise hated, then English, which she wasn't very good at, but it finished with music and then art both of which she loved. Nearly all the gang liked art, all except Livvy.

As the lesson came to an end and the girls were packing up ready to leave, they all congregated around Tina. She was most definitely the leader as far as the gang was concerned. It was very much a case of natural selection as she was the bossiest and most difficult of them all. Louise had only joined the gang a few months ago, but she quickly recognised who to obey and who to argue with. You didn't argue with Tina.

"Are we all going down to Doc's then?" Melanie asked.

"Yes!" The reply came from nearly everyone.

"What about you?" Tina turned to Louise.

"What about me?"

"Are you working again?"

"Well, I'm supposed to."

"Huh." Tina replied. She almost turned her back on Louise as if to give her the cold shoulder.

"Well, that's all right, isn't it Tina? Louise will come and sit with us beforehand," Gillian added, sensing there was a bit of tension. Tina didn't reply. The girls all picked up their bags and made their way out of school and towards the coffee bar.

As they all took their places around their usual table Tina tried to make it obvious that Louise wasn't to sit on the inside of the table but on the outside. It was cleverly done as she chatted to each of the girls in turn.

"You sit there Gillian. You sit there Melanie," and so on until there was only a small space left for Louise at the far side of the table. Louise felt the brush off as clearly as if Tina had swept her away with a broom. Ness knew how Louise was probably feeling, but didn't want it to change as it meant she had moved up in the ranks of the gang.

"Whose turn to buy?" Tina looked at Louise. "Your turn."

"I got some the other day," Louise pleaded. The others all looked at Tina with anticipation.

"You've got more money than the rest of us. Your turn," Tina ordered. There was no getting away from it, Louise was getting the rough treatment. She had put herself in a position that made her different from the rest of the gang and Tina didn't like it.

"Okay, I'll go." Louise wasn't happy but she felt

she ought to get the drinks in case Tina started to have a real go at her.

As Louise made her way over to the counter Kathy waved. "All right Louise? Did you have a good weekend?"

"Yes, thanks Kathy."

"Do you want anything?"

"Yes, please. Can you get me five different cans of drink?"

"Five!" Kathy was a bit surprised. "We're not low on straws, you know."

"I know. Five it is."

Kathy opened the cooler and took out five different cans of drink, placing them all on a tray. "That'll be two pounds eighty-five please, Louise."

"Okay." Louise opened her purse and searched for some change. "Any chance you can take them over to my table?" Louise knew it was a bit cheeky and Kathy gave her a look which confirmed it.

"Please? I need to go and see Doc."

"Yes, all right."

Louise went behind the counter, through the door, up the stairs and to the office where Doc sat at his desk. As he heard her approach his office he turned around.

"Hello, Louise. Wasn't sure if we'd see you today or not."

"Why?"

"How are things with your dad?"

"Oh, that. Well." Louise was about to say that everything had been sorted out when she realised that a situation had arisen. "He's not happy I'm working here, you know?"

"Huh, yeah. I did realise." Doc half laughed as he replied.

"So, I think it would be best if I gave in my notice." Louise thought there would be uproar from Doc but he was quite calm.

"Yes, I suppose it is."

"You'll probably need me to work a couple of days until you get someone else."

"No. If your dad isn't pleased, then you shouldn't continue working. We'll manage."

"Oh, thanks," Louise smiled as she replied. She then realised that perhaps she should pretend to be a bit more upset about it all but the moment had gone. She turned to go downstairs, but Doc called her back.

"Louise."

"Yes, Doc."

"Thanks for the work you have done here. It meant a lot to me." Doc handed her a ten-pound note.

"What's this for?"

"I have to pay you some severance pay."

"Oh, right." Louise looked at the money in her hand and then back up at Doc. He gave a smile that felt warm and friendly. He seemed almost sad at the same time. Louise couldn't really understand why the moment was as it was, but it was strange. She went back downstairs. 'I wish he was my dad,' she thought to herself. When she got to the counter, Kathy was there.

"Can I have another coke, please, Kathy?"

Louise returned to the table with her coke happy that she didn't have to leave the gang to go and work. She didn't tell any of them when she first returned, but when four o'clock came around and Louise was still sat there, they all asked what had happened. When she explained that she had resigned, they all seemed upset but pleased at the same time. Tina said nothing. By the time the girls got ready to go home though, Louise was sat next to Tina and very much a full member of the gang again.

June 1995

Michael had another driving lesson. He had had seven or eight lessons now, and was getting used to it. Glen would always put him through the usual routine when he first got in the car.

"Okay, adjust your seat." Glen waited until Michael slid the seat backwards and forwards to the right place. "Now check your rear view mirror and adjust that accordingly." Michael obliged. "Just a little thing to mention here. When you go to do your driving test you'll have driven up in this car, we hope."

"Yes, I hope so."

"Well just before you get out to go and see the examiner, I will move your rear view mirror so you have to adjust it when you get back in."

"Oh, right." Michael answered with an affirmative, but he had missed the reasoning and Glen realised he had.

"It's so that the examiner can see you adjust the mirror."

Glen continued to give Michael some little tips and they were soon on their way. Michael was quite comfortable driving now and it showed. His speed was starting to increase and his concentration would sometimes get distracted by things going on outside of the car.

"I think you should try and book your test, Mr Riddell." Glen said, as the lesson came to an end. "I think you'll be ready by the time you get a date but we won't stop the lessons. Just get one booked and as soon as we know when it'll be, we can work towards it." Michael was over the moon.

The weekend was soon around again and David slept in before eventually getting up around half past ten. He wandered into the kitchen yawning, dressed only in his pyjama bottoms.

"Hey, Mum. Can I have some milk?"

"Yes, darling. There's plenty in the fridge," Sue replied. David opened the fridge and took the bottle over to the kitchen table. He sat down on one of the chairs, and started to drink straight from the bottle.

"Don't do that, dear," Sue said in an angry tone.

"I can't be bothered to get a glass."

"You can't be bothered to get anything." Sue

grabbed a glass from the cupboard and brought it over to the table. "There. Drink out of that."

David poured some milk into the glass and then slowly drank some of it. He watched what his mum was doing as she programmed the washing machine. He looked out of the front window to see if anything was going on outside. It wasn't.

"I'm bored," David declared.

"What do you want to do?"

"I could go into town."

"And do what?"

"Buy some cds."

"Have you got any money, then?" Sue didn't think he had.

"Can I have a fiver?"

"Not unless you're prepared to do something for it."

"Like what?"

"Weed the garden." Sue waited for her suggestion to sink in before turning to look at David's reaction. She wasn't surprised. He looked as if he'd just sucked a lemon. There was a pause in the conversation.

"I'm bored."

"Why don't you try and get a job?"

David's first instinct was to totally disregard his mum's latest idea, but then she added, "Perhaps you can get a job in one of the amusement arcades or a shop on the seafront."

"Hm..." David pondered the idea. It wasn't completely insane after all. He tried to imagine himself serving in one of the restaurants. Getting tips. A big wage packet. The idea was growing on him.

After a few days asking around David found himself working in the bars at Buntin's holiday camp in Shelby Beach. He collected glasses and washed them up mainly which wasn't a great job but there were loads of girls on holiday at the camp and he enjoyed chatting to them.

On his first day he found himself chatting to a girl he liked the look of called Jenny.
"Where do you live then?" David asked her. Although she was wearing sunglasses she had pushed them on to her forehead to reveal her brown eyes.
"Gravesend. Ever 'eard of it?"
"Yes I think it's near Southend."
"No, ducks. It's near Maidstone." Jenny giggled as she replied.
"Have you got a girlfriend?" Pam asked him straight away.
"No, not really."
"Well either you have or you haven't."
"I used to go out with a girl, but not anymore." As David thought about Mary for a split second he wondered what she might have been doing. The thought didn't last long though.

Chapter 11
LIFE CAN BE HARD

Sunday 1st July 1995

It was Sunday morning, and David was up early as he was working now. Having told his mum and dad, everyone in the house was very excited for him. Louise was particularly pleased as it deflected the pressure away from herself.

"It's nearly eight o'clock, are you ready?" Sue shouted to David, who was still in the bathroom. There was the sound of the toilet flushing, the bathroom door unlocking and David appeared.

"Yes, I'm ready."

"Well okay darling. How long will it take you to get to Shelby?"

"It took me about twenty minutes, so I'm going to leave about half past." David had it all sorted in his mind.

David rushed through to the kitchen where he grabbed a warm slice of toast.

"What time are you going to be home?"

"Don't know." David took a bite out of the toast. "I was never told how long I'd be working."

"Well what are you going to do about dinner?" Sue wiped her hands on the tea cloth and considered what she could prepare for David for lunch. "I can do you some cheese sandwiches."

"No, don't worry. I'm sure I can get something there." David wasn't really that concerned about eating. He just wanted to get to work.

"Will you be home for dinner?" Sue persisted.

"Er, I don't know." David truly had no real idea. "Look, Mum, I don't know what time I'm working till."

"Well darling, try and give me a ring when you can to let me know." Sue would have to be content with that. "There must be a pay phone somewhere nearby."

"If I had a mobile phone, I'd definitely be able to ring you." David wanted a mobile phone and took the opportunity to explain why he should have one.

"Don't be daft. You make sure you ring me." Sue said it in a way that David knew he would be in trouble if he didn't ring home.

David enjoyed working at the holiday camp and he was able to meet up with Jenny that evening and kiss her. He was quite pleased with how things had turned out but Mary was still in his thoughts. He worried about how her life might be.

Tuesday came along and it was just another usual morning as David caught the school coach. He saw Mary and he again thought just how beautiful she looked. He felt a little guilty at the thought of what he had been doing with Jenny at the weekend, but as things with Mary had gone quiet he didn't really think of it as cheating. He just knew that Mary was the girl he really wanted.

David hadn't really spoken to Mary for while so he was surprised to see her looking at him as he made his way to the back seats. At the normal time, he walked up and sat next to her.

"Hello," she said, "I haven't seen you for ages."

"Well, I'm always on the coach in the mornings," David replied. "Anyway, you've not been on the coach, so I guess not at school for a while."

"No, I had to help my mum at home as we have had problems and she couldn't cope."

"What, and you have to stay at home?" David was a bit surprised.

"Yes. My mum can't always cope with all the work."

"But she's all right now?"

"Yes." The coach arrived at Mary's school. "Excuse me, I've got to get off." David stood up to get out of her way. "Might see you tonight?" It was a question, but David received no reply.

David didn't get the chance to sit with Mary on the way back so never got to talk to her again that day. In fact, he only said hello a couple of times during the rest of the week as Mary either wasn't on the coach or had someone sat next to her. David guessed she didn't really want anything to do with him and tried to put her out of his mind. It wasn't that difficult most of the time.

Thursday was the last day of term and most of the kids were pretty excited. There was a certain buzz around the bus stop at Somerby and David was pretty excited himself. He had walked down to the bus stop with Alice but Suzanne was already there when they arrived so he had time to think about what he was going to do today. He hadn't spoken to Mary for ages and he was determined to at least wish her a pleasant summer if nothing else. As the coach arrived, David looked for a sign of Mary at the window but he couldn't see her. As he boarded the coach and walked down the gangway, his disappointment grew as he realised that she wasn't on there. It was annoying but not devastating.

Being the first day of the school holidays Sue had expected David and Louise to lie in until quite late, but they were both up earlier than usual. Michael had just left for work but Sue was busy in the kitchen as always.

"What are you two doing up? It's the school holidays!" Sue exclaimed.

"Yes, and that's why I'm up," Louise replied. "Mum, can I go down to Doc's?"

"But it won't be open yet, surely?"

"I think it opens at seven."

"What do you want to go there for now, anyway?" Sue wasn't keen but was struggling to find a reason why her daughter shouldn't go.

"I'm meeting up with the girls."

"They won't be there yet, will they?"

"Should be. Livvy's mum is dropping her off sometime this morning, and I said I'd meet her down there."

"Well, you shouldn't have promised."

"Oh, Mum!" Louise put her hands on her hips and huffed. Sue thought quickly.

"Is your bedroom tidy?"

"Yes."

"I'll come and check."

"You can." Louise knew she was winning. "I'm going to the bathroom." Louise turned and dashed out of the kitchen just as David appeared. They bumped into each other as they passed in the doorway.

"Oy, watch where you're going," David moaned as he pushed Louise out of the way. Louise hit the wall and usually she would have made something of it, but she ignored her stupid brother and continued down to the bathroom.

"And what's your excuse?" Sue asked.

"What?" David didn't understand the question.

"Why are you up so early?"

"I just woke up." David slumped on to one of the kitchen chairs and grabbed for the television remote control. "What's on telly?"

By half past eight, Louise had eaten her breakfast and was on her way out of the house.

"See you later, Mum."

"Bye, darling," Sue replied as she heard the door close. David was still watching the television.

"I think I'll go and listen to some of my music."

"Good idea, my son." Sue walked over to him and

wiped the sand out of his eyes. "Did your sister say whether she was coming home for lunch?"

"I don't know."

"Perhaps you'll nip down to Doc's and find out what she's doing for me in a little while, please."

"Do I have to?" David moaned.

"No, you don't have to but..." Sue started to reply but David interrupted her.

"Yes, I know. I'll go in a while."

"Thank you, darling."

An hour later, David was washed and dressed and ready to go on his errand. He had woken up properly and was feeling a lot better. He looked out of the window. The sun was out and things looked warm and pleasant. He was ready to go out.

"Mum, I'm nipping down to Doc's. Do you want anything from the shops?"

"No, darling. Just find out what Louise is doing please."

"Okay." David set off down Rawthorn Drive and within ten minutes was at Doc's. It was quite obvious that the summer holidays were underway, as there were already a number of kids inside and hanging around outside, and none were in school uniform. Some of the kids were sat on the benches positioned around the big oak tree and everyone was generally having a good time. There were the usual little groups all chatting amongst themselves but no real problems.

David quickly spotted Louise sat inside with Livvy and Melanie so he nipped in to ask what he had been sent down to ask.

"Luce, Mum wants to know if you're coming home for lunch?"

"Oh, I don't know," Louise replied.

"I've got to tell her a time, so what's it to be?"

"Say I won't be back till five."

"Are you sure?"

"Yeah. Tell her five." Louise turned back to chat with Livvy and Melanie, who were both looking at David. "Stop it, you two!" Louise was embarrassed.

David had a quick look around to see if there was anyone he wanted to say hello to but there wasn't. He did notice Bob Packham over the other side of the café at his usual table. There hadn't been any trouble with him for a while so David dismissed him. Terry, his mate, was also over there but that was no problem either. David left Doc's but as he got outside the door he bumped into little Ricky Pascoe who was making his way in.

"Oy, wanker. Watch it!" Ricky said, pushing David out of the way. Ricky was another of the Burgh Boys, and although not really in Bob Packham's gang more or less a friend of his.

"Watch it your bloody self!"

"Yeah? You fancy making something of it?" Ricky Pascoe turned around and pushed David again. David stood and looked him straight in the eye. He considered saying something, but then thought better of it. He noticed out of the corner of his eye that Bob and Terry had started to make their way to the door. Louise and the girls also sensed that something was going on as the rest of the kids in the café all turned and looked.

"Look, there's nothing to be made of it," David said.

"What, you too frightened?"

David was in a quandary. He didn't want this talk of him being afraid to stand up for himself continuing to do the rounds but then he didn't really want to fight. He wasn't quite sure what to do.

"Look, I'm not afraid of you, Packham or any of you Burgh lot," David said. Bob Packham now made his way nearer to Ricky Pascoe.

"What's going on?" Bob asked.

"It's nothing. Just a misunderstanding," David replied.

"Sorry, can someone who can speak proper tell me what's going on?" Bob turned to Ricky.

"This London twat just wants to throw his weight around," Ricky replied.

Louise watched with great concern. She wanted to go and stick up for her brother, but didn't want to cause any problems for herself and the girls.

"What's happening, Louise?" Melanie asked.

"I don't really know."

Terry had by now joined the other two and stood by Bob's side. David watched intently waiting for one or more of them to make a move on him.

"My mate Ricky's waiting for an apology." Bob took a step closer to David. Bob wasn't really interested in a fight either but he saw this as an opportunity to get one over on David.

"Well he's going to have to wait then," David replied. He noticed that Ricky had already clenched his right fist. He guessed he knew who would probably try and get the first punch in. It was a bloody pain but David daren't stand down now. He would have to battle this one out.

"Are we going to make him apologise then?" Ricky said out loud.

"Yeah, let's show him." Terry added. Both lads looked keen to get into a fight with David. Bob looked David straight in the eye. He knew that David probably wouldn't back down. So, he took two steps back and turned to go back into Doc's.

"Go on then, Ricky. If you think you can make him apologise. I'm going back in."

"Er, what?" Ricky said, as the colour suddenly drained from his face. Terry was quick to also follow Bob back into Doc's. David meanwhile stood his ground. Ricky thought better of it. "I'll leave it this time." Ricky quickly followed the other two back inside and the tension disappeared. All the kids saw this as a victory for David. David sighed with relief but as quietly as he could.

Livvy and Melanie had by now got to a position where they could watch what had been happening.

"Your brother's so cool," Melanie said.

"Is he?" Louise tried to play it down but she was also proud of him. "He's always been a bit of a fighter, apparently."

"What do you mean, apparently?" Livvy queried.

"Well, Mum told me that when he was born everybody thought he was going to die."

"Oh," replied Livvy and Melanie almost in harmony.

"Yeah, but after a few days he got stronger and the doctors said he must have some fight in him to stay alive."

"Ah, that's sweet." Melanie tried to picture David as a little baby.

David was by now well established at the holiday camp and he found himself working most days or evenings. This was great as it kept him occupied and brought some well needed cash in for him but he was a bit down that he wasn't able to be with the girl he couldn't get out of his head. David had decided he really wanted to try and ask Mary out again. He couldn't help it, but despite liking all the girls he had chatted to whilst at work, it was always Mary he really wanted to be with.

The school holidays were now in full swing and already the days were getting boring. Louise was okay because she spent most of her time with her friends in Doc's, and David found working at Buntins meant the time passed easily. The family had their holiday planned for next Saturday and David couldn't wait. They were going to a house in York. It was going to be something different as they had really only been to holiday camps previously but now Michael had learnt how to drive, they had a little bit more freedom. Louise, on the other hand, wasn't that keen to go. She had made some good friends and didn't want to leave them, even for a week.

David didn't spend much time at Doc's, and would only go in there if he needed to meet Luce for any reason. This Saturday afternoon, after he had returned from working in the morning, he was sent down to give Louise a message about dinner. He knew where Louise would be, and she was told to be home by five as the rest of the family were going into town to have dinner. She understood the message even though all the girls tried their best to confuse the situation.

"Are you coming with us?" Louise asked.

"No, I've got to work," David replied. David decided to leave Doc's. As he left, who should he see outside but Mary. She was standing there as if she was just waiting for him. Dressed in jeans and trainers and a long t-shirt with a cardigan around her shoulders, it was the first time that David had managed to see her out of her school uniform. Her long hair was left free flowing and she had a shoulder bag. His heart beat a little faster and he smiled. He looked around for her mother's car.

"Hello," David said.

"Hello," Mary replied. There was an embarrassing silence for a few seconds before David spoke again.

"Is your mum picking you up?"

"No." Mary shook her head and smiled as she replied.

"So, are you shopping for her?" David was confused about what she might be doing in Somerby. He hadn't been able to speak to her for ages, and since the fight with Arthur they had hardly said a word. David wondered how things might be between them.

"No," Mary answered.

"So, what are you doing here?" David stepped nearer to her.

"I'm with my sister. She's in there." Mary pointed at Doc's.

"But you're out here?"

"I don't really like it in there." Mary wasn't prepared to say that the real reason she was here was in the hope of bumping into David.

"I'm going for a walk up to the post office. Can you come?" David assumed there would be some reason why she couldn't.

"Yes. I've just got to tell my sister. Wait there." Mary ran into Doc's. David saw her in a very different light. She was happy and jolly. In seconds she had returned. "Right. Where's the post office?"

"This way." David turned to walk in that direction and Mary walked next to him. "How long have you been here?"

"Not long," Mary lied.

"I've got to post a letter. This is where I have to wait for the school coach..." David and Mary chatted as they walked around Somerby.

The two of them talked for ages, talked about things in Yarmouth, the amusements and shops. What Leafby was like and how much Mary liked Somerby. David couldn't stop looking at Mary, her face, her skin, her eyes. He found them all incredibly amazing. He wished she was a little bit more like some of the girls he had met at Buntins, but knew that she just wasn't. They were getting on well but like all good things, Mary was being picked up by her mum and the time had come to an inevitable end. As it turned out, David himself had to be home, so he left Mary at Doc's.

"Will you be here next week?" Mary asked.

"Yes, of course," David replied.

"Good, then I'll see you here?" Mary was about to arrange a time when David realised he had a problem.

"I've just realised. We're going on holiday next Saturday. I won't be here."

"Oh." Mary said nothing else.

"Can I see you during the week at all?"

"I don't think I can get away during the week but I'll try."

"Look, have you got a piece of paper?"

"I think so. In my bag." Mary searched through her shoulder bag and pulled out a small scrap of paper.

Then she found a pen. She handed them to David. He wrote down his address and telephone number and then handed the piece of paper back to Mary.

"You can ring me or call round anytime. If I'm not in, someone will tell you where I am." David held Mary's hands. "Please try and get over here." David thought for a second. "Or I could come over and see you in Leafby."

"No, you can't do that. I'll come and see you." Mary was adamant. David wanted to kiss her there and then but he didn't want to spoil anything. Mary wasn't like the girls he'd been seeing at the holiday camp. He would wait until she kissed him. There wasn't anything else to be said, really.

"Okay, bye, then." David started to walk home waving as he did so.

Thursday 8th August 1995

It was about two o'clock on Thursday afternoon and David was at home watching the telly. Louise was out with the girls, and Michael was at work. The telephone rang and Sue answered it.

"David, it's for you," Sue shouted, holding the phone out to him. David came into the hall and took the receiver from her.

"Hello."

"Hello, David, it's Mary."

"Mary! Hello."

"You told me to ring."

"Yes, and you have. Are you all right?"

"Yeah, I'm okay."

"Are you coming to Somerby?"

"No, but I've got to go into town to get some things for my uncle."

"What, into Yarmouth?"

"Yes. I just wondered if you might also be going?"

"I can."

"I'll be catching -" Mary stopped rather abruptly and obviously put her hand over the phone. David couldn't hear much. Suddenly she came back on. "I'll be at St. Nick's school at three if you can make it, bye." It was a hurried message and the phone went down. David replaced the receiver and went in to chat to his mum.

"Do you mind if I go into town?"

"No, son. What are you going in for?" Sue asked.

"Nothing. Just need to sort something out."

"Okay."

David made his way down to the bus stop and was pleased to find that he wouldn't have to wait too long, only twenty minutes. This would have been a long time in London, but in Somerby it was almost like the bus waiting for you. David worked out that it would get him into town by about ten to three which would be just right. He could get to Mary's school by three. In fact, he got there at five to. Mary was already there. As she saw him approach she started to move towards him. David could see her happy eyes and he smiled. He wanted to cuddle her and held his arms out to invite her but she kept her distance.

"Thanks for coming," Mary said.

"No probs. What's happening then?" David looked at Mary and in particularly how she was dressed. The weather was fine, the sun out and the temperature quite hot but here she was dressed in jeans and a knitted long sleeved blouse that seemed to David to be quite a heavy garment to be wearing. She had a denim jacket over the top, but it seemed to be a bit big for her. All the other girls were wearing sleeveless tops and shortish skirts, but not Mary. David tried not to let her notice that he was looking at her in such a way.

"Oh, I hope you don't mind, but I've got to do some shopping for Mum."

"What shopping?"

"Some things from Wilkinson's mainly, and she needs me to get some toiletries from the cheap shop."

"Perhaps we can then go for a walk down Regent Road?" David asked.

"My sister is always telling me about Regent Road."

"Your sister?" David looked at Mary as she replied.

"Yes, she's been down Regent Road a few times."

"And you?"

"I think I walked down there last summer with Mum."

"You don't get out much, do you?" David was almost laughing as he said it but then he noticed that Mary wasn't finding it that funny. "Oh, sorry." David put his hands together in a praying form as if to ask for her forgiveness. She just shook her head.

"Come on then, where are we going first?"

"To Wilkinson's."

The two of them went around the shops to buy the things on Mary's list. When David was satisfied that she had got everything she needed, he asked again about Regent Road.

"Let's go and have a look down Regent Road."

"Yeah, okay, but I've got to catch the four thirty bus back."

"That's early!" David exclaimed.

"Mum will tell me off if I don't catch it."

"Okay." David looked at his watch and it was just ten to four. "Look, we've got about twenty minutes. We can walk a little way."

"Come on, then." Mary started over the pedestrian crossing and David took the shopping bag from her.

"What are you doing?" Mary asked.

"Let me carry that for you." Mary wouldn't let go.

"No, I must carry the shopping."

"Who says?" David wouldn't give in. "I'll give it back to you before you go home." Mary gave in and let him carry it but it was obvious that she wasn't entirely happy about it. They made their way down Regent Road and David moved his arm out to invite Mary to put her arm in his. She did nothing.

"What are you doing?"

"We can walk together down the road." He looked around and pointed out other couples who were walking arm in arm. "Look like them." Mary looked at the other couples.

"But they are all stupid."

"What do you mean by stupid?" David wasn't quite sure what she meant.

"They are all in love." Mary replied. David found this a bit difficult to answer.

"Well maybe some are but they are only walking arm in arm so they don't lose contact with each other." David stuck his arm out again. "You don't want to lose me, do you?"

"Not really." Mary reluctantly put her arm in David's. David almost smirked from ear to ear with the result but he could sense that she wasn't happy with the situation, but she didn't take her arm away and David was content with that. They looked in a shop which sold metal jewellery, some with coloured glass in. There was all manner of different styles. "I like that one," Mary said as she used her free arm to point to a necklace. David thought it was all a bit ugly, but he didn't say so.

"Which one?"

"The one with the blue diamond in it."

"It's not a diamond, Mary."

"Well, whatever it is. The blue one."

"Don't you like that little one up there with the red glass?" David saw what he thought was probably the better looking piece of jewellery in the window, but Mary didn't agree.

"No, I like the blue one."

They moved down to the next shop which was a glass stall. There was a man making small ornaments. They stood and watched for a few minutes. Mary was in awe of how the basic glass turned into little shapes.

"I like them," Mary said.

"Yeah they look quite nice."

"They are expensive though." Mary looked at some of the prices in the window. "It's good down here, isn't it?"

"We've only just started. The road goes right down to the seafront."

"Wow." Mary looked down to where the sea was. "I don't think I have walked down here before, and I'd like to walk down there one day."

"Well let's go now." David had forgotten the time.

"I've got to get home."

"Oh, yes. Sorry, I'd forgotten." He looked at his watch. "We better start making our way back," David said and they did. They headed straight for the bus stop but stopped at the rock shop on the way. As they walked back to the bus stop, David realised that Mary had by now got her arm properly in his and she was holding him tight. It was a nice feeling. Mary hadn't really realised that she had held him tighter but she was just happy at being there with him. As they got to the bus stop, Mary's bus was waiting. There was still five minutes before it was due to leave, though.

"What time does your bus leave?" Mary asked as she took her arm out of David's and started to take her bag of shopping back.

"I can get the same bus as you."

"What? Does it go through Somerby on the way back?"

"No, I'll get off at Leafby and walk from there." David sensed the tension in Mary as he said it.

"No, you can't get off at Leafby, please." There it was again, the worry in Mary's face.

"Okay, I won't." David held Mary's free hand and moved forward to kiss her. She moved back.

"What are you doing?"

"I was just going to say goodbye with a kiss."

"No, none of that kissy stuff. I don't kiss." Mary was in a panic. "Bye." Mary turned and got on the bus. She made her way to her seat and looked at David through the window. As the bus started to move she waved at David. He waved back and then blew her a kiss. She just waved.

David stood bemused. He just couldn't make her out. Mary wasn't like the other girls he had met this summer. Mary seemed to want to be with him but then he'd do something to scare her off. It was most confusing. David made his way back to Regent Road. He wasn't going home yet. He walked back down the same route and looked at the same shops. He thought about what had happened and whether he had done something wrong. Very soon though it was time to get off to work so he made his way back to the bus stop.

A few weeks had passed and the Riddell's had had their holiday in York. It was Saturday morning again, and the Riddells had been home a week. David was having a lie in having worked the previous evening, and had Saturday morning off, but by nine thirty he had woken up and after some coercion had managed to get washed and dressed. He wasn't going to work till one so had a few hours to waste. David hadn't heard the doorbell or any knocking, but he was aware that his mum was talking to someone. It wasn't Louise as she had already left to go down to Doc's. Sue shouted him.

"David!" It was a call to come into the kitchen so he did as he was told. As he entered he almost fell over when he saw Mary stood there.

"Mary." David gulped and looked at his mum who was giving him one of those cheeky looks. "Mary," David said again. "Er, sit down." He pointed to the kitchen seats and Mary took up his invitation. "Sorry, I wasn't expecting you."

"You're bloody lucky that he's got dressed," Sue added.

"Mum!" David wanted to say shut up but he didn't.

"Do you want to go for a walk?" David asked Mary. She didn't reply but just nodded hurriedly. "Give me a mo." David went back to his bedroom returning quickly with his glass collecting coat. As he returned he heard Sue was trying to engage Mary in conversation. It wasn't working. When he came back in he could see that Mary was uncomfortable.

"Oh! This is Mary," David said to his mum.

"Hello, Mary," Sue replied.

"Mary, this is my mum. She's mad," David said to

Mary.

"That's why he's so mad, so don't blame him, will you?" Sue added. Mary said nothing.

"I'm going to go out but will probably go straight to work. I'll see you tonight."

"Okay, son. Be careful," Sue said as she went to open the door. "Nice to meet you, Mary." Mary still didn't reply.

David wasn't surprised to see Mary in jeans and a long-sleeved t-shirt. It wasn't as if she was flat chested, as she clearly wasn't. On many occasions David had seen evidence that Mary wore a bra, but she always seemed to dress in an unflattering manner. David and Mary walked over the fields towards the cliffs that overlooked the sea. David had established that Mary had all day, and he had until one o'clock so there was time to walk some of the way at least. David didn't want to push anything so he just walked with Mary.

"Sorry to just come round without being asked," Mary said apologetically.

"Bloody hell, Mary! You don't have to apologise. I said to come round whenever."

"But you seemed annoyed I'd called round."

"No, I was just surprised as you have never come round before." David hoped she understood. They made their way across a half-ploughed field and to the entrance of a small wood. David started to make his way into the wood but Mary stopped. David turned around and looked at her.

"It looks a bit spooky," Mary said, frightened to take just one step into the woods.

"It's not. I've been through this wood loads of times, come on." David held his hand out and Mary grabbed it. They walked through the wood at a quick pace avoiding any large fallen trees. Mary let go of David's hand. They found themselves at the start of a narrow path that ran along the side of the wood. David led the way and Mary followed.

As the path came to its natural end they stood in front of a stile. There was a signpost showing the direction of the public footpath.

"Once we get over this stile, we cross the field and we're almost down to the beach." David said.

"I don't know if I can get over that," Mary said, looking at the style.

"It's not that hard. I'll help." David tried to reassure her. He got up on to the stile and held out his hand to help Mary up. As she got up the two of them got very close to each other and there was a moment where David couldn't be sure what Mary was thinking. He wanted to kiss her again but remembered his promise. He sat on the top of the stile, then Mary lifted one leg over and sat in front of him. David held her waist with one hand and felt her long hair touching the back of it. He breathed in the smell of her body. That wasn't to say that it was anything perfumed, just a nice clean smell. David could have sat there for ever.

He stroked her hair with his hand and he sensed that Mary wasn't happy with what he was doing, so he took his hand away quickly, and held her waist with his other hand. She was thin but perfectly shaped. The moment lingered, and Mary attempted to lift her left leg over to get off the stile.

"No, hang on a minute. From here we can just about see the sea." David pointed in the direction she should look. She tried.

"I can't see it."

"Stand up. You'll see it then." David was certain she would be able to. As Mary started to get to her feet she found it hard to keep her balance and she started to topple but stopped herself by putting her hand down on David's leg. He put both hands on her waist which by now was right in front of his face, in order to help her keep her balance. As Mary turned to look and try and catch sight of the sea, her long hair swished and swayed in front of David. It was almost magical. As she stretched to look at the sea David could see her bare flesh around her waist. The little hairs on her skin were visible and she was all goose fleshed.

"I can see it. I can see it!" Mary shouted. "Can you hear it, David? Isn't it just wonderful?"

Mary was almost in heaven. She could make out the crashing of the waves in the distance and see the sea. The wind was blowing through her hair, and the green fields were in full colour. There were yellow daisies all around and the world was just beautiful. That was until she saw what looked like a bull in the field. She sat back down and started to climb down from the stile the way they had come. "David, there's a bull!" David kept hold of her waist and stopped her from moving freely.

"I know it's a bull. It's always here."

"And you were going to let me walk across that field?"

"It's okay to walk across the field. I've done it before."

"But there's a bull in the field."

"It's okay." David tried to calm her down, while Mary still tried to get off of the stile.

"Trust me. It's alright."

David got down into the bull's field and looked up at Mary holding his arms out. "The bull's probably more scared of what we might do." Mary wasn't convinced. "Look I've walked through the field before and I know it's fine." David moved his arms to indicate that she should join him. Mary moved her leg over the top of the stile and sat looking down at David.

"Are you sure?"

"It's all right, come on." Mary jumped down and David caught her. They were in an embrace and Mary was breathing rather deeply. David felt her body next to his, and he wanted to give her a hug. All Mary wanted to do was hide from the bull. From her relative safety behind David, she decided to have to have a look and see where the bull was. She put her hands on David's shoulders and peeked over. She put her head back almost immediately.

"Is it there?" David asked.

"I don't know. I can't see it," Mary said and she laughed at the whole situation. She looked again but this time caught a glimpse of the bull. She rested her head lightly on David's arm to look more, and as she did the bull looked up. "Ooh!" Mary screamed, and hid herself behind David again. David held her close to him and it seemed to make her feel safer. David turned around to check where the bull was, and noting that it was well over on the far side he grabbed hold of Mary's hand and started to pull her.

"Come on, let's get to the other side."

They didn't run, but swiftly made their way across the field to another stile and into a little grassed area on the other side. David helped Mary down and they found themselves holding each other. David looked into Mary's eyes and he decided that he could wait no longer. He moved his mouth nearer to Mary's, and just went for it. He managed to kiss her a little before she pulled away again.

"Kissing! You men always want to kiss!" Mary said. David thought it was a strange thing to say, and felt it required some response.

"Was it horrible, then?" David asked. Mary licked her lips and pondered. She looked at him.

"No. In fact it was quite nice." This time Mary made the first move and they kissed again. It probably only lasted a few seconds, but it felt like an hour. Both of them were slightly uncomfortable with the effects the kissing was having but they both wanted to carry on, and they did. David would have liked the moment to have gone on for longer but he had to go to work. He walked Mary back to Doc's before catching the minibus to work. Standing outside, they discussed when they might meet again.

"Can you get out on Monday?" David asked.

"No, not really. That would be difficult. I can do Tuesday, though," Mary suggested.

"No, I can't." David sighed. He kissed Mary again. "What about Thursday? I'm off Thursday."

"I think so, but it would probably only be till about four."

"Tell your mum that you're coming out with me for tea!" David thought this was a brilliant idea.

"She doesn't know who you are. I haven't told her I'm with you."

"Oh."

"Look, I'll see what I can do. I'll ring you on Thursday morning, okay?" They kissed again before David had to go.

Thursday seemed a long time coming although David had been working extra hours and he was quite tired. He still made sure he was up reasonably early so he could be ready when Mary rang. He didn't have to wait long. The phone rang not long afterwards. Sue answered it.

"Hello!" It was Sue's usual greeting. "Oh, hello Mary, do you want to talk to David?" There was a brief pause and then Sue shouted for David. He was already there. He grabbed the phone.

"Hello, Mary, are you okay?"

There was a little conversation and Sue went back to her chores in the kitchen. Suddenly, David appeared. "Mum, can you tell Mary's mum that we'll make sure she gets her tea? Otherwise she'll have to go home at four," David said.

"Are you inviting her round here for tea?" Sue looked at him.

"Please, Mum." Sue went out to the phone.

"Hello, is that Mary's mum?" asked Sue. "Oh, sorry Mary, I thought your mum was on the phone." There was a pause. "Would you like to come round here for tea?" There was another pause. "Alright darling, go and get her." Sue turned to David. "I'll have a word with you later." Sue dismissed David and he went off to get ready. Sue continued to chat on the phone, but it didn't last too long. She entered David's bedroom. "Was this your idea?"

"What, Mum?"

"Inviting Mary round for tea."

"No, it was hers."

"Yeah, might have guessed. It was a nice idea. I might have guessed it wouldn't have been yours."

"Anyway, I don't think she would want to come and have tea with us."

"What? I've just told her mum we'll feed her."

"That's only so she can stay out longer than four o'clock." David continued getting ready.

"Well, that's very bad, getting me to tell lies. She'll just have to come round for tea now."

"No, Mum, honest. She's very shy and won't want to meet everyone. I was hoping that we could go into town anyway."

"Well, now you've made me say Mary will be fed, I'm afraid I've got to make sure she gets fed."

"Oh, Mum!" David sulked. "When I tell her, she'll probably go home at four."

"Do you really think so?" Sue asked but David didn't reply. "So, what are you going to do?"

"Mary's mum is dropping her off at Doc's. We were going to go into town from there."

"Look, I'll do a deal with you." Sue sat down. David wasn't looking forward to this. "The only way you're going to stop me from phoning Mary's mum is by agreeing that we have tea together before she goes home."

"Okay. I'll ask her but don't think she'll come."

"No, look, I have a better idea. I want to go into town to get one or two things so if you two are going into town, you agree to meet me at Pizza Hut and we'll have tea." Sue smiled.

"Mum, that'll be great. Are you sure?"

"Yes. Is Mary's mum picking her up at seven?"

"Yes, from Doc's."

"Right, okay. I'll meet you outside Pizza Hut at five." Sue thought a while. "I'll get Dad to cook for Louise." It was all agreed. David went off to meet Mary.

David and Mary got on the bus to Yarmouth after her mum had left and David explained what he had agreed with his mum. Mary seemed quite happy with the deal, especially as she had never been to Pizza Hut before. As they travelled on the bus they held hands and sat as close to each other as they could. When they got into town David pulled Mary down to Regent Road immediately.

"We're gonna walk all the way down to the seafront today." He looked at Mary.

"Yes, we are!" Mary confirmed. The two looked in all the shops, including the jewellery shop, the glass making shop and the rock factory, and Mary was overwhelmed by it all. Part of the way down there was an indoor market with little shops in it and Mary thought this was marvellous. David thought the shops were crap but he never let on. There was a waxworks museum that Mary didn't know much about so David suggested they went in to have a look. Mary didn't think he would have the money to pay.

"Come on. If you want to have a look at the waxworks, we'll go in."

"You'll pay for me?" Mary was still uncertain.

"Yes, of course. Come on," David said. Mary gave him a big hug and a kiss. It was becoming more like a dream for her.

The rest of the walk down Regent Road passed very quickly. They went on to the pier and spent ages holding hands and looking at the sea. David and Mary were pretty much a couple now and they were talking about all sorts of things. Music, television, school, everything. David also had a little surprise for her.

"Close your eyes, Mary."

"What?"

"Just close your eyes. I've got a present for you." Mary didn't respond how he hoped. She wouldn't shut her eyes, and recoiled a bit.

"I don't like presents," she said, most indignantly.

"I've bought you something." David was disappointed at her response, but almost immediately her tone changed.

"Oh, what have you bought?" Mary seemed keen to find out. She started searching his pockets.

"Wait a minute." David couldn't fathom the change. He withdrew a square box from one of his trouser pockets. "This is for you," he said as he handed her the box. Mary took hold of it, looked at David and then back at the box. "Open it then." She did, and inside was the necklace with the blue glass stone that she had seen in the jewellery shop the other day. She let the necklace dangle down and it twirled around. David took it from her and placed it around her neck. Mary couldn't stop looking at it.

"It's lovely." A tear ran down her cheek. "I can't have it though. My...my...my mum wouldn't be happy." Mary was almost in tears, and stuttered as she spoke.

"I bought it for you." David hugged her. "I can't take it back." He tried to kiss her but she was having none of it. She had stopped crying, but was obviously upset with the gift. David picked up the box and stuck it back in his trouser pocket. Mary meanwhile regained her composure and looked at the necklace again.

"It's lovely. Thank you." She kissed him.

Soon afterwards they set off back towards town and Pizza Hut where they were due to meet Sue. Mary had got over all the fuss and was now wearing the necklace as if it had been given to her years ago. They chatted about various things and all the time they either held hands or walked arm in arm. There were occasional stops for a kiss as well on the way back. Neither seemed to have a care in the world.

Suddenly, David changed the mood.

"So, what is it with you and Arthur Davison?"

"Nothing." Mary gave him a one word answer.

"No, look, please, I think he believes you and he are some kind of item."

"Item?" Mary wasn't fully conversant with the term.

"You know, boyfriend and girlfriend."

"No, I'm not his girlfriend." Mary was now a bit less talkative.

"So, have you ever been?"

"No."

"Or said you might be in the future?"

"Look, no. He's just a…" Mary couldn't get the next word out. "He lives in Leafby, and that's all there is."

"What do you mean, that's all there is. He's a

bloody wanker."

"Dave, don't. Don't let's talk about him. Please."
Mary obviously didn't want to discuss the situation
any more but it was clear that Arthur caused her
some concern.

"Okay, but if he starts causing you any problems,
tell me and I'll come and sort it."

Mary hoped that was the end of the subject.

They met Sue at Pizza Hut, enjoyed a meal, and
then they all caught the bus back to Somerby. Mary
had managed to get David to give her the box that
the necklace came in. The necklace itself was still
proudly hanging around her neck, and David and
Mary were holding hands. Sue thought it was sweet
that her boy might be finding his first love. They
were still chatting away to each other.

"Can you get over to Somerby on Saturday?" David
asked

"I think so. I'll be outside Doc's from about ten
o'clock," Mary said.

"I'll see you then," David replied.

As the bus turned the corner into Somerby, Mary
spotted her mum already waiting for her. The car
was parked beside the bus stop. Mary got ready to
get off the bus almost before it had stopped. She
made her way off and David followed her but she
wouldn't allow him to hold her hand. He tried to
kiss her but she was having none of that either. As
the bus drove away, Mary kissed David very
quickly, but only when she was certain nobody else

could see her. As soon as the bus passed, she crossed the road and made her way to the car. David and his mum crossed normally and were soon some distance from Mary. She ran to the other side of the car but stopped and waved before she got in it. David looked at her but couldn't see the necklace. He waved, and she waved back. Sue also waved. Mary's mum wound her window down as she drove away.

"Thank you for feeding Mary."

"She's always welcome," Sue said.

"Thank you," Mary's mum replied, and then drove off. Sue looked at David who watched the car disappear. As he turned back, she spoke.

"Funny family."

The summer was nearly over and September had already arrived. Saturday was a busy day for David. He had football in the afternoon, and then had to go to work at the holiday camp in the evening. It would be his last day for the summer. He was going to see Mary before he went off to football. He couldn't remember if he'd told her he about the football or not, but hoped she would understand if he'd forgotten.

By ten o'clock David was at Doc's. He was half expecting Mary to be there already, but she wasn't. He walked around for a while and considered going in to the café, but then thought better of it. David considered walking around a circular route that would bring him back to Doc's, just to pass the time but then thought if Mary turned up and he wasn't there, she might not know what to do. He wondered what to do next. He assumed that Mary's mum would drop her off, so it might be that she was delayed for some reason. Maybe some extra cleaning duties came up, he didn't really know. Over by the petrol station there was a wall he could sit on to make waiting a little easier. The clock at the garage said ten thirty-five. David sat there for over an hour. Mary never arrived.

It was the first day of school and it was back to the old routine for David. As far as Louise was concerned it was quite a test, as it was her first day at senior school. She wasn't allowed to catch the same free coach that David caught as she was going to Caister School and the distance didn't warrant free travel. Tina, Melanie and Livvy were all going to Burgh High, whilst Gillian was going to Yarmouth High School. She would be on the coach with David, but so would Vanessa who was going to St. Nicholas' School.

As the coach arrived, Gillian followed what David did.
"Do we just get on when we like?" Gillian asked.
"It can be a bit of a battle sometimes but yes, just get on when you can."
"And we can sit anywhere?"
"More or less."

"Hopefully I'll find Ness on there already and can sit next to her," Gillian said. They got on the coach and Ness was already waving at Gillian. They managed to get seats together. David saw that Mary was sat on her own. He waved to Phil at the back and sat down next to Mary. This was a new thing for him to do and he guessed that the lads on the back seat would all be talking about him. Mary looked at him and smiled briefly then turned back.

"Hi."

"Hello." Mary seemed to have gone back to her shy reluctant ways which David found a bit strange after how far they had come during the summer.

"You didn't make it on Saturday."

"I had to work."

"You didn't ring?"

"I wasn't able to."

"Can I see you after school one day this week?" David knew it wouldn't be easy but was sure there would be a way they could meet up.

"No. I don't think that would be a good idea." Mary replied.

"What. Why not?" David was again confused.

"My mum found out I was with you, and she didn't like it."

"Well, she knew you were with me."

"No, on our own." Mary was sobbing a little. "It's no good talking about it, I won't be able to see you."

David sat there in disbelief. They had got to know

each other so well, and as far as David was concerned they were practically going out, then it all comes to a stop because of her mum. David remembered what Sue had said - funny family. They were certainly that. David tried to engage Mary in further conversation, but she wasn't very talkative. As the coach pulled up outside the High School, the lads from the back started to make their way off of the coach. As they passed David they all slapped him on the back and said cheerio but not Arthur. He was the last one to come down the gangway and he stopped at the seat where David and Mary were sat.

"I hear Mary's been a naughty girl," Arthur sniggered. "Hope she doesn't blame you, London boy." Arthur said no more. David didn't know what to say in reply. Mary just hid her face from both Arthur and David.

"You don't blame me, do you?" David asked but Mary didn't answer. "I thought we were getting on well." David just wanted an answer out of her. "Did I do something wrong?" Whatever the question, Mary wasn't going to answer. Then David asked one more. "Will you see me again?"

"No, I can't." Mary was tearful. David went to the back seat of the coach to join Phil and the girls. His world was in a mess. As it happened, not as much of a mess as Mary's but David didn't know that.

October 1995

The new school year was well into its second month

and David had been working hard studying for his GCSEs, or at least the ones he was having to retake. He hadn't seen Mary for nearly three weeks, and had accepted that she wasn't ever going to be comfortable in his company. It didn't stop him from thinking about her though.

He still had quite a lot of the money he had earned from working at the holiday camp and it had suddenly dawned on him what he wanted to spend some of it on. It wasn't new football boots or an updated music system. He wanted a mobile phone. Several kids had already got them and initially David wasn't that keen but over time he began to see some advantages in having one.

"Mum."

"Yes, son."

"Would you mind if I spent some of my summer job money?"

"I thought you were going to save that?"

"Well, I was, but now I'd like to spend some of it."

"I guess it's yours." Sue sat down to discuss what he wanted to buy. "And what would you like to spend your hard-earned money on, Mr Riddell?"

"I want a mobile phone."

"What do you want one of those for?"

"So I can ring the lads from school, and football."

"But you can do that from here, dear."

"No, I need to be able to ring them when I'm on my way to football. From the bus or in town." David was convinced he wanted a phone. Sue wasn't happy. She thought for a brief second.

"They cost lots of money."

"No, they don't. You can buy one for about fifty pounds." David had already found out the cost.

"But you then have to pay a monthly fee." Sue knew a little bit about mobile phones.

"No, you can get pay as you talk."

"Oh." Sue found it hard to argue.

As it turned out, all the pay as you go phones were nearer to a hundred pounds, but Sue came to an arrangement with David that she would pay half. David got his phone. He was happy. Sue thought she was happy. She hadn't bargained for Louise, who wanted a phone as well. Tina already had one and Louise now had to have one too. Now that her brother had been allowed one, she didn't see why she shouldn't. Sue tried to put her off, but without much success. In the end, all she could do was delay the inevitable for a month or so.

November 1995

It was a very cold November morning and the coach was late getting to Somerby because of the weather. David and Gillian were chatting, waiting for the coach to arrive.

"How are you getting on, Gillian?" David asked.

"What, at the High School?"

"Yes."

"Oh, not too bad really." Gillian thought for a second. "Yeah, in fact pretty well."

"That's good. And you sit with your friend Ness on the coach?"

"Usually. She doesn't come in to Doc's much now."

"She's not one of the gang?"

"Well, I suppose she is, but not as much as she used to be." Gillian tried to explain but couldn't quite do it. Fortunately, the coach arrived. Mary was looking out of the window as it pulled up, and she waved in David's direction. David wasn't sure if she was waving at him, so he turned around but there was no-one else. Perhaps she *was* waving at him. As he made his way down the coach, Mary actually spoke to him.

"Hello." David looked at her, a little bemused. "Come and sit with me later, please," Mary said. David continued to the back seats, looking to see if Arthur had been watching. He didn't seem to have noticed or if he had, didn't seem to care.

As requested, after the High School lads had got off, David moved down and sat next to Mary.

"Thanks for coming down. I'm sorry if I've been horrible to you," Mary said.

"That's ok. I was just a little confused."

"It's my fault, and I can't really explain," Mary said. She held David's hand as she spoke which made him feel better.

"You don't have to explain." David considered his next question carefully. "Have you had any problems with Arthur?"

"No. Don't start talking about him again." Mary

stood up to get ready to get off the coach as it was approaching her school. She picked up her bag and David let her out. She turned and gave him a little kiss. "I just want to know that you and I are still friends. I've missed you," Mary said, and then got off the coach. David sat back down and pondered what she had just said. He looked out of the window and watched Mary make her way to the school gates. She turned and waved. He waved back. Bloody hell, David thought.

Chapter 12
THE PARTY INVITATION

Saturday 1st December 1995
Saturday was a funny day. Nobody in the Riddell household felt like doing anything, and they all had a lie in. As Michael got back into bed after making a cup of tea, Sue sat up and started to discuss what the agenda was for the day.

"I need to get some washing in as soon as I get up. David is off to football, of course." Sue sipped at the tea but it was too hot to drink. "What are you doing?"

"Think I'll have another go at that wardrobe door."

"Yeah, that would be good."

The wardrobe door had fallen off about three weeks ago and Michael had put it back on, but after a couple of days, it was off again. It was now leaning against the bedroom wall and was beginning to be a bit of a nuisance. Sue sipped at her tea again and thought hard. "Aren't you going to watch David play football today?"

"No, I said I wasn't."

"Why?"

"Can't remember to be honest. I just know I said I wasn't going." Michael drank his tea and the suddenly stopped. He turned and looked at Sue who must have had the same thought at the same time. They both said together, "Driving Test." It was Michael's driving test today. His third, to be exact.

"Perhaps I can ring up and cancel." Michael looked at the bedside clock.

"Don't be stupid. You've paid for it, you're doing it. Come on." Sue pushed him out of bed.

It was a bit of a rush, but Michael was washed and dressed just in time for Glen when he pulled up outside. Michael grabbed a half slice of toast and took a bite.

"Bye, see you later," Michael said, although it was muffled and just came out as a series of grunts.

"Yes, dear," Sue replied as she blew him a kiss. He rushed down the drive and into the car. He drove off a bit quickly, and Sue could see Glen talking to him as they went. 'Probably won't see him now for a couple of hours' Sue thought to herself, so she had time to get the washing sorted and David ready for football. It was a busy day just doing the normal things.

David eventually got up, as did Louise, and they both argued over using the bathroom. Sue ignored them and let them get on with it. The fuss quietened down and they both appeared in the kitchen looking for food.

"What's for breakfast, Mum?" David was the first to ask. Louise followed suit shortly afterwards. Sue made them both some bacon and toast with a little bit of scrambled egg which they lapped up. By twelve, both were on their way out.

Twenty minutes or so later, Michael was back. He

pushed open the door with a noise Sue couldn't fail to hear. She was ready to console him on another failure but it wasn't necessary.

"I've passed! I've only bloody passed!" Michael shouted as he opened his arms wide and waited to be congratulated. Sue did so, and the two jumped up and down as Michael sang a nonsense song which resembled the seven dwarfs' singing from Snow White. "I've passed, I've passed, I've only bloody passed!" He was making sure that Sue knew he was pleased. It was a big relief to both of them

"Does this mean we have to buy a car now?" Sue always considered the financial issues.

"Of course." Michael sat down, slightly out of breath. "In fact, we'll go and have a look at some tomorrow."

David caught the school bus on Monday morning as usual and the lads were in a good mood. Even Arthur seemed quite friendly for a change. He was talking to David as if they were friends, and that was really unusual. David had been chatting to Mary and he was sure that Arthur knew it, and it seemed he wasn't really that bothered. When the High School lads got off, David went and sat down next to Mary.

"Hello, sexy," David said. Mary went a little red.

"Don't say things like that, you know I don't like it," Mary replied.

"Sorry." David gulped. "Look I know it's going to be difficult but I would like to see you again sometime."

"Yes, I'd like to as well."

"Can you get away at all?" David assumed she wouldn't be able to.

"I should be able to, but not all the time."

"Will you tell your mum?"

"Yes. We've had a talk and she knows how I feel." Mary seemed proud of this, as it had been quite an accomplishment.

"That's good, then. Does it mean I can come over to Leafby and see you there?"

"Er, no, I don't think that would be a good idea. Somerby is better." Mary looked out of the window and realised that they had reached her school. "Look, how about tomorrow?"

"What, after school?" David asked.

"Yes. I'll probably need to be home by seven, but I'd like to see you if you would still see me."

"Yeah, of course I'll see you." David held Mary's hand. "Does this mean we are going out?" Mary shrugged her shoulders briefly.

"I suppose so."

On Tuesday afternoon David and Mary sat together on the coach back to Somerby and when it arrived, David got up to get off, but so did Mary. Before she did, she turned and spoke to a younger girl on the bus. David and Mary stepped off the coach and stood back to allow others to make their way through. He held Mary's hand.

"Shall we go in to Doc's?"

"We can do," Mary replied. David led her across the road and they made their way to the café. It was strange for him to be with her when she wasn't wearing jeans. Both were in their school uniforms which meant that Mary was wearing a skirt. David thought she looked great in anything. By the time they got into Doc's, the place was pretty full but David spotted a free table in the far corner. Gillian and the girls said hello.

"Luce not here yet?"

"No, she normally gets here late," Gillian replied. David continued over to the table and said hello to Pete on his way. Mary sat against the wall.

"What would you like? A coffee, tea, chocolate, or coke perhaps?" David asked.

"Oh, a chocolate please. Is that a hot drink?"

"Yes. Do you want anything to eat?"

"No, thanks." Mary looked around the place while David was getting the drinks. Mary had heard so much about Doc's, but this was the first time she had really been in there. David and Mary spent most of their time in Doc's that afternoon. They held hands and touched feet under the table. They kissed a few times. It was quite normal and they both felt good. David wondered if Mary had really liked the necklace and didn't want to make too much of it but was desperate to ask.

"Was the necklace okay?"

"Yes, I love it. It will always be my special necklace." Mary's eyes lit up as she spoke.

"So, will you wear it tomorrow?"

"Oh no, I need to keep it safe. In its box." Mary had already found a little hiding place for it where it wouldn't be found as she was worried a member of her family might ask where she got it. David wasn't quite sure how to take this comment. He didn't think she would think that much of a cheap present, but he didn't want to upset her.

"Oh, right."

"I'll only wear it on special occasions when I'm with you." Mary kissed David after saying this. She imagined them standing at the altar waiting to get married, and she would be wearing her special necklace.

It was one of the few times they stayed in Doc's as Mary wasn't keen to be in there when Vanessa was also there. David understood because he felt the same about Louise. They didn't avoid the place, but never stayed in there too long when they met. Most times they would walk around Somerby. David felt that they now really were boyfriend and girlfriend at last.

On Friday afternoon, Michael ensured that he had got his work finished early so he could get away from the bank by three. It was going to be a very exciting trip he made next, as one of the bank staff had a car for sale and Michael had arranged to see it that afternoon. He had already organised a loan, so the money wasn't going to be a problem, he just needed to see if the car was okay and what he wanted.

Michael caught the bus out to Bob's house, and he looked at the car standing on the drive. It was a Toyota, just a three-door model, but a nice one, and one that Michael felt he could get used to. Bob took him out for a test drive and Michael was happy with it. The deal was done.

Michael then realised that he was actually going to drive it home. For some reason this hadn't crossed his mind before, and he'd thought about getting the bus back, but despite being slightly daunted, he drove home through the rush hour traffic. He turned into the drive at home and Sue waved out of the kitchen window as she saw him.
"What do you think, then?" Michael asked.
"Yes, it looks quite nice," Sue replied. David and Louise came and joined her to look at the new car.
"It's a bit small," David said. "And it's only got two doors." Sue laughed as Michael looked annoyed.
"It's got enough doors for us," Michael replied.

Although Sue had cooked a tea and Michael had sat down to enjoy what she had prepared there was only one thing on his mind. The car. Sue was also thinking about how things might change now the family had transport, and she was happy in the knowledge that shopping would be a lot easier from now on. Michael could take her to one of the big supermarkets each weekend and she could buy more. This was good. Michael suddenly broke the silence. "I think I'm going for a drive after tea, who's coming with me?"

"Yes, please Dad!" Louise jumped up. The whole family wanted to try the new car out so washing up was postponed and off they all went for a drive around the village.

Michael didn't really know where he was going and together with the fact that he wasn't too confident driving, and had three critics in his car, he took things rather slowly.

"Speed up a bit, Dad."

"Your father can't drive too fast, David, as he is only just getting used to the car, and it's too dangerous to drive fast." Sue gave David a stern look. The journey of three miles or so around the village took nearly half an hour. David was embarrassed to be in a car driving so slowly and was relieved to get back home again. Michael promised he would get better as he drove more, but for now he was extremely cautious.

The next day was yet another milestone in the relationship between David and Mary. The schools had broken up for Christmas and David had a father who could drive. It changed a lot of things. Not only that, but Mary seemed to be getting on better with her mother over seeing David. She still had her duties but there seemed to be a lot more freedom for her, and she made the most of it.

Mary still had cleaning chores to finish but with the agreement of her mum she did a lot of them Friday and just finished up on Saturday morning before she went out. She was going to watch David play football this afternoon. When everyone was ready, Mary's mum drove her and her sister to Somerby.

"Are you coming in to Doc's?" Vanessa asked. Mary looked at the time on the petrol station clock.

"Yes, alright, I think I will," Mary replied. Vanessa went in first and made her way straight over to the girls who were already occupying a table.

"Hi, girls," she said as she got to the table.

"Hello, Ness," Livvy and Louise replied. Tina was busy writing a letter, and Gillian and Melanie were busy trying to see what it was she was writing. Mary stood by Vanessa's side not quite sure what to do.

"Hello, Mary," Gillian said as she looked up.

"Hello," Mary replied. Mary and Vanessa half whispered and Mary went and sat down at an empty table. Louise looked around to make sure she couldn't be overheard.

"Who's that then?" Louise asked Gillian.

"Mary, Ness's sister," she replied in a tone that suggested that Louise should have already known that.

"I didn't know that was Ness's sister." Louise spoke a bit too loudly.

"Yes, she's my sister," Ness interrupted. "And she's going out with your brother," she added. Louise knew that but still got embarrassed at the way that Ness had come out with it.

David came in to Doc's and quickly spotted Mary. He said hello to the girls then made his way over to her. He lent across and gave her a kiss which she was happy to receive. The kiss went on for a few seconds more than perhaps it should have done, and they both became aware that some people were watching them. They pulled away and looked at each other. They both laughed and it felt good.

"Do you want a coffee?" David asked.

"Yes, please." Mary fidgeted on the bench seat as she replied. David made his way up to the counter and bought a couple of drinks. As he placed them down on the table he slid himself on to the seat next to Mary making sure their legs touched. Mary turned to him as if she was going to kiss him. David grabbed her leg and squeezed it, but Mary pulled her leg away to stop him from touching it.

"Ooh, that tickles." Mary shook. They kissed again.

David was playing football at Gorleston that afternoon and Mary had managed to get approval from home to go and watch him. She was really excited, as she felt quite important, almost like royalty she would think to herself. As they left Doc's, Mitch's dad pulled up in the pub car park. Mitch was in the passenger seat so Mary and David got in the back. Mitch had never met Mary before but was pleased to meet a mate's girlfriend. He was also pleased for David. The whole afternoon had Mary in awe. She said very little in the car and stood shivering by the side of the pitch during the game. She didn't really understand the rules but knew the general idea and was able to see that David's team had won. She kissed him when he emerged from the dressing room after the game and David felt good about that. They were beginning to become a proper item.

As it was going to be Christmas on Tuesday there was a real holiday feeling around this weekend. David and Mary returned in Mitch's dad's car and they both got dropped off in Somerby.

"Is your mum picking you up?" David asked.

"Yes," she answered, looking at her watch. As she replied her mum pulled up.

"When can I get to see you again?"

"I'm not quite sure." Mary walked over to her mum's side of the car. "Mum, can I come to Somerby tomorrow?"

"You promised you would help me with the cooking, Mary." Mary's mum needed help for the preparation of food ready for Christmas, and had previously relied on her eldest daughter.

"Look, I can't really get over tomorrow but I'll try on Monday. Will you be at home?" Mary asked.

"Yes. I'm not going anywhere." David walked over to Mary. They hugged each other and discreetly kissed whilst doing so.

"Come on Mary, time to go," Mary's mum called

out.

"Hope to see you Monday." Mary waved as she got into the car and David watched as it drove off.

As it turned out, Mary wasn't able to get over to Somerby on Monday either and David missed seeing her. He knew she had a lot to do for her mum over Christmas, pretty much in the same way he was expected to be at home with his family. He hoped she would be thinking of him. Christmas came and went, and Mary called round just the once. She was allowed a couple of hours away from home whilst her mum went shopping. By the sound of things, it seemed that her mum had created the excuse just to get Mary away for a little while. They spent the little time they had kissing and cuddling. They were both happy and in love. It wasn't easy but David understood that Mary had problems at home. He was patient enough but hated letting her go back when her mum came to pick her up.

Sue managed to persuade Michael to drive to the local supermarket so that she could buy all the shopping she needed in one go. Michael had a couple of problems on the way, stalling at some traffic lights, and getting a couple of irate drivers overtaking him as he slowly made his way into town. They spent nearly two hours shopping and Sue was impressed with Michael's driving on the way home. It was still slow but she felt safe, and that was the most important thing.

Michael didn't do any further driving over Christmas, but being slightly bored by the day after Boxing Day he felt it was time to have another go. This time he went out on his own but things didn't go too well. He hit the kerb and had to swerve to miss an approaching car which he thought was going to hit him. It was all quite exhausting and it knocked his confidence a little.

Monday was New Year's Eve. The Riddells had celebrated last year in their house at Goodmayes, the first time they had been in their own house for New Year. Sue quite liked the idea, and ensured that all four of them were at home this year. David and Louise were allowed to go out during the day if they wanted to, but were under strict instructions to be home by six so that the family could have the evening together.

Louise went off to Gillian's house for the afternoon and David listened to CDs in his bedroom. There wasn't much he wanted to do, so he lay on his bed doing nothing.

"David!" There was a shout from the kitchen. "David!" Sue shouted again. David turned his music down a bit, guessing that was what she would ask him to do anyway, and poked his head round the kitchen door.

"What?"

"Can you do me a favour?"

"I know, turn the music down."

"No. I need something from the bakers. Would you be a darling and see if you can get me a couple of French sticks?"

"But Mum..." David was comfortable in his bedroom and didn't want to go to the effort of putting his shoes on.

"No buts. Here's a fiver. I want two or three French sticks or similar." Sue put the note on the work top near the outside door. "Now go down to the bakers. Please."

"Will they be open today?"

"Yes, they should be."

David made his way down towards the bakers but stopped at the little shop at the bottom of his road first to see if they had any French sticks, but they hadn't so he continued round to the bakers. The bakery was quite busy and there were three people waiting to be served when David arrived. He saw what looked to him like French sticks so he was happy to wait. His turn soon arrived.

"Three French sticks please." David took the bread and paid his money. He turned to leave the shop but saw out of the corner of his eye a coat he recognised in the queue. He looked up and saw it was Mary's mum. "Hello, Mrs Matthews," David said. Mary's mum looked at him, and then looked again.

"Oh, it's you. Hello, David. Mary's in the car." She pointed to the pub car park. David rushed towards the door but then stopped and turned back.

"Thanks, Mrs Matthews."

David ran over to the car and Mary saw him as he got closer. She got out of the car and David ran towards her holding his arms open out wide. They embraced and kissed.

"Mary, are you okay?" David asked as they stopped kissing.

"Of course I am, now I've seen you," Mary replied. They kissed again. "I was hoping I might see you. Mum said she wouldn't drive up your road."

"Have you been all right?" David asked again.

"Yes. You know how it is, boring relations." As Mary spoke she saw her mum leaving the bakers. "Look, quickly, it's my birthday on Friday and we're having a family party. Would you come?"

"Birthday! Friday? Am I invited?" David asked just as Mary's mum arrived.

"Mum, is it alright if David comes to the party on Friday?" Mary asked. Her mum stood and thought for a second.

"Well, your sister has invited some friends so I don't see why not." Mary jumped up in excitement and then kissed David again.

"Where is the party?"

"At Leafby Village Hall," Mary replied.

"We'll send you an invitation," Mary's mum added. "In fact, I think your sister is already invited."

"Will you come?" Mary asked.

"I should be available." David teased her a while. "Of course I'll be there."

"I might even wear the blue necklace," Mary smiled.

David started back home trying to take stock of what had just taken place. He had never been able to find out when Mary's birthday was as whenever the subject came up, she would change it. Then she just came out with it there and then. It then hit him that he would have to get her a present. He ran through in his mind what he might be able to get her, but nothing seemed quite right. He was also considering to himself what kind of party it would be. Mary's family were a bit strange, he thought, so perhaps the party would be also. He imagined everyone sat around Leafby Village Hall just staring into space. No music. No food. Then he dismissed that idea as stupid. Of course she'll have food, he thought to himself. Then he remembered Mary's mum saying that Luce had also been invited. Oh God, he almost said out loud. Loads of screaming little girls.

Initially he considered this to be an absolute disaster but then it dawned on him that perhaps he and Mary could sneak out of the way and be alone together. That would be good, he decided. Then of course she would be the centre of attention, it being her birthday, so guessed that this might not be as easy as he had first imagined. Within minutes he was back home.

"There you are." David dumped the bag with the

bread in, on the work top.

"Thanks, darling," Sue replied. "Do I get any change?"

"I didn't think you wanted any."

"Give it here." Sue held her hand out.

"I saw Mary and her mum while I was out."

"Oh, that's nice. Is she okay?" Sue didn't really know much about Mary but she found her to be a rather sullen young girl, and thought she might not have one of the happiest home lives.

"Yeah, she seemed okay." David sat down on one of the chairs. "She's invited me to her birthday party on Friday."

"Her birthday party?" Sue thought perhaps he had misheard what Mary had said to him.

"Yes, her birthday. I'll have to get her a present, won't I?"

"Where is the party?"

"Oh, at Leafby Village Hall."

"Are you sure it's her birthday?" Sue wanted to make sure she had heard David correctly.

"That's what she said."

"Is anyone else going?"

"Er, I don't know." David thought this a bit of a strange question. He suddenly remembered about Louise. "Oh, you mean Luce." Sue nodded slowly. "Yes, Mary's mum said that Vanessa, Mary's sister, had invited her."

"As long as you know."

Sue was enjoying preparing lots of food for

tonight's family night in. She and Michael had a number of things planned, including various games to play. In the past, they had usually spent New Year with Michael's parents and other members of his family, but as everyone had grown older, fewer and fewer members stayed much beyond nine in the evening. They would all be going off to other parties, but would call on the family do out of respect more than anything else. Sue and Michael made the decision last year to celebrate on their own and they had enjoyed it. Sue guessed that before too long, David would be off celebrating with his friends, so she was very keen to make sure that this year they all stayed in and spent the evening together.

Dinner was going to be more like a Sunday roast, which she usually tried to serve about four or five in the afternoon. This would typically leave the family full up and happy to sit around doing very little for the rest of the evening, then feeling hungry again later. This year, Sue was preparing a chilli to be served as an Old Year's supper. The French bread, of course, was needed to go with it.

The evening went off without any hitches and everyone enjoyed it. They played Trivial Pursuits to start with then a game of Monopoly. As always, David and Louise fought hard to beat each other, whilst Sue and Michael did their best to keep things on as even a keel as possible. This would sometimes mean cheating a bit if one or other of their children didn't have enough money to pay a hotel bill. David and Louise always complained but eventually the game would be won and all arguments forgotten.

The chilli came out around ten o'clock, and Sue also whipped up a quick salad to eat with it. They then watched the telly till around one o'clock in the morning, giving each other hugs at the midnight hour. Michael looked at Sue as they both watched their children actually hugging each other. They felt content. Michael gave Sue a big hug and then a kiss. Louise hugged them and then David joined in. It was the end of the old year, and the start of a new one.

Tuesday was New Year's Day but it was a nothing day. Both David and Louise were late getting up after last night's celebrations and although Sue had been up at her usual hour, she had made some tea and got back into bed.

"That was a good night last night," Michael said.

"Yes, it went well. I'm not sure we'll all be doing it next year though."

"What do you mean?"

"Well, David will be sixteen and he'll probably be off with his mates."

"Yeah. You could be right." Michael tried to think back to when he was sixteen. He couldn't remember if he was out doing his own thing or not. Then he had to admit, that was a long time ago. He would be turning thirty-six this year and although he didn't feel that old, when he mentioned his age he had to agree that he was older than he would have wished to be. Sue was a year younger but her outlook was younger still. She had no hangups about her age and regularly forgot exactly how old she was.

Nobody really felt like doing much today as they were all still tired but eventually the whole family managed to get themselves out of bed.
"David, can you clear up the games and put them away in the cupboard please," Michael shouted out. David had only just got dressed.
"Yeah. In a minute."
"Are you going out today, Louise?" Sue popped her head around Louise's bedroom door to ask.
"No, not today."
"What about you, David?"
"No, Mum."

Sue looked around the kitchen thoughtfully. She tidied up the old newspapers then looked in the fridge. She was bored. All of a sudden, an old magazine caught her eye so she sat down at the table and fingered through a few pages of it. It was full of those true life stories which of course Sue never ever believed could be anything but total fiction. This only helped pass a few minutes and soon she was bored again. Sue tossed the magazine across the table as if to dispose of it, and suddenly remembered the family's forthcoming holiday. She tried to remember where she had put those holiday brochures that she and Michael had been looking through. She walked back to the bedroom where Michael was sorting clothes. It was difficult to work out exactly what he was doing but Sue didn't much care.

"Where did we put those holiday brochures?"

"What brochures?" Michael quickly shut the drawer.

"You know. The Florida ones."

"Oh, them. They're on top of the wardrobe." Michael stood up and reached up to feel half blindly across the top of the wardrobe. He produced one, then another magazine.

"I thought we had more than that."

"Don't think so." Michael felt again and found another three brochures.

"That's better." Sue laid them all out on top of the bed. "Ah yes." Sue picked out the one she had been particularly looking for. "This one shows the best pictures of where we'll be staying."

"What do you want them for anyway?"

"It's about time we had a good look at them as a family."

Five minutes later all four of the Riddells were sat around the kitchen table pouring over holiday magazines featuring Florida, the USA or North America. Each brochure was very different.

"What's the name of the hotel where we're staying?" David asked.

"It's the Orange Beach Resort and it isn't a hotel." Sue replied.

"What is it then?"

"Well it's more like a holiday camp."

"But they're not like chalets, are they?"

"No, darling." Sue laughed. She wasn't quite sure whether she was laughing more at David's concern that they might be staying in chalets or the thought of what the place would be like if they were staying in chalets.

Louise and Michael shared a brochure between them. This one showed pictures of all the different theme parks that you could go to.

"I want to go there!" Louise exclaimed. Michael looked to check where exactly 'there' was. It was the MGM Studios. He turned the page. "Oh, and I want to go there." Louise pointed to a picture of the parade taking place at Disneyworld.

"You probably want to go everywhere."

"Can we?"

"It all depends really." Michael looked at Sue. "We should remember that visiting any of the parks will be tiring so it makes sense to have a day off from them every now and then."

"But Dad, we want to go and see all of the places."

"We'll see." Michael had never been to any of the parks before, but he had taken the family to Alton Towers and had been to places like Chessington before, and he knew how tired everyone would be by the end of the day.

For the next half hour or so all four of them chatted about what they wanted to go and visit, what they didn't want to go and visit, how much rest they needed and what they could fit in during their two week holiday.

"Do you two want to go to the Kennedy Space Centre?" Michael asked. He asked mainly because he wanted to go. Louise pulled a funny face at the mere mention of the place. David didn't seem to be bothered one way of the other.

"I take it you'd like to go there dear?" Sue asked.

"If we can fit it in!" Michael didn't want the holiday to be planned around him. It was for the kids and they should decide where and when to go within reason. He considered that Sue and himself were really only there to give advice.

After about twenty minutes, Sue grabbed a pencil and paper and started to jot down some of their plans. Nothing would be set in stone but it would give her and Michael some idea of what would be required in way of tickets.

"We can spend a day swimming, can't we?" Sue proposed.

"Hey, yeah, that'll be great. I've heard that Splashdown is the best place to go," David added.

"Splashdown? No!" Sue realised what she had said. "No, I mean just have a lazy swim in the pool at the resort."

"Oh." David and Louise were both disappointed. There was a short spell where all four said nothing but concentrated on looking at different pictures in the brochures. "Dad," David said.

"Yes, son?"

"Are you going to drive in Florida?"

"Hmm." Michael slumped back on his chair. "You know, I'd not really given it any thought." Michael searched through the brochure he was holding and stopped turning when he came to a map. "Well it's quite a way from the resort to the fun parks I suppose."

"You don't have to drive, darling. I'm sure there'll be buses or taxis we can get." Sue added.

"Yes, that's true. I think Disney do special coaches, don't they?" Michael hoped they did, as he wasn't keen on driving on the wrong side of the road. "I'll need to get a bit of practice in when I can then, just in case."

"A lot," David added quietly.

"I'll take you two on Friday."

"Friday?" Louise queried. "I'm going to a party on Friday."

Louise looked at Sue with a look that said she wasn't happy. She assumed that everyone had forgotten that she was going to the party and arranged some other event for Friday that she would now be expected to come along to.

"Yes, dear, it's the party that your dad is talking about." Sue tried to calm things.

"Oh, that's alright then." Louise turned it all over in her mind. "But Dad said two."

"Yes, darling. You and David."

"Why will David be in the car?"

"In the car?" Now David was getting confused. "I'm going to the party."

"How come you're going to the party?" Louise was beginning to feel a bit picked on. "It's Ness's party. You're not invited." Louise was getting a bit worked up.

"Huh! You're wrong. I've been invited as well." David tried to make the most of the situation and get one over on his little sister.

"Mum!" Louise appealed.

"He's right. It's Mary's party as well, apparently." Sue expected a tirade from her daughter, but nothing came. Louise weighed it all up and accepted it.

Michael was also quite surprised at the silence. He kept an eye on both David and Louise but both seemed to have finished for the time being.

"By the way, where exactly is this party?"

"At Leafby Village Hall," Louise answered.

"I thought the party might be at Doc's," Michael said. "Or is he invited too?"

"No, I don't think so," Louise replied. Once again there was a pause in the conversation.

"You get on well with him, though, don't you dear?" Sue said, almost without considering what the consequences of her words might be. Michael gave Sue a strange look.

"Yes, I suppose so. He seems to talk to me more than the other girls."

"Yes, and when he came round here he asked after you. To see if you were alright. And he called you Luce, not Louise."

"Oh, he's picked that up from David. Even a couple of the girls sometimes call me Luce now."

"He never enquired about David though." Sue was deep in thought. "He comes from London, you know."

"Does he? How do you know that?" Michael asked.

"Oh, he said once." Sue's mind was wandering back to when Doc was there. "Yes, I'm sure he said he used to live in London." She was sure that he had said so, but his exact words couldn't be recalled.

"I think he lost his mum and dad when he was young." Louise added.

"Did he, darling?" Sue started to feel a bit sorry for Doc. "How do you know that?"

"When I worked there he used to chat to me."

"Yes, he seems to have struck up a good relationship with you."

Again Michael gave Sue a stern look as she spoke.

"He kept going on about this tree."

"Tree. What tree?" Michael asked.

"Oh, I don't really know. He just kept saying it was his special place." Louise pictured Doc sitting up in the big oak tree on the green. Then an image of her dad also sitting in the tree came into her mind.

"Oh yeah. He said I should tell you about it." Louise looked at Michael.

"Tell me?" Michael was surprised. "Now I think about it he did mention some bloody tree when I went to see him."

Michael, Sue and Louise were all deep in thought. David sat there bemused by it all.

"No, he said I was to tell both of you about the tree."

"Tell us what, darling?" Sue asked.

"Oh, I don't know. I just ignored him. He said it was his special place. He's a bit weird sometimes, you know."

"Yeah, you can say that again." Sue replied. "But at least he is someone from the village who speaks to us all."

"He's never spoken to me." David felt left out a bit. Sue put her arm around him.

"Ah. You're feeling left out." She realised that this moody conversation had gone on too long. "Right." Sue slapped her hand down on the kitchen table. "Who wants to go to Universal Studios?"

Chapter 13
THE ACCIDENT

Friday 4th January 1996
It was Friday afternoon and Louise had made her way home quite early this afternoon as she was going to Vanessa's party later. She wasn't quite sure who else was going to be there apart from the gang, but of course David had been invited as it was also Mary's fifteenth birthday. The fact that David was going might be a bonus, but then again it might not. Louise would make that decision later.

Louise knew that there would be a number of Ness's relatives there as well, but by all accounts, including Ness's own, they were a bit of a weird bunch and Louise wasn't quite sure what to expect. She started to get herself ready for the party. She had Ness's present already wrapped and a card written out for her, and she just needed to add some finishing touches to the envelope. Nothing too intricate, but a little bit of glue and glitter to make her card just a bit different to the others. She had written out the front of the envelope in a bubble-type writing and she was just going to put glitter in the letters to make it look special. Sue had helped with the idea and Louise was pleased with the suggestion. Then came the difficult task of deciding what to wear.

Sue had suggested wearing a dress that had been

bought for a wedding they had gone to a year ago but Louise didn't want to wear that. She had almost made her mind up: the black trousers she had just got out of the catalogue, but she wasn't quite sure what to wear with them. She tried on her red round-necked top but she didn't think it was right. She also had a nice bluish coloured blouse but it was a bit worn in places. It was one of Louise's favourites and had seen a lot of use. Then there was a long-sleeved white top that she had hanging up on the wardrobe door, but it was a bit too party. This wasn't quite the right occasion to wear the white top. It was nice though. In the end, she chose to wear her blue blouse. That trusted old top. Next it was time to put on a little make-up.

David wasn't even getting ready yet, but it was only five thirty. He had Mary's presents already wrapped. He had bought her a watch as her main present. She had seen something like it when they were in town one day and he saved up some money to get it. It was quite expensive but he didn't want to appear to scrimp on Mary's present. His mum had also helped him with another present, some vouchers to spend in Top Shop. This was from Sue as much as it was David as she had heard him talking about what Mary wore all the time and thought this might come in useful. David didn't spend much time getting ready. He had his best trousers to wear, and a new black buttoned up shirt he'd bought at the end of last summer. A little bit of aftershave and he would be ready.

Sue was on hand to make sure the kids were on schedule and Michael got home at a quarter to six so he could change before he had to go out again. He just wanted to get out of his bank suit. He would change properly when he got back home.

"Hello, darling," Michael said as he came in.

"Hello." Sue gave him a hug. "What's it like out there at the moment?"

"Well it's raining but not too hard. Mind you it looks like it could get worse." Michael looked out of the kitchen window. "It's not as if I've got to go far."

"So how was your day today?" Sue asked.

"Yeah, not too bad. Because of the time of year things are a bit slow, really."

"Have you been driving today?" Sue knew Michael wasn't keen on driving far yet.

"No, I've been in the office all day. It's just great having the car there in case I need to go anywhere." Michael heard a lashing as the rain hit the window. "Sounds like it's getting worse out there." He shook his head. "What are we having for tea, then?"

"Oh, I don't know yet. I'll probably open a tin of something when you get in." Sue knew exactly what she was cooking but didn't want Michael to know. It was going to be a little surprise.

"Okay," Michael replied. "David. Louise. Are you two getting ready? I want to leave about half past." It was now just a minute after six o'clock.

As six thirty approached the weather seemed to get much worse. The wind had really got up, and the rain seemed to be falling harder and harder. It was almost pitch black outside, and Michael wasn't going to enjoy the drive.

"Okay you two, let's get going!" Michael shouted out. David came in almost immediately. He had his leather bomber jacket on. Louise followed. She had changed her mind at the last moment and was now wearing the white sparkly top.

"Aren't you going to put a coat on?" Sue asked her.

"No, I don't need one."

"It's going to be cold out there."

"Yeah, but we'll be inside." Louise didn't want to put a coat on and that was that.

"But you know what it can be like in those old halls. It won't be that warm to start with." Sue was persistent. "Look, dear, just put a cardigan on. You can always take it off when you get there if it's warm enough."

"Oh, alright." Louise gave in. Michael had already opened the door. "Chewing gum. I haven't got any chewing gum." Louise looked in her bag. She couldn't find any. "Dad, we'll have to stop at the shop so I can get some."

"Okay, as long as you're quick." Michael just wanted to get them to Leafby so he could get home again.

As they sat in the car waiting for Michael to start the engine the rain seemed to get even heavier. The noise of it falling on to the car roof was quite worrying. It sounded as if very soon the drops would fall right through. David looked out and saw how dark the sky had got. In the distance he could see lightning.

"Hey, Luce, look." David pointed to where he had seen the lightning. Louise turned but by the time she looked, there was nothing to be seen.

"What?"

"Lightning. There was a lot of lightning."

"I hate it when it storms." Louise honestly felt a little frightened. She could almost imagine the car being struck by lightning.

Michael got the car started and he took his time putting the windscreen wipers on and then his lights. The inside of the windscreen had misted up so he put on the blower to try and clear it. It took a couple of minutes but eventually the screen started to clear.

"Come on, Dad," Louise encouraged.

"Don't be impatient," Michael replied as he looked over his shoulder before starting to reverse out of the drive. He couldn't see as well as he would have liked but knew that if any other cars were on the road they would be lit up. He was a little worried that someone might be walking on the pavement but he drove extra slowly.

It was only half past six but as Michael wasn't quite sure exactly where he was dropping the kids off, and even less sure exactly which route to take, he preferred to leave a little bit earlier so he didn't have to rush. The fact that the weather conditions made driving even harder, meant he was even happier to leave early. He drove down to Coopers and parked the car as near to the shop as possible. He then pulled on the handbrake and turned the engine off. All three sat still for a few moments before Michael turned round to Louise.

"I thought you wanted to get some chewing gum?"

"Oh, Dad, I can't get out of the car in this rain."

"What? You expect me to go for you?"

"Please, Dad." Louise pulled one of her helpless faces. The rain seemed to ease off a bit.

"I don't know what it is you want." Michael replied.

"Oh, I'll go!" Louise knew she would probably lose the battle so she undid her seat belt, opened the car door and made a quick dash for the shop. It was still raining and she got a little bit damp but not too wet. Coopers was quite busy with people in the shop buying lottery tickets and evening newspapers, as well as those last-minute bits of shopping that were always needed. Louise stood back from the queue of people waiting to pay and she looked at the counter display for the chewing gum. It took her a few seconds but then she spotted the packet she wanted. It was a menthol type chewing gum that helped freshen your breath.

There were only two staff working this evening. Judy was doing general counter work. She was about seventeen or eighteen and dressed in the old goth style with dyed black hair, pale face powder and dark lipstick and eye shadow. Louise had spoken to her a couple of times but as she was that much older she didn't say much. The other person was Karen. She was working the lottery machine but also dealing with other purchases if nobody wanted tickets. She was probably the friendliest of all the staff and would always ask how you were when she served you, even if it was busy.

"Oh, hello, you've done well keeping out of the rain," Karen said to Louise as she took the chewing gum from her to pass it under the scanner. Karen had a way of speaking to you as if she knew exactly who you were and had been a friend for ages.

"Well, Dad has driven me round so I didn't have far to come."

"You're all dressed up this evening." Karen swiped the chewing gum under the infrared reader again as it failed to register the first time.

"Off to a party."

"Oh, anyone I know?"

"Do you know Ness? I mean Vanessa from Leafby?" Louise looked at Karen who tried hard, but couldn't disguise that confused look on her face. "Sorry, of course you wouldn't, I mean Vanessa Matthews." Louise waited to see if that had made any difference.

"No, I don't think I've met her. That'll be thirty-five pence please."

"Thank you." Louise handed Karen a fifty pence piece. The shop had started to empty a bit by now and there was only one other customer. As Karen was scratching around in the till for change there was a loud crack of thunder.

"Ooh, listen to that out there," Karen said in a pretend frightened way to anyone who was prepared to listen.

"Bloody terrible out there. Can't wait to get home," Judy replied, having handed the old man she was serving his change. She walked over towards Karen.

"Yes, I hate storms," Louise added.

"So, is the party in Leafby?" Judy asked as if she had been part of the conversation all the time. Louise was a bit taken aback. Not only was Judy actually conversing with her but she had obviously been listening to the previous conversation and seemed interested.

"Yes, it's at the village hall."

"Oh, I've been to a couple of parties there before. It can be a bit cold but I seem to remember that they have heaters all around the room."

"Oh, that'll be good," Louise replied.

"Is it Vanessa's birthday?" Karen asked.

"Yes, she's thirteen."

"Oh, lucky girl. Becoming a teenager." Karen thought for a brief second. "Oh, how I wish I was a teenager again."

"Well, I can't wait to stop being a teenager," Judy added in a miserable tone. Louise and Karen both looked at Judy. Karen winked at Louise.

"You have a good time," Karen said as Louise turned and left the shop. "Do you know who

Vanessa Matthews is?" Karen asked Judy.

"No, but I think I might know her sister. Weird girl."

Louise ran back to the car and quickly got back in. The rain was falling down even harder, and there was another strike of lightning.

"That was pretty close," Michael said.

"Does that mean the storm is practically overhead?" David asked.

"Yes, in a way. I think it means we are nearer to the centre of the storm anyway." Michael turned to watch Louise put her seat belt on. "Where have you been?"

"Sorry Dad, but the shop was busy."

"Well it's made us a little late," Michael said looking at his watch.

"We're not that late, are we, Dad?" David looked at his own watch. It said that the time was a quarter to seven.

"Yes, we are. I don't know how long it will take to drive to Leafby."

"It doesn't matter if we a little late," Louise added

"You might not think so but I do." Michael was a little stressed out. "Anyway, we don't know where we've got to go yet."

"Dad, it's easy," David replied.

"You might think so, but you're not driving."

Michael started the car again and began to reverse out of the parking space. It wasn't the easiest of manoeuvres and with reduced visibility it was even harder. As soon as any glimmer of a headlight could be seen, Michael stopped reversing, as cars would come round the bend at quite a speed. It seemed to be taking ages. David watched intently whilst Louise opened her chewing gum.

"Do you want some gum?" Louise asked David.

"Yes, please." He took a piece and popped it in his mouth. Michael huffed. He was getting angrier as more and more cars seemed to be driving round the bend. At last Michael reversed out on to the road, got into first gear and moved forwards. He pulled up behind two other vehicles waiting to get out at the crossroads. The rain got heavier.

This particular junction was tricky, as it was blind to both the right and left. Even the most experienced driver would have to edge out slowly to avoid causing an unseen obstruction. Michael had only ever approached it from this direction once before. He usually tried to avoid it but here he was. The rain came crashing down, the windscreen wipers moved at double speed, it was almost pitch dark and he was late. The two cars in front of him took a while to turn, but very soon Michael was at the junction. He edged forward, but still couldn't see properly. He moved forward again, but was forced back by a car turning into his road. This forward and backward movement seemed to go on for ages, and the stress was evident inside the car. David turned to Louise. "All right?" he asked.

The Somerby Tree

David could sense that his dad was getting more and more distressed. He wanted to reassure Louise that it was only a temporary thing. Michael wasn't usually as upset as this. Louise nodded at David. "I just think that something horrible is going to happen," she told him.

"It'll be alright, Luce, you'll see," David replied quietly, so Michael didn't hear.

"I'm not sure it will. I have this feeling that something's going to explode."

"This is just a difficult junction for Dad. He'll be across in a minute."

As David spoke, the car jerked forward and into Leafby Lane. "There you are, told you. It'll be alright now," David told Louise, with some relief.

"No, I still think something is going to happen," she replied, but David was facing forward again and didn't hear her.

As the car entered Leafby Lane, there was a deafening crack of thunder and, almost immediately afterwards, a big lightning flash that lit up the whole wood. The storm was right overhead. The rain continued to lash down on the roof of the car and visibility was very poor. Michael was relieved to be across the junction but he was still a bit uncertain of what direction to take at the end of the lane. It should be an easier one, though, whether he turned left or right. He knew that time was getting on so he accelerated, but the rain got worse and it was more difficult to see. At times, Michael found it hard to make out the road. The wind was stronger, and the car was blown about as gusts caught it. On the right, there was a high bank that protected them, but to the left was the old wood which left the car open to the elements and it was from this side that the wind was causing problems. Nevertheless, Michael was aware of the time and didn't slow down. He approached a bend but couldn't see round it properly. Even with the aid of his full beam headlights, the road had almost disappeared.

Michael saw that he was veering into the bank and quickly wrenched the steering wheel. As the car lurched, Louise screamed. Michael heard her, but before he could reassure her the car had started skidding off the road. Once again, the lightning briefly made the whole wood visible and he could just pick out the road ahead. He managed to get the car back on to the road safely, but then a loud crack of thunder made them all jump. A broken branch hit the windscreen and Louise screamed again. Michael turned the steering wheel, but the car skidded across the road. He felt David stiffen next to him and lost concentration for a split second. As he focussed again, he saw that the car was off the road and hurtling into the woods. He steered wildly right, then left, but the car was heading towards a tree with no change of direction. The car was sliding and Louise was screaming loudly now. The rain deafened them, and the tree was close now. Michael had to do something so he pulled on the handbrake while trying to steer away from the tree. The car spun, around and around, and another flash lit up the inside. Michael saw it all in slow motion. He saw David, stiff and motionless as if in a trance, and Louise screaming and obviously terrified. The noise grew louder and the light was blinding. There was a crunch, audible even over the storm, and a sudden stop. Then a terrible silence.

Chapter 14
SUE'S STORY

Sue started to prepare dinner. As the kids were going to the party it meant that she and Michael could actually sit down and have a meal together for a change. It had been a long time since that had happened and Sue hoped that they would be able to make it a little romantic, even though wine was out of the question as Michael would have to go and pick David and Louise up again afterwards. She had managed to get a couple of steaks that afternoon without Michael being aware, so the dinner was going to be her little surprise. It was about ten to seven, and Sue had calculated that Michael would be home about quarter past. She looked out of the kitchen window at the weather. The rain was pelting down, seemingly heavier than before. She knew Michael wasn't happy about driving in these conditions but knew he'd take it carefully and would find the place. He might drive a bit too slowly sometimes but he was safe. She could imagine him swearing quietly to himself about the rain.

As the clock turned the hour, Sue turned the heat up to fry some mushrooms and turned on the grill. She was in two minds when to put the steaks under as she didn't want to spoil the meal by cooking them before Michael got home so she decided to get everything ready and then turn it up as he returned.

The grill was now hot enough and ready for when Sue wanted to put the steaks under. She gave the potatoes one last look before sitting down at the kitchen dining table. She looked at the time. It was quarter past seven. Sue guessed that Michael would be home very soon, and she looked out of the kitchen window in case she could see the car. The weather was getting worse. The wind had really got up now and the rain was being lashed against the window. Sue checked the mushrooms which were starting to turn colour. She looked up at the clock again. It was now just after twenty past seven. Sue huffed. It was obvious that the weather had caused Michael some problems but she thought even he would have got home by now. Twenty-five past came and went and very soon it was half past seven. Sue turned off the mushrooms and turned the grill down.

"Where are you?" She said out loud to herself. Then it struck her that Michael might have his mobile phone with him. She checked around in the kitchen and then in the bedroom but there was no sign of it so she rang the number. There was a strange beeping noise to start with but it was obvious that the phone was turned off. 'David's mobile' she said to herself. Sue wondered if David had his mobile with him, but she checked and found it in his bedroom. She went back to the kitchen and looked out of the window again in case she might will him home quicker, but of course it was useless. She sat back down again and rubbed her forehead. Then she twiddled her fingers but all that happened was that time passed faster. It was nearly twenty-five to eight and Michael had been gone over an hour. She looked at the plates set on the table. The candle and napkins. She was getting angry. How could he spoil her surprise? She turned the grill and oven off completely and looked at the half cooked meal. A tear came to her eye and she fought it back. "Bloody men!" she shouted.

There was a lot of pacing up and down the hallway from the living room to the kitchen and back again. It was now quarter to eight. Sue wondered if there was any reason for Michael to have gone anywhere else and not told her, but she couldn't think of anywhere. Perhaps he had broken down and was stuck in the mud somewhere. She thought of him struggling to make his way back home in this ghastly weather and was uncertain what she could do. In the end, she decided that she would have a cup of tea and sit down in the living room and wait. That was all she could do really. She was upset and would tell Michael so when he got home.

Eight o'clock came and went. Sue suddenly became aware that other problems would present themselves. It would be alright if Michael did get the car going again. He wouldn't be happy going out to collect them but he would have to. But if he couldn't get the car working again then Sue would have to make some other arrangements to pick the kids up. Without too much effort she decided that she could get a taxi firm to go and get them. She checked to see if she had enough money. She did. Then it crossed her mind that the phones might be down in this weather so she picked up the receiver. It was okay. So, she had worked out a contingency plan, now she was just waiting for Michael. It was fast approaching nine o'clock, and Sue was convinced that there had been a problem with the car. She thought about whether she should do anything with the food that was still half cooked in the kitchen but she didn't. Sue knew that the party was due to end about ten thirty, so if Michael hadn't got home by quarter to ten, she would ring a taxi. She tried hard to relax and not worry, but it was a pointless exercise. It was a difficult situation as she wasn't quite sure what to do for the best. It was obvious that all she really could do was to sit and wait. It was very irritating.

As the time reached ten o'clock and Michael had still not got home, Sue started to look for a telephone number for a taxi firm. There was one in Somerby but she couldn't remember the name so she searched through the Yellow Pages to try and find it. It took a couple of minutes but eventually Sue found a number. She noted it down on a piece of scrap paper. She was uncertain whether or not to ring Ness's parents to let them know what was going on but she decided to ring the taxi firm first. "Hello, White Star taxis."

"Oh, hello. I need a taxi to pick up my kids please."

"At what time, madam?"

"Ten-thirty."

"I'm sorry, but we have no taxis free till about eleven thirty."

"What, none?"

"Sorry, madam, but it's Friday night and they are all out on bookings. I'm sorry we can't help. Have you tried Beeline?"

"No, I haven't heard of them. Have you got a number for them please?" Sue took down the details and replaced the receiver. She looked at her watch. It was now ten past ten and time was getting tighter. Sue rang the number she had been given but got an engaged signal. She rang again with the same result. 'They're probably all busy' she thought to herself. She then rang the number she had for Vanessa. All she got this time was a ringing tone. Nobody was at home. She doubted whether she had rung the correct number so she dialled again. Still no answer. Sue then realised everyone was at the party. She had forgotten that it was being held at the village hall. One more try at ringing Beeline Taxis but again the phone was engaged. She had almost forgotten about Michael.

She tried Vanessa's again and was almost taken by surprise when the phone was actually answered.

"Hello."

"Oh, hello, is that Vanessa's mum?" Sue felt the relief as she heard the phone being answered.

"No. I'm Harry's friend, Jane. Can I help you?"

"Oh, I hope so. I'm Louise's mum. Louise is one of Vanessa friends." Sue stopped to give the woman a chance to take that in. "My two are there at the party, Louise and David."

"Yes, okay."

"It's just that my husband was supposed to be picking them up but he won't be able to and I'm trying to get a taxi but haven't had much luck yet."

"Look, I don't know who Louise is or David for that matter. I'll pop over and tell Harry. Where do you live? In Leafby?"

"No, we live in Somerby."

"Look, don't worry. I'll see if we can get one of the other parents to give them a lift back, if not I'll drive them back myself. Don't you worry, we'll get them home." The phone went dead. Sue wanted to thank the woman on the other end but she had gone. Sue hoped that she had gone straight back to the party to get things sorted. She felt a little better but was still concerned as Michael was still not home. 'I'm going to give him a right piece of my mind' Sue thought. He was nearly three hours late and hadn't got home or bothered to phone. Sue wasn't happy with him, and was he going to know it. Then it struck Sue that he might have been involved in an accident. He might be hurt. 'It would only serve him right if he was' she thought.

At a quarter to eleven the phone rang.

"At last!" Sue said guessing it would be her

embarrassed husband. "Hello, where have you been?" Sue spoke in a most sarcastic tone, and anybody hearing her would have known how she was feeling.

"Er, hello." The woman's voice on the other end was a bit uncertain.

"Oops, sorry. I thought you were someone else."

"Hello. Is that Louise's mum?"

"Yes. Is that Vanessa's mum?"

"Yes. Sorry I couldn't ring back earlier."

"No problem. Have you managed to find a lift for them or do you want me to arrange for a taxi to come and pick them up?" Sue was hoping they were already on the way home.

"Er, well." The voice on the other end was dithering so Sue now guessed she would need to get a taxi. "You did say Louise and David were at Vanessa's party?"

"Yes. At Leafby Village Hall." Sue was a bit confused by the question.

"How were they getting here?" Sue again found the question strange.

"Well, my husband dropped them off."

"I'm not quite sure how to tell you this but neither Louise nor David have been to the party this evening."

"What?" Sue found it hard to take it in. There was a silence.

"Hello. Sorry I don't know your name, but neither Louise nor David came to the party, in fact both Vanessa and Mary were quite upset that they didn't." Sue was stunned. Without even thinking she just hung up the phone and tried to work out what might have happened. It soon dawned on her that the car must have broken down on the way to the party with David and Louise still in the car. So why hadn't they been in touch? Then she tried to imagine what Michael might do. If the car was broken down he would have tried to get it started. If he couldn't then he would have to walk to get help or walk back home. But then he wouldn't leave the kids in the car, would he? She was beginning to understand what a difficult situation her husband had faced. So, he would have had to persuade them all to walk somewhere. Probably back home, if not to the party. But they had been out there for over four hours now. It wouldn't have taken that long, would it? Surely, they would have got back home by now. Could they have got lost? Sue had been to Leafby only once before but she was certain it was a fairly simple route from Somerby. Then she thought it might not have been the car breaking down but an accident. What if they were injured? Lying in the road. All sorts of thoughts were now going through Sue's head. The phone rang. Sue picked it up but said nothing.

"Hello, is that Louise's mum?"

"Yes," Sue said slowly.

"This is Vanessa's mum again. Are you all right?"

"Yes." Sue was practically in auto response mode.

"Is there anything I can do to help?" Vanessa's mum sounded concerned. "Have you called the police?"

"Thank you." Sue just hung up. She had half taken in what had been said. Police. Yes, she should ring the police. Sue picked up the phone and dialled 999. "Hello, Emergency Services, which service do you require?" The actual words took Sue by surprise again.

"Er, oh. I want to find out if there's been an accident please."

"Are you calling to report an accident madam?"

"I want to find out if there has been an accident. My husband and children are missing."

"Madam, if you are not reporting an accident you need to go through to the police. I will put you through." There were a few clicks and another person came on to the line.

"Hello. Police Control Room, how can I help?"

The officer dealing with the call in the Control Room was very patient and took time with Sue to get the details of her problem. Sue was starting to panic and the officer couldn't help but notice. She had managed to ask if there had been any road accidents in the Somerby or Leafby area that evening and he was able to tell her that none had been reported, but she then went on to say that her family were missing and she wanted to report it. He knew that there was very little that the police would do at this stage as they required at least twenty-four hours to lapse before treating anyone as officially missing but he sensed that this situation was a bit different and would probably lead to an enquiry of some sort. He tried to keep her as calm as he could, but decided that it would be best to get someone to call round and see her personally. He knew that a patrol from the town's police station could be there reasonably quickly and he told Sue he would get someone to call round. The time was now quarter past eleven.

At half past eleven the doorbell rang, and Sue found two uniformed officers waiting outside in the pouring rain.

"Come in, please." She stepped back to allow them access into the kitchen.

"Hello, Mrs Riddell?" The first officer went through the correct procedure to ensure that they were talking to the right person although they were certain they had the right place.

"Yes, I called you."

"You say your husband and children are missing?"

"Yes. They went out to a party, and then I expected them back…" Sue was talking quickly and erratically, but she was interrupted by the officer.

"Can we just take it one step at a time, please, Mrs Riddell." Sue stopped talking. "Do you mind if John here makes a cup of tea?"

"Oh, sorry I should have offered." Sue looked over at the kettle.

"No, that's okay. How do you take your tea Mrs Riddell?"

"Milk and half a sugar." Sue sat down and her head

fell into her hands. She wanted to cry but not in front of the police.

"Let's just start from the beginning, please." The officer waited for Sue to regain her composure and when she was sat up properly, he asked his first question. "Can you give me the names of the people who are missing?"

"My husband. Michael. My son David…" Sue was interrupted again.

"No, sorry, Mrs Riddell, but I need their full names and dates of birth if you can please."

"Oh, of course. Michael Robert Riddell. His date of birth is the ninth of February nineteen-sixty." Sue paused to allow the officer time to write that down. "Then there's my son David Michael Riddell, whose birthday is the ninth of July nineteen eighty." Again, Sue waited. "And my daughter Louise Elaine Riddell. Date of birth, fifteenth March nineteen-eighty-three." Sue watched the officer write all the details into his notebook. "So there haven't been any accidents tonight?" Sue just wanted to check. The officer took a deep breath before answering.

"No, none that we've been made aware of. But we don't get to hear about all accidents."

"So, it might be that there is an accident, one you don't know about?" Sue was getting confused.

"It's very unlikely, but is a possibility. Now can you just tell me what time your family left this evening?"

"Well, David and Louise were going to a party in

Leafby. At Leafby Village Hall." Sue paused but
noticed that the officer wasn't writing anything.
"Are you making a note of this?"

"No, not at the moment. Please continue."

"Well, the party was at seven but my husband
wasn't quite sure about how to get there or how
long it would take so he wanted to leave a bit
earlier. They left at six thirty."

"Do you know what route they would have taken?"

"Route?" Sue didn't know. In fact she thought that
there was only one route to take. "I didn't know
there was more than one route."

"Yes, there are one or two routes. Would your
husband normally take one of the little lanes to get
to Leafby or would he drive towards Caister first?"

"I don't think he's ever driven to Leafby before to
be honest. He only passed his test last month." As
Sue spoke, the two officers looked at each other.

"When exactly?"

"Oh, yes. It was the first of December."

"Does he drive much?"

"Yes, he uses the car for work every day." This
reply seemed to satisfy the officers more.

"Did you say you've spoken to the mother who was
holding the party?"

"Yes, and she said that David and Louise never
arrived."

"Can you give me her name please?"

"Well, no, not really as I only know her as
Vanessa's mum. I do have a telephone number
though, would that help?"

"Yes, that would do nicely. You say she lives in Leafby?"

"Yes, obviously quite near to the Village Hall but I don't know where."

"Okay." The officer made a few quick scribbles in his notebook and then got up to quietly converse with his colleague. Sue tried to listen but couldn't make out everything. "Oh, could you tell me the details of the car, you know make, model and registration number?" Sue knew where the documents were and went off to retrieve them. She handed them to the police officer who made some more notes. He paused for a while and turned and looked at Sue. "We are going to look at the different routes to see if there are any broken-down cars anywhere, or accidents, and check the hospitals again and let you know when we locate them. They'll probably be stuck out in the wilds somewhere. We'll get them." The officer gave a half smile to Sue. "Are you going to be all right on your own, or can you call a relative or friend to come and sit with you for a while?"

"There isn't anyone I could really ask. I'll be all right. Please find them." Sue sat staring at nothing.

The two officers left and got back into their control car. After a little discussion, they decided that they would make a couple of sweeps around the various routes themselves to see if they could see any signs of an accident or breakdown, but get the station to check the hospitals. It was also suggested that they get a female officer to make the return call back to Mrs Riddell. So, after making the arrangements with the station, they drove around for about an hour and a half. The rain was still coming down but it had eased slightly. They looked for signs of cars driving off the road or into ditches, but they came up with nothing. They had to admit that it wasn't as thorough a search as they could have carried out in daylight, but they were confident that they would have seen any cars if they had been there. At two in the morning, two other officers called at Sue's house to let her have the current news. This time one of the officers was a female and she persuaded Sue to get some sleep. She offered to stay with her if she wanted but Sue refused. It was also explained that they would want to come and see her again the following morning to ask her some further questions to try and help find her family. Sue accepted that it would be so.

Friday evening turned into Saturday morning and at nine thirty the doorbell rang. Sue had already been up for at least a couple of hours and knew who it was going to be. She opened the door to allow in two plain clothed officers. They both showed their identification cards. "Hello, Mrs Riddell, sorry to hear about your current situation."

"Thank you, but I'm doing fine. Can I make you tea?"

"No, thank you. We don't want to stay too long, we just have a couple of other questions to ask you.

First, though, I take it you haven't heard from your husband?"

"I would have told you if I had."

"Okay, so I just need to confirm some details of the car your husband is driving." The officer had his notebook out ready to take down the details. Sue went to the bedroom and picked up the big envelope with the various documents in which she brought back to the kitchen with her. She handed the envelope to the officer who went through papers inside before finding what he wanted. He wrote down some details and handed the envelope back to Sue.

"There isn't much else we need to know at this stage. Obviously if you hear anything at all, we would appreciate it if you could ring and tell us."

"So, are you looking for them as missing persons now?"

"No, not at the moment. We have to wait twenty-four hours before we can class them as missing. Usually people will turn up within that time and we still hope we'll find your family somewhere soon. They've possibly had to find shelter for the night and will make contact with you later today." The officer didn't really think it would happen like that but his job was to make Mrs Riddell as positive as he could.

"So what are you going to do now?"

"We're going to run the car through some computers to see if there have been any reports of it anywhere. We'll let you know if we find anything."

He sounded positive. Sue opened the door to let them back out and then sat back down at the kitchen table. She looked at the half cooked mushrooms and remembered she still had potatoes in the oven. She didn't know what to do. She didn't feel like doing anything.

Only half an hour later there was someone else at the door. Sue hoped it was Michael or the police to tell her that they had found them, but it was neither. It was Doc. Sue's immediate thoughts were 'oh no not you' but there was something about Doc that she found relaxing.

"Hello. Mrs Riddell, I've heard the news and I was just passing. I wondered if there was anything I could do to help you all?"

"Help us all?" Sue wasn't sure whether to laugh or cry at this statement as she opened the door to allow Doc in. "It's only me who needs help, Doc."

"Well, yes, okay." Doc wasn't sure what to make of this comment as he made his way into the kitchen. "Isn't D…" Doc stopped himself from talking and coughed to hide his words. "Isn't your husband here?" Doc listened out to see if he could hear Michael but there was nothing. "I assume he is out looking?"

"Out looking?" This upset Sue. "Out bloody looking where?" Sue started to cry and Doc hugged her and tried to comfort her. He guessed he had got something wrong, and felt he shouldn't jump to his conclusions. "I heard that David had gone missing."

"Oh, sorry Doc. I shouldn't have a go at you." Sue tried to compose herself a little. "It's not just David. My husband and daughter have also gone missing." Sue sighed and sat herself back down.

"All three have gone missing?" This was a big surprise to Doc and it seemed to surprise him. "Sorry, I only thought David had gone."

Sue cried again and the two gave each other another hug before she regained her composure and sat up. "So, there it is. The police are making enquiries and nobody seems to know what has happened to them." Doc was deep in thought and only half heard what Sue was telling him.

"Don't the police have any idea what has happened?"

"No, not at all."

"Haven't they checked down Leafby Lane at all?" Doc seemed annoyed but then decided not to make any further comments.

"Yes, they've checked down there apparently but have found nothing." Sue stood up as she spotted another car park outside of the bungalow. It was an official looking car and she guessed that it was going to be the police. "The police are here, so perhaps you ought to go, Doc." Sue moved towards the door. As she opened it, a detective was already standing waiting to come in.

"Mrs Riddell, I'm Detective Sergeant Bailey." The officer showed her his identity card. "I would like to have a few words with you, if that's okay."

"Yes, please come in." Sue opened the door to allow both officers in. They looked at Doc with a little confusion.

"Good to see that the neighbours are looking after you." Sue realised that she hadn't introduced him.

"Oh, this is Doc from the local café," Sue said as she shut the door.

"Ah, yes, Doc." The detective spoke as if he knew the name. "It would be preferable if you could leave us now so we can talk to Mrs Riddell in private please." The police officer beckoned towards the door and Doc took the hint.

Sergeant Bailey knew the village well and many of the people who lived in it. He knew Doc and much of his background, and wasn't concerned too much about him being there. He knew he was friendly with many of the villagers because of the café, and assumed Doc was just round trying to comfort Mrs Riddell. Now the Riddells were a different kettle of fish. He knew almost nothing about them. He knew they hadn't lived in the village very long and he needed to find out a bit more about them, especially Mr Riddell. He sat Sue down at the kitchen table and took out a notebook.

"So, what does your husband do for a living, Mrs Riddell, or can I call you Sue?"

"Yes, please call me Sue. He works at a bank." This caused an eyebrow to be raised, but only for a moment.

"And how do you and your husband get on?" The

police continued to question Sue for nearly an hour, trying to establish whether there was any reason for Michael Riddell to run off with the kids, or possibly commit suicide. They couldn't find any reason at all.

Detective Bailey left Sue, telling her that the police would be doing everything they possibly could to find her husband and children, and that she would be sensible to ask for a relative to come and stay with her. Sue nodded and thanked him. The two police officers got back into their car and discussed the case.

"Let's go and take another drive down Leafby Lane, shall we?" They drove to the spot where it seemed obvious a car had skidded off the road and got out but there were no signs of any crashed car.

"I don't think there's any car here, Sarge."

"No, you're right." Detective Bailey scratched his head, as he couldn't see how the car could have driven back on to the road unless it had reversed. "I think we'll need to get a team down here to give the area a good going over." They headed back to the station.

In the incident room, officers were sat around a table and whiteboard trying to piece things together. "We know the three of them left home at six thirty or thereabouts, so by now he could have got to a port or airport quite easily." Detective Inspector Baldry spoke out loud to his team.

"Yes, Guv, but there is nothing that we have found to suggest that he would do that. He was perfectly happy, no marital problems and no money troubles."

"True, but you never know." The inspector rubbed his chin. "Put out a request to all ports and airports for the three of them and see if we can pick up the car on the ANPR system. Meanwhile I want a team searching that wood and interview the staff at the café to see if Doc has anything to hide."

Sue had been left thinking over what had just taken place. Did the police really think that Michael had run off with the kids? There was obviously no accident and he hadn't phoned anyone to say he was in trouble so what else could have happened to them? Sue looked through some of Michael's clothes and papers for any sign. Did he have another woman somewhere? Was he depressed? Sue dismissed both considerations. There was another ring on the doorbell.

"Oh, hello Doc," Sue said, as she opened the door.

"Are you okay? Is there anything you want me to do or get for you?" Doc wasn't quite sure what he should do for the best.

"Thanks, but no. Look I need to get my head around all of this so if you don't mind…" Sue started to close the door.

"Please ask if you need anything. Anything at all." Doc stood as the door closed. He knew she was hurting and wanted to comfort her but he also knew it wasn't his place to do so. He put his mind to where Michael and Louise might be and decided to make his way back down to the woods.

A search team consisting of six officers made their way to the woods to start their inch by inch search. It was an unusual situation as there were indications of a car skidding into the woods, but they were also asked to look on it as a possible missing person's case. The team followed the skid marks from the road as far as they could which took them past a damaged tree that looked as if it might have been hit by a car. It was half felled, and there was a trace of silver paint on it, which matched the colour of the missing car. The team's leader took an overall look at what they had found and deduced that the car had skidded off the road, hit the tree and spun when it should have then hit two other trees and come to a halt. Perhaps the car had been somehow lucky enough to spin around one hundred and eighty degrees and found itself in a position where it could just drive back on to the road the same way it had skidded off but he wasn't convinced.

The positioning of the trees would have had him expecting to find the car bashed and broken but there were no indications at all of this. No broken glass, no bits of metal, nothing. The team went no further than about twenty yards into the woods as there seemed no use in doing so. The car couldn't have gone any further in this direction so they kept their search to this area. They looked for foot prints, blood spatter, anything to show that someone had been there and they eventually found some footprints, an adult's. They followed the prints and they seemed to lead in from the road, walk around a bit and then lead back to the road.

Doc made his way back to the wood and saw the team searching in the area he would have chosen to search himself. He hadn't gone much further into the wood than that himself, and he hoped to have found some indication of the crashed car exactly where they were searching. Perhaps they had got out of the car and walked into the woods a bit further, he thought to himself, so he walked around the search team and made for a point deeper in the wood. No more than two minutes had passed when he thought what a stupid idea it was as if they had left the car then it would have still been there. He was at a loss himself. As he stood and tried to work out what might have happened he failed to spot a police officer walking in his direction.

"Hello, are you injured?" The officer called out. Doc looked up and saw his predicament immediately. He thought as quickly as possible.

"No, I've just come from the village to help you search." Doc hoped that this would be received with some thanks.

"Sorry, sir, but we need to do this ourselves." The officer walked up to Doc and took his arm. "If you could come this way please." The officer led him back to the search site. He wasn't under arrest but they weren't going to let him go. The team leader spoke next.

"What's your name?"

"I'm Doc."

"What's that supposed to mean? Do you think you're a time traveller from Gallifrey or something?" The officers laughed.

"No that's what I'm known as. Doc."

"So, what's your real name?" Doc wasn't happy to give him a name. After leaving the orphanage he lost his real identity and just went by the name of Doc but his documents showed his registered name which he gave the police.

After a quick call, another squad car was despatched to the woods and Doc was arrested. They suspected he was involved with the disappearance of the three missing persons but couldn't really say how or why so they took him back to the police station to interview him and generally keep him out of the way whilst they continued their own enquiries. He was held overnight but never charged.

Sunday was very similar to Saturday. The police called round to see Sue, but had no further information. They asked a number of further questions, but even they had no real idea as to where Michael and the kids might be. It was a total mystery to all of them. A policewoman was sent to stay with Sue but she argued that she wanted her privacy. This wasn't met with great acceptance.

Sue wondered if they thought she was being blackmailed, but surely, they knew there was nothing anyone could get from her. She wasn't rich and didn't have much. The police for their part never seriously considered blackmail. Sue wasn't acting in a way that suggested such. The policewoman agreed that if Sue was happy to get some sleep and take a sleeping tablet so she would definitely get some sleep then she would leave her. There was a card with a telephone number that Sue could ring anytime of the day and there would be regular patrols passing her home just in case. Sue agreed and by ten o'clock that evening she was tucked up in bed asleep.

Monday morning was disturbed by a ring on the front doorbell. It half stirred Sue, but it wasn't enough to wake her. It rang again. Sue woke suddenly but she wasn't quite sure where she was. She had heard the noise, but couldn't quite make out what it was. It was almost as if she was in a dream but everything was dark. Her eyes fell upon the clock on her bedside cabinet. It told her it was just after five in the morning. This seemed to bring her back to reality and she suddenly remembered she was in bed and that the ringing she had heard was the front doorbell. She would many times in the future wonder how or why, but there was something that told her she must get up. An inner self was letting her know that she mustn't go back to sleep. Sue jumped out of bed.

It was cold but she put the light on and grabbed her dressing gown. The bell hadn't rung again, but Sue rushed to see who was there. She would normally see through the window, but there was nobody there. Was it the police? Was it a neighbour? Sue went to the living room window to see if there were any vehicles waiting in the road. There were none. She thought about going back to bed. Her head was aching and she was tired. She went back to her bedroom but decided she would have a drink first. A nice hot drink would do her good. She made her way into the kitchen again and grabbed the kettle. As she started to fill it up at the sink she became aware that something had been left outside the front door. She couldn't make it out too clearly, but there were shadows that indicated that a parcel had been left there. She put the kettle on and then unlocked the front door.

As Sue pushed, something stopped her opening the door. She pushed again, and the door opened a bit. The package started to move, as Louise struggled to her feet. It was Louise! Sue wasn't quite sure if this was real or she was still dreaming.

"Louise!" Sue shrieked. She opened the door and put her arms around Louise. "Are you alright?" Sue squeezed her tight. "Where have you been?" Sue

squeezed her a bit tighter. "Oh, darling, I love you!"
"Mum, you're hurting me," Louise complained as Sue squeezed her even tighter.

"Oh, my darling, you're safe." Sue let her go. She took a step back to look at her daughter. She was bloodied and bruised, and her clothes looked as if they had been half ripped from her. Sue didn't know what to do.

"Can I come in please?" Louise was ready to drop. Sue helped her into the kitchen.

Sue sat Louise down on one of the chairs in the kitchen but as soon as she left her she dropped onto the table and almost fell asleep. "Mum, can I go to bed?" Louise pleaded.

"Yes, of course you can, darling." Sue stroked Louise's head to comfort her whilst taking the opportunity to look at the wounds on her arms and legs. "Where have you been?" Sue queried. Louise didn't seem to understand the question and it was almost as if they were speaking different languages.

"Where's Dad?" Louise replied in an extremely tired and pathetic voice. Sue just needed to know what had happened.

"Where's David?" Sue was concerned.

"Mum, I just need to go to bed." Louise was already half asleep. "Dad will tell you all about it." Sue realised that Louise was completely shattered and guessed that sleep was the best thing for her at the moment. She could ask her more when she had had some rest. There was a little bit more conversation and Sue helped Louise to bed. "I just need to sleep. Don't get me up too early will you?" Louise said wearily. Sue just wanted what was best for her daughter at that very moment and sleep it was. Louise went to bed and fell asleep within seconds.

Tuesday morning came and the police were keen to talk to Louise as soon as they could. Sue had informed them the previous evening about her return but had refused to allow anyone to come and question her then. She had told them that Louise was tired and had gone to sleep, and that the following morning was quite soon enough to ask her lots of questions. Sue was concerned that they would upset Louise, so even though she knew she had to let the police ask, she was going to be right there with her in case they went too far.

At nine o'clock, Sergeant Bailey and two other detectives were at the door. Sue let them in and was pleased to see that one of them was a woman. Louise would feel more comfortable with a woman, she thought.

"Has she told you what happened to her, Mrs Riddell?" Sergeant Bailey was keen to find out if there was any explanation of what might have happened.

"No, I'm afraid not. She was extremely tired so I put her to bed."

"Yes, I see." Sergeant Bailey nodded. "And your husband and son?"

"Nothing. They haven't turned up, but Louise seemed to think that they were here." Sue started to cry and the policewoman put an arm around her shoulder. "I don't know where they are." The tears made it hard for Sue to talk as she spluttered these few words. "Don't you know where they are?" Sue continued to cry and the policewoman sat her down on the chair and worked at calming her down.

Suddenly, Louise appeared at the kitchen door. "Are you alright, Mummy?" she asked, as she clung on to the door frame tightly. Sue got up and opened her arms.
"Yes, Louise. Mummy's alright but she needs a hug."
Louise ran to her and they embraced, hard. Louise began to cry. "I don't know where Daddy is!" she sobbed. "Has he left? Where's David?"
Louise wept and moaned while Sue tried her best to comfort her. "I don't feel too well," she groaned, but wouldn't let her mum go.

The police knew how difficult the situation was, but also knew that soon they might be able to ask a few questions. Louise did eventually settle down and told them her story, but it wasn't what they were expecting. She told them about the car skidding off the road, and then spinning around into the woods. Louise told them about road workers, and cow horns, which seemed most strange, but for them, the biggest problem was that she didn't know where her dad and brother were. The whole thing seemed like a little girl's fantasy.

They left the house, wondering if Louise was making it up. She did seem to have been in an accident, but had no idea where she had been for the past few days. The woods she described sounded like the place they had searched, so they took another drive down Leafby Lane. This time, they found debris exactly where she said it should be. The police had searched this area before and found nothing, but there it was: part of a wrecked car, and obvious signs of an accident. They also saw blood on the ground. It made no sense. There was only half a car. Where was the rest of it? The enquiry was far from over.

Louise was questioned again and again over the next few days, but her story never changed. She kept talking about men with shovels, men with furry coats and other puzzling things, but at no time could she say where she had been for the days she was missing. Sue couldn't figure out exactly what had happened, but she knew that Louise was very shaken by it all and just wanted her to get back to normal as quickly as she could.

Chapter 15
LOUISE'S STORY

Friday 4th January 1996

Louise felt the car swerve and she was convinced that they were going to have an accident. Almost as if it was automatic, she gave out a little scream. She could see her dad struggling with the wheel of the car but it didn't seem to be making any difference. She looked at her brother and could see that he was also frightened. He was holding on for dear life to anything he could. Michael was swearing and muttering. A branch hit the windscreen with an almighty whack which frightened Louise even more. She screamed again. She guessed that what she was witnessing was what happened to you before you died. She screamed again. And again. She didn't want to die. The car started to spin. Louise continued to scream. She just wanted it all to end.

There was a loud crack and a flash of light. Louise wasn't quite sure what the light was or where it came from but it lit up the whole car. She could see every little detail of the inside of the car. Despite all this, she was aware that the car was spinning around and that her dad was still struggling with the wheel trying to get control of the car. She could see him from an odd angle, as if she had come loose from her seat and had floated above her father and could see him from an elevated position. She was still screaming but didn't quite know why. She could also see David from above. David was in one seat, her dad was in another, but they had been separated. All three of them seemed to have been separated. The car appeared to have split into three pieces. They were all spinning around, but slowly, while everything else was spinning around quickly, a bit like being in the eye of a storm. There were other objects moving in and out of the spiral that the three were in. There was a man in a vest, a bit dirty, but just looking at the three of them. He spun around with them for a few seconds and then drifted out of their view.

There was also a shovel moving around with them, no, a spade rather than a shovel. The sort for digging the garden with. There was a cow's horn. These items spun around with the three of them for a few seconds before disappearing. The light was bright but not as blinding as it had been. Louise had stopped screaming but was feeling dizzy and sick. She saw a tree appear and it too spun around before moving on, then a yellow hard hat appeared. There was a quick turn then Louise noticed what looked like a space vehicle. It was silver and seemed to have no controls at all. She was hardly able to take it in before it disappeared, and then a big bearded man appeared. He was wearing a fur garment and a helmet with horns. Louise felt sick again and was dropping. She lost sight of her dad and brother and began falling quicker and quicker. There was a bump. There was silence.

The Somerby Tree

Monday 7th January 1996

Louise regained consciousness slowly. She looked around as she opened her eyes, and she could see she was in a wood. It was darkish, but there was enough light to make out trees. She was restrained in some way and couldn't move. She started to cry but the feeling of cold stopped her from crying too much. She couldn't work out where she was or how she had got there. Perhaps it was a dream but it felt so real. After a few minutes, she realised she was strapped down on a mattress. The strapping resembled a car seat belt. She looked at the metal cage next to her and it became apparent that she was in fact strapped down on a piece of old car. She struggled with the belt release clip, but it wasn't coming free. She started to cry again.

Her efforts only made her feel worse and she started shivering. She had another go at the seat belt catch and this time it opened. She jumped up and ran about twenty yards before coming to an abrupt stop. She had no idea where she was running to, she just wanted to get away. She could see the sky getting a bit brighter as the sun began to rise. As the light got better, Louise looked around her recognised exactly where she was. She was in the wood next to Leafby Lane. As if a big cover had been taken away, she remembered that she was on her way to Ness's party. She was in the car with Dad and David. Where had they gone? Louise ran back to where she had been strapped down and she called out.

"Dad! Dad!" The effort needed to shout out was immense and she realised that she had hurt her neck. Her arm felt sore as well. She looked at her right arm. Her blue blouse had been ripped and there was blood coming from a cut on her arm. She slumped to the ground and began crying again.

"David!" She tried to shout but it was no good, she just couldn't get the energy. "David..." She sobbed. Feeling cold again she looked around for her cardigan but it was nowhere to be found. It then struck her that part of the car was missing. What she could see in front of her was just the back section of the car.

"Dad!" She gave out one last shout.

The rain had stopped but the ground around and about was still damp. There was a breeze, but it wasn't that bad. Louise wondered where her dad and David could have gone. 'They've just gone off and left me' she thought to herself. The more she considered it, the more she cried. She thought about Ness's party and was upset at the thought of missing it even though she hadn't been that keen to go in the first place. The light was getting brighter by the minute. Louise sat on the car seat for about half an hour before deciding that she would have to walk back home.

As she sat there, she had slipped off the seat a bit and her trousers were covered in mud. The first thought she had was that Mum would murder her if she went home with mud on her new trousers. She tried to rub the mess off with her hands but it did no good. It didn't matter how hard she rubbed, the mud just stayed on there. She needed something hard to really get to it. She removed her belt and used the buckle pin in the hope that it would be more successful. It wasn't. She saw a large twig and had a go with that. All it did was to rip a hole in her trousers. She gave up.

She started to walk. Her arm hurt and her ankle hurt but she stumbled through the muddy woodland back to the road. There was a cleared path from where she was to the road, which had obviously been made by the car when it crashed. The wind blew. Louise shivered. She was in pain but she was walking. She rubbed her arm a bit more and got mud on her blouse. She looked around for signs of where Dad or David might have gone or indeed where the rest of the car was. She remembered the accident but not too much detail.

Making her way to Leafby Lane, Louise looked up at the sky to see that the sun had now fully risen. The light was a friendly one after such an ordeal. She was angry that her dad had left her. Almost as angry that David had also left her behind. She walked with a stumble and after about ten minutes had reached the old cottages on Leafby Lane. Nobody was about. No cars were driving around. The birds were twittering though. Louise got to the newer houses on the green and from here she made a diagonal path over to Doc's, and from there back home. She saw a couple of cars, but Louise just had her mind set on getting home. She didn't really notice what else was going on. It was early and there wasn't anyone around to see her.

Louise stumbled along and fought her way up Rawthorn Drive to her front door. She didn't have a front door key so she had to ring the bell which she did almost without thinking. She was tired, cold and upset. It didn't really cross her mind but there were no signs that there had been any troubles at the bungalow. If she had thought about it at the time, she would have thought that her mum would have been waiting up for her to return. Why was nobody worried that she had spent the night in the woods? Having stood there for a while it was obvious that nobody was coming to answer the door. She rang the bell again. Had her mum and dad run off somewhere and left her behind? Had her brother been part of it or had he been left in the woods as well? She slumped to the ground and rested against the front door completely worn out.

It seemed like ages before she felt the front door push her forwards. Someone was in. Someone was opening the door. Louise struggled to her feet. It was Mum.

"Louise!" Sue shrieked. Sue opened the door and put her arms around Louise. "Are you alright?" Sue squeezed her tight. "Where have you been?" Sue squeezed her a bit tighter. "Oh darling I love you."

"Mum, you're hurting me." Louise said. Her mum was squeezing her so tight that she was finding it hard to breath.

"Oh, my darling you're safe!" Sue spoke as she took a step back. Sue looked her up and down and Louise wasn't quite sure what to say. In the end her reply was simple.

"Can I come in, please?" Louise was ready to drop. Sue helped her into the kitchen.

As Sue sat her down on one of the chairs in the kitchen she flopped over onto the table ready to sleep. "Mum, can I go to bed?" Louise pleaded.

"Yes, of course you can darling." Sue caressed her head and looked at the wounds on her arms and legs. "Where have you been?" Sue wanted to know.

"Where's Dad?" Louise was tired but felt that either David or her dad could have explained what had happened by now.

"Where's David?" Sue was concerned.

"Mum, I just need to go to bed." Louise was already half asleep. "Dad will tell you all about it." Sue realised that Louise was shattered. Perhaps sleep was going to be the best thing for her.

"Do you want to have a wash first?" Sue asked as she started to take Louise's clothes off her.

"No, Mum. I just need to sleep. Don't get me up too early will you?"

"Of course not, darling. I'll tell the school you're

safe but you won't be going in." Sue seemed worried about the silliest of things and telling the school that Louise wouldn't be back was probably the last thing she should have been worried about.

"School." Louise shook her head. "There's no school on Saturdays, Mum."

"No, I know that darling, now you get off to bed." Sue couldn't quite understand the relevance of the comment.

"But I haven't got to go back to school till Tuesday, have I?"

"No, darling that's right. It's Tuesday tomorrow so you'll be alright."

"No, Mum. It's Sunday tomorrow."

"No, darling, it was Sunday yesterday," Sue replied. Louise was confused but far too tired to work it all out. She went to bed and fell asleep within seconds.

The next morning Louise was woken up by a ring at the door and the murmur of voices coming from the kitchen. She was aching all over and had a headache but she was home and that was all she was worried about at that very moment. The talking continued and Louise wondered who it might be. She could make out a couple of voices and then it dawned on her that it might be her dad and brother. She gingerly made her way out of bed and across to the kitchen.

Louise made it to the kitchen door and saw her mum sat on the kitchen bench next to another woman who had her arm around her shoulder. Mum was crying and spluttering.

"Don't you know where they are?" Sue continued to cry.

"Are you all right, Mummy?" Louise was worried that her mum was in trouble and wasn't sure who these people were in her house. She stayed by the door. Her mum stood up and held her arms out wide asking for a hug.

"Yes, Louise, Mummy's all right but she needs a hug." Louise ran to her and they hugged hard. Louise cried.

"I don't know where Daddy is." Louise cried harder. "Has he left Mummy? Where's David?" Louise cried and sobbed a bit more whilst her mum held on to her tightly. "I don't feel too well." Louise felt her head but she wouldn't let go of her mum.

After a while, Louise was persuaded to tell the strangers what had happened to her. They were police officers which Louise was a bit frightened about, and they seemed to want her to tell them where she had been for the last few days. It was all very confusing as she had been nowhere but they seemed to think she had been kept locked up somewhere. She told them what she could remember but they didn't seem happy with what she was telling them.

After the police left she told her mum the whole story again. Sue had been concerned that Louise had in fact been locked up somewhere but believed her daughter when she told her she hadn't been. The police had mentioned Doc but Louise didn't seem to understand where he fitted into the whole thing at all. Sue was certain that she would have been able to see something in Louise's eyes if he had been. Louise was questioned another couple of times over the next few days but her story never changed. She told them about her Dad's driving, how the storm was loud, and the rain crashing against the windscreen, and how the car went off the road. She told them about the work men with shovels, the men with furry coats, the cow horns, the axes, and a number of other things that she could recall but that was it.

Louise couldn't work out herself what had happened. Where was Dad? Where was David? Had they been taken from the woods whilst she was buckled up in her part of the car? It was all so very confusing. She remembered talking to her brother just as they first turned into Leafby Lane telling him that she had a bad feeling about that night. She had meant the party, of course. Things weren't getting any clearer and Louise found life quite difficult over the following weeks.

Chapter 16
MICHAEL'S STORY

Friday 4th January 1996
Michael wasn't quite sure what to make of it all. He was still trying to get control of the car, but as he turned the steering wheel left and then right, it was being spun around by some outside force which Michael assumed was the strong wind. He had seen the lightning but hadn't immediately noticed that the light remained. He heard Louise screaming behind him, and David, obviously frightened, by his side, but he continued to try and steer the car to relative safety. Everything was spinning dizzily.

Michael looked again to see how David was coping, but was suddenly aware that he was not where Michael expected. David was still belted into his seat, but the car had split so the front seats were drifting apart. He looked behind him to see if he could see Louise, but there was nothing there. The back of the car had gone. They had somehow been separated. Michael felt himself spinning faster. He looked down at his arms, and then his hands, which were firmly gripping the steering wheel. His seat was intact, but something that had ripped the car into parts. Louise suddenly came into view, still screaming. They were spinning, but slowly, whilst everything around them was moving quickly. It felt like being in the eye of a storm. Oddly, they could see other objects flying around them. There was a workman in a vest. His face was dirty and he was sweating as if he had been working hard, but he was just looking at them. He spun around with them for a few seconds, and then drifted out of their view. There was also a shovel, the sort you would use to dig the garden. There was a carved cow horn, the kind of thing the Swiss use to make musical instruments. The light was quite bright but not as blinding as it had been. Michael tried to keep track of his children but couldn't watch both at once. He could see Louise. She was holding her hands over her ears. The noise was loud, but he could distinctly make out several different sounds. There was the noise of a whirring electrical motor. A silver vehicle came into view. Beyond it he could see Louise looking at the same vehicle. It had no obvious way of propulsion but it moved between them, quite unaware of their turmoil.

Michael tried to look for David. He couldn't see him anywhere. Louise was still there but David had gone. Michael tried to loosen the seat belt but he was unable to. He felt himself falling. The speed of the fall increased and he continued to spin. He closed his eyes. There was a bump. There was silence.

The next morning Michael suddenly became aware of the fact that he was in pain. He was a bit confused and aching all over. A number of questions went through his mind almost at once.

The Somerby Tree

Where was he? How did he get there? What day was it? What he did know was that his name was Michael Riddell which he thought was quite a useful thing to know.

First, he felt the pain in his head. It was as if he had hit it or had been hit with something very hard. He was convinced that there was a bump on his head so he tried to rub it. His automatic response was to try and move his right arm but this was more difficult than he had first thought as he was laying on his right arm and not only was it difficult to move from under his body but it had lost much of its feeling. His arm was practically numb so instead he moved his left arm which was free. He rubbed the bruise on his head. It only made it hurt more but it was an instinctive thing to do. Gradually things were coming back to him.

Michael found he was still buckled into the seat of his car. The front of the car had bent away from him but he was laying on the car door. He struggled with his left hand to release the seat belt and although it took a few moments it came away quite easily. His recollection of the accident was beginning to come back to him. The rain. The wind. The skidding. Michael got to his feet and looked back at where he had been lying, whilst rubbing his right arm to try and get some feeling back in it. His head was throbbing and his left leg was giving him pain as well. He rubbed his head once more with his right hand and this time noticed the blood on his fingers. He must have been cut.

As things started to take shape Michael remembered exactly what it was he was doing. 'I was driving to Leafby' he said to himself. It was dark. This caused a bit of confusion as it was now clearly daylight. He remembered that it was raining, in fact it was a storm. Perhaps I must have knocked myself out? Michael continued to try and piece things together. I was taking David and Louise to that birthday party. Louise was screaming. Where are they? He looked around but as he turned his leg gave way and he fell to the ground. David and Louise were nowhere to be seen. What have I done? He got back to his feet and looked around slowly this time. The wood seemed quite normal. No sign of rain. No sign of wind damage and certainly no sign of any car accident. He kicked at the seat of the car he had previously freed himself from. It moved a bit but all he really did was to hurt his toe.

"David!" Michael shouted out. A few birds flew off from their high perches. "Louise!" Michael tried to move a bit and walk. The pain was excruciating. "David, Louise!" There was no reply. Michael looked at his watch. It had stopped. The time said five past seven. Michael felt a trickle run down his cheek. He rubbed it with his hand and found it to be blood. He walked around a little bit but it wasn't that easy. The car couldn't be far away. He stopped and turned back to look at the part of the car that he had crawled away from. There wasn't much of it left, he thought to himself. What if the car had broken up into pieces when he drove off the road? He then got the idea to follow the cars tracks back to the road. He made his way back to the crumpled piece of metal.

Looking around again he tried to establish where exactly the road was. He knew he couldn't have travelled that far, so the road could only be about twenty or thirty yards away and he had expected to see a trail or path leading from the car back to the road. He must have made some tracks as he drove through the wood but there were none that he could see. Fairly happy with his bearings he walked a little way through the wood towards what he hoped would be Leafby Lane. The wood took a bit of an incline in the direction he was walking. Michael was happy with this as he could remember slightly that the car went down a dip. As he walked a bit further there was a steeper incline and at the top what looked like a lane. A feeling of success went through him. He tried to walk up the incline but it was difficult with the way his leg was. He walked along by the side of the lane when a strange noise caught his attention.

It was a strange humming noise, with the occasional whirring sound just a little bit louder. He looked in the direction of the sound and was dumbstruck at the sight of a rather shiny man-made structure there in the woods. It was about twenty feet high and made of metal. At the top of it was what looked like a plastic shield and it was from up there the sounds were coming. The structure, which by now seemed more like a wall cut right across Leafby Lane and continued for as far as he could see both left and right. Michael didn't know what to make of it. Whatever it was, he couldn't remember it being there before. Perhaps it was some electrical substation that was in the woods, that he hadn't realised was there. Had this been the cause of the accident? Michael tried to think but couldn't remember exactly what had happened. He just wasn't sure. What he was sure about was that he wouldn't be able to climb it, so he turned around and started to make his way back along the side of Leafby Lane, away from the structure.

He could see the remains of the wrecked car where he had awoken in the distance. There was still only a very little bit of it.

"David! David, can you hear me?" Michael called out again. "Louise!" Michael shouted at the top of his voice before falling to his knees. He beat the ground with his fist. It was useless. There was nobody left in the woods apart from him. He tried hard to work out a solution but he couldn't come up with one. Perhaps they had already been found and taken home. That sounded like a great answer. If that was the case though, why had nobody found him? He couldn't answer that. His head hurt. His leg was giving him much pain. He walked a little bit further and found a flatter route to Leafby Lane. As he got to the road he looked up to see the walled structure again. He was confused but more importantly he was tired and hurt. He needed to make his way back home.

Michael made his way across the village green and past the café, Doc's, as Michael knew it, but he saw nobody and didn't really look around very much. He just put his head down and made his way back home. He assumed it was quite early on the Saturday morning and that everyone was still in bed. Surely David and Louise hadn't just left him back in the woods but then if they had all been split up if the car broke apart, they might all have finished up in different places.

The walk up Rawthorn Drive was difficult because Michael's leg was hurting badly. He couldn't understand why but things just seemed a bit different to how he thought he remembered them. The gardens all seemed very uniform but he didn't have time to give them a closer look as he was just so tired. All he really wanted to do was go to bed.

He eventually found his way to number twenty-six and he walked up to the front door. He searched around in his pockets to find his front door key, but took a couple of minutes. With a bit of a struggle the key went into the lock and the front door opened. Michael threw off his coat. He assumed that Sue would be annoyed or worried.

"Sue, I'm home." Michael shouted out. There was no reply. "Sorry I'm late." There was a deathly silence. "Are the kids in?" Michael walked from the kitchen into the hall. The place seemed to be empty. Nobody was at home. He was uncertain as to what time it really was and wondered if Sue had gone out looking for him. He made his way to their bedroom and found the room freshly made up. The bed had been changed. It was too much of a temptation to resist so he took his clothes off and got into bed. Sue would understand why he had gone to bed, he thought. Within seconds he was asleep.

Michael slept for nearly twenty-four hours and woke up about six the next morning. He had dreamt about Viking warriors and workmen. It was all very confusing and he didn't feel quite right when he did wake up. He felt to his right hand side expecting Sue to be lying there next to him, but he was alone. He then reached out for the alarm clock but it wasn't there. 'What has Sue moved that for' he said to himself. He had taken off his wristwatch and that was lying on the bedside cabinet, so he looked at that, but it still said five past seven. The early sun was prising its way through the curtains so Michael was assured it was morning. 'Where on earth has Sue got to?' he said to himself

He began to take stock of all of his limbs and see

which ones were aching and which ones weren't. The effort of getting out of bed was much more than Michael expected, but eventually he got himself sat up with his legs hanging over the side of the bed. He rubbed his eyes and gave out another call. "Morning!" It was met with a strange dull quiet. More than a house being empty, Michael thought. He looked at the bedside cabinet and noted that it had nothing on top of it. Sue has moved the bedside lamp as well, he again thought to himself. As he pulled open the cabinet drawer he was surprised to find it empty. He then opened the other drawers to find them empty as well. He jumped to his feet but slowly made his way around the bedroom checking all drawers and wardrobes on the way. They were all empty. Had Sue left him? This was a further confusion. Had she planned to leave him whilst he was taking the kids to the party? He hadn't foreseen this. Michael next noted that the light switch had gone. He looked up at the ceiling and was even more surprised to find the light had gone as well. What had happened?

Michael made his way to the lounge. There was a settee and another matching chair but otherwise the room was empty. No television. No lights. He quickly checked the other bedrooms and the kitchen and they too were all different. They looked a bit like they should have done but they were all different. Michael went back to the bedroom, sat on the side of the bed and scratched his head. He needed to have a wash so made his way to the bathroom. This was completely different. It had a shower cubicle where the bath should have been, and a new sink. Michael put his hands to the sink and then realised there were no taps but the water came out regardless. It was quite automatic. As he took his hands away the water stopped. He put them back under and the water started running again. In only ten or fifteen seconds the water was hot so Michael splashed water over his face and washed himself. He felt better. He put his old clothes back on again which weren't brilliant but he felt happier.

Michael made his way back to the kitchen looking for a kettle so he could make a cup of tea. He couldn't find one. There were strange square things inset into the wall and on the worktop which all looked like microwave ovens, but he wasn't sure what they were. He noted a calendar on the wall for the year 2023. Michael squinted, looking closer. Did it really say that? As he grabbed the calendar, the string it was hanging from broke as if it was decayed. Michael flicked through the pages and sure enough, it was for the year 2023. Michael threw it onto the kitchen table and it knocked over an envelope he had failed to notice. He picked it up and saw that it was addressed to Dad. Michael assumed it was for him, and ripped open the envelope. Inside was a folded piece of paper and another, smaller, envelope. He unfolded the paper first, and saw it was a note signed by Louise which was addressed to Dad too. He read it a couple of times.

'Dad, not sure if you'll ever get this note but if you're reading it please try and get in touch with me if you can. If you remember the car accident back in 1996 you should know that things all went wrong from there. Not sure where you've been since, but I need to see you. David thought you might have gone into the future. I'm not sure he's right, but just in case you have, please read the enclosed letter which will help you. I love you, and have missed you all these years, and can't wait to see you. Your loving daughter, Louise.'

Michael started to cry. What had happened? He looked at the enclosed envelope. There was no name, but he opened it. Inside was yet another note, and a neatly folded piece of thicker paper. The note read 'This should be presented by Michael Riddell to the solicitor's offices of Ellis and Son on South Quay where they will advise as to what funds are available to him'. Michael shook his head. There was a date: 9th July 2020. He looked at the note, and this made things even more confusing. It was addressed to Dad but had Michael written in brackets after it. It was signed Doc, followed by (David). Michael found this all a bit strange. The note told of Doc's illness, and his reluctance to give up the hope of meeting his dad again. He said he was increasingly certain that his dad had been thrown into the future and could appear some time, but he wasn't sure if he would still be alive when this happened. He felt it necessary to make arrangements for such an event should it happen after he died. It finished very much as Louise's note had, saying how he missed his dad and loved him, and it was signed Doc. Michael wondered if he was going mad, or someone was playing a trick on him. He sat and stared at the papers in front of him for nearly twenty minutes.

Michael decided that Dawn next door would let him know what was happening so he made his way outside. He looked at the bungalow next door but it was very different to how he had remembered it with lots of black glass and shiny metal. The kitchen window suddenly turned from black to see through, and Michael spotted a woman drying her hands on a towel. It wasn't Dawn. The woman appeared at her front door. "Can I help you at all?"
"Is Dawn there?" Michael wondered if Dawn had some guests.
"Dawn? Who's Dawn?"
"Dawn…er, I don't know her surname." Michael had a sad tone in his voice. "Can I just speak to Dawn who lives there?"
"Sorry, there is no Dawn lives here. I'm Donna and I've been here for nearly twelve years. The person here before me was called Stephanie so I don't know who Dawn is." The woman saw his confusion. "Are you looking for the woman who

used to live at that place?"

"Yes, I am. Do you know where Sue is?" Michael hoped that at last there would be some answers but he wasn't.

"Sue. No, her name was Louise."

"Yes, Louise. Where is she?"

"She moved away when Doc died. It was his house really, I thought, but he left it all to her in his will, I think." This confused Michael even more. He didn't really want to ask much more in case the answers followed along the same path as the previous ones. He started to make his way back indoors but then thought of one last question.

"Sorry to ask, but what is the date?"

"The date?" Donna thought it a strange question. "It's the 6th of January."

Michael felt this was okay, but then realised it didn't actually answer the question completely.

"Yes, but what year?"

"Year! Twenty twenty-six of course. What year did you think it was?" Michael didn't reply.

Michael went back indoors and started to look a lot closer to the various things in there that he hadn't properly recognised. Obviously, the main style of the house was very much how it should have been but there were many gadgets or new bits of equipment that he couldn't recognise at all. Bit by bit he had to conclude that he was somewhere other than where he thought he might be. He was very confused and not sure what to do next so his first thought was to see if he could buy any food from the local shop. He went off on his way down to the shop but then realised he had very little money on him. He felt around in his pocket and pulled out about three pound fifty. That wouldn't buy much but perhaps he could buy a loaf of bread and something to put in it. He was starving. He hadn't got too far down Rawthorn Drive when he started to notice all the other bungalows in the road were very different to his. Their doors were very strange, more like shower doors and the whole place always seemed to be made of dark glass and metal. Michael stopped and studied one of the bungalows when suddenly the front door seemed to disappear and a woman appeared in the doorway. "Can I help you?" She asked softly.

"Oh, sorry, I was just admiring your bungalow." Michael pretended to look over the place. The woman went back into her bungalow although Michael didn't actually notice how she did it. All of a sudden, the door was back again almost like magic.

He carried on down to the little shop at the bottom of the road and made his way in through the open gap at the front of the store. The doors had been taken off by the looks of it he thought to himself. Quickly he walked around the store and grabbed a loaf of bread, a packet of ham, some butter and some crisps. All the packaging looked strange but he didn't really care, he just wanted to buy some food. He made his way to a young girl stood at the counter and placed the items on the counter.

"Er, sorry mate, what do you want me to do with these?" The girl looked confused.

"Can you tell me how much I've got to pay perhaps?" Michael replied in a sarcastic tone.

"Not really. You need to put them all in a basket." Michael thought that this was a bit petty. Most people might use a basket but he was able to carry the few things he wanted. "Er, well, I can't serve unless you put them in a basket." The girl pointed to where the baskets were and Michael went and picked one up. As he did, it buzzed so he put it back down again and the buzzing stopped. He picked it up again but far more carefully this time but still it buzzed. He looked over towards the girl. "Put your card in mate, blimey!" She tutted and shook her head in annoyance. Michael walked back over to where he had placed the bread and other items and took out the change from his pocket and held it open in the palm of his hand.

"Card? I haven't got a card, all I have is some money. Will that do?" The girl peered over at the strange coins in Michael's hand.

"Do ya think I'm stupid or what, mate? Nobody buys without a card, and anyways that's old money there."

"What do you mean old money?"

"Well it's not Euros, is it?" The girl stood there with an arrogant stance. Michael looked at the coins in his hand and then back at the girl.

"So I can't buy anything with this?"

"Not with the coins, but put your card in and you can." Michael had heard enough and left the shop.

A woman followed Michael out of the shop and called out to him. "Excuse me sir, are you okay?" The woman had seen how frustrated Michael had looked and thought he was in need of some help and it was everyone's duty to help someone in need.

"Oh, I just need to buy some food, I haven't eaten in a couple of days but I seem to have the wrong money." Michael showed the woman his coins. She picked one up and sifted through the others.

"I don't know where you got these from but they seem in pretty good condition for their age."

"For their age?" Michael repeated. "What do you mean, for their age?"

"Well this coin here has a date of 1994 on it so it is obviously an old English coin and is thirty-two years old. I'd say it was in very good condition for a coin that age, wouldn't you?" The woman wasn't sure if Michael had some mental problems or was just very confused. He seemed quite okay but it was hard to tell nowadays. Michael regained himself a little.

"Oh, yes. What year is it now, twenty twenty-six or something isn't it?"

"That's right, the sixth of January twenty twenty-six. Look, is there anyone who can help you, dear?"

"No, I'm on my own it would appear. I seem to have lost my family somewhere but I'm sure it's only temporary." Michael started to feel giddy so leant against the wall. Where was he? What was going on? He felt ill but he felt hungry even more. "I just need some food," he pleaded.

"Where do you live, darling?"

"Oh up Rawthorn Drive."

"So do I! Perhaps I can get you some biscuits to see you over. Let's make our way up the road." The woman wanted to know exactly where he lived and was a bit surprised she didn't already know him as she thought she knew nearly everyone in Rawthorn Drive.

They walked for a while and as they approached number twenty-six Michael stopped.

"This is where I live," he pointed to the old bungalow. Michael was beginning to notice more and more just how different his house was from the rest. It seemed old fashioned whilst all the others were sparkling and new.

"What, Doc's house!" The woman replied. "You don't live here, do you?"

"Yes, this is where I live and it isn't Doc's house, it's mine." Michael was beginning to get fed up with hearing Doc's name all the time.

"Well yes I suppose it would be yours now dear but it used to be Doc's." The woman was adamant.

"So, do you know who else lives here?" Michael asked her. "Susan Riddell? Michael Riddell?" He watched the woman's face as she struggled with the names.

"Don't know them but I think that was Louise's name, Riddell." Michael's jaw dropped.

"Did you say Louise?"

"Yes, I think her name was Louise Riddell."

"And she lives here?"

"Well she did, but she moved away when Doc died."

"Moved away, where?" Michael had so many questions that he couldn't get them all out at once.

"Oh, I don't know dear, she had a boyfriend, or was it a husband, who wanted her to move abroad I think, but she wouldn't leave Doc. I mean she lived in her own house but wouldn't move away from the area. When Doc died, she just upped and left." Michael suddenly realised what else the woman had said.

"Doc died?"

"Oh yes, dear. About three years ago now but he was seventy-three." Michael tried to take all this in. Doc was dead and was seventy-three about three years ago.

"And David Riddell?" Michael hoped the woman would know where his son was. She thought long and hard.

"Nope, don't recognise that name either, sorry, just Louise Riddell."

Michael made his way back inside the bungalow whilst the woman watched. She was pleased to see someone using a key for a change. Michael sat back down at the kitchen table and tried to come to terms with the fact that he had missed the last thirty years or so. Had he been in a coma somewhere? Doubtful, as he would surely have come around in a hospital. He just couldn't fathom at all what might have happened to himself. He was still hungry but could find nothing at all to eat. He called at Donna's house again and managed to persuade her to give him some bread and a cup of tea. He didn't explain why he had no food himself and she didn't ask. It was her duty to help out someone in need and she was just pleased to do so. The more Michael looked around the more he tried to come to terms with his predicament. He looked at the letters from Doc and Louise again. Was the letter about the solicitors from David rather than Doc? It was a bit complicated so he knew that first thing tomorrow morning he would have to make his way into town to call at Ellis & Son and find out just exactly what was going on.

Michael slept quite well again through the night even though he had so many things going through his mind. He managed somehow to get some running water again in the bathroom and had a wash but he was beginning to feel uncomfortable. Perhaps I can get someone to show me how this thing works. He stepped into the shower type cubicle but again there were no taps. He checked all down the chrome piping but there was nothing to push. He waved his hand under the shower head but again it was just bone dry. It was useless. He dressed back into the only clothes he had, picked up the letters and made his way down to the village centre where he knew he could catch a bus. Then he wondered what had happened to his car. If it had crashed and it was thirty years ago then someone else would have sorted that out by now he thought. I'll have to catch a bus he concluded but then realised he had no money. Looks like I'll have to walk.

Michael knew that there was a slightly shorter route he could walk into town if he went the back road, but then thought if he followed the main road he might be able to hitch a lift with someone. He started walking down towards the green and noticed a couple of vehicles passing him. He held out his thumb but nobody really took any notice. The cars all turned right at the end of the road which was in the opposite direction to town so none would have been going his way anyway. He watched ahead to look for cars heading towards town but none seemed to be driving that way at all. It was another strange thing that he hadn't really spotted before, but nobody had their cars on their drives. He assumed that they all parked them in their garages but then realised that he hadn't seen any cars going up or down Rawthorn Drive at all. Reaching the green, Michael stopped and looked around to see where all of the cars seemed to be heading. There was a massive car park that he hadn't really noticed before when he had been making his way back home from the wood but sure enough, it was there.

There were cars coming in to an entrance near to where he could see the car park and what looked like a load of cars leaving from an exit on the far side of the car park. They all seemed to be making their way up a slope but he couldn't see properly to work out where they were heading. He wondered if there was anyone who might give him a lift so thought it would be worth having a look.

Michael reached the entrance to the car park, and saw that people seemed to be dropping their cars off at the entrance leaving someone in a white uniform to park them while they left by foot. It was a continual process, as one car was driven off by a valet, another car arrived. Michael made his way over to a group of three young men in white uniforms.

"Hello, sir, are you wanting a car?" The three jumped to attention as if he was royalty.

"No, just wondered if there was anyone going into town who could give me a lift?" Michael replied, but was surprised at the confused looks from the men.

"Well, possibly there is sir, but why don't you just take a car yourself?"

Michael wondered if they were being sarcastic. He was not in the business of stealing cars and thought it a bit of a cheek to suggest that he might be.

"Steal a car! I wouldn't do anything like that. I just need a lift. I don't have my own car." The men all laughed.

"I don't have a car myself!" one repeated.

"That's a funny one," said another as he bent over double in laughter. Michael looked on in astonishment.

"But what's so funny about me not having a car?"

The three men controlled their merriment and looked quizzically at each other.

"Well, nobody's got a car themselves, have they? That's why we're here," one of the men replied. "You have used Autotron before, haven't you, sir?" The young man quickly resumed the polite manner that Michael had noticed when he first arrived.

"Sorry, but I don't know what Autotron is!" Michael was beginning to realise he would have to be careful about what he said and did, since everything was so different. This looked like another new situation he was going to have to get used to. "Can you tell me about Autotron?"

The young man explained the Autotron system. Everyone was entitled to the use of a car anytime they needed one. You just turned up at one of the car parks, picked up a car, and off you went. The car had to be driven from the car park around the village, but then you could head up the slope to the Autotron system, just sit back and tell the car where you wanted to go. The car would then do the rest. Michael asked how much it cost but the young man explained that there was no charge, it was all paid for out of taxes. Unfortunately, Michael had no identity card which seemed to be needed to do anything. Shop, drive, relax, he couldn't do anything without his card. Michael needed a story, quickly. He told the young men that he had lost his card, and was trying to get to town to sort it out.

"Ah, well, sir, you just need to take the pedestrian travellator. You do know that the fast-move booths are out of order again, don't you, sir?" Michael confirmed that he did, without having a clue. "Yes, there was another mass destruction in Manchester last month, so they're out of use until the problem is solved."

One of the young men accompanied Michael across the car park towards the travellator. Michael looked at the cars as he passed. They were all very similar with a small steering wheel tucked away under the dashboard, which was all lights and dials. Very modern, he thought. The young man explained further as they walked. Anyone can take a car, anywhere, but you never keep it. It is dropped off at the nearest car park to your destination, and you then walk the rest of the way. Once the car is switched to automatic it will go wherever you want, it just needs programming. No driving, just sit back and enjoy the ride. There is music and a screen. Everyone uses them.

The two reached a large bright metal wall very much like the one Michael had seen in the woods. There was a set of double doors, very like a shower cubicle, and the young man made straight for them.

"This is the entrance to the pedestrian travel centre." He waved his hand in front of a sensor. The doors disappeared. "There, you see, just like your front door."

"Not like *my* front door," said Michael, quietly. They were in a large room with metal walls. Along one side were what looked like telephone booths, all roped and cordoned off with big Out of Use signs. Michael gave them a glance.

"The fast-move booths. I told you they were out of use, didn't I?"

"Fast-move booths," repeated Michael, forgetting to hide his confusion at all this strangeness.

"Yes. You have heard of these, haven't you?" The young man looked as if he was about to launch into a long explanation when a buzz sounded. He touched his wrist lightly and started to talk. "Hello, Malcolm 75/358." The young man took a couple of steps away from Michael, his attention obviously elsewhere. "Yes, I'm with a customer, won't be too long." There was another brief pause. "Tell him he can have whatever car he wants, but he might have to wait." The young man turned back to Michael. "This way." He led him around a corner where there was a sparkling new looking escalator. "I'll come up with you, sir."

Michael followed the young man onto the escalator. At the top, they found themselves on a glass covered walkway where Michael could look out across the village. It was nothing like he had seen before, and it took his breath away.

"Just round here." The young man led them down a corridor to a conveyor belt. It was very much like a baggage carousel at an airport, Michael thought. "You just take the travellator out to the main track, and you need to go left for town." The young man waited to see Michael onto the moving walkway, but he was very reticent. "Okay, sir?" The young man wondered if Michael was going to be a problem.

"Oh, yes, I'm okay."

"Don't forget, if you don't want to walk, there are seats about every five minutes, you just have to wait for them to come along." Michael nodded, and tried to reassure the young man that he was okay to be left. The young man shook his hand and went.

Michael stepped on to the moving path, and it was quite a strange sensation for him. He had heard about such things but this was the first time he had been on a moving pavement. Within seconds he had reached the junction with the main track, but he was too slow and carried on past it. He just stayed on and went all the way around. The second time he managed to step onto the straight, which took him to another junction. He was ready to step off as it arrived at a waiting area. He took a few moments to gather himself and take in where he was. There were a couple of stairways which he followed with his eyes, and it looked quite straightforward. Obviously, these led to and from the opposite travellator. He was only a dozen steps from the slowly moving conveyor. He looked at where it went. There was nobody else on the path as far as he could see. He looked the other way, and a bench appeared, moving slowly. This must be the seating that the young man had told him about. There was still nobody on the travellator, and Michael let the bench move past and away from him without any attempt to get on it.

Suddenly Michael could see someone walking on the travelator heading the opposite way. He tried to look casual as he watched the man who never looked up, he just went on past. He seemed quite at home on the moving pavement. It gave Michael a bit more confidence and he felt it was time to step onto the thing and see what happened. As he got nearer to the travelator he heard voices. A quick glance to the right and Michael saw two people on the travelator approaching. They were both walking and chatting to each other and within seconds they passed him. Michael took a step back, as if a fast-moving train had just passed him in the station. They were soon out of sight and earshot and he was surprised just how quickly they had passed. It was time for him to take the plunge and gingerly he stepped onto the moving pavement. The motion forced him forward and his left leg jerked onto the travelator sending his body forward slightly and making him wobble. Quickly he regained his posture and stood upright looking at the passing scenery. Very quickly Somerby became a distant view. He passed a couple of other exits where he could have got off if he wanted to. Michael stayed on until he heard a computerised voice calling out. "End of section, please step off. End of section, please step off," the voice repeated. Michael noticed that the pavement he was on was due to bend around to the right and start its journey back to where it had come from. He stepped off and found himself in an open section of walkway where he could sit down and wait. There was a further moving pavement that continued his journey towards town, or stairs to take him down to the ground below. There were a few more people here, some joining the travelator, others leaving it, and they were all going on their way as if this was just a regular occurrence.

As Michael stood up and looked through the glass cover, he could see the road below. It too was automated, and cars were driving along while the occupants sat back reading magazines, or putting on make-up. Whatever they were doing, they certainly weren't driving. All the cars seemed very much the same although mostly different, pale, colours. Every now and then there would be one that stood out, in a dark colour. He stood for nearly twenty minutes watching them all go past.

Eventually Michael made his way into town and felt a natural on the travelator. It was very easy really and a very convenient way of getting around. He calculated that the distance of about six miles took him only twenty-five minutes to walk. 'How brilliant was that?' he thought. Michael was now walking on a more conventional pavement and he made his way to South Quay and entered the building marked Ellis & Son. He was getting quite used to the clever doors which would disappear as you waved your hand over the sensor, and he presented himself to the young woman behind the reception desk.

"Hello, sir, do you have an appointment?"

"No, not really, but I do have a letter of introduction and I think I need to see someone." Michael waved the envelope as he spoke. The young woman read the note a couple of times and then looked at a screen.

"I'm not sure if Barnaby can see you straightaway, but if you could take a seat please." She indicated some chairs against the wall and Michael sat down. She knocked on another door in the office, and went into another room. Very quickly she reappeared. "Mr Ellis will see you now." She showed him into a rather grand big office full of old oak furniture with leather insets which smelt of money. Behind the desk was a smartly dressed man, who rose and shook Michael's hand.

"Mr Riddell?" he asked.

After a number of formalities to confirm that Michael's identity, the solicitor took a deep breath and opened a file he thought he would never have to open. It was labelled 'Doc' and was quite a size. Michael was there for nearly three hours during which the whole story was explained to him. Doc had died three years ago, and he had made a will some years prior to that where Michael was named as the beneficiary of a number of his possessions. Michael found it odd that the property at twenty-six Rawthorn Drive was part of the bequest, because Michael thought that he was already the owner, but apparently when Susan died she left the house to Doc. The solicitor explained that Louise had been access, and lived there, but he had had a letter from her dated two or three years previously, stating that she had moved away. The solicitor said that she would normally write each year, and the last letter had come from somewhere in Florida though he didn't have an address. Doc had also set up a bank account in Michael's name which had been accruing interest and was now worth nearly two million Euros, a very tidy sum. So, Michael had money but no way of spending it, however instructions had been left to arrange for Michael to obtain a Citizen's Card so that he could survive. Everything had been thought of, and Michael was relieved. There was also a brief history of what had changed in the last thirty years, and Michael tried to take it all in. Life wasn't going to be easy though; Susan had died, Louise had moved away, and nobody could explain what had happened to David. Michael wondered if he would suddenly appear, like he had.

February 2026

Over the next few weeks Michael settled into his new life but found it hard when he came across something that mentioned Sue. There were some photos he often looked at and had the odd evening when he just cried, but over time this reduced, and he started to live a normal life. The money Doc had left him meant that he didn't have to work. He made various enquiries to try and locate Louise, but they never came to anything. He often thought about Doc, and how he had infiltrated the family. Did he move in with Sue when Michael disappeared? Then he lived with Louise. It was all very confusing still.

March 2026

Michael got on well with his new neighbours and spent much of his time around the village of Somerby, even spending time in the café bar, which was still called Doc's. Michael thought it quite a reasonable place. He made occasional visits to the crash site in the woods. Once, he was wandering around the area when a young boy came over to him and asked what he was doing.

"I'm looking at this area where there was a car crash," Michael told him.

"Oh, yes, we learnt about that at school," the boy replied.

"Did you! And what did you learn exactly?"

"There were at least three cars that crashed here on the same site, and it is supposed to be a Viking

burial site dating back thousands of years."
"Three crashes?"
"That's what they told us."
The boy went on his way whilst Michael thought about what he had said. 'Three crashes. I wonder what they were? Mine was obviously one of them. I wonder what happened to Louise and David.' Michael guessed he might never know.

Chapter 17
DAVID'S STORY

Friday 4th January 1996
David felt the car skidding, first left and then right, and he held on to whatever he could. His left hand was clutching the door handle and his right gripped a part of the central console. He didn't know what he had hold of but he wasn't going to let it go. David was aware that his dad was struggling with the steering wheel, and he could hear him swearing and muttering under his breath. A flying piece of tree hit the windscreen with an almighty whack which caused his sister to scream. She screamed again. David wanted to tell her to shut up but he was still too frightened himself to speak. The car started to spin. Louise continued to scream. David started to get a headache.

There was a loud crack like thunder and a flash of light. David opened his eyes to see that the whole car seemed to be lit up and he could see the whole of the inside of the car. The car began to spin and David was certain that this was the end. They were going to crash big style. He braced for an impact but it never came. The car just slowly spun around. David noticed that he could see his sister without having to turn around to look at the back seat.

"Luce, can you hear me?" David called out. "Luce! Luce!" Louise couldn't hear a thing, she was still screaming. David looked around again and saw his dad. All three of them seemed to have been separated. The car had split into three pieces. They were all spinning around, but slowly, whilst everything else was whirling around them at speed. It felt a bit like being in the eye of a storm. It was strange, they were all somehow suspended, but slowly spinning around inside a funnel of wild weather. David held out his right hand and felt the rain. There were just the three of them, or so David thought, but he realised in fact they weren't completely alone. There were other people, and things, moving in and out of his field of vision. A man appeared. He was wearing orange trousers and a vest. He was sweating and a little dirty but was just looking at the three of them. He spun around them for a few seconds and then drifted out of view. A workman's spade danced around for a few seconds, and then there was a cow horn looking like something a Viking would wear on a helmet. Various other items swirled around them for a few seconds before disappearing out of view. The light was still bright, but not as blinding as it had been. David saw a yellow hard hat appear, just as he felt a dropping sensation. He had lost sight of both his dad and Louise as he started falling faster and faster. There was a bump. There was silence.

"Dad!" David cried out. He was in some pain as he regained consciousness but immediately recalled he had been in a road accident. He tried to release his seat belt to get himself out. "Dad!" David called out again. He noticed that the rest of the car had gone, and he was on his own. "Luce! Where are you, Luce?" David fell out of the car seat and landed hard on the ground. 'What has happened?' he thought to himself. There was a path back to the road, but where had Dad and Luce gone? His first thought was to get back home.

David trudged back down Leafby Lane and made his way around to Rawthorn Drive, but to his astonishment all he could see were fields, furrowed fields as far as he could see. In the distance was a small steam train making its way along the line but where his house should have been were just fields. He was beginning to ache from the effects of the accident, but he put the pain to the back of his mind. David wasn't quite sure what to do, so he found a way through the hedge and walked up the field to where his home should be. There was nothing. Where had all the bungalows gone?

David stood in the middle of the field for a few minutes before making his way back to the hedge. An old man was walking along the lane on the other side of the hedge as David made his way back through.

"What you up to, you little rascal?" The old man spoke to him, lifting his walking stick.

"Err nothing sir, I'm just looking for my house." David thought it was a reasonable response but the old man thought otherwise.

"Don't be cheeky! On your way." The old man

waved his stick at David, so David took off down the lane back towards Doc's.

As David approached Doc's he was surprised by the petrol station on the opposite corner. It had changed, it was an older building, with just a couple of vintage looking petrol pumps. The metal canopy had gone, as had the supermarket and in its place was an old workshop. David looked hard at it as he got nearer, but then saw that Doc's café wasn't there, either. There was a flat piece of land behind the old cottage, but there was no café. Doc's just wasn't there. The shops around the corner weren't there either. Everything had changed. Suddenly, he remembered Mary, and her party. Hopefully she wouldn't be upset that he hadn't got there. He wasn't sure he fully understood why he hadn't got to the party, as he stood in front of the old cottage. He was standing there, pondering, when the old man from down the lane caught up with him again.
"What are you looking at now, son?"
"The shops and café have gone." David pointed to the open ground which was part of the cottage's land.
"What are you talking about? Who are you? Where do you live, boy?" The old man was suspicious of his intentions. "I'm David Riddell and I live at 26 Rawthorn Drive, but it seems to have gone. Is this Somerby?"
The old man was getting angry, and had had enough.

The Somerby Tree

"Yes, of course this is Somerby. Be on your way!" He went into the cottage that David was staring at. When he looked out of the window and saw David still standing there, he telephoned the police.

Not being sure about what was going on, or where he was, David was pleased to see that the old oak tree was still where it had always been. He walked over to it and climbed into the branches, although every stretch brought pain. He didn't climb too high, as he wasn't up to it, but to just be able to sit on the lower branches and look around seemed to bring him some peace of mind. He decided to climb back down and have another walk along to where he thought he lived.

Ten minutes later the local constable arrived at the cottage, but David had moved on. He hadn't moved far, though, and he was found back on the field where he thought his house should be. The constable propped his bike up against the hedge and called out to him. "Oi, son, over here a moment." David came straight over.

"Hello. Sorry, I suppose I shouldn't be on the farm land." David guessed he was in the wrong.

"No, you shouldn't but if you climb back over now I won't take any further action about it." David jumped back over to the road at a low point in the hedge and a pain shot up his back. He walked up to the policeman.

"Do you know where Rawthorn Drive is?"

The Somerby Tree

David thought if anyone would know, a policeman would. The constable scratched his head.

"This is part of Rawthorn Farm, but I've never heard of Rawthorn Drive, son. Let's go back to the station and I'll get the maps out, what do you say?" David was happy to oblige.

The two of them walked to the little police station in the village whilst the policeman chatted to David, and tried to find out a bit more about him. David told him which school he went to, which was miles away in Southtown, but the policeman had never heard of any of the teachers that David mentioned. He was also uncertain why David wasn't in school and wanted to check whether he was a known truant. When they got back to the police station the constable got a little more formal.

"So, what is your full name?" David thought this was a bit unusual, but answered anyway.

"David Michael Riddell." David watched as his name was written down. "Am I in trouble for being in that field? It wasn't much and I didn't do any harm, did I?"

"No, it's not the field, I'm just trying to establish who you are. Now what's your date of birth?"

"Ninth of July nineteen-eighty." David said, like he had a hundred times before. The constable dropped his pen and gave David a stern look.

"Now look, son, if you're not going to tell me the truth then you might finish up in trouble." At that moment the door opened and in walked another uniformed officer.

"What we got here then, constable?"

"A David Riddell who says he was born in nineteen-eighty, Sarge."

"Is that so? That would make you how old, then, son?" The sergeant turned to David.

"I'll be sixteen later this year." The two officers looked at each other and said, almost at the same time, "Nineteen-fifty."

"What do you mean, nineteen-fifty?" David asked.

"That was the year you were born, son, nineteen fifty."

"No, I was born in nineteen-eighty. What year is this?"

"It's nineteen sixty-six, what year did you think it was?"

David decided that his best course of action was to say nothing further, tell them nothing about the accident, his dad and sister, nothing at all. This didn't go down well with the police and he was eventually arrested and taken to the big station in town.

It was now Friday morning and David tried to come to terms with the fact that he appeared to be living in the past - nineteen sixty-six, to be precise. The police ignored David's claims of when and where he was born, and worked on the nineteen-fifty date. They ran his name through what records they had, but could find no trace of him, certainly not living in Somerby. The sergeant made a call, and arrangements were made for David to be taken to a children's home in the town. The police would have to make some enquiries about the other place where he had said he had lived, Goodmayes, but until then, he would have to be looked after.

David received the news with some indifference. He wasn't keen on the idea of going to a children's home, as he had heard of them from his mum and dad and they didn't sound like the type of place he wanted to be, but he considered his situation and realised that there any other options for him. There was too much happening for him to take everything in properly. David ran through in his mind just exactly what had happened. It was all very strange and he felt confused and lost. He wanted to cry, but he held back. Perhaps he would get a chance to see someone who he could explain it all to, but he wanted to try and understand it himself first. In the meantime, he wouldn't say much else about what he had been through.

The first day in the children's home wasn't too bad. There was a rather stern looking woman who greeted him at the entrance.
"Welcome to Hedley House. This is going to be your home for the immediate future, so treat it properly and we'll all get along." The woman held David's arm as she took the relevant paperwork from the constable and signed it. As soon as the door was shut she turned back to David. "Now, I

run a tight ship here and any trouble, you'll be in the brig." She whacked him around the head for good luck, and David stood there stunned.

"Okay, okay, I won't be any trouble."

"You better not be." The woman grabbed his arm again and took him into a room to the right of the hall. It was full of tables and chairs. "This is where we all eat. Breakfast is at half past seven sharp, if you're late you miss it. Lunch is served when the gong rings once, and dinner when the gong rings twice. If you're not here, you miss out. You can go out after breakfast and must be in before it gets dark, because the doors are locked."

David tried to take it all in as he was dragged by the arm out of the room. He struggled to get free of the woman's hold but she was practised at it.

"You don't have to drag me, Miss, I can walk on my own quite easily." David looked up at the woman and she gave him another whack around his right ear. It hurt and he stumbled from the shock. The woman kept hold of him so he didn't fall.

She led him around the whole house giving him a guided tour and a few blows on the way. David had tears in his eyes. He just wanted to be on his own. At the end of his tour he was shown to a small bed in a room of six.

"This one is yours. Keep it clean. Change the bedclothes every Friday. Don't make any noise when lights have been put out. Right, get your things." The woman let go of him and looked at the paperwork she had received from the police. "Oh, you don't have any things. All right then, empty your pockets." David did as he was told. There wasn't much. A dirty handkerchief and a little bit of change. David looked at it, he only had about two pounds. "What's this?" The old woman picked up the coins and looked at them. "What are these?"

"It's the only money I have."

"What country does it come from? Are you from the Channel Islands or somewhere like that?"

The woman noticed that the coins seemed to have a picture of the Queen on them, and wording similar to normal coinage, but she didn't recognise them at all. She held up a pound coin. "What's this, for instance?"

"It's a pound coin," David told her.

"Yes, I can see it says that but what country does it come from?"

"Well, England, of course." David replied. He was saying too much without thinking, but he had forgotten already the response he would get from this woman. He got a whack around the left ear.

"Don't be insolent!" the woman said. David cried briefly, and thought that he would rather be dead than where he was now. The woman still seemed to be wanting an answer about the coins so David came up with something.

"I found them in Somerby, Miss."

The woman thought about his answer, and was putting the coins down on the bedside cabinet when she noted the date on one of them. Nineteen ninety-two. She looked at the coin again, and then gave up. "Okay, I'll check through your paperwork. Your clothes need washing so get them off. We'll bring you some other clothes to put on, and then when I'm ready you can come to my office."

The woman left David alone at last. David laid on the bed and cried.

About ten minutes later a lad came into his room carrying some clothes. He placed them on David's bed.

"These are for you."

David looked up at him. "Thanks."

"You'd better get your own clothes to the washroom as soon as you can, or else Mrs Bulley will be after you again." David assumed it was a nickname but understood exactly who he was talking about.

"Does she hit everybody?"

"Most of us get hit every now and then."

"And what do I call her?" David needed to know how to address her if he was going to speak to her again.

"Mrs Bulley," the lad replied.

"No, what's her real name?"

"That is her real name. Mrs Bulley. I think her first name is Ruth but everyone calls her Mrs Bulley."

"Oh, I thought that was a nickname."

David looked at the clothes. They weren't in very good condition, but they were near enough his size. He looked back at the lad. "Have I got to wear these?" David noticed that the lad had better clothes himself, although they did seem very old fashioned.

"Yes, you'll probably get your own clothes back eventually, and when you've earned some money you can buy some new ones. Come on, I'll show you where the washroom is." The lad seemed happy to try and help David fit in. "I'm Simon, by the way." He held out his hand ready for a handshake. David grabbed it and shook it.

"I'm David."

That afternoon and evening Simon introduced him to the various young people who lived at Hedley House. As he pointed them out, he would also tell David who was ok, and who to watch out for. Most of them were fine, but David was advised to steer clear of a brother and sister, George and Harriet. They were trouble. David duly noted his new friend's advice, but he would make up his own mind in time.

Mrs Bulley had a brief interview with David that evening, and tried to get out of David exactly where he had come from. David's story wasn't easy to believe so he invented an excuse of losing his memory. He mentioned Goodmayes again, and gave his address there. He told her about Rawthorn Drive in Somerby, but only briefly, as he knew the road didn't exist anymore, and then he mentioned the car accident in the woods. He told her about his mum, dad and sister, and Mrs Bulley took down some details. It was all kept in a file with his name on the front. David made sure he was as polite as he could be when talking to Mrs Bulley, and wanted to ask her lots of questions about what would happen next but it made sense to him to just let things carry on as they were for now.

The next morning, David was up in time for his breakfast. He looked out for Simon and they sat together. There was only porridge available which David tried but didn't like. Simon laughed at him as he pushed the bowl away.

"In a couple of weeks, you'll get to like it," Simon told him. David didn't think he'd be right but smiled anyway.

"What are you doing today, then?" David asked him.

"Well, I'll go into town and see if there's any work I can get, or find any old bottles that I can get some money back on."

"Old bottles?"

"Yes, you get ha'pence back on old beer bottles, and I know where there are a couple of houses where they drink a lot."

"What's a ha'pence?" David asked, thinking it was some slang word that Simon had used.

"Ha'pence! Half a penny, you fool!" Simon gave David a strange look. "I also have a couple of places where I can sometimes get a job or find some old rags, and it all mounts up."

Simon took David around the town that day,

showing him all the different places he went to. It was a funny day, as David knew many of the places he was taken to, but not in the form that they could now be seen. He was getting more used to being in nineteen sixty-six, and remembering to keep his mouth shut. Simon knew lots of places to try and find things that he could then sell. By the end of the afternoon, they had managed to collect nine pennies.

"Here, I normally collect sixpence, and I knew where to go so I'll let you have the extra thruppence." Simon placed three big pennies in David's hand. "Keep it safe, there are those back home who'll nick it as soon as you can say Jack Robinson," Simon warned him.

They made their way back towards Hedley House and chatted about girls. There was a younger girl at the home called Sarah that Simon quite liked, but he explained that it was not really possible to talk to the girls, and he hadn't managed to speak to her much. David mentioned that he used to have a girlfriend called Mary, but didn't know what had happened to her. They then talked about football.

"I'm a Spurs fan, I wonder who they are playing today?" David had forgotten it was a Saturday.

"Oh, I can look it up in the paper. We always keep a record of the football results. I'm for Norwich City, like most of us, but there are one or two who support other teams. I think Charlie supports Sheffield Wednesday so we look out for that result."

"Sheffield Wednesday. Yes, he'll be looking forward to the cup final then." David realised what he had said as soon as he had said it.

"What cup final?" Simon asked.

"Oh, nothing." David refused to say anything further but Simon was interested in his comment.

When they got back Simon checked the football results. Someone would always be listening to the radio and writing down the results.

"Ha, Spurs lost two-one to Chelsea," Simon kidded David.

"Oh, typical. We can never beat them."

"Norwich drew nil-nil. Sheffield Wednesday lost two-one as well, Charlie won't be happy."

"How did Everton get on?"

"Why Everton?" Simon asked.

"Oh, Mum supports Everton." Simon looked up the result.

"They won two-nil," Simon advised. The two made their way back to their bedroom and David saw a brown jumper on his bed. He picked it up.

"Whose is this?"

"It'll be yours, probably. Has it got your initials on it?" David looked and saw that it had. "We all have a jumper with our initials on so the blokes from the Health Ministry know who we are." Simon explained.

Life settled down for David and although he had one or two run-ins with George, there was nothing he couldn't handle, and he began to get on with things.

Over the next few days, David got to know some of the other lads a bit better, and he found that one of them, a lad called Tom, had an old football. After a bit of persuasion Tom agreed to let the boys use it. Simon was up for it, as were a couple of others, but David wanted to try and get more of the boys to play, and he even asked George. Simon was surprised that David had asked him, and even more surprised when George said yes. Plans were put in place for a game on the coming Thursday afternoon at the local park.

Thursday soon came and the football match took place. David thought he might be a better player than most of the others, and thought it best to get George on his side. The game was all over the place, but very competitive and Simon captained the opposite side to David.

David organised his team quickly, and he put various kids in various positions, although the names they used were not quite the ones he was familiar with. George was asked if he wanted to score the goals, and got put up front. This was a bit of a master stroke really, as although David ran most of the team, and beat the others single handed, he was able to set George up to score the winning goals. David thought that George had shown some promise, and certainly knew how to control a ball and pass it properly, so he made a point of telling him how well he had played. David thought this might help bring George into the group but he still kept himself to himself. David tried to chat to Harriet, George's sister, as well, but this was very much hard going.

The following Thursday, the boys wanted to have another game of football so it was arranged. George didn't join them this time, which David was disappointed about, but some of the girls came and watched, including Sarah. David made sure Simon got to talk to her after the game, and told him to explain the rules to her as something to chat to her about. They made their own way back to the home, whilst the other lads walked back with David. They were all going on about his control of the ball, and the way he could do all sorts of tricks. They asked him if he had thought about becoming a professional footballer when he got older, but he played down the idea and didn't answer any questions about where he had learnt his skills. As they reached the home they had got on to the subject of the World Cup.

"It's in England this year, isn't it exciting?" Billy said.

"Well, yes it will be, and the final will be just fantastic, we'll give those Germans a good hiding." Again, he spoke without thinking.

"So, you think England will win the cup then?" Mark asked.

"I think they might do, yes." David tried to change

the subject. "It's the FA Cup this weekend, isn't it?"
"Yes. Norwich are playing Walsall, I think," said
Simon who had waited at the front door for David.
"Do you think they'll win?" Simon had heard one
or two comments that David had made about how
Sheffield Wednesday were going to get to the cup
final, and England were going to win the World
Cup, but he also noted that David was a bit guarded
when he said them. This was an attempt to get him
to open up a bit.
"I don't know, Simon," David replied.
"What about West Ham, will they win?" Mark
asked.
"I don't know that either." David tried to speak to
all the lads at the same time. One called Ben spoke
up. "What about my team, Sunderland. Do you
think they might win?" David liked Ben, and
wanted to make him feel happy, so he told him,
"Yes, I think they could win this round. Who are
they playing?"
"Everton," Ben replied. David's face showed his
dismay.
"But if they don't win, Ben, you know that they are
still a very good team, don't you?" David tried not
to give Ben too much hope, but also tried not to
make too much of his predictions.

The lads made their way back inside leaving just
Simon and David outside the front door. Simon
turned to him and thought now was as good a time
as any to tackle him on the subject that had been

bothering him for quite a while now.

"You know that Sunderland aren't going to win, don't you?" Simon stared at David, to see if his face would give anything away, and it did. "How do you know these things?"

"Look, I can't really tell you how, but I just know." David wasn't sure how he was going to explain this but he didn't want to lie to Simon. He had been his only real friend here and he didn't want to put that in jeopardy.

"But how do you know? Do you know what the score will be?"

"No, I just know that Everton will win."

"What, because your mum supports them?"

"No, not just that. I just know they'll win the cup this year, that's all." David hoped that would be enough for Simon but it wasn't. They made their way into the house and up to their bedroom whilst the conversation continued.

"But I thought you said Sheffield Wednesday would win the cup this year?"

"No, that's who they'll beat in the final," David laughed. "Well, that's what I think anyway.

Saturday was the day of the cup games, and David had forgotten that he'd mentioned the games the previous Thursday. Simon hadn't. That evening, he made certain he checked the scores and he was amazed to hear that both Sheffield Wednesday and Everton had won. Simon let the idea roam around his head, and decided that he would give it a go for the next round of the cup.

The next round of the cup arrived, and Everton had been drawn to play non-league Bedford. It wouldn't be that difficult to predict a win for Everton, but Sheffield Wednesday were drawn to play away at Newcastle and that was a very different matter. Simon had a few contacts in town, and had spent the previous few days trying to engage a friend of his who was old enough to put a bet on for him, Sheffield Wednesday to win. Football betting wasn't a big thing in nineteen sixty-six but some bookies would take your money for any bet. Simon wasn't sure just how much he trusted David's confidence, but paid for the bet. That evening he checked the results, and sure enough, Sheffield Wednesday had beaten Newcastle away. Charlie was happy, but not as happy as Simon although he wished he had trusted David's words more. He calculated that he had won just under three shillings and that was good.

On Monday morning Simon was up early, and went into town on his own. He had to pay a bit more in tax than he had first thought, but he picked up his winnings of two shillings and eightpence, plus his original shilling. Simon wanted to tell David what he had done, and went off in search of his friend as soon as he returned. He found David in one of the back rooms chatting to Harriet. They seemed to be getting on quite well, but Simon knew that she could be violent and that if George turned up and found them talking, he too could cause a scene. Simon coughed. The two of them looked up and almost immediately Harriet got up.

"I'll see you later, Harriet," David called but she did not respond but left the room. "Oh. I thought we were getting on quite well there."

"Sorry to disturb you, but it's probably for the best." Simon thought he was doing the right thing in breaking the two of them up.

"Why do you say that? Harriet is okay once you get to know her." David tried to stick up for her.

"But she's not right." Simon pointed to his head. "Nor is George." Simon quietened his voice. "You know they have both been in trouble for being violent? George was in lots of fights last year and Harriet has had a couple as well, and they seem so weird. I bet they could be really nasty if they wanted to."

"Oh, I don't think they're that bad. George is a bit quiet but Harriet is just shy."

"Shy! Shy!" Simon half laughed. "You know why they are in here don't you?" David obviously didn't know and he shook his head. "The rumours are they murdered their father, that's what I heard."

"Don't be daft, Simon. If they had, they would be in prison."

"They're too young to be in prison. Anyway, the rumours are they buried him somewhere and nobody can find the body, but they did it. Anyway, I came here to give you some money."

"Money?" David thought he might have left his money on the bedside cabinet, so he felt his pockets, and was satisfied that he had all his money with him. "What money?" Simon handed him a shilling.

"There you are. A shilling."

"What's that for?"

"I won a bet, and have you to thank for it," Simon explained.

"Me? Oh, you've bet on the football, haven't you?" David had never given it a thought before. He could have done that! He was too young to go into a betting shop, but he might see if he could get someone older to put the bet on for him. Simon might be able to put him in touch with someone.

"Yes, I did. And Sheffield Wednesday won."

The two chatted for a while and Simon said he would bring David with him for the next round of the cup so they could both put bets on. David thought this sounded like quite a good idea, and was keen to see how Simon got his bets put on. They chatted for a while and talked about Simon's past. His father had run off with another woman after his mother had died and left him alone at the age of twelve. He had been in the home ever since but knew that when he reached eighteen he could leave and get a job with some proper money. That would be towards the end of this year, and he just couldn't wait. Simon asked David what his full name was and how he had finished up at the home. He knew that the police had been back a couple of times to talk to him, but nobody really knew what had taken place. David said he had lost his parents in a car accident and that his sister had gone missing, telling some of the story as truthfully as he could, but didn't tell him all of it. The two of them got on well and Simon was also thankful to David for getting him talking to Sarah.

David was getting on better with Harriet. They would have regular chats whenever they happened to meet but Harriet would change if ever George were to appear. David wasn't quite sure why. Was she afraid of him, or did she feel she was betraying his trust by talking to David? On one occasion, when he was chatting to Harriet, he thought he would try and find out a bit more about her background.

"Why are you and George in here?" Harriet looked away as if she was not prepared to hear the question or maybe she was looking to see if George was about, but David didn't think she would give him an answer when she suddenly replied.

"Our dad is a fisherman and he goes away for a long time, and then when he comes home he's always drunk."

"What about your mother?"

"She ran away years ago." David felt bad at hearing her story. He wasn't quite sure what to say when Harriet continued. "George doesn't like me talking to you, and he'd not be happy if he knew I was telling you about dad so please don't say anything to anyone, will you?" David gave his word.

David and Harriet talked more and more, and George made it clear that he wasn't happy at what was going on. He would give Harriet a hard look that even David could feel. Harriet for her part obviously needed someone to trust other than George, and David seemed to fill that void. On one occasion, the two of them managed to get out and walk towards the town. They weren't in love, although David had a soft spot for her, but they were becoming very good friends. Harriet took the opportunity to open up.

"My dad is a fisherman," Harriet exclaimed.

"I know, you told me."

"Yes, and our mum did run away, but Dad is actually in prison."

"Prison!"

"Yes. He used to look after our cousin when he was home from the sea and he used to treat her special, like." David wasn't quite sure what she meant. "You know, he would love her more than George and me." Harriet didn't really want to talk about it in detail. "George saw them together many times, I don't know." She started to cry. David put his arm around her and she quickly cheered up. He asked another couple of questions to try and see if he could fully understand what Harriet was trying to tell him, but she changed the subject each time.

The subject only really came up once more when David and Harriet were chatting alone. She said that horrible things would happen between her dad and her cousin and George was made to stand and watch, or take part. She guessed that she only knew a little bit of what George had seen. She then explained that George had gone a bit mad, which led to him running away and the police being involved, and that was what led to their father being put in prison. She explained that they wanted to put George into an asylum, but it never happened. David tried to ask if her dad had ever done anything to her, but she never answered such questions.

The next day, Harriet was with one of the other girls when they were playing dress up. Harriet wouldn't get too involved but she was encouraged to put a necklace on. George came in and saw his sister with the necklace on. He went mad immediately. He rushed up to her and ripped the necklace from her neck, catching her lip as he did. Harriet cried but George went into a proper rant.

"How could you? Only bad girls wear jewellery! Whores and prostitutes wear jewellery! Are you a whore? Do you want to be like our cousin? You bad girl!"

George was oblivious to anything else as he hit Harriet around the face. Harriet cried. "And I don't like you talking to Doctor either. He will dress you up!" George was by now being pulled away by Mrs Bulley and the other staff, as he continued swearing. David witnessed the end of the incident. As George was being dragged away he looked at David. "Yes, there's the Doctor, he wants to dress you up!" George was taken away. David went to Harriet to see how she was but she would have nothing to do with him. She cried again and ran upstairs.

The whole incident was over in minutes and most of the other residents had by now come to see what was going on. Simon took David to one side.

"I told you he was mad. You're lucky he didn't have a knife or something. You'd have been dead meat." Simon seemed quite sincere with his warning.

"He referred to me as a doctor. What was that all about?"

"Oh, that's what he's been calling you almost ever since you've been here. He calls you Doctor," Simon explained. David couldn't understand why.

"Why?"

"Your initials, stupid." Simon pointed to David's initials that were sewn onto his jumper: DR. "George just calls you Doctor because of your initials." The nickname became common knowledge around the home, and stuck. The next day, George and Harriet were taken away in a car. They had bags with them, and it was assumed that they would be going to another home. David never saw George again.

David found himself a proper role at Hedley House, and although he wanted to find his own home as soon as he could he made the best of his time there. Mrs Bulley even took a shine to him. She called him Doctor or Doc as did most of the others and she was sad when he finally left. David took all the boys for football training. Nearly every other day they would make their way to the park for a morning or afternoon to learn how to play football. David would teach them the basics, but would often show off his skills. Simon came along and helped as often as he could.

Saturday 5th March 1966

It was time for the fifth round of the FA Cup. Everyone was excited as Norwich City, the local team, and the team most of the boys supported, were playing at home to the mighty Blackburn Rovers. Simon and David were excited for other reasons, as they were putting bets on.

"Come on, Doc, have you got your money?" Simon asked him.

"Shh!" David was a little annoyed. "Don't tell everyone." David found his secret stash of money. It was of course old money to him, and he was still trying to get used to it. He counted it carefully, and found he had four shillings and tuppence. Not bad, he thought. Simon had given him the shilling to start with and he had managed to get the rest by selling back bottles. Simon meanwhile had about six shillings to bet with.

They made their way into town and Simon sought

out his friend who put the bets on. He introduced Doc to Bob, and David got on quite well with him.

"You'll put some bets on for me, won't you?" Simon asked him.

"Yes, I will. Is it another football bet, or are you doing horses this time?" Bob replied.

"More football."

"Are you happy to put bets on at different betting shops?" David asked.

"How much you laying out then, son?" Bob thought that this would be the question one would ask if they were betting thirty or forty quid.

"I've got four shillings," David replied. Bob laughed. "No bookie is going to worry about that much money."

"No, I know, but I'd like to go to some other betting shops." Bob thought about his request and said he would go to a couple of shops, but didn't have time to walk all around town putting bets on.

"How much are you paying me for all this, anyway?" David looked at Simon. Simon raised his eyebrows.

"Well, you can put your own money on the same bets." David hoped this was enough for Bob, and after a moment's pause it seemed it was. The bets were made including Everton to win the cup outright, and the slips passed over to Simon and David.

"Did you bet, then?" David asked Bob.

"I put something on Sheffield Wednesday, but not much. Newcastle should beat them really."

They carried on betting into the sixth round, but Simon was very disappointed when he found that one of his bets didn't win. Manchester City and Everton drew and the match went into a replay, but it meant that the bet was a loser.

"Hey, Doc, you never told me that they drew." Simon said.

"Ah, yes, I forgot. I know they get through to the final but don't actually know how, who they beat or what the scores are." David was himself a bit miffed at the result but he knew Everton would beat City in the replay. "Anyway, we're still up on the money and as long as we don't bet too much, we'll do okay in the other rounds." David tried to convince Simon to carry on and bet in the replay but Simon wasn't sure.

The replay was on the Tuesday, and David dragged Simon into town that afternoon. They found Bob who was also not pleased with David about losing his bet.

"You putting another bet on?" Bob asked Simon.

"Yes. Doc has convinced me we should, so I'm putting a quid on. What about you?"

"No, I'll give it a miss this time, I think." Bob replied. David was a bit more cautious, only betting four shillings. It was another disaster, as yet again the teams drew, and the bets were lost. This time Simon gave up, but David having met Bob, was able to carry on betting. He also spent some time trying to get to know a couple of other men in town who he persuaded to put bets on for him at other bookies'. It was a real network of contacts.

When the day of the Cup Final arrived, David found he had one pound ten shillings to bet with, keeping a couple of shillings in reserve. He knew the outcome of this game, and in particular knew that it didn't go to a replay so he split his money up amongst three people he had managed to find who would bet for him and placed it all on Everton to win by three goals to two. He got an average price of six to one, and with all his other bets he found himself with over twelve pounds. That wouldn't have sounded much to David once, but in 1966 it went a long way and he was pleased with what he had. Simon had by now lost faith in David's predictions, but he had put a bet on Everton to win the cup at the beginning so he was happy enough to chat about what David had won.

"Are you going to bet on England winning the World Cup then, Doc?" Simon asked.

"Yes, I think I will. I don't know much more than that though." David lied. By now David didn't want to let on just how much he knew, as he hoped he could make a bit of money. He opened a bank account and although the bank wasn't quite sure what to make of a young lad who lived at a children's home, they seemed quite happy to accept his money

The Somerby Tree

After the World Cup Final, David was a relatively rich young man. He had over five hundred pounds in his account, and was able to increase his money with regular bets. It was a bit of a problem that he still wasn't old enough to place the bets himself but he continued to recruit friends around the town and over time he found his way to Norwich where there were more opportunities. There were even a couple of horses in the Grand National he could remember, especially Foinavon, which came in at a hundred to one. This was a great day but he always considered the 1966 World Cup Final as his turning point, where he made a start on his fortune.

December 1966

During December there was another occasion to celebrate. Simon West reached the age of eighteen, and was ready to leave the home. He had managed to save some of his money and get himself a little one bedroomed flat in town where Doc was invited to visit whenever he wanted to. Mrs Bulley had made a cake to mark the occasion and although he was sad to see his friend leaving, David was pleased that Simon had made it. Although officially David should have stayed at Hedley House until he too was eighteen he was lucky enough to be able to make plans to move out well before that. It was a strange situation and he discussed things with Simon one day, talking about how he could rent a property and exactly how much it all cost.

David realised that he certainly had enough money

to put down a deposit on a house, but wasn't old enough to obtain a mortgage. Even if had been old enough, he didn't have any work, and wasn't able to use his betting as his main income. There was only one thing for it, he would have to bet as often and as much as he could until he could buy his own house.

David managed to get a bus to Somerby and looked around to see what places there were for sale. There weren't many. Two little cottages that he thought might not cost too much, which he made a note of. He knocked at the door of one in the hope that someone might be in and show him around but nobody answered. He looked through the window and it seemed quite warm and comfortable. David was surprised to find that the total cost was less than two thousand pounds, so it was a target figure he aimed for. Whilst he was in Somerby, he met a couple of local lads from the village. One was called Peter Phillips and he and David seemed to get on very well. They chatted about various things and David told him that he had been arrested by the police the last time he was in the village. Peter said he wanted to be a policeman when he left school.

The two of them chatted for a while as they reached the big oak tree. "I do like this tree, Peter."
"Yes, so do I. It's been there a long time, you know."
"Well, yes, I can see it is an old tree."
"Do you know that this tree is why the Vikings

settled in this village?"

"I had heard."

"Yes, apparently they found a number of trees in Leafby Wood that had magic powers."

"Magic powers!" David exclaimed.

"Yes, magic powers."

"What magic powers?"

"Oh, I don't know. All sorts." Peter tried to tell David what he had been told as a child but couldn't remember much. He only knew a little bit about the Vikings, but he told David all that he knew. After giving David the benefit of his knowledge, Peter made his excuses and left to go home.

There was a lot going through David's mind. It was 1966, and he tried to work out what year his parents moved to Goodmayes. He knew that police enquiries had shown that nobody by the name of Riddell lived at his old home at the moment, so obviously, they were yet to move in there. Thinking about it, he tried to work out what year they got married, and guessed that they probably hadn't even met yet. He could make his way to London and try and find his parents, but thought that for now this was probably not the best idea. He needed to get his new life in order. It was around this time that he started to climb the big oak tree in Somerby. Peter had shown him different ways to get up there and David often went to sit and watch the village whilst pondering on his life. He found himself a knife, and started to carve his initials in the tree, but then changed his mind and carved David. He left his mum and dad a message. David cried a few times in that tree, and it became his place to think.

1967

By nineteen sixty-seven, David had enough money to buy a little cottage in Somerby. The bank was a bit surprised about a seventeen-year-old with all this money, and the police had called into Hedley House to question both David and Mrs Bulley about the subject, but they could find nothing fraudulent and had to accept that the money had been acquired properly. David was warned that he was too young to place any bets in betting shops, but as he didn't place the bets himself, he was okay. A solicitor was engaged to help him purchase his first property, and they advised him to rent it out and make some money while he stayed at Hedley House. It was another year before he could live in the cottage on his own, but he was able to go and visit the place most days and Doc was by now a familiar site in Somerby.

1968

In nineteen sixty-eight, David left the children's home for good. He moved into his cottage and went about his business. The cottage he had purchased was next to the site where the café and shops should have been. It was strange looking at the open land where the café should be, and Doc soon set himself his next task. He saved to buy the land and by the middle of nineteen sixty-nine it was his.

1969
In the latter part of this year, several farmers were selling up. The owner of Rawthorn Farm was one such and David did enquire about how much he was selling the farm for, but a big developer had plans to build an estate and David was quite happy to let them go ahead with their purchase. He knew it was what was destined and he knew pretty much exactly where each road and house would go. As the estate started to take shape, Doc would spend hours looking at the site of twenty-six Rawthorn Drive. He made very early enquiries to buy the bungalow and he made sure that he purchased it when it was built. He would often refer to it as his home, but he always had his first little cottage plus a growing number of other properties as time went on. He continued betting, and his fortune grew, and sometime in nineteen seventy-three, he bought the last property on the plot where he would now build a café which would become known as Doc's.

Wednesday 9th July 1980
It was Doc's birthday. By now he had his café to keep him busy, and it was a very popular place. Coffee bars were becoming increasingly popular and Doc found that even Somerby could attract loads of people from miles around. He did a lot of the work himself, but employed a couple of local people to help him when he couldn't cope.

It was Doc's thirtieth birthday but it was quite a special day, as it was also the true date of his real birthday. The whole event had crept up on Doc and although he had wondered if he should visit the hospital where he was born on that day the café had taken his mind off things, and time was too short to arrange anything. He employed a local woman called Kathy who worked for him more and more, while there was also a chap called Brian who would do an odd shift, and Doc was lucky that they were both working this morning. Doc thought that this birthday in particular was going to be one of the best but during the morning he started to become quite ill. It was strange, he felt as though his whole body was being sucked dry of strength, and by lunchtime he wasn't easily able to stand, let alone walk. Brian got him back home and waited until the local GP arrived. Doc was examined but no illness could be diagnosed, so he was told to get some sleep and see how things were in the morning. Doc felt like he was dying. Was this the end? He knew it couldn't be, of course, but it felt like it. He slept for nearly thirty hours, and had no thought of whatever else might be going on. Kathy had things in hand, anyway.

After three or four days, Doc was able to get back on his feet and Kathy and Brian called in regularly to make sure he was all right. There was often talk of Kathy and Doc marrying, but she knew otherwise. Doc's heart was still as cold as it had been almost ever since she knew him. She guessed that there was another love somewhere. Nobody else knew who that love was, but Doc would often think about Mary. Sometimes it was thinking of her that got him through the pain. It was at least three weeks before Doc felt anything like back to normal, and the strength started to come back to his body, but he would for evermore have to be prepared for attacks of pain. These happened more frequently the nearer he got to London.

September 1994

Doc went to London a few times, mainly to conclude business deals, but also to watch football or see a West End show, but each time he felt his pain increase. In nineteen ninety-four Doc was on another such visit. He had to go and see a solicitor to sign some documents but he knew that t he could probably find some free time to do what else he wanted to. Doc was at his appointment at ten o'clock, on the dot. The business took no more than forty minutes to conclude and by eleven, he was out and free to do whatever he wanted to.

There were so many things he could do but Doc couldn't decide, and found himself on The Embankment looking at the Thames and Tower Bridge. He just stood against a wall and watched as the barges towed their loads up and down the river. It was most relaxing. There were many things on his mind at the moment, the biggest of which was the possible impending reunion with his family early next year, at least he hoped it would be a reunion. He knew it was the day they were due to move. Then that same old thought crossed his mind again. He could go to Goodmayes now and see them. He could talk to them today if he wanted. He could go and see his dad at the bank. Then of course the whole idea became ridiculous. What would he say? What reason would he have to go and visit the bank? None, of course. Doc made his way back to his hotel.

After an hour of throwing things over in his mind he decided that he would at least go to Goodmayes and look at his old house, the place where his childhood was spent, where everything seemed so happy. He caught the train and quickly made his way down to the road where he used to live. He could see the house, and it was almost exactly how he remembered it. He wondered if he could knock on the front door and meet his mum or dad. But then he wondered what might happen if David answered the door. He begun to feel more pains shooting through his body, and he concluded that perhaps he couldn't call that easily. He made his way around the area and looked at the old shops again. He found a great warmth seeing them again. He looked at his watch, it was time to leave, he thought. The pain in his body had got worse but he was used to these attacks, and he knew he would be able to cope. They seemed to get slightly easier the more he had them but today's was a big one.

Doc was making his way back to the station when he noticed the sweet shop he used to go to as a boy. He went in and asked for some chewing gum.

"I used to come in this shop as a boy, you know." Doc spoke as he waited for his change. It was probably a stupid thing to say but he wanted to fill the quiet pause.

"Oh, did you. I didn't know this shop was a sweet shop before. It was haberdashery when we took it over." The woman looked a bit confused.

"Oh, it must have been another place then." Doc checked his change.

"So you lived around here?"

"Yes, just around the corner, actually." Doc pointed towards his old house. The woman looked at him strangely. The bell rang as another customer entered, a young girl. She walked right past Doc and up to the counter, looking at the penny sweets you could help yourself to.

"Can I help you, dear?" the woman behind the counter said, keeping her eyes on the girl.

"No, thanks, I'm alright," the she replied.

Doc almost collapsed when he heard the reply. It was a voice he recognised immediately.

"Luce, it's you!" Doc said. The young girl glanced at him, and then turned back to what she was doing.

"Luce, are you okay?"

"Sorry, are you talking to me?" Louise replied. Doc looked at her and walked over to give her a hug, as the woman behind the counter coughed. He stopped, very quickly realising what he might be getting into here. He also then remembered that his sister wasn't known as Luce.

"Yes, hello, Louise. It's great to see you."

"Err, I don't actually know who you are." Louise turned towards the woman behind the counter who was now concerned about what might be taking place. Doc had to think quickly.

"You'll be moving home soon, to the seaside."

Doc saw the growing concern on the shopkeeper's face, so he stopped. Louise asked for a big bar of Cadbury's Dairy Milk which the woman behind the counter handed to her, and she paid with a five pound note before collecting the change and turning to leave. "Bye, Luce." Doc watched as she skipped out of the shop and past the window. Doc turned to the woman behind the counter. "Lovely girl. I know the whole family you know." He quickly made his excuses and left the shop hoping to catch up with his sister. Doc wasn't sure if Luce might have run home, but he was in luck. She had stopped a few yards down the street, and was looking into the window of another shop.

Doc caught up with Luce and approached her again, but tried this time to engage her properly so he could at least talk to her for a few moments. He remembered as well to call her by her proper name.

"Louise, I just wanted to say hello." Doc wanted to give her a big hug, but as he reached out to her, Luce muttered a shaky response.

"Must get home." She turned and set off. The words seemed to echo in his mind and he thought Luce sounded afraid. It was then Doc remembered what his sister had told him all those years ago, about how frightened she was when a strange man made a grab for her. It was all beginning to make sense. The sweet shop. Him and Luce! Of course, it was all making sense now. Doc could have walked after his sister, but knew he had to let her go and he watched her turn the corner and disappear out of sight.

He knew there would be problems trying to communicate with his family, and there were probably far better ways in which he could try and get his situation across to them. More opportunities would come along soon enough, he was convinced of that. Next year would be a different. He consoled himself with this thought as he made his way back to his hotel and eventually, his way back home.

Thursday 26th October 1994
September soon moved into October, and Doc spent many hours working in his little office in the coffee bar. Business was booming as far as he was concerned. Footfall was well up, and losses and damages were down, so it was a good month.

Today was a Thursday, very much like any other day of the week. Kathy was busy down in the café and everyone seemed happy as Doc flicked through some outstanding bills. He had his plans for January next year well underway, with orders for a number of different items and delivery planned, and all was going well when suddenly he felt peculiar, first in his head and then his stomach. He nearly fell off his chair. This was a feeling he hadn't experienced for a number of years, and although it caught him by surprise he knew well enough how to get through the pain. It lasted about five minutes and fortunately nobody had seen him suffering. It was a pain he wanted to keep to himself although he wasn't sure what the problem was.

Days turned to weeks and then to months and quite soon it was 1995. Sunday 15th of January, and Doc was feeling an incredible sense of anticipation. He was well aware that tomorrow was a day he had been waiting for, but as it grew ever nearer he felt a pang of uncertainty as well. It was a strange feeling, really. Obviously, he knew about tomorrow and what was going to happen, but he wanted more. Initially, Doc had planned to be at the bungalow when the Riddells arrived, and then he considered going into Yarmouth and meeting them at the hotel but as time went on, he knew that he couldn't, because it wasn't what had happened. Whatever he wanted to do now, he was frightened to change anything. After such a long time, he just wanted to hug his father, and kiss his mother and sister, to be part of a family again. But it wasn't the way things happened. In fact, he knew that he, Doc, didn't really meet the family for a long time. It was all very weird. So much he wanted to do, but so much he daren't do. In the end, he settled for flags, lights and bunting which he could remember had been put up when he first lived through tomorrow. It was going to be an historic day.

Over the last year, he had been arranging and planning things and the intensity of his involvement had meant the coffee bar had been neglected a little. Luckily, he had some trusted staff who he was sure wouldn't take advantage of his absences. He knew that he should spend a bit more time in the bar, but his other plans were more important. Flags, flagpoles, banners and some lights. All had to be purchased, checked and erected ready for tomorrow. It hadn't cost a great deal of money, it was mainly time it had taken that was hard. Doc was feeling a bit breathless, but he was happy with his general state of health. There were just the last little bits to do and then he could relax a little in the satisfaction that he had played his part. It was nearly nine o'clock, so the coffee bar would be opening soon, and then the day would keep him busy. There was a knock on the window, and Kathy was waiting outside. Doc went and unlocked the front door, let Kathy in and re-locked the door.

"Hi, Doc. How are you today?" Kathy was her usual bouncy self.

"I'm feeling good today, thank you, Kathy."

"Is Steve coming in?"

"Not till eleven but he is due. I don't think we'll be too busy until later, so we should be able to cope," Doc answered, as much in hope as in belief. As it happened, the day was quite busy, but everyone managed and by half past five only Kathy and Doc were left.

"Do you want to go?" Doc asked. Kathy looked at her watch.

"Are you sure?"

"Of course. There's only half an hour left, and I can't see there being many others coming along so get going if you want to." Doc made a panoramic sweep of the café to reiterate his point that in fact the place was empty.

"I'll go, then." Kathy laughed at Doc's antics and made her way out of the door. Doc took up his place behind the bar, but as he guessed would be the case, nobody else came in. The whole village knew that Doc's closed at six on a Sunday, and it would only be the odd bit of passing trade that might look to see if the place was open.

Doc locked the front door and turned off the main lights both outside and inside. He had most of the banners and flags he needed in the back of his van and the next twenty minutes was spent getting the things into the café where he could prepare everything. Doc had parked the van round the corner, so a brisk walk took just a couple of minutes. As he parked outside the café, Ken from the Chinese take-away was outside, and said hello.

"You are late home today, Doc."
"I have some things to do tonight, so I'll be here for a while yet. In fact, I'll pick up some food on the way out."
"Okay, Doc. See you then."

Doc got the boxes out of the van and into the café. The lights were going to be the most difficult thing as he wanted to hang one set around the oak tree and another across the top of the shop. He had brought his extendable ladders and with a little bit of climbing he was sure he could get the lights around the tree. The power would come from an extension lead that he would run from the roof of the café to a nearby telegraph pole, and from there to the lights. He had done a similar thing for the summer fair a couple of years ago, so was sure that it would work. Doc was heavily involved in all sorts of things that were going on around Somerby so nobody was too surprised to find him up ladders, up a tree or on the roof of his coffee bar. Usually there would be others around to give him a helping hand, but of course these plans were only known to Doc, so he had to do everything himself. It took longer and made him tired, but he knew he would get there. Lan, from the Chinese take-away, came out and chatted briefly but Sunday was one of their busier nights so she wasn't able to hang around long. She helped for a short while the electrical lead was drooping across the road, but nobody wanted to drive by, so she didn't have to do much.

The Somerby Tree

Eventually, the lights in the oak tree were ready. They were more like Christmas lights, which Lan had pointed out to Doc when she said that she thought he was putting them up too late. The other lights and the flags were easy, which just left the banner. Doc had decided that this would not go up till tomorrow morning. He made sure that everything was in place to tie the banner but then left the actual hanging it up until the morning. He looked at his watch and thought about going into Yarmouth, but the craving didn't last. Doc knew it wouldn't be right to interfere this early into his family's move. He could at least wait until tomorrow. One last look around and he was sure that everything was ready. If memory served him, it would be late morning that the family arrived. He knew they would be coming by taxi, but he could not at all recall what type of taxi it was or even the colour. He would just have to be on the lookout. With his task almost complete, Doc got himself a Chinese meal and made his way back home. It was going to be an early start tomorrow but despite that, with all the things going on in his head, and the overall excitement, there was no way Doc was going to sleep tonight.

Monday was probably one of the biggest anti-climaxes of Doc's long and unusual life. By six thirty, the banner was unfurled and in place. It was in bright blue and white and announced 'Somerby welcomes the Riddells'. He had tried to remember exactly what the banner said when he first saw it thirty-odd years ago, and he had considered many different versions of this slogan. In the end, he was happy with what he had written. The lights both in the oak tree, and along the café roofline, had been turned on and were working perfectly. Doc took a couple of minutes to admire what he had done. The three flags were flying from the flagpoles on top of his coffee bar. He could have stood and looked at them all day but at seven thirty on the dot, Doc opened up. There would be the usual mass of school kids this morning, and a number of villagers waiting for the bus into town would call in and have a coffee or while they were waiting. This kept the place ticking over until the later rush started. The coffee bar's busiest time was probably between the hours of four and seven when they closed. Kathy would be in at her usual time, but she would be the only one, so Doc was kept quite busy for most of the early part of the day. The cafe did good business most days, but the requirements differed, depending on the weather and the school holidays. Today there would be very little need to serve more than drinks and crisps in the morning, but for the afternoon rush there would be kids in who would want cokes and burgers, or hot dogs and chips. Doc was quite conscious of healthy eating but found that however cheap he made healthy food, the kids only wanted junk. It was a bit unusual, but both Steve and Brian had been asked to come into work at ten thirty. Both men were quite efficient at working all the grills and deep-fryers, and usually only one would be on duty working with Kathy and Doc, but today was different. Doc told them both that although he would be around, he wanted to spend most of his time out the front today.

"What're all the lights and flags for then, Doc?" Steve was the first to ask.

"Oh, I've just put a welcome out for some important visitors who are arriving today."

"That would be the Riddells then, I guess."

"That's them."

"Who are the Riddells then?" Steve asked what he thought was a sensible enough question.

"The name doesn't mean anything to you, I suppose?" Doc wasn't sure whether to expect an answer or not.

"No, not really. Brian, do you know who the Riddells are?" Steve shouted.

"Are they American sports people?" Brian thought he had heard the name before but automatically considered the name synonymous with a company or business.

"Are they American?" Steve asked Doc.

"No, they are British." Steve didn't bother to ask again. Doc wasn't completely surprised that neither Steve nor Brian had managed to see the significance of the name as he had been known just as Doc for so many years now. He got asked the same question another few times before the day was out but nobody ever found out what all the fuss was about.

The Somerby Tree

Doc moved one of the brooms from the cleaning cupboard to the yard outside the front and he spent a lot of his time either brushing the yard or just leaning on the broom looking at the road from Yarmouth. Every time a taxi came into view, he would try and work out how many passengers it was carrying. He was looking for a full car but once again he couldn't remember much about who would be sitting where. They had a case and bags as well so perhaps they travelled in a people carrier. He just couldn't bloody remember. At about eleven fifteen, a white taxi swung round the green and passed in front of the café bar. It was a big saloon and looked to be full of passengers. He tried to make out who was sitting in the front seat but they were facing the wrong way and then he caught a glimpse of someone in the back seat. An image of his mother overtook him. He knew instantly that it was her. He could see that the back-seat passengers were looking at the banner and as he looked at her face staring out of the car, his knees went weak and he almost collapsed. The intention had been to give them all a big wave as the car drove by but it had already got to the end of the road before he could make even a feeble attempt. There, in that moment, all he had been planning for almost a year had passed him by. 'I don't think they even saw me,' Doc thought to himself. Feeling a bit depressed, he went back in to the café bar and sat down on one of the seats at an empty table. Steve came over.
"You alright, Doc?"

"Yes, I'll be okay. Just get me a cup of tea, please, will you?"

"Right away, boss." Steve fetched the drink and left Doc to his contemplations. He sat there and drunk his tea slowly while he considered whether it had all been worth it. It was a bit of a stupid question really as even if it hadn't been worth it he knew it was necessary that he did it, and that was all he had to know. In many ways, now that it had been done it was quite a relief. This was an event that he knew he had to play a part in and it was all over. All sorts of thoughts went through his mind about what he would do in the coming year. He looked up and just caught a glimpse of the removal lorry driving past the front of the green.

All during the rest of Monday, Doc toyed with the idea of calling on the family but knew why he shouldn't. He hadn't set foot on Rawthorn Drive for years, and that alone was going to be a bit of a test for him. As the café closed, he thought again of going to visit them but he decided against it. The lights were taken down from the oak tree a lot quicker than they were put up, and Doc also removed the banner and the lights from the coffee bar. He left the flags flying. It had been a stressful day all in all, and Doc was pleased to get home. The evening was a difficult one. He wished he had some photos to look at. He had none of course. The image of his mum, looking out of the taxi window, was strong in his mind. He tried to think back to other times with her, but could recall very few. A solitary tear trickled down his cheek, and it found its way to his mouth where the taste made his eyes water a bit more. He wiped away the tears with the back of his hand in a masculine way, but he was not embarrassed about how today made him feel. A part of him had returned from the dark side of nowhere. It was a massive reunion, and, to Doc, the return to normality. All of this was of course one sided, as The Riddells had no idea what would happen in the coming months. Doc reached up for the shoe box on top of the wardrobe. It was all he had to remind him of his life, and then it only reflected part of it. Perhaps if he were to make contact he could help this time round. He decided that he would go and say hello to the family tomorrow morning.

Tuesday morning was very much the same as usual. Doc and Kathy had opened at seven-thirty, and there was the usual onslaught of school kids wanting cokes and crisps. They were both used to the routine, and when there was the odd order for a hot dog, Doc did the honours, whilst Kathy took over serving. Steve came in at ten-thirty and Doc took this opportunity to make his little trip.
"I've got to pop out for a while. Can you manage for me, Steve?"
"Yes, I think so."
"I'm not sure how long, I'll be but may be a couple of hours. Are you sure you'll be alright?"
"Of course. What could go wrong?" Steve was

insistent he could deal with any problems and was happy to show he could manage.

"See you a bit later."

Doc left the coffee bar. He made his way around the corner and towards Rawthorn Drive. It wasn't the first time he had walked this way, as the grocer's shop was down here, but usually he would look away from Rawthorn Drive, whereas today he was focussing on it all the way. As he got nearer there was that strange feeling in his stomach again. Nerves? Uncertainty? He wondered what he would say, depending on who might answer the door. He hoped, of course, that it wasn't his father who answered, and preferably not David, but his mother sister. He guessed that regardless of how many times he practised, when it came to it he wouldn't know what to say.

Doc came to Rawthorn Drive, and then stopped. It was very difficult to take that first step into the road, and he considered turning round and approaching from another direction, but then something in his mind clicked, and he just started walking. He closed his eyes for the first few yards, and then he looked at the bungalows he had not seen for so many years. One or two looked remarkably different due to extensions and the like but the scenery was calmingly familiar. As the road curved a little, and he reached the bottom of the rise, Doc could see his old home. It was there in the distance exactly how he remembered. He took a brief moment to stop and take it in, what he hadn't seen for such a long time. His stomach began to feel much worse, and he had a pain in his head, like a migraine starting. He was vaguely aware of someone walking towards him on the other side of the road, but he couldn't have said whether it was a man or a woman. His head got rapidly worse, and he was almost frozen, finding it impossible to walk another step. The giddiness became more apparent and Doc knew what was to follow. How stupid he had been to think that this wouldn't have happened. He knew that worse was to come, but he was powerless to do anything about it. The other pedestrian had obviously spotted that Doc was having problems and had slowed down to see what might happen. The pain in Doc's head got worse and the world around him started to spin. He reached out for some support, but there was nothing to grab hold of. He knew he had to hold on tight to something, but it was too late, he was already falling. He fell on the pavement and hit his head. The pedestrian witnessed the whole thing and rushed to his aid. It was Margaret Brown from Buxton Drive. She knew Doc from the café, and she was happy to help if she could. Doc appeared unconscious when she reached him, but within a few seconds he stirred. She helped him sit up and a bit and then she tried to talk to him.

"Hey, Doc, are you okay?" All Doc could make out was the image of a kitchen. He was a bit confused. Margaret Brown continued talking. "Doc? Can you hear me?"

"Yes, I can hear you. Where am I?" Doc replied quite sensibly. Margaret Brown was happy to hear a normal response but she could see his eyes were not right. She tried to help. "You're in Somerby." "Yes, I know that, but where exactly? Oh, yes, I'm in Rawthorn Drive." Doc was remembering how the kitchen looked in his old home. Margaret Brown was reasonably happy with his response, as indeed he was in Rawthorn Drive, so she helped him back to his feet. Doc rubbed his head and felt a bump. Things were starting to come back to him. How could he have forgotten? He made his way back to the coffee bar, where Steve was quick to sit him down. Doc was still not right and his head, although better, was still aching. He remained in his small office for the rest of the day. He did occasionally look out of the window and on one occasion caught sight of the Riddell family staring up at the coffee bar from the oak tree. 'The tree', Doc thought to himself. How apt that we should have visited there so soon. He looked at Michael and Sue. He missed them so much. 'I wonder what Dad did after the accident?' he thought to himself. He then looked at Louise and wondered what the future might hold for her. Lastly, he looked at David. 'If only I could let him know' he thought, briefly. The more he thought about it the more difficult it became. It was really a bit of a paradox. If he did warn David and something different took place, then what would become of him? Now that was a question he couldn't answer. In the end, he decided that he still wanted to try and give the whole family some warning, so that they might be prepared for what was to come. He knew it couldn't happen how he wanted it to, but he would try. Doc's head was starting to hurt again and he laid back down in the chair up in the office.

Although Doc helped to open the café and get the tills ready, he spent most of the following day upstairs in the office taking it relatively easy. It had been a long time since he had felt this unwell and the whole thing had taken its toll. Doc was tired and stayed off his feet as much as he could. He tried to remember back to the 80s when he first started to feel like this and recalled how wore him out at first. He was sure that he would get used to it, if the attacks were to continue.

As the day went on, the café got busier. Doc popped down to see how things were going, but returned to his office quite quickly. Brian had given him a progress report an hour or so ago, but the noise was growing down there, so Doc decided he would make sure that everything was going well. He made his way to the bottom of the stairs and stood in the doorway, surveying the scene.

"Are you all right, Doc?" Brian asked, as he served.

"Yeah, I'm ok. Just making sure you're coping down here."

"We're coping." Brian and Kathy were quite

capable, and Doc was confident they could handle most events. He looked to see what Kathy was doing, and noticed a table full of girls in the corner. Almost immediately he saw that one of the girls was Louise. Doc hadn't realised that she came into the café so soon after moving to Somerby, but sure enough there she was. Doc looked at the other girls around the table and started to identify them. Tina Phillips, of course, and Melanie Huggins, but he struggled a bit to name the other two. Gillian was familiar, but he couldn't be sure if that was because she'd been coming into the café for a while. As he tried to think back, suddenly he realised that Louise was looking at him. They made eye contact. Doc wanted to wait for the right moment before talking to Luce, and it wouldn't be right to go and talk to her now, so he smiled and turned back up to the office.

Thursday was very similar to the day before as far as Doc was concerned. He was feeling much better, but still spent most of the day upstairs. As before, he decided to give the bar a quick look to make sure all was ok, and he made his way down the stairs. Just as he got to the doorway, he saw Louise at the counter buying two cokes. Brian was serving, of course, but Doc felt the urge to make a comment.

"Are they both for you?" Doc looked at Luce.

"No, they're for my friends," Louise replied indicating the table in the corner where Kathy was currently cleaning.

"As long as you're not being made to buy them." Doc had said it before he had time to think what he was saying. He thought it might have sounded strange, but Louise replied quite normally. She grabbed the cokes and started back to the girls. Doc was desperate to talk more with her but knew he had to wait.

Monday morning was quite uneventful. Doc helped open up and served the first few customers, then Kathy took over. Brian had orders for bacon sandwiches so he was busy cooking. As the queue disappeared, Doc heard the phone ringing upstairs.
"I'm just going to answer the phone."
"Okay," Kathy replied.
"Give me a shout if you need me." Doc made his way up to the office but the phone stopped before he got to it. He sat down at the desk and started to open his mail. It was all bills, so nothing he wasn't expecting. Suddenly, there was a shout from downstairs. It was Kathy asking for some help. Doc reacted immediately, and skipped down the stairs. He couldn't be sure that he didn't miss a step, but half way down, his head suddenly started throbbing and the accompanying dizziness disorientated him, so that he fell down the last five or so steps. It was another attack. Doc knew the feeling, he couldn't mistake it really.

Kathy heard the noise and ran to see what had happened. In a slight panic, she shouted for Brian, and between them came to Doc's rescue. Kathy made sure he was okay before returning to the café. Brian helped Doc back upstairs. Doc was exhausted. He wondered if David was in the café. He wanted to go and look, but Brian was in charge and he hadn't the strength so he never found out. His recovery was quicker than before, and as he had guessed he was getting more used to the attacks.

It was just another ordinary day. January had become February, his family had arrived in Somerby and were starting to settle in, and as yet he had not managed to speak to any of them very much. He was aware that time was running out. It was difficult for him to know exactly what to do next. He had to carry on living as much as normal as he knew that was what happened. He knew that he wasn't going to get to speak to David, or else he would have known, but he still wondered if it was possible to change things. In the end, he comforted himself with the thought that he might get a warning through Luce or his mum or dad, but at the back of his mind he wasn't convinced.

Day turned into evening as the light disappeared and Doc kept an eye on how things were in the coffee bar. He hadn't yet seen much of David, but Luce had been in a few times. She was in again today.

"Doc, are you alright?" Kathy asked as she ventured to the upstairs office.

"Yeah, I'm okay. Is there a problem?"

"No, it's just that we don't see that much of you out front anymore and I wondered if there was anything wrong?" Kathy was genuinely concerned. She knew he had had that fall recently, and guessed that he might be feeling ill.

"No, nothing's wrong, really. I've a lot on my mind."

"If you need to chat, let me know."

"Thanks, Kathy."

Kathy made her way back to the counter and got on with her job. Doc thought about coming down but knew that the place would be filling up with school kids and he didn't want to take any chances. He looked at the calendar, the eighth of February. He thought about the date for a while but couldn't recall any importance. He sat back down and mulled over the figures. He concluded that they were well up on last year. He made a few quick calculations, and then put away the ledgers for the evening. He was making his way downstairs when he began to feel queasy. He guessed what the problem was, but continued. Then suddenly he felt as though someone had given him a right hook, and his eye hurt like hell. 'What was that?' he thought to himself? Shocked, but used to anything now, he made his way back upstairs to the cloakroom. He looked at his eye, in the mirror but there was nothing wrong with it. What had the pain been? Then he remembered. He had been hit outside the coffee bar and that could well have been today. He started to feel a bit better, so made his way back down to the coffee bar.

"Hi Doc," Kathy said as he appeared. Doc looked around and saw a group of Burgh High School pupils over by the front door. It looked as if they had just come in.

"That lot over there…" said Doc.

"Which lot?" Kathy asked.

"Bob Packham, Marksy and the other two." Doc pointed them out.

"What about them?"

"Have they been causing any trouble?"

"No, I don't think so." Kathy was confused by Doc's question. He came out from behind the counter, and wasn't quite sure what to do next but as he considered, the four lads started to leave. Doc watched them as they left and then followed them outside. The four moved swiftly and were already turning the corner, heading towards the pub.

"Oi, you lot!" Doc shouted. The four of them stopped and turned. There was Bob Packham, Terry Marks, Roger Turrell and Micky Tranyer. They already had attitude. "I know what you lot have been up to."

"What do you mean, Doc?" Terry replied.

"I'm just going to tell you once. If I see you picking on the new lad again I'll sort it out." Doc was fuming. His recollection of the incident was beginning to come back to him. It was nearly thirty years ago, but he remembered.

"Picking on who?" Bob was next to speak.

"You know. I'll be keeping an eye out." Doc knew it was stupid to do anything now even though he wanted to so much. The boys turned and started on their way again. Doc could hear their laughter.

The next day, Doc called both Kathy and Brian into the office.

"There was some fighting in the coffee bar yesterday, and I don't want it to continue."

"Fighting?" Brian queried. "With us?"

"No, some of the kids were picking on David Riddell." As Doc said, it he thought it really strange.

"I didn't see anything." Kathy said.

"Nor did I!"

"Well, I know it happened. Packham, Marks and those other two were picking on David."

"David?" Kathy thought she knew who Doc meant but wasn't sure.

"The new lad from London. David Riddell."

"Well, I'm sorry boss, but we didn't see anything."

"Keep an eye on them and make sure it doesn't turn into anything, please." Doc was worked up. It was unusual for him to lecture the staff at all, let alone give them a telling off.

"There was a little bit of bag kicking the other week, but nothing serious," Kathy added, remembering.

"I…" Doc started to reply, but stopped himself and coughed to hide the intentional pause. "He got punched in the face."

"What, the London lad?"

"Yes."

"I don't think so. We would have seen it, wouldn't we, Brian?"

"Yes, we would have seen a scuffle if any punches had been thrown." Brian backed Kathy up.

"I'm not arguing, I'm just saying he got punched." Doc tried to draw a line under it. He left the two of them and went to set up the tills. Brian and Kathy stared at each other.

"I think Doc is mistaken," Kathy said, as she slumped down onto a chair.

"Yeah, I think you're right. We'd have seen it, wouldn't we?" Brian wasn't fully convinced.

March arrived and it was another ordinary day in the café, but today Doc was going to make sure he spoke to Luce. He had noticed that she was coming into the place and Doc felt a great happiness at seeing her. He would have liked her to stay all day but he knew he had to be careful in the way he approached her. She didn't know who he was and she might not believe him if he tried to tell her. He decided that he wouldn't tell her straight away, but try and gain her friendship and trust before dropping the bombshell. It wasn't as if he knew what to tell her, anyway. Just how could he warn her about her impending future? It wasn't a subject you could just bring up. He could always let her know nearer to the event if necessary, but he knew he must get a message to her or David. He just wasn't quite sure what message, as yet.

Doc looked over to see who was sitting with Luce, and today there were three other girls: Tina Phillips he knew, and Melanie Huggins, but he couldn't remember who the third one was. He thought it was something like Libby or Livvy, so perhaps it was her, but it was too long ago to remember. He also knew Gillian Fortescue was one of Luce's friends but she wasn't there. He went over and briefly spoke to all the girls, but made a point of saying something to Luce. It wasn't brilliant as all they were concerned about was a free coke, but at least he had spoken to her. It was great to hear her voice and he could have listened to her all day, but with the other girls there he didn't want to appear weird or perverted.

Doc saw another opportunity to talk to Luce a little later. Only the girl he couldn't name was with her and he seized the chance to casually go over and chat. 'Bloody Hell', Doc thought to himself. He had a flutter in his stomach as if he was trying to chat someone up. It was something he hadn't felt for years, in fact a feeling he hadn't had since he first talked to Mary. As he got to Luce's table, he started to speak, but almost immediately he had an attack, and he fell. He managed to stay on his knees and didn't fall over completely, but it was very painful this time. He felt dizzy and sick, and had pains going through his head and stomach. Wow! this was a good 'un! He almost lost consciousness, but he could tell that Brian and Louise were holding him up and walking him back to the counter. Louise said something, and left Brian to get him up the stairs where Kathy took over. It wasn't exactly a complete success but at least he had spoken to Luce.

Thursday 16th March 1995

Doc remembered that it was Luce's birthday yesterday. He had calculated that she would have been twelve. He kept an eye open for her all day, but she hadn't come into the café. In fact, none of her friends of Luce's had come in yesterday. This afternoon was a different story, and all of them were in. He took his opportunity to walk over, pretending to clean a few tables before getting to Louise's. He wished her a happy birthday. It was a great feeling, and he was pleased with her response. It may not have been much but to him it was a big step.

April 1995

Doc had pick up a few things from town Tuesday afternoon. Kathy volunteered to go, but her place was at the counter so Doc went himself. The whole trip only took about an hour and he was back by about five. As he drove into the village he could see that the café was buzzing. It made him feel good.

He drove round the back where the deliveries were normally made, and he got out and opened the boot. Picking up a couple of the boxes, he decided to go into the café, and see if Kathy or Brian could help him unload. The first two boxes weren't heavy, so he carried them right into the counter area and looked to see what his staff were doing. As he stood there, he could see they were busy, and it was obvious he would have to do his own unloading, then his head started to throb and he lost his balance. The boxes fell and Doc hit his head on the counter on the way down. It was another one of those bloody attacks he thought. Within minutes, he was back up on his feet and starting to feel better. It was more embarrassing than anything else.

Saturday 15th April 1995
Doc decided to go for a short walk this morning. It was a Saturday and the weather was warming up, so he left Kathy and Brian working in the café and set off. Firstly, he went for a stroll up to the post office. He didn't want anything but fancied a chat with Jean.

"Hello, Jean, how are you?"

"Morning, Doc. I'm okay. The legs are playing up a bit, and I still have to be careful with my back but I'm doing okay."

"Good to hear it."

"Did you want anything?"

"No. Just came down to have a little chat. Catch up with what's going on in the village."

"Nothing new really. You know they are going ahead with that new by-pass."

"I thought that had gone back to planning."

"No, Doc. It's all going ahead. They will start building early next year, I'm told." Jean usually knew what was going on.

After the post office, Doc made his way back to the crash site in the woods. He didn't stay long but just gave it a look, as if it might give up some clues. It didn't. Doc set off back to the coffee bar but not before chatting to Ken in the Chinese take-away and then seeing Doris in the bakery. While he was in there, he saw someone he hadn't seen for years.

"Harriet?" Doc said it more as a question. The woman turned to look at him.

"Bloody hell. It's, it's…"

"Doc. Call me Doc."

"Oh, Doc." The woman obviously didn't recognise the name.

"You're Harriet. Harriet...?" Doc never did know Harriet's surname.

"Harriet Matthews." They chatted generally for a minute.

"How is George?" Doc asked.

"Oh, he's ok I suppose." Harriet didn't sound too keen to divulge anything more.

"Is he living locally?"

"Yes, he's in Leafby."

"And did he marry?"

"Well. He just lives at home with his son now. It was a marriage doomed to fail." Harriet obviously didn't like talking about it.

"He had a son, then?"

"Oh, yes. Trouble. You see, boys are always trouble."

"I'm sure he's not that bad." Doc remembered that Harriet could sometimes exaggerate.

"Well, I suppose Art has his good points." Harriet seemed reasonably happy to give her nephew some benefit. Doc stood and pondered. "Well it's nice to meet you again but I must get in the queue to buy some bread. I've got a busy day shopping ahead of me.

"Yeah, okay. It's good to see you again, Harriet." Doc made his way around the baker's, but then stopped. He was thinking about Harriet and George, and the problems they had before he ever knew them. They had a hard childhood. He went back up to Harriet. "Harriet, sorry to ask again, but you said your name was Matthews?"

"Yes, that's right. Harriet Matthews."

"Is that your married name?"

"Yes."

"So, what was your maiden name?"

"Oh, Davison. My father was Scottish," Harriet replied. Doc suddenly forgot all about buying his loaf of bread. He walked out of the bakery and stood outside, stunned. He kept repeating the name Mary over and over. He had a bit of a headache coming on again. He tried to sort out all the information he had just got. It would explain a lot. Doc just stood there gazing at nothing. He kept repeating himself, 'Mary, Mary'.

Doc made his way back to the café bar where Kathy sat waiting for him.

"Everything alright, Doc?"

"Yes," he lied. All sorts of things were going on in his head. He felt giddy. He almost fell into the seat opposite Kathy.

"Do you need any help?" Kathy asked.

"No, not really. I've just been talking to an old friend in the baker's."

"Oh, yes? Anyone I know?" Kathy thought there was going to be a revelation at the end of this conversation.

"I doubt it. Someone I knew many years ago, Harriet Matthews." Doc looked at Kathy as he said her name.

"Don't think I know her. Where does she live?"

"Not in Somerby. She lives in Leafby."

"Oh, that's probably little Ness's mum." Kathy was sure she knew who Doc meant.

"You know Vanessa?" Doc tried not to sound interested but couldn't hide his curiosity.

"Well of course. She comes in here most days."

"Does she?"

"Yes, she sits with the Huggins girl and the rest of them."

Doc started put everything into place. Vanessa was a friend of Louise's. Harriet was Mary's mum. No wonder he got on well with Harriet. He hadn't noticed the family resemblance before of course, but now it was all starting to fit. That wasn't the only thing falling into place, either. The problems, their childhood. It all made sense.

Doc also tried to get to know the Riddells as much as he could. He knew that he would rarely get to chat to David but he was getting on with Louise and had talked a few times to their mother. Doc tried to enhance this friendship but Michael, the father, wasn't over keen and it became obvious that Doc would have to nurture any relationships with the others secretly.

It was a busy day in the café and Doc found himself having to help out with serving in order to keep the queue down a bit. Kathy and Brian were extremely busy. He looked to see if Luce was helping but he couldn't see her. She was there alright, working away trying to keep Kathy and Brian stocked up with plates and glasses. It was pandemonium in there. Doc caught sight of Louise looking at the clock on the wall. It was nearly a quarter past five.

"Are you happy to stay until half past?" Doc asked her.

"Yeah," Louise replied.

Soon, the rush had been dealt with, and the coffee bar was back under control. Doc told Louise that she could go home but he was rather pleased that she found time to engage him in some idle conversation.

"You know, when I was young, I had a special place to go when I was sad," Doc told Louise. It may have seemed a strange comment to make but it fitted in with the conversation at the time, or at least Doc thought so. "I go and sit in a tree."

"In a tree?" Louise looked at him strangely. "That's a daft place."

"No, really, it's a place you could also go to." Doc knew she wouldn't understand what he was trying to tell her. The conversation went on briefly about the tree and Doc explained exactly which tree he was talking about. Louise didn't take much of it in.

Towards the end of the conversation, Doc asked Louise to tell her mum and dad about the tree as well. This was obviously the last straw of this conversation as far as she was concerned, and she passed some remark about how stupid to think her dad might want to climb a tree, before picking up her things and leaving. Doc had at least managed to broach the subject. He would try again when the opportunity arose.

Friday 20th May 1995
Doc had guessed he wouldn't have too many opportunities to talk to Louise, so he made the most of this week, trying to talk to her every chance he got. It almost became a bit of a joke that he would always bring up the tree when they talked, but Doc felt Louise was quite happy about it.

Doc knew what he wanted to tell her, but it was never going to be the right time for him to explain everything. If he started to try she'd just find him strange. At least whilst she was working there, he could gently prepare her for what was to come. It was a big shock when Louise came into his office crying and said that she wasn't happy working there. Doc tried to sort it all out but she just wanted to go home. It was probably the best thing for her.

Saturday 21st May 1995

Although he hadn't been expecting him, Doc wasn't surprised to see Michael the next day. Louise was upset. He knew her dad wasn't keen on her working at the coffee bar, so when Michael came to tell Doc, it was quite expected. Michael started off quite angry but by the end of their meeting he was uncertain what to think. Doc didn't take any offence, already had answers to Michael's questions, and was generally very polite. He was of course pleased to actually be talking to his dad, so everything else was totally irrelevant. This took out all of the anger that Michael initially felt and he found that Doc was a nice bloke, but he wouldn't let his resolve slip. Michael said what he needed to say, and that would be enough. Doc mentioned the tree again but guessed it had fallen on deaf ears. He felt he would have no option but to have to explain all at some later date.

Chapter 18
A REUNION

Friday 4th January 1996

Doc sat upstairs in his office, looking intently at the date circled on his calendar. It was the fourth of January nineteen ninety-six. It was another one of those dates that had long featured in his life. Downstairs in the coffee bar, things were starting to ease off. The appalling weather meant that fewer kids had made the journey to Doc's today and those that were in just wanted to get home. A storm was in full flow outside and everyone wanted to be indoors. There was a knock on the office door, even though it was open.

"Doc, there's only about half a dozen in now and nobody has bought anything for at least twenty minutes. Do you still want me?" Kathy asked.

"No, not really Kath. You start packing up and I'll be down in a couple of minutes." Doc looked at his watch. It was quarter past six. He tried to imagine what he would have been doing at this very moment in Rawthorn Drive.

Doc made his way downstairs where Kathy was already to go. She walked over to him and saw that he had things on his mind.

"What's the problem?"

"Oh, nothing Kath." Doc smiled at her. "You get off now, I'll close tonight." Kathy sensed that there was a problem that she was unaware of. She had seen

Doc in varying states of misery and this looked like another big one. She put her bag down on the counter and gave him a hug.

"Tell me what's worrying you?"

"I can't really explain."

"Have you had another attack?"

"No." Doc smiled at her question. "No, no more attacks." Doc thought about adding that there wouldn't be any more attacks from now on, but then thought better of it. Kathy gave him a kiss, an affectionate, friendly one, on the lips. They looked at each other for a few seconds. "Go on, you get home." Kathy picked up her bag and left the café. She had an umbrella with her which she opened as she got outside. Doc watched her walk out of view. He looked at the clock. It was half past six.

"Ok, let's be having you. Closing in five minutes," Doc shouted as he started to collect the few glasses and plates that were still on tables. Kathy had washed up nearly everything else. The kids were a bit surprised as Doc's was nearly always open until just after seven, but they slowly obliged and made their way home.

The weather had not improved at all, but then Doc knew it wouldn't. The thunder and lightning got worse and the wind was starting to pick up a bit. Doc got changed ready to go out. He was in waterproof trousers, a nice thick cagoule and good strong walking boots. He knew that there might be a bit of walking this evening, and he wanted to be prepared. Having previously got his equipment ready, he placed the selected items in his various pockets and then pulled on his gloves and woolly hat. He was ready.

It was about quarter past seven, and Doc was fine about going to look for Michael and Louise. He knew that David wouldn't be there, of course, but at least he would be able to help the other two back home. He might even be able to find an opportunity to explain where David had gone, but first things first. He needed to ensure that his dad and Louise were back home and safe.

The rain was torrential by the time Doc got halfway down Leafby Lane. He had seen the lightning strike all around Somerby. There was a massive bolt that seemed to hit the woods. Doc guessed that this must have been the one that hit the car. The wind had worsened but he was ready for that. The one thing Doc was a little concerned about was just how much energy he would be able to put into it all. He would probably weaken after an hour or so but he would do what he could.

As he walked further down Leafby Lane, he looked ahead into the woods for signs of the accident. The bend where it all started was about fifty yards away, so he hoped he'd be able to see something soon. There were skid marks on the road, and in the mud to the side of the road, and Doc followed these to where it was obvious that Michael had left the road. There was a big clearing and a track, which could only have been where the car had gone through the woods, and a track down a slope further into the woods. Doc was feeling quite energetic for a change and trotted along the path. He got out the torch he had previously put in his pocket and followed the path until it came to an end about a hundred yards into the woods. He looked around to see if there was any possibility of the car veering away from this course, but there was no way for anything to have gone any further into the woods. What was more, he recognised the spot where he was now standing as where he had regained consciousness some thirty years ago. This had to be the spot, but there was no sign of any car, let alone any bodies.

Doc scratched his head as he walked all over the place looking for signs of wreckage, but there was nothing. He wasn't going to give up, so he made his way back up the path to the road, to look at it in a different way. He spent the next four or five hours walking all around the woods, but there was absolutely no sign of any wreckage. At midnight, Doc decided he should call it a night. He would be able to come back tomorrow when the light was better. He couldn't understand what had happened, but then he knew that he wasn't going to be there, so nothing should have been unexpected. Doc started to make his way back to where he knew his bit of the car had come to a stop. From there he would make his way up the path and back to the road. He was surprised to find someone with a torch further along the path when he got there. His first thought was that it was his dad and Louise, so he ran towards the light. As he got closer, he was able to make out that the person with the torch was wearing a uniform so he stopped immediately, but it was too late. The policeman had seen him.

A beam of light was shone in his direction and it landed on him straightaway.

"Hello, who's there?" the policeman shouted. Doc tried to think of what to do next, but it was impossible to run away so he thought that honesty would be the best policy. Well, up to a point anyway.

"Hello, Officer, it's me."

"Just stay where you are. I'm going to come to you." Doc stood where he was. The policeman came towards him still shining the torch. His colleague also had a torch set on Doc. "Hello, are you Mr Riddell?" The policeman stood about three feet away from Doc shining the torch in his face. Doc almost answered 'Yes' but he stopped himself.

"It's Doc, officer." Fortunately, it was one of the local officers who recognised him immediately.

"What the hell are you doing out here at this time of night, Doc?" Again, Doc wanted to tell him the truth but thought better of it.

"I just saw the skid marks on the road up there, and then saw this track and wondered if there had been a car crash."

"Have you found a car?"

"No, there's nothing here at all," Doc answered. "Can I continue on my way now?" The policeman lowered the torch.

"Sorry, Doc. Yes, of course you can." The police spent another ten minutes looking around the woods while Doc went back home to bed. He would give it another look tomorrow.

Doc hadn't slept well, and was going over in his mind what had happened to him thirty years ago. He concluded that he must have been the only one to be affected by the incident, and that Michael and Luce must have made their way back home. He was a bit annoyed that they hadn't looked for him for very long, but then guessed that they too had been a bit shaken and just wanted to get the police involved. Perhaps they thought he had fallen out of the car. He had an urge to call at the family home in Rawthorn Drive and make sure that they were all there, and see if the opportunity might arise where he could explain exactly what had happened to him, so he got himself washed and ready.

He waited for Kathy and Brian to arrive so that the café was open and running, and then he made his way up to the bungalow. Doc looked at his watch as he rang the doorbell and saw that it was just about ten o'clock. Sue opened the door and Doc could see she had been up all night crying. He wanted to give her a big hug but knew she wouldn't have been expecting him to be calling, especially on today of all days.

"Hello Mrs Riddell, I've just heard the news and I wondered if there was anything I could do to help you all?" Doc tried to sound as sympathetic as possible.

"Help us all?" Sue replied. She seemed rather shaken at his statement, but opened the door a bit more to allow him in. "It's only me who needs help, Doc," she added.

"Well, yes, okay." Doc wasn't sure what to make of her comment, but still made his way into the kitchen. "Isn't D..." Doc stopped himself quickly and coughed to hide his words. "Isn't your husband here?" Doc listened, to see if he could hear Michael or Luce, but there was nothing. He wondered if they had tried to get some sleep. "I assume he is out looking?"

"Out looking?" Sue caught her breath. "Out bloody looking where?" She started to cry, and Doc managed to position himself where he could cuddle her and try to comfort her. He suddenly wondered if he had got something wrong and felt he shouldn't jump to expected conclusions. "I heard that David had gone missing."

"Oh, sorry, Doc. I shouldn't have a go at you." Sue composed herself as she apologised. "It's not just David. My husband and daughter have also gone missing." She sighed and sat herself back down.

"All three have gone missing?" Doc was astonished.

"I only thought David had gone."

Sue cried again, and they had another hug before she composed herself, removed herself from Doc's arms and sat up. "So, there it is. The police are making enquiries, and nobody seems to know what has happened to them." Doc was deep in thought and only half listening to what Sue was saying.

"Don't the police have any idea what has happened?"

"No, not at all."

"Haven't they checked down Leafby Lane at all?" Doc was referring to the skid marks but then realised that he knew the police had searched, as he had seen them there, so decided not to make any further comments.

"Yes, they've checked down there apparently, but have found nothing." Sue stood up. A car pulled up outside the bungalow. "The police are here now, so perhaps you ought to go, Doc." Sue moved towards the door. As she opened it a detective was already waiting to come in.

"Hello, Mrs Riddell, I'm Detective Sergeant Bailey." The officer flashed his identity card. "I would like to have a few words with you if that's ok."

"Yes, please come in." Sue allowed the two officers in and they looked at Doc, not absolutely sure who he was.

"Good to see that neighbours are looking after you." The detective felt he should say something. Sue realised that she hadn't introduced them.

"Oh, this is Doc from the local café."

"Ah yes, Doc." The officer spoke in a knowing tone. The name had already been mentioned back at the station. The officer turned towards Doc. "It would be preferable if you could leave us now so we can talk to Mrs Riddell in private please." He pointed towards the door and Doc took the hint.

Doc made his way down Rawthorn Drive to the road at the bottom. He knew that from a point on this road he would be able to see the car in front of number twenty-six so he spent the next hour or so leaning against the wall. A number of villagers said hello to him as they passed by, but he kept looking up the road until the police left. He wanted to get back and see Sue, but he was worried what the police might have said to her. He was annoyed to have been seen at the woods last night, and pondered over whether or not he should have just run away. It was too late now to worry, he had been seen and that was that.

He saw the police leave by car and he gave it ten minutes before making his way back up to the bungalow. He prepared himself for a different reception but hoped that Sue would still be friendly towards him. He rang the doorbell. Quite quickly she opened the door and didn't seem surprised to see him. "Oh, hello Doc," Sue said.

"Are you okay? Is there anything you want me to do

or get for you?" Doc just wanted to help in any way he could. He didn't know what to do for the best, but he was going to make sure that Sue knew he was there for her anytime she needed him.

"Thanks, but no. Look I need to get my head around everything, so if you don't mind…" Sue gave a half smile as she closed the door on him. Doc quickly added some of what he wanted to say before she closed it completely.

"Please ask if you need anything. Anything at all." He wanted to comfort her but he knew he couldn't, and besides, he had other things to think about, such as where on earth could Michael and Louise have got to? He knew that his only option was to make his way back down to the woods.

Doc went back to the wood and spotted the police team still searching. They were in exactly the area he would have chosen to search himself if he had been in charge. He knew that he hadn't finished up much further into the wood those thirty years ago and he would have expected to have found some signs of the accident just exactly where they were all searching. Perhaps Dad and Luce had got out of the car and walked further into the woods, but then he realised what a stupid idea that was, because if they had left the car and walked then the car would have still been there. It was all a bit of a mystery but he knew he had himself gone through a strange time shift so anything was possible he supposed. As he stood and pondered over what might have been he missed the police officer walking in his direction.

"Hello, are you injured?" The officer called out to him. Doc weighed up his options and realised his situation. 'Bugger!' he thought to himself. He considered his best reply.

"No, I've just come from the village to help you search." Doc hoped that this would be good enough but it wasn't.

"Sorry, sir, but we need to do this ourselves. If you could come this way please." The officer led him back to the search site. He was placed under arrest.

The team leader came over and spoke to him next.

"What's your name?"

"I'm Doc." Doc hoped the officer would have heard of him but he was unlucky.

"What's that supposed to mean? Do you think you're a time traveller from Gallifrey or something?" The officers laughed. Doc groaned

"No, that's what I'm known as. Doc."

Doc wasn't happy but he had to give them a name. Almost immediately another police car arrived, and Doc was taken off to the station 'to help with their enquiries' as they say, and he guessed they suspected he was involved. Nobody was going to believe his story, but he would have to try and think of a way of convincing them. In the end, he was held overnight but never actually charged.

Doc awoke in a cell. He looked around and began to feel all the aches and pains he had encountered through the night. The bed wasn't the most comfortable but at least it was warm. He was served breakfast on a tray, which consisted of toast, scrambled egg and tea, but the plastic cutlery was useless and it made eating very difficult. Doc assumed he would be interviewed most of the day, and hopefully be home by the evening. He was interviewed, but for only about an hour. It was a strange interview, as the police were asking about what reasons Doc might have to harm the Riddell family, but each time they came up against a brick wall. His place of business had been searched, as had his little house in the village, and there was no evidence at all to suggest that he had anything to do with an abduction.

Doc knew what they were thinking, and the only real stumbling block was the fact that he had been seen on Friday evening around the accident spot. Doc himself was trying to work out what might have happened to Michael and Luce. He had assumed that they had crashed, and only he had had the misfortune to find himself thirty years in the past. He was now wondering if in fact he had come off far more lightly than his dad and sister. He told the police that he had heard something like a crash, and went to look around, knowing that the road was quite dangerous. He had even said that he had seen his dad's car drive down there, but his times were a bit out. Unfortunately, his memory from thirty years ago wasn't spot on, and he was sure it was around seven o'clock when they set off. The police questioned his timings, but that led to no satisfactory conclusion. Doc wasn't going to tell them the true story as he knew he'd be locked up. The police didn't really have anything on him but they didn't want him interfering with Mrs Riddell or their current enquiries, and the order had gone out to try and keep him locked up for a couple of days. Doc was never charged with anything but consented to being held at the station until the matter was resolved. He had no idea how long that might take.

Sunday came and went, and soon it was Monday. Doc was getting fed up with his confinement but didn't want to cause any problems. He considered phoning a solicitor, but then decided to go along with the police in the hope that they would just release him. The police had no idea what they were going to do with him. They had no evidence of a crime, and knew that fairly soon they would have to let him go, but they kept him locked up for as long as was legally possible in the hope that some development might turn things. They didn't have to wait too long.

The police received the call the evening before, but by the time they had decided to let Doc go, he was already bedded down for the night, so they surprised him this morning. It was a Tuesday morning and at six o'clock sharp, the custody officer brought Doc his breakfast tray and gave him the good news.

"You're being released, Doc," he said. "Just as soon as you've finished your breakfast we'll get the forms signed and you can go."

"About bloody time."

"Yes, the young girl has turned up and she says you've had nothing to do with it, so for now we have no further use for you."

The custody officer looked at Doc and wondered what was going through his mind. If he'd been in his position he felt he might be a little bit more annoyed than Doc was, but then, everyone was different. Doc meanwhile was trying to get his mind around things. He was pleased to hear that Louise had got back home, but where had his dad got to? He would have to see what Luce had to say, just in case his dad was lying injured somewhere.

After sorting out the release papers, Doc made his way back to Somerby and home. He needed a bath and it gave him some time to take in what he had been told. By ten o'clock he was making his way up Rawthorn Drive, but he could see that Sue and Louise had visitors. The car looked again like it was probably the police, so Doc waited until they had gone. He called at the house and spoke briefly to Sue but she was in no mood to talk and asked him to go. He confirmed that Louise was all right and left it at that. All he could do, really, was to go back to the woods and see whether anything else was there. Again, he couldn't look around too much as the police were present, and busy checking around, but what he could see was the back half of a car, the same car he was in thirty years ago. It was strange that this should turn up now, as he knew it hadn't been there over the last thirty years, but sure enough it was part of the same car that he had been in, and in the same part of the woods that he had crashed in some time ago. Was his dad going to arrive later? If so, how much later? Perhaps he wouldn't arrive for another thirty years? Wow! The thought of it all was quite enough to cope with for now.

Louise took the whole incident badly and came close to having a breakdown. She would often have nightmares, seeing the men working on the road and the Viking warriors, all spinning around in her mind. Sometimes she screamed out, and Sue spent several nights trying to comfort her daughter. Doc called in and tried to speak to Louise, but Sue wasn't keen. When he started to also mention the car accident it was enough for her to say no to him seeing her, and in fact she put a halt to Doc's visits altogether. Louise did pull through though.

February 1996
Some weeks later Louise was back at school and feeling almost as good as new. She made an appearance or two at Doc's but never stayed for very long. She just wanted to get home to her mum, and hoped each day that this would be the day when she got her dad and brother back. Doc bided his

time until Louise felt able to chat to him. He kept the conversation light at first, but then mentioned the accident.

"Sorry I mentioned the accident when I came to see you," Doc said sympathetically.

"I didn't know you had been to see me. What, at home?"

"Yes, I called round. I wanted to help you"

"How can you help?" Louise was confused.

"I can just tell you about my own experiences. We've both been through similar problems, but I've had time to get over mine. If you ever want to talk about anything, let me know."

Doc thought it would be ages before he would get another chance to talk to Louise but to his surprise only three days later Louise appeared at the counter and asked if he would let her know what had happened to him. Doc and Louise went upstairs to his office and he began to explain what he felt he could.

"I was in a car accident just like you." Doc started.

"When was that?"

"Huh! Now that's a difficult question." Doc pondered briefly. "It was just over thirty years ago, but it feels as if it happened only yesterday." Doc tried to stick to the truth as much as possible.

"And were you driving?"

"No, I was in the front passenger seat and my dad was driving. My younger sister was in the back."

"Just like I was."

"Yes, and just like you I was on the way to a party."
Doc didn't want to push this too much as things
were going quite well he thought.

"Yes, I was going to Vanessa's party. You know
Vanessa, don't you?"

"Yes, I know Vanessa."

"So, I was going to a party too." Louise thought
back. "Did you get to your party?"

"No." Doc shook his head and thought about Mary.
He imagined her standing in the village hall waiting
for him. "No, I never got to my party either." Doc
watched as Louise sat and looked around at all the
different things in his office. "So, Luce, how do you
feel now about the accident?"

"Oh, okay I suppose." She lied. "I don't really think
about it too much now."

"Well, I think that the accident I had is connected to
the accident you had." Doc made some complicated
explanation to try and describe a connection, but
Louise wasn't listening. "Are you okay, Luce?"

"Yes, I think so." Louise quickly snapped back to
realise where she was. "I think I'd better go, Doc."
He was glad they had at least broken the ice on the
subject but thought it was right to leave it alone for
now.

Over the next few weeks Doc and Louise had a few
further conversations on the subject. He'd explained
that his accident took place exactly in the same
place as hers, and produced a newspaper report
describing where the spot was. Louise was quite

surprised. It almost made her wonder if there was some true connection between them. She knew she liked Doc, but could never really put her finger on exactly why.

"This might sound strange, but I lost a lot of time when I had my accident." Doc said. "I think you lost a few days, didn't you?" Doc waited for an answer. Louise thought long and hard about the question.

"Yes, I think I lost a couple of days. How many days did you lose then?" It was Doc's turn to think.

"A lot more than you did. A lot more." Doc smiled. "Having said that I didn't really lose any days at all but actually gained days. You know, my life all repeated." The conversation went on and both Louise and Doc got deeper and deeper into their respective stories. Doc closed by coming out with what he'd wanted to tell her for so long. "I'm David, your brother." This didn't go down quite the way Doc had expected it to. Louise saw things all fall into place at first, and accepted the claim with all positivity. The more she thought about it, though, the more it scared her.

"If you're my brother, then why are you so old?"

"As I said, I gained thirty years. I went back in time." Doc started to shed a tear. Louise grimaced as she churned over the prospect that Doc might be her brother.

"So, if you're my brother then what accident were you in thirty years ago?"

"It was the same accident as you."

"But it couldn't have been."
"Yes, it was the same car, our dad's car but I crashed thirty years before you did."

Louise didn't freak out, which was Doc's biggest fear. In the end, Louise begun to warm to the idea of Doc being David.
"Prove you're my brother, then."
"And how do you want me to do that?" Doc started to get excited at the thought of Luce accepting him after all these years. It would be good to have his sister back to talk to. Louise was still not certain, but prepared to give him the chance.

"Okay, tell me something that only David would know," Louise demanded. Doc thought for a while.
"Hmm, on the way to the party you said that you had a feeling that the party was going to be a bad one, or the day was not going to be good. You only said it as you got in the car."
Louise mulled this statement over in her head. It was true, she had thought that something wasn't right, but it didn't convince her.
"Whose party were we going to?" Louise asked, before realising that she had already told him.
"Well, *you* were going to Vanessa's but *I* was going to Mary's," replied Doc, looking sad. Louise thought the reply was very convincing.
"And," he continued, I can tell you how you came to be called Luce."
"What do you mean? My name's Louise."

"Yes, but I called you Luce. There was a strange man who called you Luce in the sweetshop on the High Road."

Louise recalled the strange incident, and knew that David was the only person she had told. It was almost enough to convince her.

Over the next few weeks, Louise talked to her mum about David and things she remembered about him, and checked some of them out with Doc. Most of the time he answered believably. Louise invited him back to their home so that Sue could chat to him. Despite both Louise's and Doc's attempts, Sue was never convinced by his story. They had further meetings, and Louise became more and more positive that Doc and David were the same person, however bizarre that was. Sue agreed that certain things Doc knew could only have come from David, but she found it hard to accept his time-slip theory. Doc also mentioned the oak tree a couple of times and tried to persuade Sue and Louise that they needed to climb up into it to see the carvings there but it fell on deaf ears.

Just to add insult to injury, Sue started to get grief from her bank. As Michael had only been declared missing and not dead, she wasn't able to get access to their bank account which was only in Michaels' name. Money was beginning to run out. Doc got to hear what problems Sue was having and offered to pay the mortgage for her. At first, Sue refused, but after a few months she had no choice. She also spent endless hours putting out posters asking for information about the whereabouts of Michael and David. She felt they were out there somewhere, confused or with lost memories, and that someone somewhere would find them. Doc tried to convince her that this was probably not the case, but she never gave up hope that one day they would just reappear.

March 1996

Doc and Louise continued to be great friends. Neither treated this relationship in quite the same way as before, but they were almost as close. Doc eventually did persuade Louise to climb the big oak tree, where she found the carving from David. It said he loved his mum, dad and Luce, but it was dated 1966. Louise found it hard to believe that it was from her brother, but she still carved her own message for her dad next to it. Doc continued to try and convince Sue who he was, but she was becoming ill, and found talking about the whole incident very tiring. Louise suggested that Doc gave her some space, and although he still helped out with money, he kept away more often than not. Sue grew weaker but continued to talk about Doc every now and then. She liked to hear Louise's news of what he'd been up to, and had a picture of David in her mind when visualising it. Many an evening they spent talking, which usually finished up with them crying.

After a few years, Sue decided that she needed to thank Doc for his help. A meeting was organised between the three of them, but Louise was concerned that it might prove too much for Sue. It would probably be too much for Doc, too, but her mum was her biggest concern. In the end, though, they went ahead, and the meeting went well. Doc agreed to stop trying to convince them that he was David, and just be a friend called Doc. This was difficult but he felt it was probably for the best. They got along quite well, each leading their own lives without too much interference from each other. Doc would call round and visit regularly but had his own little cottage, while Louise remained at home with her mum.

2002

It was a few more years before Sue finally began to accept Doc as part of her family. They actually hugged now and then, and talked more like mother and son, but Louise was concerned about Sue because she began to refer to Doc as David, and talk to him as if he was a teenager. Doc loved it, and Sue seemed okay with it, but Louise found it very uncomfortable. Later, Doc persuaded Sue to get into the village more. She had remained indoors for months recently, but on the tenth anniversary of the crash, Doc got Sue to come with him to the oak and say a prayer for Michael, wherever he may be. Sue also said a little prayer for David but Doc didn't join in.

2005

"I want to go to the crash site, Doc, will you take us there please?" Sue asked. She wanted to remind herself what her son and husband might have seen when they came round. Doc chatted to Louise on the way, and when they arrived at the site he started to point out to Sue exactly where the accident took place. Louise listened, and heard an exact description of what she recalled. She looked at Doc and wondered if she would ever know what he had gone through. If it was David, and she was ninety-nine per cent sure now, just what life had he had? Sue didn't want to hear anymore.

"Could you leave us now please, Doc? I just want to be here with Louise." She smiled and Doc complied.

"I'll see you both later." Doc made his way back to the café.

After Doc had gone Louise asked Sue why she had sent him away.

"I just want to be here with you, darling."

"But Doc is also part of our family, and he is suffering as much as we are," Louise pleaded.

"Yes, I know, but we've lost your dad." Sue didn't mention David, knowing that Louise would argue that Doc was David.

"But so has Doc. He's lost Dad just as much as we have, and in fact may have lost him for longer than we have." Louise thought about the fact that he had already suffered thirty more years of this.

"Yes, I know. It's sad." But Sue refused to discuss the subject anymore. "Let's make our way home." Sue grabbed Louise's hand and they walked back towards the village centre. As they crossed the green they bumped into Vanessa.

"Hello, Ness!" Louise greeted her old friend with great enthusiasm. The two girls hugged and kissed.

"Hi, Louise, it's good to see you. Hello Mrs Riddell, how are you?"

"I'm okay, Vanessa, thank you." Sue let the two girls gossip a little bit before asking the only question on her mind. "How's your sister, Vanessa?"

"Oh, she's okay, I suppose, I don't see her very much now she's married."

"Married!" Sue exclaimed. "I didn't know she was getting married." Vanessa explained that it was a quiet wedding with only about half a dozen people there. Louise asked who she married but Sue missed the name. It was obvious from how Vanessa talked about him that she didn't like him very much.

"To be fair," Vanessa continued, "I don't think she likes him either but she agreed to marry him. I'm a bit scared of him and hope I don't finish up like her."

"But she would have enjoyed her day?" Louise asked.

"Yes, I think she enjoyed all the dressing up. She did that traditional stuff as well."

"What do you mean?" Louise wasn't sure.

The Somerby Tree

"You know, something borrowed, no that's not right, something old, something new I think. Anyway, part of it is that she is supposed to wear something blue and she wore this ghastly cheap metal necklace with a blue bit of glass on it. It looked awful but she insisted. Nobody knows why." The girls chatted for another couple of minutes before going on their way.

In 2009, the council finally agreed to build a bypass around Somerby. There had been many alternatives suggested, and there was a lot of arguing about how such a construction would spoil this or that but a plan was finally in place. Part of the site was in Somerby woods close the where the car had crashed. There was a lot of excitement for a few days as archaeologists found some interesting old items. To start with nobody could confirm exactly what they were, but soon identified them as Viking, and the official word was that this must have been a site of great importance to them. Louise and Doc both visited the site on hearing what had been found but neither said anything. They weren't at all surprised by the findings.

A lot of changes took place over the coming years. Sue died in 2015, still relatively young, and Doc a year later. Both had lived, loved and lost and it was a great burden on them in the end. Louise stayed in Somerby for a few more years but then a new love in her life enabled her to move away, though never entirely forgetting her ties to the village.

Even further into the future, in 2029, Michael was settling into his new existence when he suddenly remembered what Louise had said to him about the tree in the village. What had happened to him and his family would never be properly accepted and he grieved hard. Many times, Michael had considered climbing up to look at the carvings she had told him about, but in the end, he never did. He visited Sue's grave regularly, and sent out many letters to try and contact his daughter Louise. It was a difficult thing for him to accept that she would be seven years older than him, so if they ever did meet it would be a strange experience.

Michael took over the running of the café. He found it ironic that he had inherited the place, but he got used to it, and in fact enjoyed it. He got to know many of the villagers, who tended to think of him as a new Doc, some incorrectly supposing that he might be Doc's son. Every now and then, though, he would see something that made him wonder. Once, he was sat at one of the tables talking to anyone who wanted to chat. A young girl, about fourteen, strolled into the café, and walked up to Michael as bold as anything.
"I want a coffee."
"Well, do you now? Perhaps if you say please, you might even get one." Michael looked at her. She was a good looking girl with long black hair. She

watched him as he got up and went behind the counter to prepare the coffee. Michael got so far and stopped. He turned and looked at the girl.

"Please." She said it in a most sarcastic tone. Michael prepared the coffee and took her money.

"So, what are you doing here today? Shouldn't you be at school?"

"I'm allowed to have the day off, today."

"I'm sure your mother wouldn't agree with that."

"Nobody listens to her," she replied, taking Michael by surprise. The girl was sipping from her coffee when a woman entered the café. She also had long black hair, but she was rather thin and looked very tired.

"Jenny!" the woman called out. The girl looked up.

"Just drinking my coffee."

The woman heard the answer and made her way over.

"Come on, your father is waiting." The woman watched, but there was no sign of urgency from Jenny. She then spotted Michael at the counter. "Hello, you must be in charge?" The woman seemed to almost melt as she spoke to him. He reminded her of a lost love, and they exchanged brief comments. The moment was interrupted when a man walked rudely into the cafe.

"Where the fuck is everyone? I'm waiting out here." The woman quickly snapped back to the tired looking woman she had been before, but Michael saw a glint of something in her eye.

"Sorry, Jenny is still drinking her coffee."

"I've told you, Mary, you daft cow, I'm waiting. Bloody sort things out." He approached the woman in a threatening way. Michael watched the scene unfurl.

"It's not my fault..." Mary had started to explain, when the man slapped her around the mouth with the back of his hand. Michael almost felt the blow, in his shock.

"Don't you backchat me, woman!" The man grabbed Jenny's hand and pulled her up from the table. He put his arm around her shoulder and they both made their way towards the exit door.

"Sorry, Arthur," Mary said, as she trudged behind them. She wanted to find the courage to turn back to Michael and apologise but she didn't. Michael watched them all leave, noticing that the man was holding his daughter very closely, in a rather more than fatherly manner. Michael shook his head. Despite everything he had experienced, people were still able to surprise him, and not always in a good way.

THE END

About the Author

David was born in the heart of London 1957, the only son of middle class working parents, themselves both North Londoners. They moved from Euston Road in Kings Cross to the growing town of Goodmayes, but moved to East Anglia when David was a teenager.

He completed his education in Gorleston before joining the civil service in the form of H.M. Customs & Excise in 1973. After nearly 40 years of service he retired in 2012.

He has been writing seriously since 2000 when a football injury left him with time on his hands. David has always been imaginative and enjoyed writing. He is interested in social aspects of future earth societies rather than space travel and alien life forms. He is also interested in time travel too, but his novels are diverse and not easy to categorise, featuring romance, drama and crime.

David has always written in various forms, including poetry, short stories and plays as well as novels but until recently his writing always had to be fitted in around full-time work.

He now lives with his second wife Louise and her son in Lowestoft with the ability to devote more time to writing.

David is on Facebook and Twitter so feel free to get in touch.

Also by David Merrifield from MindsEye:

I've Got Your
Number

A life changing experience
can change more than one life

David E. Merrifield